I0603818

Shades Of Crimson

Colors of Evil, book 1

Cynthia Hickey

Acknowledgements

Thank you to God for the wonderful story ideas he continues to give me. Many thanks to my husband and children who are patient when I'm on deadline and not afraid of the dust bunnies that tend to collect when I'm writing. The beautiful model on the cover is my niece who happily "played dead" for me.

1

*A*islinn McFarland stared at the envelope on her desk. Her mouth filled with cotton. Her gut turned to ice. She knew what the 12 x 9 inch package contained; knew it was a cry for help from a sick mind.

Regardless, at this point, the culprit could look somewhere else for compassion. That well had run dry.

Her hands shook as she reached for her mug. When would the deaths end? The taunts?

She choked on the gulp of bitter coffee. Why did the Upton Falls police station have brew that tasted like burnt tires? She redirected her attention to the manila envelope with the all too familiar computer printed label on the front. The interval between deliveries grew shorter before the next arrival, and they always coincided with a woman's murder.

The bulge at one end told Linn it contained more photos. Her heart beat like the pounding of a race horse's hooves, and she pressed a trembling hand to her chest. The bold letters of her name shouted at her. Mocking her for being helpless to stop him.

Some detective she proved to be.

She pulled open the bottom desk drawer and withdrew a pair of latex gloves. The snap of the rubber as she pulled them over her hands echoed in the small office. Her partner glanced up from his desk. Linn crooked the corner of her mouth.

A frown marred Steve's handsome olive complexion. "Linn?"

Grabbing the letter opener next to her desk blotter, she shook her head. Her hand continued to shake like someone with palsy as she ripped the thin metal blade under the envelope's lip. Turning the envelope upside down, she dumped out the contents.

Photographs landed face down. She grasped a pencil from the chipped mug beside her and gently tipped the pictures over with the sharpened tip.

The first one was similar to the others she'd received in the past. A woman in a red evening gown posed elaborately on a bed of thick moss, wide eyes staring into the camera. Moonlight filtered through tree branches, streaking her with silver light.

Linn's gaze cut to the next picture. Her own face stared back at her, super-imposed onto the body of the woman from the first photo. Written in black marker across the front were the words, "I'm watching you. Why don't you see me?"

"Getting too close, aren't we, buddy?" Her voice shook as if to laugh at the bravado of her words, and she tried to swallow past the lump in her throat, and glanced out the window. Could he see her now? Why her? Why choose to stalk a small-town, overworked detective?

"Did you say something, Linn?"

"Got some more, Steve. Take a look." She rolled her chair back, allowing him room to step beside her.

Steve withdrew a pair of tweezers from his pocket and lifted one of the photos. "This one's of you." He placed a hand on her shoulder and turned her chair to face him. His brow wrinkled. "Are you okay?"

She looked up into her partner's gold-green eyes and forced herself to relax. "I'm fine. Shook up, but I'll get over it." She always did.

"Uh-huh. Tough as nails, that's you." Steve drummed the fingers of his right hand against his lips as he studied the photograph. "There has to be a clue; something we're missing."

Linn pulled a plastic Ziploc bag from her drawer and held it out to him. "He's getting personal."

He dropped the photo in the bag and reached for the other one. "Pretty lady. Someone we're looking for?"

"She fits the description of a woman reported missing a month ago."

"They've all fit the description. *You* fit the description."

"As our friend here has so kindly pointed out. Except my hair is red, the vic is a blond." Linn slid the locking tab across the baggy and tossed it on her desk. "I'll have it checked for prints. Doubt they'll find any. These photos will be like the others. Clean."

"Your hair is barely red. Strawberry blond, I believe people call it." Steve perched on the corner of her desk. "How many does this make now—three, four?"

"Four."

He swung his leg, his shoe heel tapping against the metal panel. "The FBI completely took over the conference room last night. They sent another man in today. Looks like a country hick cowboy."

Feds were everywhere, interfering in her job, taking over the station. She sighed. Now, she and Steve were crammed into an office barely big enough for one person. Desks so close together there was hardly room to walk, much less pace and brainstorm.

The phone rang. Linn flinched and reached for the receiver. Steve rested his hand on her shoulder and gave her a gentle squeeze before turning back to his desk.

"McFarland here." Linn leaned back in her chair. Her eyes widened as a voice void of emotion rattled off an address. She slowly hung up the phone.

"They've found another body. Let's go. I'll drive." She grabbed her navy jacket from a nearby chair and slid the pictures into the pocket before swinging the blazer to her shoulders.

"You always drive." Steve slipped his arms into his suit jacket.

"Do you have any gas?" She speared him with a glance.

"A little. Enough to drive across town."

Linn strode to the doorway then paused. "A quarter of a tank?"

He shrugged. "Think so. Maybe."

"Thought so, and you know that isn't enough." She led the way out, their heels clattering on the tiled floor as they marched down the hall and to the parking garage.

"Almost."

Linn pressed the button on her car fob, releasing the door locks on her candy-apple red mustang, then slid inside. "This woman is in a warehouse by the river. You know I'm uncomfortable with anything less than a quarter of a tank." Less than that left a girl vulnerable to the evil in the world.

Steve set the stopwatch on his Timex, glancing at it often as they drove. "Wow." He pointed to his watch for a final time as they parked in front of the warehouse. "A whole fifteen minutes. I'm positive my car wouldn't have had enough gas. When are you going to tell me why you're so hung up on never going below a quarter of a tank?"

"Don't be sarcastic. Save that for the suits. Maybe I'll never tell you." Partner or not, Steve pried into her personal life too much for

Linn's comfort. Her past was better left behind her. She had no desire to revisit such a dark and desperate place.

Two police cars, lights flashing, idled in front of the square, gray-bricked building. Linn sighed and cut the ignition. "I hope they didn't touch anything." She popped the trunk and retrieved the square aluminum case. "Sometimes, first responders lacks common sense."

"McFarland. Chavez." Chief Madden's bald head shone in the Ozark summer sun like a brand-new eight ball. The seams of his dark suit strained against his bulging bulk. A cigarette dangled from full lips. Obviously, his diet wasn't working.

Linn stifled a smile. "Mad Dog."

"I've told you not to call me that." Madden frowned down at her. "I never should have told you my college nickname."

"You know you like it." She wiggled her eyebrows.

The captain took her by the elbow. He tossed a glance at Steve as they walked. "The medical examiner thinks she's been here since early this morning. Might be Sara Vern, but we haven't made a positive ID. We're waiting for her file."

Linn paused in the cavernous doorway of the warehouse. The block walls kept the area cool, despite the summer humidity. A breeze blew through the door and out an open window, taking with it the faint stench of death.

A man stood next to the woman's body.

Linn's quick glance took in the faded jeans, scuffed cowboy boots, and a black tee-shirt that fit smoothly across a toned back. The man squatted, his gloved hand cradling the woman's. The dress she wore, a spot of bright color against the cement floor. Her hair fanned out around her head.

"Who is that?" Linn glared into Mad Dog's face. "And why is he touching the body?"

"FBI."

"Why is the FBI here ahead of us?" Linn planted fists on her hips. "Granted, the body count warrants the feds coming in, but common courtesy would be to let us know. This is *our* case."

"You did know. The FBI have been holed up at the station for a day already. They're working with us. The call went in to the feds from the little old lady who found the body. I called you as soon as I got here."

"Fine. We've got more pictures," Linn informed Madden. "One is from the last batch of missing persons."

The man studying the body uncurled himself and turned. He looked even better from the front. Eyes the color of a stormy sea focused on

Linn. "Pictures? May I see them?" He spoke with a soft, rich, southern drawl; the sound like distant thunder during a summer rain.

Linn yanked her gaze away, determined not to be sucked in. She gave up men a long time ago.

"Detective McFarland, this is Special Agent Andrew Wayne. Drew for short. Or Wayne. He answers to both. He's been assigned to assist us." Madden's lip twitched with the hint of a smile. "The silent partner over there is Detective Chavez."

Madden had something up his sleeve, and she was bound not to like it. She had a job to do, and she wouldn't let some pretty cowboy get in her way, no matter how well his jeans fit.

"We've received a photograph of each of the victims after their murder, some immediately after, others much later." Linn set her case on the ground beside her feet. "This morning, two more photographs arrived." She took a deep breath and squared her shoulders. "One minor deviation from his prior MO. One of the photographs is of me. And unless I'm mistaken, I'm very much alive."

The agent's gaze caressed her. "I'd have to agree."

"What?" Madden's voice boomed through the warehouse.

Linn cringed then turned to Madden, forcing herself to stand firm beneath his glare. "My face is superimposed onto the photograph of the woman in the other picture."

"Did you bring them with you?" Special Agent Wayne rubbed his chin, his hand rasping on what looked like a day's growth of whiskers.

Nodding, Linn withdrew the baggy from her pocket and handed it to Madden, trying to ignore the agent. The man definitely didn't look like FBI. Instead, he belonged on the cover of an outdoor magazine. From the corner of her eye, she spotted a slow smile spread across the agent's face. Embarrassed at being caught checking him out, Linn's face heated.

Madden glanced at the photos then passed them to Wayne. The agent snatched them from his hand.

Linn tilted her head and watched his face as the agent perused the photographs. His features remained expressionless, except for a muscle twitching in his jaw. The man's raven hair waved over his head, barely brushing against his shoulders. Chiseled lips pressed into a line as he handed the photos back to her. Definitely not like any fed she'd ever seen. This man did not fit the mold of an emotionless clone. Anger vibrated from him. His hands clenched. Linn took a step back.

Their gazes locked. His eyes were such a dark blue, they appeared black. Way too pretty for FBI. He said something she missed. "Excuse me?"

"He air-brushed your scar."

Linn's hand flew to her lip. Her other hand flipped the photos over. The scar from an accident years ago was gone.

"Why would he remove the scar?" Madden frowned.

"I'm guessing here, but maybe he doesn't want his women imperfect. We know the man has some expectations of beauty. He takes his time arranging each body to bring out that woman's individual beauty. Look." He directed their attention to the photographs. "In this one, he spotlighted her hands. See how one is folded beneath her chin? The long fingers and sculpted nails?"

Imperfection! As if Linn needed reminding. She'd spent her life trying to push aside memories of that night. Sometimes, she succeeded. Other times she woke in a cold sweat, heart racing.

Drew took a manila folder from the hood of the nearest squad car. "In this other photograph, the victim's thick hair is fanned out over the leaves." He skimmed through the papers in the folder. "Here, it's the woman's skin. Pale, porcelain-like. This woman's dress reveals much more skin than the other victims. The deep plunge emphasizes her full breasts, which are natural, not plastic. See the belly button ring? He's dressed her so the skin and ring are emphasized."

Give me a break! Linn rolled her eyes.

"Our perpetrator is taking the best parts of his victims. I think he's trying to build his image of the perfect woman."

~

Drew noted the quick flash of pink on McFarland's cheeks. She's sensitive about her scar. He studied the lines of her frame in the dark suit. She stood about five-foot-nine, curly strawberry-blond hair tied severely back in a ponytail. She wore no makeup to hide the scattering of freckles across her nose. Despite her attempt at being a no-nonsense girl, the severe clothes and hairstyle still didn't hide her beauty. The suit couldn't hide her feminine curves.

The camera's flash illuminated their area of the warehouse as the pretty detective walked around the body, photographing it from each angle. She bent closer and snapped a close-up of the victim's face.

He transferred his attention to the man beside her. Dark hair slicked away from his face, expensive suit, shined shoes. For a second, Drew's gaze clashed with Chavez's. Yellow eyes? Well, some would call them green, but they seemed yellow to him. The man's brows drew together. Drew smirked and turned away, accepting the file offered him by one of the other detectives.

Opening the folder, he compared the dead woman to the twenty-eight-year-old divorced mother of two. He sighed and returned the file to Madden. "Matches the photo of Sara Vern. Get the ME to verify."

The officer swore under his breath. "I was afraid it would."

Drew watched as McFarland and Chavez moved carefully around the woman's body, searching the crime scene. They worked in unison, dancers accustomed to how the other moved. Never bumping into each other. No tripping over the equipment.

"They won't find any trace evidence." Drew nodded toward McFarland and Chavez.

"How do you know?" Madden followed his gaze.

"The scenes are always clean." Drew tapped the file. "Any idea why he sends the photos to her?"

"No idea." Madden shrugged. "Linn received the first one a few months ago. This is the first time he's done that thing with her face."

"Notice any resemblance?"

The officer shrugged.

"A shade or two difference in the hair, maybe." Drew pointed in Linn's direction. "They're all pretty, tall, and thin like McFarland." He tapped the photograph. "Now, with this latest picture, I'm thinking he's more fixated on her than before. He's recreating her. This is someone she knows."

"Crazy mother, son-of-a bitch. Sorry. I'm trying to stop the cussing, but this job—" Madden slapped Drew's shoulder. "Good thing your college education wasn't a waste."

"At least I got one." Drew laughed. "I graduated by using my brain. Not like you, playing your way through by knocking down other muscle-clad bozos."

"Ha ha. Yeah, you're the smart one." Madden grew serious. "He's getting closer. That's the toughest, sweetest girl a guy could meet. A bit gun shy about men, but, well…I've wanted to put her in protective custody before, but she resisted."

"I'll keep a close eye on her, now that I'm working the case."

"I'm counting on it. Thanks for coming. It'll be a difficult job."

"Yeah, it'll be tough watching a good-looking woman, living in her house." Drew chuckled. "You want to tell her the good news? I don't think she likes me."

"Didn't I tell you she's smart? Let's go see if they've uncovered anything."

Linn slipped a brown bag over Sara's hand and secured it with a rubber band before straightening to face Drew and Madden. "We haven't found a thing." She jerked her head toward Chavez. "Steve will check for prints and fibers, but it looks the same as all the others. Nothing."

"Make friends with Drew, Linn. You'll be working closely with him for a while. He's your new best friend." Madden shook Drew's hand and turned away.

"Mad Dog!" Linn jogged to catch up with the big man, her voice carrying through the warehouse. "I told you I don't want a bodyguard. Steve works with me every day. We're used to each other. He'll watch out for me, since you're so insistent I need a babysitter."

"He's a good guy. Drew will be with you twenty-four-seven, Linn." Madden gave her a stern look. "One of the best. I've known him since my college days."

"You have *got* to be kidding! I will not have a stranger in my house."

The chief strode back to his car. "I'm serious. This is not open for discussion. Either you accept the protection, or you're off the case and sent on vacation until this is over."

She turned a sullen look to Drew, who smiled and waved.

"I can't believe this." She stalked past him and slammed the lid to her case. "I'm going to check for tire tracks. The victim got here somehow, and I don't think she walked."

"Over there." He motioned with his head. "Standard..." Drew checked the clipboard in his hand. "Firestone issue 65R15's." He handed the clipboard to a passing rookie officer. "Fits a lot of cars."

"Is there anything you've left for us to do?"

Chavez stepped behind her and crossed his arms. "Linn doesn't need your protection. She's got me."

"You're too close to her." Did these two have a relationship outside the professional boundaries? He hoped not. His job didn't need to be any harder than it already was. "I'll carry that for you." He grabbed the case then reached down and retrieved a black cowboy hat from the hood of a squad car and slapped it on his head.

"Do you always dress like this?" Linn's eyes raked over him.

"Like what?"

"A hick."

"Yeah. Why?"

"You look like an idiot." He actually looked good enough to eat. She snatched the case back and stalked away, calling over her shoulder, "I carry my own things. I don't need a cowboy taking care of this lady."

~

The wind blew her blond tresses across her face. The strands stuck to the fire-engine red lipstick on her parted lips. He tenderly pulled the strands free and tucked them behind her ear.

"There now, my love." He patted her cheek and she blinked; her eyelids slow and heavy.

"Please." Her voice cracked.

"A few minutes more, and it will all be over. I wish you'd have cooperated with me a bit more. We could've avoided this, you know." He lifted the red dress from where he'd laid it across the moss-covered log. "We need to get you dressed." The silk slipped effortlessly over her head and skimmed her naked body. No underwear lines to interfere with perfection. He lifted one arm through the strap, then the other. "I don't like to hurt my girls. I want them to love me as I do them."

Her body grew heavy, and he struggled against her dead weight as he propped her against the tree. "Help…me…just a bit…now, darling." With a grunt, he positioned her with her back against the bark. "Almost ready." He lifted her arm. "Here, hold it like this. I'll get the camera." He smoothed the fabric over her body, lingering with a delicate touch on her breasts, then down to her waist. Perfection. He sighed and turned away.

He felt a flicker of pleasure at remembering to set the camera's tripod up before getting the girl ready. Last time, he hadn't gotten the effect he'd wanted. The picture had been too cold. Too lifeless.

The click of a button and whir of the camera sounded deafening in the dark woods, and he paused in his ministrations. He glanced once more through the viewfinder. The dress shimmered blood red in the night and covered curves nature intended a man to cherish. The pale moonlight cast subtle silver highlights in the girl's hair. Her head fell back against the tree, stretching her neck, and he rushed forward to correct her position.

His fingers itched to play more across her silky skin, yet he resisted. Removing the ski mask from his face, he tenderly cupped her chin in his gloved hand and kissed her. Her breath tickled his lips, drawing a moan of pleasure from his own. He held himself rigid, his lips hovering over hers until her breath ceased.

The girl's body went slack, her eyes widened, and she froze.

He felt a moment's sadness at the passing of her soul and rose to his feet, staring soundlessly down at her body. He swore he felt her spirit blow past him, and he inhaled with a deep breath, expanding his lungs. He refused to take the women physically, saving himself for Aislinn. But he could take their spirit.

A bird chirped, reminding him of where he was, and he packed up the camera and tripod, casting one last look at the masterpiece he left behind. At least he'd have the picture. He'd print out several and send them to the object of his affection. He couldn't hoard the pleasure the woman's beauty gave. It needed to be shared. It needed to be shared with *her*. The woman who haunted his dreams.

He wanted to keep himself in hers.

2

*T*he papers labeled him The Photographer. He snarled. A fitting name. From a house across the street, he peered through the Canon 10x30 IS Image Stabilized Binoculars as Linn and the agent entered her small brick home. The agent said something then laughed. The sound carried to where the watcher sat, sending sharp shivers up and down his spine, like nails on a chalkboard. If he'd had a gun, he'd have shot the agent in the street like a dog.

Linn frowned and shook her head.

Good. She wasn't encouraged by the cowboy's actions. He magnified the binoculars as the two entered the house.

Using his booted heel, the oaf of an agent closed Linn's door behind them. He was obviously no gentleman. He scoffed, releasing a puff of air from his nostrils that ruffled the sheer curtains parted on each side of the binoculars.

Linn opened window blinds that allowed him a better view into the front room and on into parts of the kitchen.

The agent dropped his bags on the floor beside the coffee table and his hat on the table itself. The Photographer frowned again at the agent's uncouthness, as the cowboy opened Linn's refrigerator, withdrew a can of soda, handed it to her, then chose another for himself.

Cowboy acts as if he lives there! The Photographer lowered the binoculars and closed his eyes. With a deep sigh, he leaned his forehead against the cool panes of the window, letting the heat recede from his brow. The cowboy made himself completely comfortable. Linn should refuse to let him stay. She should make him leave. Why was she allowing it? What about her reputation? Did she not realize how much he cared for her? How much this would hurt him? Why can't she see him!

Tears welled in The Photographer's eyes. Acid churned in his stomach, rising and burning his esophagus. He swallowed and roughly brushed his tears away with the sleeve of his shirt. He raised the binoculars again. No way would he allow his attention to be diverted when his love had a strange man in her house. She might need him.

~

"Thanks." Drew lifted his can of soda toward Linn. "I'm thirsty."

"No problem. Are you hungry? I could whip up an omelet or something." Her voice sounded surly, even to her own ears. *I may* have *to have him here, but I don't have to like it.*

Drew pulled one of the dining chairs away from the table and spun it backward, straddling it. He fixed his gaze on her. "Not yet, thanks. Let's go over some things."

Pulling out another chair, Linn sat, folding her legs at the ankles and tucking them beneath the chair, then electing to stretch them in front of her. "Like what?" Why did he look at her so intently? She hated the way he made her squirm.

Over the rim of the can, Linn allowed her eyes to travel across his face. The shadow on his cheeks and chin grew more pronounced as the day passed, but instead of making him look tired and unkempt, it increased his attractiveness, making him more rugged than pretty. He had the type of sexiness that sold magazines and romance novels. The kind of looks that made her run, under most circumstances.

She shook her head. How would she be able to stand his staying here? She needed Steve as a buffer. Good, safe, Steve. Why couldn't she love him? He was handsome, gentlemanly, and treated her like a precious piece of china. His very attractiveness made her uncomfortable.

"What?"

She jerked, realizing he'd seen the shake of her head. "Nothing."

"Okay." Drew folded his arms across the chair back and rested his chin on them. Dark eyes peered through lashes much too thick for a man. "What do you know about the perpetrator?"

"Not much." Linn set the can on the table, running her fingertip absently around the rim. "The sites are always clean. We dust for prints and come up with nothing. We check under the victim's fingernails; also nothing. Rape kits; nothing. We do know our killer uses a poison. Most likely curare. The victims die from respiratory failure."

"And he's fixated on you."

"Yes, let's not forget that important fact." She sighed. "We suspect he's a white male, mid-twenties to mid-thirties, and intelligent. Most likely works with the public, but not in a job up to his potential. The newspapers call him The Photographer."

"Has he ever tried contacting you?"

"Besides sending me the pictures? No, not yet." But, it was only a matter of time. Someday, she'd come face-to-face with the killer. She prayed she would have what it took to take him down before he got her.

She squirmed. Drew maintained eye contact with her. The intensity in his eyes made her feel as if he saw into her soul. Not a feeling she relished. There were too many secrets in her hidden places.

"We'll catch him. They always trip up somewhere."

"Yes, but in the meantime, more women will die."

"My job is to keep you safe until we catch the guy." Drew rose from his chair and strode to the window. He pulled the curtains together tightly. "Keep the curtains closed and the doors locked."

"Why? You're here. Cowboy always saves the girl. I've read the book."

"I can't stop a sniper's bullet."

"That's not his MO."

Drew stepped in front of her. "Maybe not, but it might be. He could change. Evolve. Not likely, but it could happen."

His voice rolled mockingly over her, remaining calm, his drawl more pronounced. His eyes twinkled with humor.

"Are we going to argue every time I give you an order? 'Cause if we are, the days are gonna be mighty long. I don't care to be a babysitter any more than you want to be baby-sat. I came here to catch a killer."

"How dare you." Linn narrowed her eyes.

"And don't get your Irish dander up with me. I don't fight with girls." A grin teased the corner of his lips. "Might wrestle, though. You want to?"

Linn grabbed her soda can from the table and hurled it at his chest, spraying soda over his shirt front. She stood and shoved both hands against his chest. "Don't worry about me being a girl, you chauvinistic pig! I can take care of myself." She marched into the kitchen to wash the sticky liquid off her hands. When she returned, her mouth fell open.

Drew pulled the shirt over his head, revealing a tanned, muscular chest. A sprinkling of dark hair disappeared beneath the waistband of his pants, drawing her eye, and completed the picture of masculine appeal. He tossed the shirt over the back of the sofa then unzipped his duffel bag.

Whirling, Linn stomped down the hall toward her room. She wouldn't let him in her house to distract her. She wasn't called the Ice Queen of the Ozarks for nothing.

"Don't worry about me. I'll just make myself comfortable out here on the sofa." His voice followed her, mocking. "Call me if you want company."

She slammed her bedroom door and turned the lock. Plopping on the faded quilt across her bed, she groaned, fell backwards, her arms splayed at her side. *I cannot do this! What is Mad Dog thinking?* She kicked her feet in one quick motion and turned her head toward the open window.

From outside drifted the sounds of a car passing. A dog barked. A child laughed. Innocent, every day, neighborhood sounds that Linn normally enjoyed hearing. Not anymore. Now, open windows invited murderous creeps into a person's sanctuary.

Great! She bolted to her feet and closed the window and curtains, throwing her room into the grey light of pre-dusk. She hated admitting Drew could be right about The Photographer changing his MO.

The phone rang, and she crawled across the bed to the nightstand to answer it. "Hello?"

"Linn, are you all right? How are things going with your guest?" Steve spat the words.

She rolled over onto her back. "He's insufferable. Do you know he had the audacity to tell me he doesn't fight with girls? Then he asked me if I wanted to wrestle."

"The nerve. What did you do?"

She giggled. "I threw my soda can at him."

Steve sighed. "Are you getting any work done?"

"We did talk about the case—a little." Linn held her hand out, studying her nails. Her short, no-nonsense, unpainted ones were a direct contrast to the manicured ones she'd bagged earlier that day. She rolled her fingers into a fist, then flexed them out straight again. "I told him what we know…which isn't much, and he ordered me to keep the curtains closed. Seems to think The Photographer might take a shot at me."

"He might. Where's Wayne sleeping tonight?"

"In the spare room. He thinks he's sleeping on the couch, but I'll have mercy on him in a while."

"Uh-huh."

"I will. I'm not completely heartless." She sat up. "What did you need?"

"Tonight's a full moon."

"The last one didn't disappear on a full moon." Linn sat and reached to pull the hair clasp from her hair. She caught a glimpse of her reflection in the mirror and shook her head, letting the waves cascade down her back. Pulling a few strands over her shoulder, she placed them across her upper lip like a moustache, hiding her scar. Her lip twitched against the tickling of her hair. "Last month he took two. I think he's stepping up. What do you want to do?"

"What we talked about. Each of the girls disappeared after visiting one of the local nightclubs."

"Not all of them. One was jogging."

"One. I think he finds most of his victims at a bar. It makes it easier for him to blend in."

"I'm not really in the mood, Steve."

"You'll be working. You know *I* don't inhabit those types of places. I prefer something more upscale."

"Well, I don't inhabit them either." Not anymore. She sighed. "Fine. Pick me up in half an hour." She set the phone back on the receiver and moved to her closet. She chewed the inside corner of her mouth and studied the meager choice of suitable garments hanging there. Shopping for clothes wasn't a necessity. Not when you wore a suit every day.

She grabbed a pair of black skinny jeans and tossed them on the bed. She riffled through the blouses, settling on a black gauzy thing with ruffles she'd bought on sale once in a moment of weakness. She ended up hating it. The neckline plunged, revealing pale skin dusted with freckles, and more cleavage than an officer of the law ought to show. The long sleeves were sheer, showing more skin through the fabric. Give her the familiarity of a trusty pant and jacket any day. Clothes that showed she meant business.

Leaving her suit in a heap on the floor, she pulled on the jeans and blouse, then slid her feet into a pair of silver strappy sandals, bought at the same sale as the shirt. Is this what someone wears to a nightclub nowadays? She couldn't very well go looking like a cop.

She shrugged and headed to the connecting bathroom. A quick dab of mascara, a swipe of clear gloss, and she was finished. She drew a finger along the scar on her lip, wishing for at least the millionth time in her life she could camouflage it. Not even heavy makeup concealed the reminder from a night of horror.

She sighed. *This is as good as I get.*

~

Drew glanced from where he sprawled across the sofa and almost dropped his book. His breath stopped. Linn entered the room, as beautiful and enticing to him as a flame. Her hair seemed to burn against the black of her blouse, while her pale arms shimmered through the fabric of the sleeves. Black skinny jeans showcased slim legs that seemed to go on forever.

Don't think about her. It's a bad idea to get involved with a Black Widow. And, that described Linn perfectly. She'd use him and cast him away like unwanted garbage. Something had built a wall around her heart, and he pitied the man who tried to break through.

He swung his legs to the floor. "Where are we going?"

"I'm going out with Steve." Her eyes dropped to the book.

"Are y'all a couple?"

"We are not." She tried to stuff her driver's license and keys into a pocket of her jeans, failed, then slid them into her cleavage before sticking her pistol in her waistband. Lucky keys. She stared him down. "We're working."

"Looking like that?"

"What's wrong with the way I look?" She turned to him with a frown. "Won't I blend in?"

Not for a second. "There's nothing wrong with the way you look. You're hot." He opened his bag and withdrew a clean shirt. A long-sleeve, button up one in blue cotton.

"You can't come with us." Linn propped one fist on her hip.

"I have to. Otherwise Mad Dog will have my head."

A horn beeped outside.

"I'm riding shotgun," Linn stalked out the front door.

Drew grinned. A real firecracker. Standing his distance might be harder than he thought. But he'd never compromised his job over a woman before and didn't intend to start now. Romantic notions distracted people. Got them killed.

He fished his boots from beneath the sofa where he'd kicked them, grabbed his hat from the table, and sprinted in sock-covered feet to the waiting car. He didn't put it past the other two to drive off and leave him.

"Thanks for waiting." He yanked open the rear door of the idling car, and folded his large frame into the small, modest four-door sedan.

Steve frowned at Linn, who shrugged. "He won't take no for an answer."

"Wouldn't want y'all to have all the fun." Drew tugged on a boot, his head bumping the back of Linn's seat. "Sorry."

He fell backward as the car roared to life. Tires squealed as it sped away from the curb. He chuckled and reached down to retrieve the other boot. Feet covered, he leaned back and folded his arms across his chest. "Where are we going?"

"Elmo's." Linn turned to look at him. "A nightclub and barbeque grill on the other side of town. We're going to start bar-hopping each week, hoping to pick up clues as to exactly what The Photographer is looking for. We make a point of going when there's a full moon."

"He's looking for you."

She shook her head. "He knows where I am. It's a game of cat and mouse."

"I don't think so. It's more than that." Drew patted his hair into place. The killer definitely had more on his mind than playing. Linn's thinking The Photographer played a game could get her killed.

"I didn't ask you." She pressed her lips together and raised both eyebrows.

Drew's hand rasped against the stubble covering his jaw. "Hope it's a country bar." He turned to stare out the window. Bantering with Linn seemed like a battle he'd lose.

"It is."

The drive to the other side of town took ten minutes in which none of the occupants of the car spoke. Drew studied the slicked back head of Steve. The other man drummed his fingers against his smooth upper lip. Occasionally, Steve would tilt his head just enough to take a peek at Linn.

Linn's elbow rested on the armrest, her chin propped in the cup of her hand. She seemed oblivious to Steve's covert glances.

Drew's gaze collided in the rearview mirror with Steve's. Oops. Got caught looking. He smirked. It'd been a while since someone considered him competition for a woman. If he only knew Drew didn't have time for a relationship, he'd relax. In the meantime, a friendly rivalry might be fun, and make the security job easier to get through. He rather liked the thought that Steve was jealous.

Elmo's was a typical weathered-board square of a building with a huge red neon sign flashing the proprietor's name. The melancholy strands of a country song spilled through the doorway along with the tangy aroma of barbecue.

Grinning hugely, he donned his hat and slid from the car. Two ladies in tight jeans, cowboy boots, and satin camisole tank-tops smiled flirtatiously from a nearby van. Drew tilted his hat. "Ladies."

Linn huffed and stalked past him, knocking against his shoulder.

The women laughed, and Drew spared them a wink before following Linn into the smoky, dim recesses of the bar. If there were time, he might have made their acquaintance. As it is, the beauty in front of him was all he could handle.

He reached out to take her elbow.

Steve pushed him aside with the force of a pit bull.

Sparing neither of them a glance, Linn led the way to a round table with a good view of the dance floor. Several men sent hopeful glances her way. Like a horse wearing blinders, she pulled out a chair from the table and sat down before either of the men could help.

Drew set his hat on the fourth chair and angled his seat so he could keep an eye on each of the room's entrances.

A pretty waitress in denim jeans and red-and-white-checkered blouse unbuttoned down the front and tied at the waist, smiled down at him. "May I take your order?" She leaned over just enough for him to catch a peek at her lacy red bra.

"Ladies first." He winked at Linn, who rolled her eyes.

"I'll have a diet soda and a mushroom burger with cheese." She turned to her left. "Steve?"

Steve waved his hand, ordering a glass of white wine.

"I'll have a beer in the biggest mug you got and a rack of ribs with the spiciest sauce available." Drew smiled at the waitress.

"We've got whatever you're hungry for." She beamed back, tossing her head so her hair swung behind her and her breasts thrust outward.

"I'm going to be sick." Linn plopped back in her chair and folded her arms across her chest.

"That'll do, darlin'." Drew turned sideways in his chair, stretching his legs in front of him and cased the room.

Although still early in the evening, people poured through the front doors, and soon the bar filled to capacity. Slender ladies swayed to music blaring from a jukebox as cowboy wannabes pushed drinks into their hands in hopes of becoming better looking as the night wore on. Several of the women fit The Photographer's sense of taste, at least as far as build and coloring went.

Drew scratched the stubble on his chin. Would it be one of these women tonight or someone at a different location? He smiled as one lady caught his eye and leaned against the bar, flashing big teeth in his direction and cleavage as deep as the Grand Canyon.

He directed his attention to the plate of barbecue ribs being placed in front of him.

"How can you possibly eat all of that?" Linn frowned from across the table. "And are you always such a flirt? Women are more than objects of lust."

He shrugged. "Healthy conscience. It's good for the appetite. I like to flirt. It's fun and harmless. Especially if both parties know there are no strings attached. I would never dally with a woman's affections that wasn't on the same page as I." He motioned his head toward her hamburger, lifting a rib from the basket. "That's a big burger for a little bitty thing like you."

"I am not a little bitty thing."

Drew closed his eyes and took his first bite, savoring the tangy taste of the sauce dripping off a tender rib. When he'd swallowed, he reached for a napkin. "You're tall, but about as big around as my little finger. It wouldn't hurt for you to put some meat on your bones. A man likes a woman with something to hold onto."

"I'm going to the restroom." Linn scraped her chair back.

Drew rose halfway.

"Sit down. Don't waste your manners on me." She whirled and stalked away.

"Man, she's prickly."

Steve set his glass of wine directly in the center of his napkin. "Why must you torment her? She's a fragile woman, overly concerned with her deformity. She feels a constant need to prove herself in a world of men. And yet, she's the best detective on the force."

Swiping the napkin across his mouth, Drew took his time answering. "I'm not tormenting her. She just doesn't like me, and she isn't fragile, she's frightened."

"Nothing frightens Linn." Steve scoffed.

Drew shrugged. "And as for her 'deformity', as you so delicately put it, a person doesn't even notice. If she'd stop stroking her lip, she wouldn't draw attention. Linn is a beautiful woman. I know she's a good detective. I've read her file."

Pounding the table with one fist, Steve rose to his feet. "You had no right."

"I have every right." Drew stared up at him. A muscle twitched in his jaw. "It's my job. I've been assigned to protect her and needed to know all I could before I got here."

"Your presence complicates things." Steve stalked across the room to the bar.

"What did you say to him?" Linn slid back into her chair. "You're scoring points everywhere."

"Don't you find it tiring working with a partner who's in love with you?" Drew dropped a rib bone into the empty basket beside his plate. "One who's love you don't return?"

Linn laughed. "Steve's attractive, but I'm not his type. That's why we get along so well. Steve likes the girly-girls. Makeup, pretty clothes, shy glances, fake boobs." She shivered. "Everything I'm not."

"And you don't like men."

"I never said that!" Her hands wrapped around her hamburger and suspended halfway between her mouth and the plate.

"It's just me you don't care for, then."

"I don't have time for men. My career is more important." She bit into her burger, avoiding his eyes. She chewed and swallowed, then set the burger back in its basket. "Why am I talking to you about this anyway? It's none of your business."

"Fine." For several minutes they ate without speaking. Drew's gaze roamed over the patrons on the dance floor. Discarding his last rib, he ripped open one of the packets of moist towelettes and wiped his hands. "Want to dance?"

"I don't dance."

He stood from the table and grasped her hand. "Tough. I'm your bodyguard, and I want to dance. You go where I go."

"But…my gun." She stuffed it more firmly into her waistband as Drew swung her into a two-step.

Bending close to her ear, he whispered, "Think what you want, but Steve is definitely in love with you."

"Don't be—"

A gunshot exploded from outside. Drew grabbed her arm and jerked her behind him. Steve darted toward them, weapon in one hand, cell phone in the other.

Drew shoved Linn beneath the closest table and yanked his revolver from his waistband.

3

"*D*on't shove me under the table like I'm helpless. I'm going with you." Linn glared at Drew. Her face reddened beneath a fine sheen of perspiration.

He shook his head. Would the woman ever listen? He squatted next to her and returned her look. "No, you're not." He'd been responsible for the lives of others and had never lost one yet. He wasn't about to start now.

"I'll go anyway once you're outside. I'm a police officer, Drew. You can't stop me from doing my job."

"You're right." He shook his head, relinquishing control to the inevitable, and grabbed her arm. "Just don't get yourself killed."

Another gunshot shattered the air. They sprinted outside, shoving aside other patrons of the bar with orders to stay down.

A man held a woman with her back to his chest. One of his beefy arms wrapped tight around her throat while his other hand brandished a pistol at the group of men ducking behind parked cars.

The woman's pencil straight blond hair fell forward, obscuring her face, and she screamed as she kicked frantically against her assailant's shins. Her pink camisole twisted, revealing the brighter Fuschia bra beneath.

The man cursed each time her booted feet connected with his legs.

Drew leveled his Kimber Eclipse Pro II and strolled forward, pausing with each step. "Let her go, man. I don't want to shoot you."

"Drop the weapon!" Linn's voice boomed beside his ear.

"Stand back, Linn." Drew spoke low from the corner of his mouth.

"I'm working," she hissed. "Drop the weapon now."

The man released his hold on the woman and shoved hard enough to send her reeling across the pavement. With the tips of his fingers, he dropped the weapon. The pistol hit the concrete with a rattle. The sound ricocheted through the night air.

With Steve at his side, Drew rushed the man. He twisted the man's arm behind his back and forced him to his knees while Steve handcuffed him. Off to the side, Linn helped the woman back to her feet.

"Leave him alone." The woman shrieked. "He's my husband. Where are you taking him?"

"Your husband?" Linn replaced her gun in her waistband. She crooked an eyebrow in Drew's direction.

"Yes. We had a fight. It didn't mean anything. He wouldn't really have hurt me. He's all talk, just a big baby." She stalked to where her husband knelt and smoothed the hair back from his face. "Tell them, Ross. Tell them what we were fighting about."

The man shook his head and swayed from side to side.

"Fine, you drunken fool. I'll tell them." She placed her hands on her hips. "He drank too much before we got here, and passed out in front of the television. I called my girlfriend…" She inclined her head toward a woman rising from the bed of a pickup truck. "And came without him. I wasn't going to wait around while he got his sorry self ready. When he woke up, I was gone, and he got mad. End of story."

"Ma'am." Drew recalled the two women who'd flirted with him when he'd arrived at the bar. Gone was the image of flirtatious beauty, replaced by enraged vixen. He shook his head. Women never ceased to amaze him.

Grabbing the man by his elbows, he yanked him to his feet. "It's still against the law for your husband to be shooting a gun in the city limits. He could have killed someone. He's going to jail."

He raised his brows at the woman's broad range of curse words and led her husband to a waiting police vehicle. Placing his hand on the man's head, he steered him inside the car and closed the door. *Thank you, Steve, for calling in the calvary.*

Linn faced the irate woman. "Calm down, Mrs…" She glanced at the driver's license she held in her hand. "Stockton."

"I don't want to calm down!" She swiped the back of her hand across her eyes, smearing her mascara. "I'm not pressing charges."

"Fine. He's still under arrest for firing his weapon in town." Linn handed back the driver's license. "Go home, Mrs. Stockton."

The woman tucked the license into the pocket of her jeans then two-hand shoved Linn. More curses exploded from her mouth.

Linn's feet slipped beneath her and she fell. She cried out as her palms slid across the pavement.

Drew and Steve dashed forward. They each grabbed one of Mrs. Stockton's arms and pulled her away from Linn.

Using a parked car, Linn pulled herself to her feet and held a bleeding hand out from her side. "I repeat, go home before we arrest you, too." She spun on one heel and marched back to Steve's car.

Steve and Drew released the irate woman.

She walked a zig-zag line back to her girlfriend.

Drew shook his head. "This happen a lot around here?"

"No more than anywhere else, I expect. Probably less. Until The Photographer showed, crime around here was pretty low." Steve turned. "I'll let the other officers know they can take Stockton downtown. Find out what Linn wants done with Mrs. Stockton. We could arrest her for assaulting a police officer."

Drew walked to where Linn leaned against Steve's car. "Let me see your hand."

"It's fine." She let her hand fall to her side and tucked it behind her.

"Let me see it." He took her right hand in his and turned it up. A three-inch gash lay across her palm. His gut clenched. Although a tall woman, Linn was small-boned, and her hand looked fragile lying in his. Blood mixed with dirt and small pebbles covered the skin. "Come with me." He wrapped his hand around her wrist and dragged her along behind him.

"You can't go in there." Linn pulled back outside the door to the women's restroom.

Drew pushed the door open a couple of inches. "Police. Anyone in here?" Not receiving an answer, he pulled Linn inside. The sharp smell of toilet deodorizer, upchucked dinner, and booze assaulted his nostrils. No wonder he hated bars. Same story, different day.

He grimaced as he took hold of the grimy faucet handle. It didn't offer them much more than a trickle. Drew shoved Linn's hand beneath the water and, grabbing a handful of paper towels, proceeded to scrub the wound.

"Ow! You're hurting me." She fought to free herself.

Drew tightened his grip. "We have to clean it. What did you cut yourself on?" Blood turned the water red as it swirled it down the rusty drain.

"I think it was a broken bottle." Her breath hissed as she drew it in.

"You need stitches and an antibiotic." He clapped another wad of paper towels on her hand and dragged her back out of the restroom and into the bar where Steve waited.

"Linn needs stitches."

Steve pulled Linn's hand from Drew's. "It's that bad? What about pressing charges?"

She yanked her hand free. "The two of you need to stop pulling and yanking on me. Now that Drew has pulverized my hand with his Neanderthal cleansing, yes, I need stitches. The worst part is, it's my gun hand."

"You needed stitches before I cleaned it." Drew stepped back. Why did he seem to rub her the wrong way no matter what he did?

"Whatever. Can we go before I bleed to death, please? Forget about Mrs. Stockton. The headache she'll have in the morning will be punishment enough."

~

Frantic parents tried consoling screaming children. Lethargic elderly people slumped in vinyl chairs. The odor of vomit, mixed with antiseptic, hung heavy in the emergency room. Linn closed her eyes and willed herself to focus on something other than the throbbing in her hand. She took shallow breaths. Her hand bled through the wad of paper towels, and blood dripped onto the floor with a steady *plop plop*.

Why'd she insist on taking her turn? All it would have taken was a look from the nurse, a flash of Linn's badge, and she would already be sewn up and on her way home. She could bleed to death waiting.

Drew grabbed a towel from an unsupervised janitor's cart and wrapped it securely around her hand, paper towels and all. If he'd leave her alone, the pain might ebb. Instead, his heavy-handed helping did anything but. It'd been a long time since she'd had to rely on the ministrations of someone else. She wasn't sure she cared for it.

"Are you cold?" Steve pulled out a chair in front of the registration desk and helped her lower onto the slick seat. "Do you need a blanket?"

"Stop fussing, Steve. You're worse than a mother." Linn laid her injured hand in her lap. "Go sit over there with Drew."

"What if you need me?" A shadow darkened his eyes.

"I'm a big girl. I'll be fine." She rested the elbow of her left arm on the chair armrest and propped her head up. She closed her eyes again, willing the din behind her to lower to a dull roar.

When she opened her eyes, Steve still watched with a hurt look on his face. Drew slumped in his seat, long legs stretched out before him, eyes stormy as he glared up from beneath lowered lashes. He frowned at a couple whose toddler insisted on crawling in and out of the chairs.

When the little guy's projectile vomit narrowly missed Drew's boots, he bolted from his chair and went to stand by the entrance.

"I'll…uh, wait out there." Steve rushed outside.

An hour and a half later, the three left the hospital with four stitches in the palm of Linn's right hand, and her woozy from painkillers. When she stumbled stepping off the curb, Drew swooped her into his arms.

"Neanderthal." Her words slurred as if she had been drinking.

"Shrew." He laughed.

His chest rumbled against her ear, and she snuggled closer, feeling an odd sense of security. Add in the fact he smelled like a musky man's cologne, and she could stay there for a while.

Steve held the car's back door open and glowered while Drew helped her inside. She curled into a ball, hugging her knees, and promptly fell asleep.

She woke from Drew digging through the pockets of her jeans. She scowled at the personal invasion of space. "What are you looking for?"

"Keys."

"Here." She dug them from inside her shirt. Her hand throbbed, keeping time to the beat in her head, which felt foreign and incredibly difficult to hold up. "Steve, do you have any more painkillers for me?"

"It's not time." He helped her out of the car then held her upright while Drew unlocked the door.

"I don't care if it's time or not. I need one."

"Then at least wait until we get inside."

Drew held the door open while Steve led her to the sofa. He set the bottle of painkillers on the coffee table and tossed her keys into her open purse. "Take good care of her, Wayne. I'm heading home. There's no need for both of us to be here. Goodnight, Linn."

"Night, Steve." She allowed her head to fall back against the softness of her plushy couch. She loved her couch. A girl could get lost in the cushions.

"Here." Drew handed her a glass of water. "Only take one."

"Call me if you need me." Steve stopped with one hand on the door handle.

"Go away. Both of you." Linn tossed the pill into her mouth and downed it with water. "Feel free to use the guest room, Drew. I won't make you sleep on the sofa. The guest room is the one with the made bed and no dirty laundry on the floor."

"Thanks. Yell if you need me. I'm going to put my things away." He dragged his bags from where he'd stashed it behind the sofa.

Linn closed her eyes. Her body grew heavy as the painkiller swept through her, filling her head with cotton. Her hand still throbbed, but she didn't mind as much.

Drew's face swam before her with his mussed curls and dark eyes, thick lashes, and a sculpted body. Too bad she'd sworn off men, having decided to put her career first. They couldn't be trusted anyway. At least none of the ones she'd met. Except maybe Steve. He'd make a wonderful brother. Or husband for some other lucky woman. Drew must have a girl in every town. "And way too pretty to be FBI."

"Thank you. I presume you're talking about me."

Her eyes snapped open. He grinned at her from across the room. Heat flooded Linn's face, and she returned his smile. "You are. Way pretty." Her words slurred and she giggled. Mortified, she clapped a hand over her mouth.

"And you're drugged. You'll hate yourself tomorrow for those flattering words." He rose from his chair. "Let's get you to bed."

"Not ready. Sit by me, while we watch the late news."

"I'll sit over here. I don't trust you to keep your hands off me. Not that I would mind too much. I'm always up for a little fun." Drew picked up the remote from the coffee table, turned on the television, and sat in the easy chair beside the sofa.

"Linn." His voice was stern enough to make her struggle to a sitting position and blink against sleep fighting to claim her. "Straighten up. Watch this."

She fought to focus on the television. The images blurred in fuzzy lines before they cleared enough for her to see. A close up of Elmo's flashed across the screen. A harried young reporter stood before the bar, holding a microphone in front of a pretty young woman in blue jeans.

"Shelly just went to the bathroom. She was gone so long, I got worried." Tears poured down the girl's face. "Thought maybe she was throwing up or something. She was pretty drunk. I went to check on her, and she was gone." Her words caught. "I looked everywhere. All I found was an earring."

The camera focused back on the reporter. "Three hours ago, Michelle Stockton went to the restroom…and didn't return. Authorities have questioned her husband after arresting him earlier for assault and illegally firing a weapon within city limits. Randy Stockton's alibi is firm. He's spending the night in jail. Is Michelle a victim of The Photographer? This is Rose Miller, reporting live from Elmo's Bar and Grill."

"Did I fall asleep?" Linn's heart stopped. "How long was I out? How could this have happened?"

"You slept about an hour." Wayne clicked the television off and pulled his cell phone from his pocket.

"Wait… just a second." Linn couldn't comprehend what had happened. She shook her head, raising her hands to rub her eyes. "Didn't we leave her at Elmo's? What time is it?"

"One a.m." He mumbled something into the phone she didn't catch.

"What?"

"I've got to go. Who can come watch you?"

She squared her shoulders. "I don't need anyone to watch me."

"Give me your car keys."

"No."

"I need your car keys. I'm going to have to take you with me. You can stay in the car. You're in no condition to walk, and I can't leave you alone. We need to get to Elmo's." He bent, his face inches from hers. His breath smelled of coffee.

"You tossed the keys in my purse. It's on the counter in the kitchen. Call Steve. He'll want to meet us there."

Drew disappeared, only to return seconds later with her purse draped over his arm. With his other arm, he helped her from the sofa. On rubbery legs and leaning heavily on his shoulder, Linn made her way outside.

Her mustang sat in the driveway. She slid into the passenger seat. Her hands slipped on the vinyl seats and she lurched, banging her hip on the gear shift. "Whoa. Dizzy." She dug into her purse for her keys. "Here." She tossed them to Drew who caught them in one hand. Fishing with her left hand, she located her cell phone and hit the speed dial for Steve's number.

"Did you see the news?"

"Yes. I'm on my way to Elmo's."

"Good. We'll meet you there." She dropped the phone back into her purse, staring absently into the dark leather of the clutch.

"How's the hand?"

"What?" Her head shot up. "Fine. Hurts. It's my gun hand."

"You won't need it." Drew steered the car into Elmo's. "You're staying in the car."

"Drew…"

He turned to look at her. "You're still woozy, Linn. We can't have you falling or shooting yourself."

"Do you baby all your partners?"

"No, just the female ones." He winked at her. "And we're not partners. I'm here to protect you and to catch a killer. There's a big difference." Drew slid from behind the wheel. "Lock the doors and take a nap."

"Lock the doors and take a nap." Her tone mocked. She hoped he caught her sarcasm despite the slurring. He needed to know how much his chauvinistic manner irritated her. Linn engaged the lock and leaned her head back against the seat, closing her eyes. A sharp rap on the window caused her to bolt up. Her eyes flew open. Steve peered at her through the glass. She rolled the window down. "You scared me." The sudden movement caused her head to reel. "And the painkiller is making me nauseous."

"Lay your head back." Steve frowned, his face registering his concern. "I was just checking on you."

"Drew's already over there somewhere." She waved her hand vaguely and let her head fall back against the headrest.

She closed her eyes as Steve tucked a strand of hair behind her ear. "Roll your window up. I'll see you later."

The click of the lock disengaging woke Linn. She blinked and glanced around, her mind clear, and her hand still throbbing.

"They found Shelly Stockton's purse." Drew slid behind the wheel. "We tried dusting for prints in the restroom, but I bet everyone in this town has been in there."

"Well, most of the women anyway. And you." Linn licked her lips. "Run all the prints. At least we can rule out some of them. Narrow the list down. I need something to drink. My mouth feels like cotton."

"I'll take you out to breakfast. You need food in your stomach along with those pain pills."

"Stop by the house first, okay? I want to clean up."

They drove in silence to Linn's house except for one short phone call from Steve checking to see how she felt. The man fussed more than a grandmother. They pulled into the driveway. Linn gripped Drew's arm.

A sheet of paper waved from her front door, welcoming them.

4

Shelly's eyes flickered open when he wiped the smeared makeup from her face.

"You have beautiful eyes." The Photographer tossed the rag he'd used into the fireplace. "You shouldn't have pushed her. I love her. She's mine." He clicked his tongue. "Blood is messy. You made her bleed and caused her pain. Two things you should not have done."

"What do you want with me?" Tears spilled from the woman's eyes, and she shivered.

He took her by the arm and pulled her to her feet. "Do you see that red dress hanging there? I made it for her, but you'll be the one to wear it. I can make another. Do you like it?" He reached out and fondled the crimson silk, the fabric cool and as soft as the finest chocolate. As soft as his love's skin, her breath against his hand as he held her. "Can you imagine her wearing it? Beautiful until death."

"I've seen you before." Her eyes widened. "At the bar at Elmo's." Her voice lowered to a croak. "You're the one who's murdering women? Wait." She clasped her head. "I've seen you before."

He tightened his grip on her arm. He felt the bone beneath her skin. "A fair assessment, considering I took you from the alley behind Elmo's while you puked your guts out. Quite disgusting. I almost changed my mind, but then you looked up and I saw your eyes. So like hers." He shrugged. "And murder is such a nasty word. I don't consider it murder, my dear, but rather an expression of my artistic abilities. Of my love."

He moved toward the kitchen, dragging the reluctant woman with him. "Someday she'll see and appreciate all I've done to win her."

She struggled against the rope binding her hands. "Please, I'll do anything you want."

The Photographer whirled, bringing his face inches from hers. He wrinkled his nose at the odor of sweat, beer, vomit, and fear that wafted on her breath. "Can you bring her to me? Can you make her love me? Will you make her *notice* me?"

"I…I…can try. I'm persuasive. Women listen to each other."

"That isn't good enough." He kicked away a rug covering a trapdoor in the kitchen floor. "I need promises. Assurances!" He bent and pulled on the iron ring. The door lifted with a groan. "Can you give me that?"

Shelly's scream echoed beneath him when he pushed her in. Her pale face stared up at him as he crouched beside the pit.

"Why don't you take her?" Shelly knelt beneath him. She clasped her hands in prayer.

His lip curled. She thought she could act pious. Virtuous.

"I'll help you." Her words broke in a sob. "I promise. I'll help you get her. Then you can let me go."

He shook his head. "I need perfection, my dear. I desire perfection. My love hasn't attained it yet, but she's very close." He lowered the door and shut off the woman's cries. The Photographer replaced the rag rug over the outline of the door and strolled outside to the small shed behind the house.

Another door lay in the floor of the shed, and he opened this to reveal a wooden ladder leading into a dark abyss. At the foot of the ladder swung a naked light bulb, hanging from a cord. The Photographer reached up and pulled the chain, illuminating a small room. His secret place. A shrine to Linn's beauty.

Photos of Linn and the murdered women papered the walls around the deep sinks he used to develop his photographs. He smiled at his latest. It was taken of Linn in the hospital, her hand cradled in her lap, head thrown back, and eyes closed.

The drops of blood from her hand stood out on the grey-white tile of the hospital floor. He'd used Photoshop to grey everything but the blood. *Beautiful Anguish.*

It'd been so easy to sneak a janitor's uniform and keep his head down long enough to get close so he could snap the picture. His love for her had grown when she'd offered to take her turn instead of being ushered into a room immediately because of her status as a law enforcement officer. The act had shown her true beauty.

He'd taken the photo at an angle that didn't reveal her scar. He couldn't wait to give it to her. But first, he needed a copy for himself.

And her partner, good-looking and favored? Well, The Photographer had plans for him. Wouldn't Officer Chavez get a shocking surprise when the two of them came face to face?

A small desk housed a laptop, a scanner, and a photo copier. He scanned the photo and printed out an 8 x 10 inch size. Lowering himself to the floor, he sat and stared at the image before him. *She really is lovely. I want her.*

The cowboy only makes things more difficult for all of them. *He* cannot have her. *He* has everything. Everything I want.

Tears welled in his eyes, and he tightened his hold on the photograph, creasing the corner. The crease was another sign of her imperfection.

Smoothing the paper across his thigh, rage rose within him. He considered taking out his frustrations on his latest acquisition. But, no, her time would come. He wadded the photo in a ball and tossed it across the room.

With a deep sigh, he rose and pushed the button to print off another copy. The soft whine of the printer filled the room. He leaned back against the desk, closed his eyes, and relished the feel of the cold metal.

Discomfort, agony, the ability to take life. It all added up to the power that belonged to him. It proved he lived.

~

Linn's heart skipped a beat as her eyes focused on the paper. She couldn't make it out clearly in the faint light of dawn, but she was certain she looked at another photograph of herself.

Her gaze cut to Drew's. Her mind raced with clarity. A sense of danger heightened her senses. No longer foggy from the effects of the pain medication, Linn realized The Photographer had taken a dangerous step forward in his dance of evil.

Drew watched her, a concerned look on his face.

She tried to smile, but failed, succeeding only in giving him a shaky baring of her teeth.

He laid a hand on her shoulder and squeezed before opening his door and sliding from the car.

Blood pounded, cold, through her veins. Linn choked back a shuddering sigh and followed. Her eyes focused on the front door with all the thrill of a man walking the Green Mile. The photo pulled her like a magnet, a force too strong for her to break.

Drew untacked the photograph before he handed it to her. It had been taken the day before, showing her closing her bedroom window.

"He watches me continuously. How can someone get so close to me without being noticed?" Linn's hand fell to her side. "Next thing, he'll be in my house."

"From the angle of the camera shot, he had to have taken it from…there." Drew's gaze swept the street. "The yellow house. Who lives there?"

"The Morrises. They're an older couple who've lived here for years. But The Photographer's smarter than that. He'd have to know we'd figure out the angle."

"Maybe he wants us to. When did you see your neighbors last?"

"Day before yesterday, I think." Linn bit the inside of her lip. "Mr. Morris was mowing his lawn. They stay pretty much to themselves. Sometimes days go by without me seeing them."

With long strides, Drew loped across the street. Linn rushed to keep up with him, tucking her injured hand close to her side. Her hand throbbed along with her head. She shouldn't be doing this. She ought to be lying in bed. Instead, her blood pounded. Adrenaline burned.

One hand on his gun, Drew rang the doorbell, then stepped to the side, motioning for Linn to follow suit.

She peered in the front window and made out the shadowy shapes of furniture. "It's dark inside. I don't think anyone's home."

"Let's check the back. Be careful, and stay behind me." Drew stepped around the corner of the house and reached over the fence to flip the latch on the gate. He followed an orange flagstone path to the back of the house.

Linn's heart chilled when she spotted the first fly, followed closely by another then another. It shouldn't have spooked her. After all, flies liked the humid summer of the Ozarks. But something was wrong. Something didn't feel right.

She dashed to the rear of the house, batting the pests away from her face. Flies swarmed from a perfect circular hole in the glass of the arcadia door. She swallowed against the lump in her throat and stepped closer to Drew.

His face tightened, and he gripped her arm. He removed his weapon from its holster. "Stay behind me."

Wishing for her weapon, Linn nodded and placed her hand lightly on the back of his waist. The metallic smell of blood grew stronger as they entered the house. The chainsaw buzzing of flies filled her ears, shutting out all other sound.

Linn's heart plummeted at the sight of the bodies in the master bedroom. Bile rose from her empty stomach, further bothered by medication. "This doesn't seem like the work of the same guy." She gagged and pulled her shirt over her nose. "This is messy."

Both victims lay in their pajamas. Multiple slashes and punctures dotted their bodies. Blood, now dried to a rusty black, soaked the blankets and mattress beneath them. The dark, rolling cover of flies rose and fell as if a dark cloud filled the room and breathed. Linn approached the bed.

"This is anger. Rage." Linn's voice sounded hoarse to her ears. She held her hand over her mouth and nose. Her poor neighbors. They had always been so kind to her, so friendly, bringing over casseroles and cookies. Mrs. Morris had said many times how Linn needed fattening up. "We've got to call this in. They did not deserve to die like this."

"I'll use the phone in the kitchen." Drew swept his gaze across the room and checked the closet. "It's got to be our man. He took the picture from this house. I don't think it's a coincidence that he walked in here, found these people dead, and then used their house to watch you. Something set him off enough to kill."

"What kind of a mad man are we dealing with?" Linn parted the curtains. She had a clear view of her front door. "You set him off. It has to be because you're staying with me."

Drew halted just outside the door. His shoulders stiffened. "We'll draw him out. Messy, angry people make mistakes."

With one more glance toward the grisly scene on the bed, Linn followed him from the room. "Draw him out? Make him more enraged, you mean. He'll kill more people."

"Yes, he will, until he finally comes after you. We have to stop him before it comes to that." Drew speared her with a gaze. "See if you can determine which room he took the photo from. Maybe he left a print this time."

He left her with her mouth hanging open as she watched his retreating back. She clenched her teeth and whirled to face the murder scene. She should have taken the time to grab her forensic bag.

Now, before the other officers arrived would be the perfect time to case the scene. As she turned to leave, she spotted a bloody footprint beside the bed. Only the upper portion, but maybe they could get something from it. It's the most evidence they'd discovered yet. She didn't think the eighty-year-old Mr. Morris wore gym shoes with a squiggly pattern on the sole.

She directed her attention back to the dark hall. Three doors faced each other, all closed. A light burning from behind cast her shadow before her, and a chill ran up her spine.

Using the hem of her shirt, she turned the first handle. It opened to a guest bathroom. The sweet scent of a sugar cookie candle greeted her and partially masked the odor from the master bedroom.

The second door opened into a bedroom which contained a single size bed, small dresser, and desk. Linn stepped into the room and gazed across the street. She couldn't see her bedroom clearly.

Behind the third door lay another bedroom. Small like the one before, but it contained only a bed and a vanity. Linn approached the only window.

She tripped on a bump in the carpet. A hissing to her right caught her attention. She turned, taking the blast of mist full in the face. Her body spasmed, then twisted. She fell to the floor with a muffled thud. Her one thought was of Drew before darkness descended.

~

Linn opened her eyes. The strap of an oxygen mask pulled her hair. Someone called out. A car door slammed. The shrill shriek of a siren pierced her ears.

Beside the gurney, Drew hunched in a plastic chair, his head cradled in his hands. A medic squatted nearby, and Linn raised her head to attract his attention, then motioned toward the oxygen mask. The medic removed the mask, replacing it instead with tubes in her nostrils.

Drew raised his head, his eyes black with worry. "How do you feel?"

"My chest hurts." She took a deep breath. "What happened?"

"I already headed down the hall when I heard you fall. Vapor released over your head, and I pulled you from the room."

"Vapor?"

"Some kind of gas." Drew ran his hand through his hair. "A very small amount, considering you're still breathing and able to speak."

"A trap?"

"He set a trip wire under a throw rug. Set to spring when anyone walked across the floor." He rested his elbows on his knees. "I'm sorry, Linn. I've done a poor job of protecting you."

The pain in his eyes tore at her heart. "It could have been anyone, and I should have been paying closer attention." If not for the shock of seeing her neighbors brutalized, she might not have been lost in her thoughts.

She placed a hand on his knee. "This just doesn't fit our guy's MO. A messy killing, then a trap. What kind of game is he playing? Besides, I thought he 'liked' me or something. He sure has a fine way of showing it."

"Maybe he hoped I would walk into that room. I don't know, but he *is* toying with us." He shook his head. "I called Steve. He's at the house looking for evidence. When he's finished there, he'll meet us at the hospital."

He looked tired. "You need to get some sleep." Dark circles ringed his eyes, as if someone had taken purple chalk and rubbed it into the skin. The dusting of a beard that seemed a permanent fixture on his cheeks and chin was darker and thicker. His hair stood up on his head, wild and curly.

"I'm fine." He looked at her with bloodshot eyes. "You, on the other hand, can't seem to stay out of the emergency room."

"Ha ha. This all started when you came around." Linn shifted on the hard gurney. "I insist on my bodyguard being in the best of shape. You can't do your job properly if you're exhausted."

"Oh, I'm in good shape. If you can stay out of the hospital, I could show you." He grinned at her. "I'll nap at the hospital. Okay?"

Yeah, he looked good to her. Tired, but gorgeous. She shrugged one shoulder. "Whatever." Fatigue overwhelmed her and weighted her body. She closed her eyes, only to open them when the ambulance stopped.

"We're here." Drew stood to the side while medics lowered the gurney to the ground.

They wheeled Linn to a private room in the ER and transferred her to a bed there. Mere seconds passed before her eyes closed again.

When she opened them, night had fallen. The moon cast silver shadows across the tile floor of the room.

Drew reclined in the only chair offered, hands folded across his stomach, his mouth open slightly. A soft snore wafted from him.

A tender smile pulled at her lips, then froze. She couldn't be falling for a pretty playboy. He was fine to look at, but nothing more. She didn't need another man to dump her and move on to greener pastures. She'd seen the way women flitted around Drew, offering their treasures like peasants before a king. Not to mention, the man enjoyed the attention. No, Linn couldn't even afford a casual dalliance. Not with someone like Agent Andrew Wayne. A handsome, upstanding officer of the law who would turn up his nose if he knew about Linn's damaged past.

No one from her past was left to tell her secrets. The few people who had been a part of her life had passed on years ago. She intended to keep the secrets buried. She pushed the button to raise the head of her bed.

Drew bolted from his chair, his eyes scanning the room.

Linn giggled, then winced at the pain.

"You're awake." Steve entered the room, carrying two Styrofoam cups of coffee and handed one to Drew.

"Where's mine?" Linn stopped the bed at a comfortable height.

"Haven't received the doctor's okay." Steve perched on the edge of her bed. His gaze bored into Drew. "Doing a good job of protection. A great one, actually. My partner has been in the hospital twice in less than twenty-four hours."

A muscle twitched in Drew's right cheek, a telltale sign that anger was rising.

"Stop it, Steve. Tell me what you discovered at the Morris's. Did you see the footprint?" Linn pulled the thin sheet higher, as protection over the thin hospital gown.

He nodded and took a sip of his coffee. "The bloody one beside the bed, and another partial outside. Standard gym shoe, size eleven, sold at just about every department store across America. We questioned the neighbors. One woman saw a man, slight of build, about five foot eleven with dark hair."

"That fits half the men in this town." Linn plucked at the hospital blanket. Disappointment flooded through her. "It fits both of you and half the police force."

"The gas was probably a nerve gas called Sarin. Our perp used a very small amount, otherwise you'd be dead. The lab's testing it now to be sure, but that's most likely the correct gas. We found no prints besides the Morris's and the lady who cleans for them once a week." Steve downed the rest of his coffee. "Madden is determined to get answers immediately and everyone at the station is jumping through hoops. I've got to type the report." He brushed a hand over Linn's hair, lingering on her cheek, and then glared at Drew. "Try to take better care of her."

"Sure thing, *buddy*." Drew's lips thinned, and he nodded. After Steve left the room, Drew turned to Linn. "Told you the man cares for you."

"Like a sister or a best friend."

"Suffer your delusions." He sat back in the chair and leaned forward, legs spread and hands hanging between them. "There's something we're missing. The Photographer has never left prints before." He straightened. "He wanted us to find them."

He grabbed the phone from beside the bed, and punched in a set of numbers. "Madden."

Linn tilted her head to watch and listen.

"It's Wayne. Have your men check all the dumpsters in town for shoes that match the prints found at the Morris's. Check all trashcans on curbsides and in alleys. My guess is he dumped them as soon as he left the premises." Drew rolled his head. "I know it'll take a while. Start at the Morris' and spread out. Put a hold on garbage pickup until they're found."

A spark of hope leaped in Linn's chest. "You really think we'll find them?"

"I'd bet on it." Drew replaced the receiver. "He's also monitoring us to see how long it takes. Somehow, our friend knows every step we take, and he is enjoying the chase."

"Why has he gotten sloppy?"

"Because I've entered the picture. It's not just about you and him anymore. I've infringed on his territory."

37

5

*T*he Photographer stared at the woman on the bed. Faded lashes lay on wrinkled, paper-thin skin. Skin so pale, he could detect the purple-blue veins running beneath it like elaborately spun spider webs. The low beep of the heart monitor filled the silence in the room. He ached to shake her awake. He needed to tell someone what he'd been doing, the accomplishments he'd achieved, and the woman on the bed was the perfect confidante. The only one to whom he could spill his secrets.

A nurse padded past the door, sending the obligatory complacent smile his way. He forced his own lips into the semblance of a grin before turning back to the bed. He sighed and rubbed his forehead. *Wake up*!

He glanced at the gold-plated imitation Rolex on his wrist. He'd already been waiting for an hour. Didn't she understand he's a busy man? The urge to hold the bed pillow over her face until her life was gone itched at the palm of his hands.

Why not? Look at her? She'd clearly outlived her usefulness. What had she ever done for him besides give him up? His eyes moved to the dark age spots on her weathered hands. Imperfect. Wrinkled. He scowled, rose from the chair, then took a step toward the bed.

The old woman's eyes flickered open. They widened and focused on him.

"Hello, mother." The Photographer bent and kissed the air beside her cheek being careful not to make contact. "I've come to visit. Sorry it's been a while, but I've been quite busy." He pulled his chair close to her. "Would you like to know what I've been up to?"

Her eyelids fluttered quick as butterfly wings.

"Too bad. I'm going to tell you anyway." The Photographer smiled. "Have you been watching the news? No? Pity."

He drummed his fingers against his lips. "The doctor told me the probability of you ever speaking again is non-existent. I'm sorry about that—for you, anyway. For me, it couldn't be better. Who knew your stroke would be such a positive thing? I thought you'd be a nuisance. Of course, your dying would have been better. I would then have been a wealthy bachelor, but we can't have it all, can we? At least not immediately."

His mother's nurse, Mrs. Green her nametag stated, padded back into the room, and he paused, doing his best to look saddened by his mother's plight. He stepped aside while Mrs. Green checked the monitors. The Photographer stared out the window. The nurse's murmurs provided background noise to the machines and grated on his nerves. Why couldn't she do her job and get the hell out?

A siren blared outside, and he craned his neck to see a squad car speed by beneath him. He laughed softly. Had they found the shoes? What would they make of them? A shame he had to get messy with the old man and woman, but this game had bendable rules. Rules made by him. It was so much fun to see the cowboy and Linn's partner scramble in their futile attempts to keep her safe.

"I'm finished here, sir." The nurse collected her tray.

The Photographer nodded. His gaze ran over the hair tucked into a loose bun. Too dark. He'd like to start a "live" collection of Linns, rather than killing them. Wouldn't that be intriguing? Take the perfect pieces and put them all together into one perfect Linn. His heartbeat quickened. After all, he had read somewhere that women liked their own kind for company. He would make sure that Linn had all the friends she needed before the end of his and her time together.

He closed the door behind the nurse and resumed his seat. "Have you guessed who I am? Does The Photographer ring a bell?" He crossed his legs, running a finger down the tight crease of his trousers. "I'm shaking things up a bit, though. I'm going to keep my girls a bit longer. Why should I have only one? Of course, I'll still kill them and send my love the picture, but I've got this wonderful place to keep them."

His mother closed her eyes and turned her head.

"Now, don't go falling asleep on me. I'm not finished." He reached over and pinched the tender skin beneath her arm.

Her eyes flew open and a whimper escaped her.

"That's better. Would you like to know how I take them? The girls? Yes? It's simple, really. I can find them anywhere. It's a gift. Sometimes I spot them walking down the street. Most of the time, it's from the local bars and nightclubs. There's such a wonderful collection there." He shook his head and leaned forward, balancing his elbows on his knees. "The one I have now…she pushed Linn during a police investigation. Cut my love's hand pretty bad. I will have to make her pay. Maybe I'll cut her."

"It's good you were so strict during my upbringing. If you hadn't have locked me away, social services would have known I existed and would have carted me away." He laughed as his gaze locked on hers. "I could have turned out so differently. As it is, you taught me to value perfection above all else." He planted a kiss on her forehead, his lips barely touching the skin. "Goodbye. I'll be back to visit soon. I'm sure I'll have plenty of entertaining stories to tell."

He stepped lightly as he exited the hospital room. Excitement caused his breath to catch. He entered the empty elevator and sagged against the wall. The thought of taking another one so soon almost overwhelmed him.

The elevator stopped at the next floor and the doors opened. The Photographer found himself joined by two overweight nurses. He pulled his suit jacket tight around him, lest it brush against their germ-infested scrubs.

One of the nurses gave him a sharp look, then rolled her eyes before turning back to her companion. "So, my daughter is home for a whole week. I managed to have someone cover most of my shift so I can spend as much time as possible with her. Would you like to see a picture? She's beautiful. Going to school to be a nurse like me." She pulled a photograph from the pocket of her coverall.

The Photographer stepped forward, just enough to peer over the nurse's shoulder. A young woman's laughing face shone forth. Long blond hair blew in the wind, and he smiled. Yes, he had a rare gift indeed.

~

"You'll have company soon." The Photographer peered into the gloom of the pit. "I've chosen my next acquisition. She'll join you within the next day or two." He grabbed his camera from the nearby table and snapped Shelly's picture. "I need to make sure everything is perfect."

"Please, let me out. My family will be worried." Shelly squinted up at him. "I won't tell a soul, I promise."

"Don't beg." He tossed down a sandwich enclosed in a plastic bag and bottle of water. "I thought you'd be pleased to have company, not naglike my mother." He slammed the trapdoor closed on her pleas.

The nurse's name tag had said Dolores Green. The Photographer climbed the stairs and entered the small room he used as his home office. The walls were papered with newspaper clippings about him. His exploits, achievements, the game he played with the Upton Falls police. The knowledge of how he stayed one step ahead of them at all times sent a delicious thrill through him. A pity it had to come to an end.

He sank into the rolling office chair and turned on his computer.

Minutes later, he leaned back and stared at the address on the screen. Ten minutes, and he could be there. He shoved the chair back from the desk and sprinted down the stairs and outside to his car. His face ached from the size of his smile.

Self-discipline kept him driving the speed limit. It wouldn't do at all to be stopped for speeding. He'd have to answer too many questions. His knuckles whitened as he gripped the steering wheel. He had managed to stay out of the eyes of the world, until now. And, soon, on his own terms, everyone would know him, especially Aislinn.

Nurse Green lived on a tree-lined street of older, well-maintained homes. He drove past the house, then turned and drove by again, slower this time. His gaze scanned the homes on each side. An alley! He turned the corner, pulling the car into the alley, and parked several doors down from Nurse Green's. The Photographer switched off the car lights and sat in silence, focused on the light spilling from the house.

Movement caught his eye. He watched as the nurse tossed a black bag into the plastic garbage bin. He glanced at his watch. Six o'clock. Was this a nightly routine? Every other night? Would her daughter offer to take out the garbage during her visit? What about recycle? He'd have to find out when the pick-up would be. There were so many details to work out. He wanted everything to be perfect.

He backed the car down the alley before turning the lights on and driving home, lost in his thoughts.

6

*L*inn sat back in her wheelchair as Drew rolled her out the front doors of the hospital and into the warm sunshine of a late summer day. Linn raised her face to let the ray's caress her skin. The hospital was growing old, fast. But, she stilled breathed, the sun still shined, and she was fit enough to work.

"We…found…the…shoes." Madden rushed toward them. His breath came in labored gasps and he leaned one arm against the hospital's stone pillars. He forced the words between pants. "Man, I…have got…to lose weight."

"I love you just the way you are." Drew laughed. "Big and squishy."

"Ha. Ha." Mad Dog pulled a yellowed handkerchief from his pocket and mopped his brow. "You were right. We found the shoes in a garbage can less than a block from the Millers. No prints. Nothing—other than smears of what we think is blood from one of the victims."

"Why didn't you call?"

"In the area." The big man straightened. "I'm headed back to the station right now."

"Hmmm." Drew pushed the wheelchair forward when Steve stopped his car beside the curb.

Something's nagging at him. Linn craned her neck to look up at him, squinting in the bright light. "Hmmm, what?"

"Just hmmm." Drew stepped in front of her and offered his hand. "Do you feel up to stopping by the precinct? I'd like to go over our notes. Have the three of us do some brain-storming."

"I'm fine." She ducked and slid into the front seat. "Work will be good for me." She turned to her partner. "Steve?"

"Sure." He turned the key in the ignition and pulled slowly away from the curb.

She sighed and stared out the window. Linn's mind ticked back over her years in the police force. Who would want to hurt her? Who hated her enough to terrorize her with photographs and murder innocent people in order to take those pictures?

"You all right?"

She turned her head to look at Steve. "Just thinking."

He reached over and patted her hand, then redirected his attention to his driving.

"Love." Drew leaned forward and whispered in Linn's ear.

Rolling her eyes, she huffed. A chuckle from the backseat caused her to pull down the car's visor. She tilted it at an angle to see Drew.

He winked.

With a huff, she flipped the visor back in place. Why did it bother her for Drew to think she had a thing going with Steve? Her partner would be a fine catch for any woman. Just not her.

Could she be falling for Drew in such a short time? She straightened. Her grandmother's words came back to haunt her. Cutting words of Linn's loose morals. Words of God's anger and punishment. After all, something had to have been bad about her? Something horrible enough for her mother to have dumped her at Grandmother's and fled as if the hounds of hell were after her. Or maybe it had just been the fear of raising a strong-willed child.

She shook off the unpleasant memories and looked up when they stopped before the police station. She *would* catch The Photographer, and if her mother were somewhere watching, she would be proud of her daughter. The one she cast away.

Drew opened the car door and held out his hand. "A penny for your thoughts." He grinned down at her, eyes crinkling at the corners.

A flush spread up her neck and across her face. Ignoring his hand, she slid from the car. "They're not worth a penny." Slinging her purse over her shoulder, she stalked into the building.

His laughter followed.

Once in her office, she plopped into her chair and thumbed through the mail on her desk. A chill of apprehension ran down her spine. The formidable manila envelope stuck out from the bottom of the pile, taunting her. Her heart thumped against her rib cage.

"Linn?"

She nodded at her desk as Drew entered. "Another envelope."

He pulled gloves from the box on her desk and snapped them over his hands. Using a pair of scissors, he ran the blade beneath the flap and dumped the contents onto her desk. Two photographs.

The terrified face of Shelly Stockton glared up at her. What looked like dirt walls rose on all sides of the woman. "She's alive in this picture. What's she in? A pit? A cellar?"

She set that photo aside and focused on the other. Time stopped. Her breath caught. It was of herself. She sat in the hospital waiting room cradling her wounded hand.

"What is it?" Steve stood in the doorway clutching a coffee mug in one hand and a batch of messages in the other.

"Another package." The words stuck in Linn's throat. She wiggled trembling fingers in Steve's direction.

He stepped closer, and she snatched the coffee cup from his hand.

"Wait…" Steve reached for his mug.

She gulped the liquid, gasping as it burned down her throat searing a painful fiery trail. "Oh. Oh."

Linn fanned her hands at her mouth, searching for something cool to wash down her throat.

Drew dashed into the hall and returned a moment later with a paper cone of water. Linn gulped it, the water a cool relief. "Sorry. Sorry." Trembling as severe as a convulsion overtook her and she slid from her chair.

"Not afraid of anything?" Drew snarled at Steve before taking Linn into his arms. "Shhh."

Steve stood, arms hanging at his side. "She's always so tough. So full of grit. I'll get us more coffee."

"I'm sorry." Linn tried to pull free. If Mad Dog came in and saw her breakdown, he'd remove her from the case. A detective did *not* fall apart. Drew's tight hold reassured her she was anchored here. Safe, at least for the moment.

She pulled her head back, glancing from him to Steve, who now stood with a mug in each hand. "It's all happening so quickly. He sees everything I do. When I'm vulnerable, he's there. He's like a parasite under my skin, eating away at me."

"You okay now?" Drew brushed her hair away from her face.

She nodded.

He released her, then pushed to his feet. He held her chair steady while she sat.

Linn's eyes flicked back to the photographs. "This isn't like me—falling apart under pressure." She raised her eyes to Drew's. "I'm not a weak person."

"I know. Maybe we need to take you off the case." He stepped back and perched on the corner of Steve's desk, accepting the offered cup of coffee.

The compassion in his eyes was almost Linn's undoing and the tears welled up again. "You can't." She needed this case. With every fiber of her being, she needed to catch The Photographer. Falling apart on the sidelines wasn't an option. Not this time.

"You won't be objective."

"I will." Linn nodded. She'd need to toughen up before Drew packed her bags and sent her away. "I definitely will not quit. This guy wants me. Keeping me around will draw him closer." She rubbed her hands together. "Okay. Let's get to work. What do you want to start with?" Her words sounded sharp to her ears and she cringed. Why did she have to be so hateful? The man was only trying to help. "I'm sorry. I really don't mean to be so nasty."

"No apology necessary." Drew rose and grabbed a dry erase marker from a mug on Steve's desk. He divided the board facing Linn's desk into sections titled: Victims, Suspects, Linn, and Clues. "Where's the photo copies of the women?"

Steve pulled them from a folder on his desk.

Once taped to the board, there were five photos. Three dead, the one of Shelly Stockton, still alive, and one of a woman still missing. Drew tapped the photograph of the missing woman. "I don't think she's part of our case."

"Why?" Steve blew into his coffee. "She fits the general description."

"This picture wasn't sent to us by The Photographer."

"That's right. Her husband gave it to us when she turned up missing."

"Have you interrogated the husband?"

She nodded. "As soon as the second victim turned up dead."

"We'll need to speak with him again. He's all we've got at this point." Drew put a check mark next to the woman's picture, then moved over to Suspects and wrote Stockton. "And now," he turned his dark-eyed stare on her. "Enemies?"

"Linn doesn't have any." Steve's eyes narrowed. "Everyone in Upton Falls loves her."

"There has to be someone. Someone she's put away, a man scorned, a jealous female?"

"The Photographer is not a woman." Linn shook her head. She ran her finger along the rim of her coffee mug. "I've been thinking about this, and I can't come up with anyone. Not a single person. Until recently, Upton Falls has been a peaceful town. Nothing more dangerous than drunken fights at Elmo's."

"No family?"

"None. I've been alone for a while now. My father died when I was four. My mother dumped me off at my grandmother's a year later. Grandmother died five years ago." Images of an unhappy childhood flashed through Linn's mind, her overbearing grandmother at the center of it. She sighed. "There's no one. I've been pretty much a loner until they partnered me with Steve."

Drew wrote Steve's name beneath Linn's.

"What are you doing?" Steve slammed his coffee mug on his desk. "I'm not a suspect here."

"That's why you're name isn't listed under Suspects." Drew glanced at him over his shoulder. "But you're the only connection to Linn we seem to have. Who are *your* enemies?"

Steve folded his arms. "I don't have any, either."

"Where did you live before you came here? Could someone have followed you?"

"I've lived here my whole life. Linn's the newbie. Thought you read the files."

"I have. Just checking to make sure the facts match." Drew leaned against the board, his gaze glued to Steve.

"Of course they match." Linn looked from one man to the other. "What's really going on here, Drew?"

"Steve is the only one close enough to you to have been at all these places and taken your picture. I can't recall him being visible during a single time. He was there, but away. He knows his forensic science, so covering his tracks would be easy."

"I cannot believe this." Steve bolted out of his chair. "I cannot believe you're insinuating I would do anything to hurt Linn."

"Nobody has intentionally hurt Linn. Just women who look like her."

Steve slapped his thigh and turned away.

"This is ridiculous." Linn pushed herself out of her chair. "You are really grasping at straws now."

"What size shoe do you wear?" Drew glanced at Steve's feet.

The other man hesitated. "Eleven."

"Good grief." Linn stood in front of Drew. "Half the men in this town probably wear that size."

"Fine." Beneath Clues, Drew wrote size eleven shoe. "Any other clues?"

Linn fought to regain control. She clenched her fists until a sharp stab of pain reminded her she had stitches in her hand. With a shaky breath, she glanced at Steve and answered. "Caucasian male, approximately five feet nine or ten inches."

Steve rolled his eyes and fell back in his chair as Drew wrote down the description. "The man also takes his own pictures and most likely develops them. We've checked with the local print shops. No one has seen any of these photos before."

"What about the red dresses? Any idea where they come from?"

"Not from anywhere around here." Steve crossed his arms.

"They aren't bought from a store."

Both men turned to Linn.

"I think he makes them. There hasn't been a clothing tag on any of the victims' dress, or anyplace a tag was cut out. If he hired someone to make them for him, he would have an accomplice to his crime." Linn sipped her coffee. "I don't see him doing that."

"Did y'all check fabric stores?"

"I did. No one has bought a large amount of red silk fabric. At least not locally."

Drew listed this information on the board. "Then it leaves the internet. I'll get someone on it. Anything else?"

"I think that just about covers it." Steve unfolded his arms and twirled a pencil on his desk blotter. "Other than the Sarin gas."

"Sarin?" Linn gulped. "I'd managed to push that piece of information aside. I should be dead."

Steve shook his head. "Drew got you out fast enough. Besides, the lab said there was only a trace. Just enough to knock you out."

"Where would someone get a hold of Sarin?" Linn felt as if someone had punched her in the stomach. Why is this guy playing with her? There were faster ways if he wanted her dead.

"Folks can get a hold of just about anything nowadays." Drew shrugged. "You just have to know where to look."

~

Drew watched the play of emotions flit across Linn's face then allowed his gaze to run across Steve's clenched jaws. The detective hadn't shown any sign of being The Photographer, but he did fit the description, and he had easy access to Linn. In Drew's book, that's all it took to become a suspect.

Would Drew be able to convince Linn to go with him to check out Steve's house? She appeared to be watching Steve herself. Her hazel gaze ran over his. He didn't dare leave her home alone.

"So, considering I'm your prime suspect," Steve crossed his arms. "What would you like me to investigate today? Is there anything you trust me with?"

"You could pick up the gym shoes from Madden."

Steve bent, retrieved a plastic bag containing a pair of shoes from beneath his desk, and tossed them at Drew. "Done. Anything else?"

"Guess you could type up what we *do* know." Drew caught the bag in one hand and smirked.

"Whatever you say, *Boss*." Steve narrowed his eyes at Drew before turning to his computer screen.

"This is ridiculous." Linn planted her hands on her hips. "Enough is enough. Steve's no more a serial killer than you are, Drew. I'm going with him to speak to the missing woman's husband."

Perfect. "I'll stay here."

"What?" Linn faltered.

"You're right. Steve's no killer. You'll be perfectly safe with him. I've got plenty of work to do."

She glanced at Steve, confusion apparent on her face. "Okay. Steve?"

He grabbed his holster from the back of his chair. "Let's go. I'll drive. I've got half a tank of gas."

Drew watched out the window until Steve's car backed out of the parking spot. He then loped to the front desk, requested keys to an unmarked car, sprinted to the garage, then sped out of the police parking yard.

Like everything else in the small town of Upton Falls, Steve's house was situated close to conveniences such as a grocery and drug store. No one in town had to go far for necessities. Drew cut the ignition and studied the small ranch-style building that sported a porch across the front. The grass was green and well-maintained. One large oak tree dominated the front yard. Its branches hung low, brushing against the house roof.

Glancing up and down the street, Drew slid from the car. The day was quiet except for the occasional bark of a dog. His feet crunched up a gravel-strewn path to the wooden porch. A simple screen door hung in front of an ornamental glass one and allowed Drew an unobstructed view into the foyer. Polished pine floors. A wooden entry table sat below a large mirror. Drew slipped on a pair of leather gloves and tried the front door handle. Locked.

He stepped around the corner, trying windows as he went. Bingo! A small window in the bathroom hung open just above his head. Stretching, he pulled himself up. It was tight, but with some clever maneuvering, a lot of grunts, and a couple of painful scrapes, Drew stood on a black-tiled floor in a black-and-white-tiled bathroom. Matching towels hung evenly from a brushed nickel towel rack, and a clear saucer held fragrant potpourri.

Drew stepped into the hall and glanced right. Three open doors beckoned, leading to three immaculate bedrooms. Prints of famous artists hung on the walls. No personal photos of any kind. Not even in the master bedroom. He turned and headed toward the living room.

A black leather sectional sofa dominated the room. Glass end tables and a coffee table held an assortment of books on profiling and forensics. A manila folder peeked from beneath them. He slid it free. Opening it, he smiled with satisfaction. Inside were photos of the murdered women along with details and penciled clues. Drew replaced the folder and reached for a small framed photograph.

It was a photo of Steve and Linn standing before the precinct. Steve's arm was thrown companionably around a smiling Linn's shoulders. Drew grunted, set the photo back on the table and headed to the kitchen.

With black and chrome appliances, the kitchen seemed stark and unwelcoming. Nothing looked out of place. He returned to the folder of murdered victim photos. It didn't really mean anything. He was working on the case, after all. Drew rubbed his chin. If he wanted to harm Linn, he'd had plenty of opportunities. He allowed his eyes to roam once again over the walls in the room. Why weren't there any pictures of his foster family? Friends?

7

*T*his would be so easy. The Photographer grinned behind the wheel of his car. His face ached from a smile stretched too far. It had taken a few days longer than he'd like to figure out the girl's schedule, but tomorrow was garbage pickup and there she was, bag in hand. The girl tossed her head, her ponytail swinging and said something to someone behind her.

"Hurry, Suzy. Dinner's ready." The call floated to where he sat. Suzy. He knew her name, and it was beautiful.

"Okay, Mom." Her voice sounded like orchestra music to his ears, and he closed his eyes for a moment.

In the shadows where he waited, The Photographer pushed the play button on his recorder and the mewling of a kitten floated across the evening air. His prey lifted her head, a frown on her lovely face, and gazed down the alley. She took a couple of steps toward him, and he pressed the pause button. When she shrugged and went to turn away, he played the cries again. A cool night breeze blew. He shivered beneath the light jacket he wore.

This time she ventured farther, only feet away from where he sat, hunched in his seat behind heavily tinted windows. He held his breath. She stopped a little past the car, her eyes searching for a kitten. Suzy's face shone pale in the moon's glow. She looked ethereal, other worldly.

The Photographer lunged from the car and pressed the cloth of ether over her nose. She gasped and kicked backward, missing his leg. Within seconds she sagged against him. In the blink of an eye, he shoved her into the back seat, closed the door as silently and rapidly as possible, and soon the car roared from the alley.

An overwhelming urge to break into laughter came over him. Tears poured down his cheeks as he fought for control. Once free from the alley, he allowed the sounds of glee to burst forth, mingling with the classical music spilling from his radio.

The girl stirred when he parked the car in his garage. Moans from the backseat spurred him to action. He bounded from the car and yanked open the door.

Long bare legs struck him, hammering his chest and face. Screams rose in volume and vibrated against his eardrums. He groped for a hand hold on the silky skin and dragged her kicking from the car. A real live firecracker! His heart swelled as adrenaline coursed through him. This girl was the closest he had found to being like Linn. Beautiful and feisty. Strong, yet vulnerable. He looked forward to taming her.

The Photographer made shushing sounds and clamped his hand over her mouth. Of course no one could hear her where he lived, but the din gave him a headache.

Holding her tight against him, he breathed in the fruity scent of her hair. He closed his eyes and wrapped his arm around her throat into a choke hold, compressing her carotid arteries for the fifteen seconds it took to render her unconscious. He exhaled as her body went limp, then scooped her in his arms and carried her into the house to position her on one of the kitchen chairs. He whipped his belt from the loops in his slacks and wrapped it around her, securing her body to the chair. Then, he pulled up a chair of his own and sat back to wait.

~

The slamming of car doors in front of the house sent Drew sprinting down the hall and into the bathroom. He stuffed his weapon in its holster, thrust himself through the window, twisting and turning until he squeezed through, and scraped his arm and shoulder. Taking a deep breath to steady himself, he retrieved his gun, examined the dent in his side from where it had dug into him, and then stepped around the corner of the house.

Steve and Linn stood beside Drew's car. Linn shaded her eyes and peered through the passenger side window while Steve stood with a stony face and surveyed the house.

"Hey!" Drew wiped the blood from his arm on the end of his dark tee shirt.

"What are you doing here?" Steve's voice was sharp enough to cut through steel.

"Thought you two were interviewing that missing woman's husband."

"I wanted my notepad." Steve's eyes cut to Drew's bleeding arm. "It has all my case notes in it."

"Steve's pretty obsessive about his notes." Linn raised her eyebrows in a clear statement of 'What the hell were you doing?'

Drew raised his eyebrows. "I brushed up against the bougainvillea bush in your backyard. Snagged myself on a thorn."

"Right." Steve marched past him and disappeared in the house.

Linn stood, hands on hips, and glared up at Drew. "Were you searching Steve's house? You have a lot of nerve."

"Have you ever been inside Steve's house?" Drew pulled her around to the back of his car.

"Once or twice." She yanked her arm free. "Why?"

"There are no family photos. Not one. Steve said he grew up here. Don't you think that's odd?" Drew leaned against the trunk of the car and folded his arms across his chest. "And not to be racist or anything, but Chavez isn't exactly a common name in these parts."

Her eyes narrowed. "You had the audacity to go inside his house?"

Drew shrugged.

Linn turned away to stare at the front of Steve's house. "Why?"

"I told you why. He fits the profile. He's close to you. No one would suspect him, and he has no family photos. I find that odd."

She threw her hands in the air. "You're being ridiculous. Steve was a foster child, taken from biological family when he was nothing but an infant. Maybe they were migrant workers. His childhood was not a happy one. That's why he doesn't have any family pictures. There wasn't anyone he cared to keep pictures of. Not because he's a lunatic or a serial killer."

Steve strode toward them, a spiral notebook tucked under his arm.

"Now be quiet, before you upset him with any more of your harebrained ideas." Linn slammed Drew with her shoulder.

Steve yanked the notebook and shoved it into Drew's face. "You were in my house. Things are not as I left them." His eyes fell on Drew's arm. "You did not cut yourself on a bush."

"Guilty as charged." Drew grinned. "I cut myself getting out your bathroom window. Sorry. I thought I was careful about putting things back." He slapped the notebook from his face.

"I ought to have you arrested for trespassing."

"And I ought to add your name to our official suspect list." Drew's gaze locked with Steve's wide-eyed one.

The other man hesitated and took a step back. "You honestly think I would harm Linn? That hurts, even coming from you."

"No, Steve, he…" Linn put a hand on Steve's arm.

"She hasn't actually *been* harmed, has she?" Drew pushed away from the car. "The things that have happened to Linn over the past day have all been accidents. Not something planned by our perp. Except for maybe the gas. And that could've been for anyone entering the room."

"I would never hurt you." Steve turned to Linn.

"I know you wouldn't." She glared at Drew. "Don't listen to him."

Drew raised his eyebrows. "Are we going to interview the woman's husband or not? We're wasting time out here." He strode to the driver's side door. "I'll drive. Y'all can ride with me or not."

The air inside the car was thick with suppressed emotion, and Drew rolled down his window, relishing the feel of the wind on his face. Linn insisted on obstinately riding in the backseat with her partner. Drew felt like a chauffeur carting around a couple in a tiff. Once they pulled up before a small red brick house, Drew rolled his head on his shoulders, easing the tension knotting there.

He slid from the car and marched forward, leaving the other two to catch up. He paused at the bottom of the steps that led to the front door. A slight breeze blew. The leaves of the maple tree shading the house rustled. A layer of dust lay over the patio furniture and dirt tracks led to the front door and back. He glanced toward the windows. Curtains were tightly closed against the day.

"Definitely lacks a woman's touch." Linn stood beside him.

"It doesn't look like anyone's home."

"Someone is." Steve pointed to an upstairs window. "The curtain moved."

Resting his hand on the butt of his weapon, Drew stepped forward and rang the doorbell. The ding echoed beyond the door. For several seconds the three stood on the front porch and waited for a response. Drew pressed the doorbell again.

"What?" The door swung open.

"Ronald Milroy?" Drew's eyes racked over the slightly overweight man. He looked like he sported five days worth of whiskers, and the odor emanating from him told Drew he obviously hadn't bathed in as long. "We'd like to ask you some questions about your wife."

"I've already answered plenty of questions. Questions aren't going to bring my Kelly back." The man tilted a beer bottle to his mouth. "Is it?"

"May we come in, Mr. Milroy?" Linn stepped closer. "We'll only take a couple minutes of your time."

Milroy peered at them through red-rimmed eyes before he stepped aside and ushered them into a gloomy room. Drew wrinkled his nose against the man's body odor and the mustiness of the closed house.

Milroy swept a hand across the seat of the sofa, dislodging and knocking several newspapers to the floor. "Have a seat." He chose a seat across from them.

"Where are your children, Mr. Milroy?" Linn leaned back and crossed her legs.

"Upstairs."

"Do you watch the news, Mr. Milroy?"

"Sometimes." The man frowned.

"Another woman disappeared." Linn leaned forward, resting her elbows on her knees. "Did you hear about that?"

Drew shifted his eyes from Linn to Milroy, then studied the room. Dust motes floated on the narrow sunbeam squeezing through the space in a back window curtain. Glass littered the floor along one wall. He squinted trying to make out the broken object. Frames. Shattered glass from picture frames glittered like ice around the edges of the room. A wooden baseball bat sat propped in a corner.

Downing the remaining beer in the bottle, Milroy belched. "Yeah. What's that got to do with me? I didn't take her."

"Did you and Mrs. Milroy have an argument the night she disappeared?" Linn's question was calm, her voice low.

Milroy slammed his empty bottle on the table beside his chair. "What're you getting at?"

Drew placed his hand on his weapon at the same instance as Steve.

Linn placed a hand on each side of her and pushed to her feet. Two steps and she stood inches from Mr. Milroy. She bent, so close her breath ruffled the long hair at his temple. "I think you killed your wife."

She straightened and stepped back. "At first, we thought she was just another victim of The Photographer, but," Linn swept an arm around the room. "I don't think so. Why are all the pictures of your wife shattered, Mr. Milroy? Was she unfaithful? Did she want to leave you? Was she going to take the children with her?"

A smile tugged at the corners of Drew's mouth at the myriad of emotions running across the cornered man's face. First outrage, then confusion, bewilderment, and then anger. The big man lunged to his feet.

Drew and Steve rushed forward, each grasping an arm and shoved the man back into his seat.

"Where is your wife?" Drew's voice was low, hard.

Milroy covered his face with his hands as sobs burst from him. "She's dead. I killed her. I put her in a bag and dumped her in the lake."

The man's shoulders shook. "She'd met somebody else. I caught them together and, one night, I waited for her to come home." He raised his tear-streaked face. "I didn't mean to kill her. I didn't. I loved my wife."

Steve pulled a pair of handcuffs from the pocket of his jacket.

Linn grinned.

Drew's heart leapt in his chest at the sight. He returned her smile. "How did you know so quickly?"

"Women look at other people's houses. I noticed the shattered pictures right away. Thought I'd take the chance and make the accusation. It worked."

"Too bad we can't catch The Photographer this easy." Drew pulled a cell phone from his pocket. "I'll call Madden to send someone down to get Mr. Milroy."

The man's wails increased in intensity as Steve stepped forward, hand-cuffs clanking together in his hands. "You have the right to remain silent. Anything…"

Mr. Milroy bolted from his chair, barreled into Steve, who rolled over the coffee table, and then fled down the hall and up the stairs.

Drew pulled his weapon and sprinted after the man.

Mr. Milroy bounded up the stairs. His footsteps thudded on the carpet runner. He stopped at the top of the stairs, long enough to give Drew a thin smile, then the man disappeared into a room. He slammed and locked the door behind him.

"Open the door." Drew jiggled the door handle. A child's cry drifted to him. "Open the door now!" He glanced at the others. "He's locked himself in the room with his kids."

"I'd like to speak with you, Mr. Milroy." Linn knocked on the door and leaned her ear against the wood. "Please open the door."

"I've got a gun in here. Go away before I shoot."

"I'm counting to three before I knock this door in." Drew yanked Linn away from the door.

Steve stood on the opposite side of the door, his weapon drawn. He nodded at Drew.

"One. Two."

Gunshots rang out. Bullets pierced the door, and Drew threw himself flat against the wall.

"Three." He reared back and slammed his foot into the door, crashing it open. His heart dropped to his stomach.

Milroy sat on the bed, two small boys next to him. In his hand he gripped a pistol, the barrel pointing to his temple. "Take one more step, and my boys are going to see their daddy die."

Linn stepped around Drew, her hands held loosely at her sides. "You don't want that, Mr. Milroy." She walked forward, halting when Milroy's hand twitched. "Your boys have been through enough. They've already lost their mother. Don't take their father away, too. Look at their faces. Look at the faces of your children, Mr. Milroy."

The boys raised tear-stained faces. Silent sobs shook their bodies. Tears poured down Milroy's cheeks. "I love my boys."

"I know you do. Please." Linn held out her hand. "Give me the gun."

"Linn, be careful." Drew put a hand on her shoulder.

She shrugged it off and continued forward. "Mr. Milroy?"

The man's shoulders sagged as he lowered his hand. The gun fell to the mattress, and he gathered the two boys close to him.

Drew breathed a sigh of relief and snatched the gun from Mr. Milroy's reach. "That was brilliant," he whispered to Linn.

Sirens rent the air.

"Madden's here." Steve turned. "I'll let them know where they can apprehend Mr. Milroy." He tossed the unused handcuffs to Drew. "Might want to get these on him."

"Mr. Milroy." Drew transferred his attention to the subdued man on the bed. Drew held up the cuffs. "If you would, please."

Linn ushered the weeping children down the stairs.

The father nodded and swung his legs over the edge of the bed. He stood and turned to offer his wrists to Drew. With a loud snap, the cuffs closed, and Drew grasped the sobbing man by the elbow.

8

Linn sat on the cool cement of the Milroy front porch, her arms around each of the two boys. Shudders passed through their small frames as their sobs faded. How old were they? Five and seven? She shook her head. To have faced such terror at their age. Her grandmother might have been a tyrant, but she'd never witnessed the murder of a loved one. It surprised her that the cruelty of the world failed to shock her anymore.

The moon's rays sliced through the branches of the tree and dappled the ground in front of them. How could there be such beauty amidst killing and horror?

"You okay?" Steve sat on the steps next to them, resting his arms on his knees.

"I'm fine. Just wondering about these two little guys." She gave them a squeeze. "And waiting for Social Services."

Drew steered Mr. Milroy down the steps to a waiting squad car. The man still cried, his wails rising and falling like an ambulance siren as he looked toward his sons. Drew said something to the man, who nodded, and ducked into the vehicle.

Linn's gaze followed him as he sauntered over to the waiting Madden. He stood, booted feet spread, arms crossed at his chest, emphasizing bulging biceps, and tossed his head, shaking the hair out of his face. He needed a haircut. She'd never known an agent who had hair long enough to brush their shirt collar.

"You're attracted to him, aren't you?" Steve's question fell flat, void of emotion.

"Is it that obvious?"

"To me it is. I've known you for three years." He stared at his folded hands. "I'm not sure what you see in an arrogant man like Wayne."

"Neither do I, but he sure is easy on the eyes." She gave him a sad smile. "I'm sorry, Steve."

He waved her words away. "A relationship between us would only complicate things at work. I just don't want you hurt, Aislinn. Your emotions are so fragile. You may be tough on the outside, but inside…well, I've never met a softer person."

"I don't plan on doing anything but look. You, better than anyone, know I don't want a steady relationship." If only her heart didn't have other ideas. That particular organ flip-flopped in her chest as Drew threw back his head and laughed at something Madden said.

A white sedan pulled along the curb and Linn rose, pulling the two boys with her. "Social Services is here. They'll take good care of you. You'll be fed and sleeping in a warm bed tonight." Keeping an arm around them, she walked them to the waiting social worker.

The African-American woman opened the car's back door, and unsmiling, ushered the boys inside. "Poor tykes. We're already so crowded and short-handed they'll have to spend several days in a group home." The woman sighed. "No help for it." She slammed the door and stalked back to the driver's side, her heels beating out a clackety-clack on the asphalt.

Linn stood back to survey the scene before her. Steve still sat on the porch, the sun beginning to set behind the house. Sympathy for him, as his eyes remained on the two children being placed into the system, flooded through her, and she squelched the desire to make a move of comfort. He'd told her of his childhood being bounced from foster home to foster home before the last one kept him on long term. He had no recollection of his birth parents.

She continued to scan the yard as police officers hopped in squad cars and prepared to head back to the station. Drew shook Madden's hand before the officer slid behind the wheel of the car transporting Milroy. Her breath hitched as Drew turned to her, smile flashing, and strode in her direction. His long legs cut the distance between them short.

"Hey." He smiled down at her.

"Hello." Her eyes cut to Steve, who turned away.

"You doing okay?"

She looked back up at him. "I'm fine. It's always a little difficult to hand children over to social services. It's really hard for Steve."

"Are you two up to heading back to the station to type up the reports?"

"Of course…"

"Wait up, Wayne," Madden yelled from his squad car window. "We've got another disappearance."

Linn glanced at Drew and, together, they quickened their pace.

"How long ago?" Drew leaned with one arm against the car.

"Approximately an hour. Girl's mother just called. Said her daughter, Suzy Green, was taking out the garbage and disappeared." Madden pressed his lips together before continuing. "If her daughter was anything but blond, we wouldn't rush on this, but, well…"

"Steve, we're heading out." Drew grabbed the paper with the girl's address from Madden's hand. "Thanks."

Drew opened his car door. "I'm driving."

"See, Steve can't be The Photographer. He's been with us." Linn clicked her seatbelt on.

Drew laughed and turned the key in the ignition. "You're tenacious, aren't you?"

She shrugged. "Just don't like my friend accused of a crime he didn't commit." Linn glanced at her hands lying in her lap. The stitches in her right hand ran like railroad ties across her palm. She flexed her fingers, stretching as far as the stitches would allow. She had a little more flexibility without the bandage, but not enough to suit her.

"It's been a rough couple of days."

Drew reached across and took her uninjured hand in his, sending sparks of electricity up her arm.

Her flesh grew warm. She tried to pull away

He held firm. "Let's see if we can't get you through this day without being hurt."

Steve crawled into the backseat, looking up and meeting Linn's eyes. She locked gazes with him, then turned away from the pain she saw there. What did Steve think as Drew held her hand? She hadn't believed Drew's declarations of Steve's love for her until she witnessed her partner's pain when she admitted her attraction for the FBI agent. She sighed. Partners in love would never work. Besides, Steve was like a brother to her.

A final squeeze to her hand, and Drew released her as they pulled up in front of the home of Suzy Green's mother. Two squad cars were parked diagonal from the sidewalk, the officers milling in the front yard. Radio static punctuated the night air with calls from dispatch.

Linn's skin quivered from the evening breeze blowing through the car windows, and she took a deep cleansing breath, allowing her gaze to roam over the small block house. Its yellow paint stood out from its more neutral-toned neighbors. Vibrant flowers shouted color beneath the streetlamp's glow. *Must be really pretty in the sunlight.* A heavy-set woman pushed open the screen door, and Linn slid from the car.

"Please find my daughter." The woman rushed toward them, her round face red and raw. Tears spilled from her eyes, leaving tracks in the woman's heavy makeup.

"Ms. Green." Linn held her hands in front of her as the woman stopped just inches away.

She grabbed Linn with two pudgy hands, and squeezed. "Please. She's all I have in this world. Does that killer have her? Does he?"

Drew pried the woman's hands from Linn's shoulders. "Ms. Green, please. We don't know anything at this point. Don't expect the worst without something to back it up. Could she have gone out with friends?"

The woman shook her head. "Not without telling me. She just flew in a few days ago, and we were going to stay in tonight and watch a movie."

Steve circled around them. "Could you show us where she was when she disappeared?"

"Oh, yes. The alley." Ms. Green huffed and sniffled her way to the back of the house. She paused once to pull a damp tissue from her bodice, and dabbed her eyes. "I just can't go on if something's happened to her." The tissue went back to its holding place. The woman's steps slowed as they neared the alley.

"She was taking out the garbage." One large arm waved. "I called to her to make it quick, dinner was almost ready, and she said okay. She looked down the alley, motioned to me to wait a minute, so I closed the door." The woman's sniffles increased. "That was the last I saw of her."

Linn put an arm around the woman's shoulders and gave her a quick squeeze. "We'll do everything we can to find her."

The woman nodded and patted Linn's hand. "I know you will, dear."

"Hey, Linn!" Drew squatted a few yards down the alley.

Linn withdrew her arm and loped to him. Steve scouted the alley at the opposite end.

"Look." Drew pointed to a set of tire tracks. "These look like the same tracks I noted at the warehouse."

"I knew it." Ms. Green wailed. "He has my Suzy." She covered her face with her hands, plump shoulders shaking.

"Please." Linn steered the woman back toward the house. "It doesn't mean that necessarily, but we do need you to let us do our job. That's our best bet for finding your daughter."

"Got signs over here." Steve shone a flashlight at his feet. "They're faint. But they're here."

"Looks like he parked here." Drew swung his flashlight beam around the ground. "He got out of his car…there's the footprints…and struggled with someone." He raised his eyes to where the victim's mother stood. Lowering his voice, he bent his head to the returning Linn. "All the signs point to The Photographer."

Linn's eyes flicked to where the girl's mother stood. "She's probably still alive, being so early since her abduction. What should we do?"

"The usual. An APB. Alert the media. Hopefully we're wrong, and someone has seen her."

"I've seen her."

Linn and Drew whirled toward the voice.

"Where are you?" Linn searched the bushes. She yanked her weapon from its holster. "Come out where we can see you."

"No." The voice faded. "I'll tell you what I saw, but that's it. I wish to remain anonymous."

"A woman?" Drew whispered.

Linn shrugged. "If you don't come out, how do we know you're on the up and up?"

"You don't. But it's the best you're going to get." The bushes rustled. "I was taking my garbage out a little over an hour ago and heard what I thought was a cat, a kitten maybe. The sound would rise, then fall, rise, then fall. I walked up to the noise real careful like. I didn't want to frighten it. I heard a car door open, gravel crunching, a scuffle, and then the car door slammed."

"That's it?" Linn frowned at Drew. "You didn't actually see anything?"

"I poked my head out. Caught a glimpse of the back of the man's head and a bit of his profile."

"In the dark." Linn shook her head. "I don't suppose you noticed the license plate, or the make of the car?"

"I'm not a detective."

Linn sighed.

"Wait." Drew placed a calming hand on her shoulder. "What did the man's head look like?"

The bushes rustled some more. "Smaller than yours. Dark hair, though. Oooh."

"What?"

"He looked like that man coming over here." The bushes rustled again.

Linn turned as Steve approached. Retreating feet slapped across the ground behind her.

Her partner's brows drew together. "What are you two doing?"

Linn and Drew glanced at each other. "Talking to a witness."

Steve looked toward the bushes. "Right." He folded his arms across the front of his suit jacket and glanced at the weapons the other two still held in their hands. "Where is this witness, and what did they say?"

Biting her lip, Linn turned her face away. "Huh. We never actually *saw* the witness, and they said the man who took Suzy looked like you."

"Right." Steve glanced toward the silent bushes again. "And this witness got a good look in the dark. Anything else?" He drummed his fingers on his lip, his brows drawn together.

Drew shook his head. "Nope. They just saw the back of the guy's head." He replaced his gun. "But, from the signs of the tire tracks, we're pretty certain The Photographer has Suzy Green."

~

The redness around her mouth from the chloroform contrasted with her fair skin, and he winced. Rising from his chair, he stepped closer, bending to get a better view. Suzy Green's eyes snapped open and startled him. He jerked, tripping and landing with a thud back in his chair.

The Photographer lunged back to his feet and clamped a hand over her mouth as she opened her lips. "Shhh. Everything will be all right." His eyes locked with hers. "I'm going to remove my hand now. Don't scream, and I won't have to hurt you. Understand?"

Suzy nodded, her eyes huge in her pallid face.

The Photographer slowly removed his hand, then smiled when she remained silent. Blue eyes glared at him from beneath her lowered brows. Perspiration beaded on her upper lip. "You're brave. Just like she is." He lifted a hand to smooth the hair that had fallen free of her ponytail. She shrank back from his touch.

"Don't be like that, Suzy. I'm going to cut you free now, but," he jerked his head toward the table. "See that knife there? I'll hurt you if you try to run." He picked up the knife and twisted it before her face. Her reflection shone back at him from the smooth edge.

He sawed through the belt binding her and hauled her to her feet. Once he'd kicked the rug away from the trapdoor, he bent and lifted, cringing at the squeak the door made.

Shelly's dirt-streaked face peered up at him from where she crouched.

"I've got company for you." He grasped Suzy by the nape of the neck and bent her over the hole. "I said I would, didn't I?"

"Please, no." Suzy's voice croaked her plea. "I'm afraid of the dark."

The Photographer shoved her forward, sending her crashing to the dirt floor beneath him. "You two get acquainted. You'll be spending some time together."

Shelly stood and cursed him.

He set his jaw, the pressure sending spasms of heat through his face. "Stop it. We don't curse here. You must act the part of a lady at all times."

She cursed again. His face flamed.

"I'll have to punish you if you curse again. You won't like what I'll have to do." He slammed the door shut on her screams and slid to the floor, his back against the counter. Tears sprang to his eyes. *Why can't they be like her? Brave, beautiful, obedient. Linn doesn't curse. She's a lady.*

Placing his palms against the floor, he pushed himself upright. He kicked the rug into place, wiped his tears on the back of his sleeve, and then rushed outside into the beginning drizzle of an autumn rain.

9

*T*he Photographer's wet shoes slapped and squeaked as he made his way down the tiled corridor. Interns and nurses gave him stern looks as he hurtled past them, sparing them little more than a glance. Tears burned the backs of his eyes. He blinked repeatedly, forcing them to stay at bay.

Upon reaching his mother's room, The Photographer leaned against the door jamb and took a deep, shuddering breath. A nurse stood beside the hospital bed, taking his mother's blood pressure. She glanced up with a smile. "Your mother is doing great. She's having a good day."

"Is she speaking?"

The nurse shook her head. "Oh, we don't think she'll be able to do that. But with luck, we hope she'll learn to communicate in some way." The woman patted his mother's hand. "I'll be back later."

Once she left, The Photographer turned his attention to the woman in the bed. "Mother."

His hands shook as he closed the door before lowering himself into the chair. He ran his hands through his hair. "I don't think she'll ever see me." His voice whined inside his head, the words droned against his eardrums. "I try so hard. I have two girls now." He waved his hand. "I'm sure you've heard it mentioned. I'm all over the news." He stood and paced. "But they just aren't *her*. I have to let one of them go today."

A quick burst of air left the woman's lungs, hissing through her lips.

Her son stopped and whipped around to face her. "Are you trying to speak, Mother?" He stepped beside her. "That wouldn't be wise, now would it? We can't have you spilling all my secrets." He flopped back into the chair and covered his eyes with his arm. "Oh, what to do, what to do. It pains me, beautiful as it is, each time I set their spirit free."

He bolted to his feet as a thought occurred to him. "Could she be laughing at me?" The force of his rising caused the chair to slam into the wall behind him. "I think she may be."

White-hot rage overwhelmed him, and his breathing quickened. The Photographer resumed his pacing. He couldn't get close enough, not with the testosterone loaded bodyguard. He'd have to show her he was serious in another way. Get her attention. Let his love really see him.

Excitement replaced his anger. He trembled so hard he had to lean against the chair for support. Both hands clenched the vinyl. The flesh across his knuckles turned white. Thoughts whirled in his head, tumbling over themselves in their ferocity.

He lifted his head and focused watery eyes on his mother who stared back at him. "Thank you, Mother. You've been an inspiration to me. Your listening has been invaluable. If only you were this attentive when I was a child."

Whirling, he yanked open the door and rushed into the hall, almost knocking aside an orderly in his haste. His feet felt as if they floated above the tiled floor, his head in the clouds. His heart beat a lively tempo. He hummed as he waited for the elevator.

Good. Empty. He stepped inside and pushed the close door button before a rushing nurse could join him. Behind the door, he twirled and laughed, the sound bouncing back from the paneled walls. *Oh, this will be fun!*

Inside his car, he punched the CD play button. Opera music blared from the speakers. His voice belted out the words to the beloved songs. All too soon, he pulled up in front of his house and entered the garage. His heartbeat accelerated. He couldn't wait to speak with his lovelies.

"Ladies!" He ran into the house and kicked aside the rug covering the trapdoor. He flung open the door. "Let's have some fun."

Shelly glared up at him and let loose a string of curses.

The Photographer narrowed his eyes and laughed. "Oh, yes. Let's have some fun. Starting with you."

He snatched the ever present knife from the kitchen table and lowered the wooden step ladder. "Shelly, you first."

Once her head was within reach, he grabbed a handful of her hair, ignoring her cry of pain, and yanked her up the ladder. With a backward thrust of his foot, he kicked the door closed. With the knife's blade poised against her throat, he led her to a kitchen chair and secured her with a rope of twine.

She flung her head forward, trying to strike him in the face.

He laughed and backhanded her. "Glad to know you have so much spirit. It's a shame to take it from you." Taking hold of a dishtowel, he stuffed it into her mouth, careful to stay away from her snapping teeth. With a six inch strip of duct tape, he secured the towel in place.

Stepping behind her, he grasped the chair in both hands and dragged her down the hall and into a white room, devoid of furnishings except for a single small table on which sat a compact disc player, a tub of wipes, and a hair brush. The only spot of color…the crimson dress hanging from a hook on the wall. The fabric blood red against the starkness of the paint. Thick white canvas covered the only window.

He had created the room as a place for Aislinn. A room as pure as he desired her to be. But, things changed, and so must his original plans.

The Photographer slapped her cheek. "Now, you be patient. I've got to collect your friend."

He sprinted outside to his studio and retrieved his camera and a video recorder. Glee bubbled in his chest, spilling out with loud laughter. He hadn't had this much fun in ages.

His running footsteps thudded across the lawn as he hurried back to the house. Depositing the cameras in the room with Shelly, he strode back to the kitchen and the waiting Suzy.

"I have a job for you, my dear." He held down a hand to help her up the ladder. "Do I need to tie you? It will be awful if I do. I need your hands free."

She shook her head. "I'll be good."

"That's my girl." The Photographer ripped off another six inch strip of tape and placed it over her mouth. "Don't remove this. I demand utmost obedience, Suzy. Do you understand?"

Suzy nodded, her eyes wide and fear-filled above the grey tape.

"Wonderful. Follow me." He once again took her hand in his, then led her to the white room and the bound Shelly.

Shelly had managed to bounce the chair several feet closer to the door, and The Photographer groaned. "Shelly, you are really trying my patience." His voice rose on the last word and he closed his eyes, struggling for control.

From his pocket, he withdrew a small, rectangular box and placed it on the table top. Without looking up, he ordered, "Suzy, push her chair back to the exact center of the room. Close the door first."

The scraping of the chair being drug across the floor echoed, and he winced. Opening the box, he revealed a single syringe nestled on black velvet. He smiled and turned to the cameras. Lifting the recorder, he handed it to the waiting Suzy. Silent tears streamed from the girl's eyes. "This is going to take team work, my dear."

She shook her head and whimpered.

"Either you work with me, or you can take her place."

He set up the camera within minutes, its black eye focused on Shelly.

The Photographer slipped a black mask from the pocket of his slacks and donned it. "Once I give our friend the injection, we have very little time. I'll set up the still shot, but I want you to film what I do. This is a first for me. Don't mess it up. I want it perfect." He turned to Shelly. "I said I would punish you for your disobedience. I would have liked keeping you around a while longer, but…" he shrugged. "I'll find someone else. Someone more perfect."

Squeals issued from beneath her tape. She struggled against her bindings.

The Photographer reached over and tapped the play button on the disc player. The lyrics of Masquerade from The Phantom of the Opera swirled through the room.

"You may begin filming, Suzy." From a hidden pocket in his suit jacket, The Photographer pulled a small pair of scissors. With quick movements, he cut through the bound woman's clothing, tossing the shreds of fabric to the side.

The dress was like liquid silk as he removed it from the hanger and laid it across his shoulder, rubbing his face against its softness. Taking up the hair brush, he stepped behind Shelly and, with long, sinuous strokes, brushed her hair. The woman trembled beneath his hands.

He pulled several of the wipes from their tub and commenced cleaning her face, neck and arms. As her glare of anger turned to fear, and her tears gushed, he clucked his tongue and wiped the wetness away. "Shhh, my love. All will be well."

Light glinted off the needle as he held it high and tapped away the air bubbles. The puncture of her arm was quick and efficient.

Positioning her head to show off the lovely curve of her neck, he waited. His breath hitched in his throat as he bent to kiss her, stealing her last breath. He closed his eyes and savored the sweetness.

"Thank you, my dear." He reached out to take the camera from Suzy's shaking hands. "I can only hope the picture isn't too out of focus. You are trembling so hard." He set the camera on the table and held out his hand. "Come. It will be easier after a while."

She placed her hand in his, and he led her back to the dark hole. With the door securely fastened above her, The Photographer rifled through a kitchen drawer until he located a meat cleaver. With his hand firmly grasping the weapon, he headed back to the white room.

10

Sunlight squeezed through the crack in the curtains, and Linn rolled over, groaning. She tossed her arm across her face. Peering with squinted eyes, she glared at the alarm clock. Six o'clock! She groaned again and flung back the covers, swinging her legs over the side of the mattress. The room carried a chill, and she shivered. Goose pimples rose on her skin.

The scent of wet cement and damp dirt floated through the open window. A shock shot through her. She leapt from the bed, her legs tangling in the blankets. She crashed to the floor. Her breath whooshed from her lungs, and she lay gasping for breath like a stranded fish and tried to pull her shirt down past her hips.

"Linn!" Drew burst through her door, flinging it open with enough force to slam it back into the wall.

Grabbing the sheet off the bed with one hand, she held up the other and took a deep breath. "I'm…fine." Linn glanced toward her window. "My window's open. I know it was closed last night."

"Where's the screen?"

"I haven't had one on for over a year." She tugged her shirt down then tossed the blanket aside. Just her luck, Drew would barge into the room while she wore nothing but a thong and tee-shirt.

With another glance at her, and a quirk of his mouth, Drew strode to the window. He flung it up as far as it would go and stuck his head out.

Within seconds, he withdrew and slid the window into place. "I didn't see anyone. Are you sure you closed it?"

"Positive." She pushed to her feet. "I closed and locked it the first night you were here and haven't opened it since." Her eyes scanned the room.

A large padded envelope lay propped against the bed's foot-board. "He came into my room." The banging of her heart threatened to drown out her words. Her voice trembled, and she raised wide eyes to Drew. "How could I not hear him? Sense him? Something." Her body filled with liquid fear, weighing her down. Her knees shook. She fell to the bed. Why hadn't he taken her?

Ridiculous. That's what she was, thinking she could overcome a fear born years ago and be a tough, brave officer of the law. Even Upton Falls had its crime. What had she been thinking? Taking a deep breath, she lifted her head and squared her shoulders. It was too late to turn back now.

Drew lunged to the closet and whipped the door open. He shoved aside the clothes hanging there. "Unless he was in here before we got home. Did you check the window before you went to bed?"

"No. I didn't see the need." She slid down the side of the bed, her eyes not leaving the forbidding vision of the envelope. "Is it safe to open?" Now, she'd have to check her closets before bed too.

He stretched out his hand.

Linn grabbed his arm. "Don't touch it."

Drew continued and moved the envelope an inch to the side. "We both know there won't be any prints."

Linn held her breath, waiting. Nothing. She exhaled hard enough to flutter her bangs. "It wasn't prints I was worried about."

"You're right. There's a pair of gloves in my bag. Could you get them for me?"

She rushed from the room, pulled his duffel bag from under the bed, and riffled through it until she located the thin, black leather gloves. Dashing back to her room, she tossed the gloves to Drew.

He caught them and tugged them on. Lifting the envelope, he turned it over in his hands.

The doorbell rang. Linn jerked.

"Come with me." Drew tucked the envelope under his arm and led the way to the front door. He grabbed his weapon from the holster hanging on the doorknob of his room.

Linn peered around him as he yanked the door open. No one stood on the porch or the sidewalk. She followed with bare feet as Drew sprinted down the steps and to the street. Linn glanced both ways. The street was empty.

They whirled and dashed to the back of the house. Still, she saw no one.

Drew shrugged and led her in a circle of the house until they ended up where they'd started.

Breathless, she stopped and leaned against the porch railing. Her eyes caught a glimpse of white at the base of a bush. "Drew."

A square box sat under the low hanging branches of a juniper bush. An icy fist grabbed Linn's heart and squeezed. She reached for the box.

Drew shot out a hand to stop her. "Wait. Let me. You step back." He laid the envelope on the ground and knelt, his gaze searching around the box.

Water splashed against the low rock wall separating Linn's property from that of her neighbor's. Drops sprayed across her feet.

"Good morning, Aislinn." An elderly woman dressed in a housedress and curlers directed a steady spray of water over a patch of late blooming flowers. The woman giggled, shrilly. "You two are chasing each other awful early, don't you think?"

Drew stood and approached the woman. Her gaze focused on the bare expanse of his chest. "Did you see anyone this morning? Someone other than us?"

She shook her head, her gaze moving to his gloved hands. "No. But I was out back until just a moment ago. Why?"

"Someone rang our doorbell and ran." Linn placed a hand on Drew's arm. "Probably kids playing a joke."

The woman drew in a sharp hiss of breath as she spotted Drew's gun. "Oh. Are you a police officer? That would explain the gloves. Linn always said she'd never date an officer."

"Uh. We're not actually dating, Mrs. Hunt. This is Special Agent Drew Wayne. He's helping with The Photographer case." Linn wrapped her arms around her middle.

Mrs. Hunt winked. "I can see he's helping." Her gaze ran over the large oxford shirt Linn wore, then over Drew's bare chest. "Especially without being fully clothed."

Linn tugged at the shirt, trying to pull the wrinkles from it. It was obvious the shirt had been slept in.

"I'll just get back to my flowers. I'll let you know if I *see* anything."

Drew laughed as the woman strolled away, sending one last mischievous glance over her shoulder. "She's a firecracker, isn't she?"

"You have no idea. It'll be all over the neighborhood that I was chasing you around the house, in my pajamas, at six in the morning, and you without a shirt." She glared at him. "It's not funny."

"Is it that bad for your neighbors to think something?" His eyes twinkled down at her. "Am I that bad? An ogre?"

She sighed. "It's not that. I have a reputation. A good one." One that took her years to obtain.

"So do I." His tone grew serious. "If I weren't working a case, I'd never be staying in your home, just the two of us, unless you invited me. I believe in treating women as ladies, not objects." He stalked back to the box, studied it for another minute, then lifted it and the envelope. "Let's go see what our friend has sent."

Linn wiped her sweaty palms on her shirt and followed Drew into the house. Dismay flooded through her as she stared at his back. Did he not find her attractive? Was her scar too noticeable for him? Did he know of her past? Maybe someone knew and put it in her file. She mentally slapped herself. What did it matter? They'd solve the case, and he'd be gone.

Drew set the ominous objects on the kitchen table. "Could you get me a knife, or a letter opener?"

She rushed to do his bidding, returning with a paring knife from the kitchen.

With careful precision, Drew slit open the envelope and slid out a disk in a hard case. Taped on the front was a note. Linn leaned closer to read the typed words. "So you will see me. Watch DVD before opening the box."

"Bossy, isn't he?" Drew rubbed the stubble on his chin. "Up to watching a movie?"

Linn swallowed against the lump threatening to lodge in her throat. "You get the popcorn. I'll get the player ready." She forced a laugh at her corny joke. Instead, it came out as a strangled sob. She lifted the disc with the hem of her shirt and slid it into the DVD player.

Drew took a deep breath.

"What?"

He looked at her. "I have to admit, I'm a little frightened about what we're going to see on that disc."

Okay. Big guy is scared. That did not reassure her. "Nothing wrong with that. I'm apprehensive myself." Linn raised her eyebrows.

"Wanna hold hands?" Drew wiggled his eyebrows. "We can pretend we're a couple of horny teenagers at the movies and make out."

She gave another shaky laugh. "If you think it will help." She hit the play button before joining Drew on the sofa. Bile rose in her throat.

The camera shook. The figures it filmed were jumpy and out of focus. "Oh, we're watching a murder." A lump of ice sat in her stomach.

"Stockton's murder."

"Who's filming?" Linn remained glued to the television screen, despite the overwhelming desire to look away. "Suzy?"

"That's my guess." He lifted his hips and fished his cell phone from his jeans. "I'm calling Madden."

"I'll call Steve." But she stayed seated. Tears flowed down her face as The Photographer brushed his victim's hair. "He loves her. In his own twisted way of loving." Her tears increased as the man on film washed Shelly's face, then kissed her.

Drew barked orders into the phone and snapped it closed. "He thinks he loves you. These women are a substitute for you, Linn. He's deluded himself into believing he loves them, but it's you. Never forget that." He rose. "Let's see what's in the box."

Using the same paring knife, he pried open the lid. Taped on a tissue wrapped bundle was another note. *So you won't forget me. And punishment for what she did to you.*

"Don't open it." The objects on the table blurred. Linn grabbed the back of a chair to steady herself. "I don't want to know what it is."

"Linn." Drew let the lid fall. "I'm right here. You're all right." He turned back to the box and opened it.

The crackle of tissue paper echoed through the room. Linn bit the inside of her lip. Blood filled her mouth, and she grimaced.

Drew tilted the box and stepped back as the last of the tissue paper fell away. A severed hand in a plastic bag hit the tabletop with a dull thump. It rolled over, revealing a gash in the meaty flesh of the palm.

Linn's own hand flew to her mouth as her eyes rose to Drew's face. "He's never dismembered them before." She lowered her hand and stared at the stitches on her own palm. "He cut off her hand because she is responsible for this."

Drew rubbed the back of his neck. "He's doing a lot he's never done before."

"Why doesn't he just take me?" She slumped into a chair. "Why torment me? Why kill these innocent women?"

"I don't know." Drew knelt before her, taking her hands in his. With a gentle touch, he traced her stitches. "I don't know why he's toying with you. I wish I did. My supervisor might have a better idea. I'll give him a call."

She winced as he squeezed. "Maybe that's what we need. A fresh look."

"I hope so." Drew loosened his grip.

"Did you recognize the music in the video?"

Drew shook his head.

"It's 'Masquerade' from the Phantom of the Opera. I love that play. It's the first Broadway play I've seen." She stared at their entwined hands. "How does he know so much about me? How does he know how to hurt me?"

"Masquerade, huh?" Drew pulled her to her feet. "You need to tell me some things. I need honest answers, Linn, whether you want to reveal them to me or not. No matter how painful. Understand?"

He sat her on the sofa and handed her one of the sofa pillows.

Linn clutched it to her chest.

Pulling up a dining chair, he swung it around and straddled it, folding his arms across the back. "Ready?"

"No."

"Tough." He smiled. "I've got to know everything I can about you. Things that aren't in your file."

"Won't Madden be here soon?"

His husky laughter washed across her, lifting her spirits. "You win, for now. But we are going through this—today." His eyes roamed over her. "As beautiful as you look all rumpled from sleep, I think you'd better get dressed." He looked down at himself. "And I need a shirt."

Not really. Seeing Drew shirtless, basketball shorts slung low on his hips, the view didn't get much better. Linn wanted his arms around her. His mouth on hers. Passion to drive away the horrid images seared in her brain.

She buried her face in the pillow, and cried for the women in the hands of a mad man.

~

Masquerade. Drew tugged the tee-shirt over his head and grabbed a denim jacket from where he'd tossed it on the bed, donned it, and slipped the holster with his Glock over his shoulder. Was the symbolism meant for Linn or The Photographer?

Sitting on the edge of the bed, Drew bent to pull on his boots. They were no closer to catching the guy than they were on Drew's first day on the job. He stood and stomped his feet, settling the boots. And what is in Linn's past that she was so afraid of revealing?

Linn stood in the frame of the door dressed in a conservative navy pantsuit and white blouse. She'd drawn her hair back into a ponytail. The sound of a car pulling into the driveway drifted through the door. "They're here."

God, she's gorgeous. He sighed and shook his head. But, he knew not to fall for his assignment. He learned from past mistakes. Loving your assignment could destroy them, and you. "I'll let them in."

Her eyes closed for a second, and her face paled as she glanced toward the white box containing the grisly gift and the recorded disc. She spun on her heel and plopped on the sofa.

"You okay?" Drew paused, his hand resting on the doorknob.

She lifted her chin. "Let them in."

He opened the door and stepped to the side.

"Still worried about that sniper's bullet?"

"You bet." He opened the door wider. "Madden. Steve."

"Wayne." Steve stepped inside. His gaze zeroed in on Linn.

She stared back for the merest second then dropped her gaze down to her hands folded in her lap. Interesting. She'd never seemed uncomfortable around Steve before. Drew would need to keep a closer eye on Linn's partner.

He studied the perfect line of her profile, the straight nose and curved lips, the bottom one full and pouting. Her skin so fair, he could detect the faint blue lines of blood vessels spread across her jaw. Drew smiled. His description of her sounded like lines from a bad romance novel. Minus the heaving bosom and throbbing manhood, although under different circumstances he wouldn't mind trying.

"Got any coffee? " Madden plopped his bulk into an easy chair.

Steve placed a hand on Linn's shoulder when she started to rise. "I'll get it. I know where it is."

They sat, quiet, staring at the box on the coffee table until Steve reappeared.

"Take a look in the box." Drew leaned against the wall. "Linn got a little present this morning. Hope you aren't squeamish."

"Wait…" Linn reached out a hand.

Steve lifted the lid with the same utensil Drew had used to open it and jumped. A squeak squeezed from his throat. He fell back into a kitchen chair and crashed over to the floor. His arms flailed. Coffee sloshed over his hand, and he dropped the mug, shattering it on the vinyl floor.

Madden peered into the box. "Damn!" His face paled beneath his coffee-colored skin.

Despite Drew's resolve not to, a snorting laugh escaped him. "Sorry, man. I should have warned you. I had no idea you hadn't seen this type of thing before."

"Not in Upton Falls. Until this crazy person came along, things were relatively peaceful." Steve picked himself off the floor, eyes flashing. "What…is…that?"

"Shelly Stockton's hand…we think." Linn handed him the DVD. "We also got this."

Steve tugged on a pair of latex gloves from his pocket, donned them, and in slow motion, reached for the video. A myriad of emotions ran across the man's face. Anger, fear, shock, and sorrow. Once the tape played through, Steve lowered himself back into his chair, his face grey. He scrubbed his hands over his face, then let them fall. "Someone needs to tell her husband. I'll go."

"Wait." Linn took a step toward him.

"No." Steve squared his shoulders and stood in front of Drew. "Did I pass the test, Agent Wayne?"

"Yes."

"What test?" Linn looked from Steve to Drew. "What's going on?"

Steve drummed his fingers on his mouth, then released his breath in a sudden expulsion of air. "Agent Wayne shocked me with the intent of judging my reaction to something so horrific he hoped to catch me unawares. Am I right? If I was The Photographer, I wouldn't have been as surprised, either that, or I would be an awesome actor."

"That's right." Drew leaned against the desk and folded his arms.

"You owe me an apology."

"Sorry."

Steve rose and pulled a set of car keys from the pocket of his slacks. "I'm going to inform Mr. Stockton that his wife is dead." He patted his suit jacket. "Call me if you need me."

Once he'd left the house, Linn whirled to face Drew. "What kind of game are you playing?"

"I'm eliminating a suspect." Drew shrugged.

"I hope you're satisfied." She plopped into her chair. "The three of us should be working together to solve this case, not jaunting off on our own pursuits like some lonesome cowboy."

Madden shook his head and rearranged his bulk into the chair. "That was bad, Wayne. Cruel."

Drew shrugged. "He matches the description of The Photographer. Every time something has happened to Linn, Steve hasn't been there. It's a natural assumption to suspect him."

"He is not a killer. How many times do I have to tell you that?" Linn's eyes sparked flames. She crossed her arms and took a deep breath. "What do you think is the significance of the music playing in the background on the disc?"

Drew rubbed his chin. "I think he's referring to a mask. Whether figuratively or literally, I'm not sure. I'm also not sure whether the reference is to you, or to him."

"Maybe both," Madden interjected. "I think our man is not who he appears to be. Hence the mask. And I *am* talking figuratively."

"Maybe." Drew ran a hand through his hair. "It's as good a guess as any."

Madden looked from Drew to Linn. "You two need to follow me to the station." He rose, grunting from the effort. "Bring that stuff with you. There are reports to file."

"Yes, sir." Linn pushed herself from her seat, suddenly all business. "We need to secure the front yard. Look for clues. The man was inside my house. He was on my front porch."

"It's already being done." Madden held up a hand. "There are two officers outside now. They should be coming in any minute."

11

*T*he phone on her desk rang. Linn grabbed it and lifted it to her ear. "McFarland."

"Hello, Aislinn. It's me." The words filtered through a voice modifier, deep and rumbling. "Did you like your gift?"

Her hand shook. She placed it on her desk blotter in an effort to steady herself. Her breathing accelerated. Nausea rose, and she bent forward to prevent herself from hyperventilating. She lifted a hand to keep Drew from grabbing the handset. "Not…particularly."

"Oh." He paused. "I thought it was a *just* gift, considering the stitches in your hand. I would hate to think you were unappreciative of my efforts."

Linn straightened and fixed her eyes on Drew's. The warmth in his dark eyes kept her glued to the present. She wanted nothing more than to drift away from the nightmare she lived. "I don't want anything that requires someone to lose their life."

He chuckled. The sound vibrated through the modifier he used. "That's what I love about you. You're beautiful and caring. Always thinking of someone other than yourself. The world needs more people like you."

"Do you have Suzy Green?"

"She's the closest thing I've found to you."

"Take me." Linn closed her eyes and let her head fall against the chair's back. She forced the words past a throat determined to hold them in. "Let her go and take me."

"Are you offering yourself to me?"

"Yes." The lump in her throat grew, threatening to choke her. Perspiration broke out on her upper lip.

The Photographer sighed. "It isn't time, Aislinn. You mustn't rush things. You haven't reached perfection yet."

"What do you mean? My scar?" Her voice rose. "Is that what's holding you back?"

The phone clicked. A dial tone buzzed.

"He hung up." Shudders shook her body, and she let the phone fall to the desktop. Wrapping her arms around her waist, she squeezed and concentrated on her breathing. She could do this.

"Does he have Suzy?" Drew pulled Steve's chair over and sat in it.

"Yes." She swiped a hand across her face. The crying was getting ridiculous. Weakness she couldn't afford.

"What else did he say?" Drew replaced the handset.

"That I haven't achieved perfection yet." She laughed, the sound bitter and hard in the room.

"You're the closest thing to perfection I've ever seen." Drew tucked an errant strand of hair behind her ear.

Linn swallowed hard. Heat burned her cheeks as she drowned in his gaze. Her heart pounded, not only from fear this time, but desire. A need to be held and loved.

The phone rang again, and they both lunged for it. Linn emerged victorious, and sighed at the close call of giving into her emotions. "McFarland."

"Tell Cowboy to keep his hands off you. You're mine." Click.

Linn sprang to her feet. "He's watching us." She dropped the phone handset, sending it banging against the side of the metal desk, whirled toward the open blinds on the window and then, like an automaton, peered outside. "He's close enough to see us. He said to tell you to keep your hands off me."

A firm grip on her arm, and Drew yanked her away from the window. "Get back. Are you crazy?" He kept hold of her and hauled her behind him as he rushed from the office shouting orders to officers to search the buildings across the street.

Yanking her arm free, Linn planted her feet and refused to budge. "He won't be there! He'll have seen us leave the room."

The ringing of the phone behind her sent her sprinting back into the office. "What? More orders you crazy, sick…"

"Hello?"

"Oh." She collapsed in her chair. "Sorry, Steve."

"What's going on?"

"The Photographer called." She released her hair from its ponytail and ran her fingers through it. She mouthed Steve's name when Drew stuck his head in the door.

"What did he want?"

Linn ran the calls through her mind. "He asked if I liked the gift and told me to tell Drew to keep his hands off me."

"Okay." His voice sounded small through the phone.

"How did Mr. Stockton take the news of his wife's death?" Linn picked up a pencil from next to her desk blotter and doodled, sending the pencil's tip into swirls and curly cues.

"Bad. He cried." Steve was silent for a moment. "*Does* Wayne touch you?"

Linn closed her eyes. "Nothing inappropriate." Yet. But she wouldn't mind forcing his hand. Anything to feel…something other than stark fear and unworthiness. "He's a gentleman, Steve."

"Really?"

"Talking about me?" Drew seemed to appear out of nowhere and whispered in her ear.

She shrieked. "Yes, and you scared me." She twirled her chair away from him. "Sorry, Steve. Drew's being a jerk."

The subject of their conversation propped himself on the corner of her desk. "Are you making fun of me? I mean, it's okay, I don't mind." Drew smiled, revealing the dimple in one cheek. "I like the fact you're thinking of me, and the price I charge for the privilege of mockery would be enjoyable for both of us."

"Oh, please. Go type the report."

"Uh huh. That's your job." He scooted off the desk and strode to the window, careful not to stand directly in front of it. Reaching up, he closed the blinds, shutting out the mid-morning sun.

The phone clipped to his belt rang, sending the tune of "I Love Rock and Roll" through the room. Drew flipped the phone open. "Wayne, here. Okay. Thanks." He closed the phone and turned to face Linn.

"Steve, I'll call you back." She replaced the receiver. "What?"

"The officers didn't find anyone."

"I told you. He's like a ghost. The Phantom from the opera he seems to like. It wouldn't surprise me if he wears a cape." Her fingers tightened around the pencil, snapping it in two. "I wonder if there's a face under that mask he wears."

"He's a man, Linn. Like me. A flesh and blood human."

She shook her head. "He's nothing like you. It pierces your heart every time you've had to pull your gun on someone, doesn't it? It does me. But I get over it. It's part of my job. This man finds glory in killing."

"Doesn't it also hurt you to have to shoot someone?"

"My heart is cold, Drew. Hardened. I do my job and move on." That's what was required of her. Linn tossed the pencil pieces in the garbage can. The wood thunked against the stainless steel canister, shouting to the world that Aislinn McFarland was a big liar. She hated pulling her gun, hated pressing the trigger.

He approached her and took her left hand in his. "Let's get a cup of coffee…and some pie."

"I don't want anything."

"I do, and you still have questions to answer." Drew tugged her along with him. "I'll drive." He smirked down at her. "Your car has half a tank of gas."

Who told him about her oddity? "What about the report?"

"Do it later."

The drive to the nearby diner took less than ten minutes. As if he were afraid she'd get away, Drew held the car door open for her and kept a firm grip on her arm.

The aroma of hot coffee and apple pie greeted them on waves of air-conditioning as Drew opened the diner doors.

Linn's stomach rumbled in response. Maybe a bite to eat wasn't such a bad idea.

A smiling, thirtyish woman dressed in a white blouse and black slacks welcomed them and led them to a back corner booth.

"Coffee and apple pie." Drew smiled, eliciting a blush from the hostess.

Linn rolled her eyes. Puh—leeze! The man flirted with every female he ran across. "I want my pie ala mode."

Drew raised his eyebrows. "Sounds good. I'll have the same." His gaze bore into Linn. "Ready for my first question?"

"No." She picked at a paper napkin, and squirmed.

"I'll start easy. Where did you grow up?"

"The South."

"No one word or simple answers, please. Those won't help us."

"Fine." She lifted her head. "I grew up in a little town of seventeen hundred people at the foot of the Ozarks."

"Any enemies?" He lifted his hips and pulled a small notebook from the rear pocket of his jeans. "Anyone worth mentioning?"

"No."

"What about your parents?"

"Not that I know of." Linn slid another napkin from the basket between them.

"Jobs. Earliest to now."

Linn swept aside the pile of shredded napkins as the waitress placed her pie in front of her. "Why these questions? Surely you read them in my file."

"I did." He smiled at the waitress. "Thank you."

"You're welcome." She batted her eyelashes.

"Stop flirting." Linn smoothed the ball of vanilla ice cream on top of the hot pie.

He laughed. "Why? I adore women. They're a curious breed. God knew what he was doing when he created the fairer sex."

Linn stared at his lips as he blew into his coffee. What would it be like to be kissed by him? Thorough enough that her knees would weaken? And that hair, thick and glossy and almost always messy from his cowboy hat. She almost laughed. Who would have thought she would find herself attracted to a cowboy?

He peered up at her through lowered lashes. "What?"

"Nothing." She flushed and speared her slice of pie with her fork. "My first job was babysitting. My grandmother insisted I work as soon as possible. Said I needed to help support myself. She gave me a month to mourn my parents then had me babysitting for a couple at her church. They had five boys." Linn grimaced. "And terrible, all of them. When I could drive, I worked at the local pizza hangout."

"Boyfriends? Jilted high school love?"

"I didn't date in school." She lifted her coffee mug, then set it back down. She swallowed hard and lifted her chin. "I had a lovely nickname. I was quite affectionately called Scar Lip, or Scar Face, or my favorite-- Hair Lip Linny."

His eyes hardened. "You're kidding. The scar is hardly noticeable."

"Kids can be cruel. What's your next question?"

"How did you get the scar?"

"I fell out of a tree house when I was five. My lip caught on a rusty nail, and it got infected before my grandmother took me to the doctor. She tried cleaning it herself. Hence, the scar."

"How did you work your way through the academy?"

She felt the blood drain from her face. "If you read my file, then you know."

"I want you to tell me."

"I was an exotic dancer. There, I said it. Happy?" She stuffed a bit of pie in her mouth. "That must shock you, I'm sure," she spoke around the food.

"Not really. About as much as you talking with your mouth full. A lot of women dance their way through college. Who am I to judge?" He sat against the vinyl back of the booth. "You were working toward a goal the best way you could. It doesn't sound as if you had much support from home."

"I didn't."

"Were you any good?"

"I was great." She grinned and returned to shredding napkins. "Heavy makeup hid my scar and working out in the gym kept me in shape."

"Did you ever go home with anyone?"

Her head snapped up. "That's none of your business."

He laughed.

The sound rolled over her like warm water, and she returned his smile. "You're just being nosey."

"Maybe, but I'm hoping to get a little piece of something to give us a clue as to why this guy is fixated on you. What are the names of your former boyfriends? Do you know what they're doing now?"

She breathed deeply. "I told you I didn't date much. When I danced, I didn't have the opportunity to meet nice guys. The ones I did meet were just faces in the dark. Once I started working for the department, I didn't have the time." She looked down at the snowy pile of shredded paper. "You were right about Steve. He does care for me." To his credit, Drew didn't say 'I told you so'. "But that doesn't make him a murderer."

"What's your obsession with having at least a quarter tank of gas in the car?"

Linn's heart plummeted to the pits of her stomach, and she squeezed her eyes closed. Horrific visions of pain and terror flashed through her mind, swirling with all the ferocity and color of a manic kaleidoscope. She broke into a cold sweat.

"Are you all right?" Drew reached across the table, placing his hand over hers.

"I left work late one night." Her eyes snapped open and focused on his eyes. "I'd worked an extra shift, covering for one of the other dancers. There wasn't anyone left to walk to the parking lot with by that time. I needed gas in my car, but thought I had enough to get me home. I told myself I'd stop by the gas station in the morning."

She shuddered. "I ran out of gas two miles from where I lived. It was winter, and the night was cold. I wore a long sweater over my dance…things. For an hour, no cars came by so I got out of my car and started walking. I guess it was about a half mile later when I spotted the first car. It slowed down and cruised beside me. I tried peering into the dark to see who drove. I couldn't tell. The interior of the car was dark so I said no thank you and kept walking. The next thing I knew, the driver swerved the car and brushed me hard enough to knock me down. I got to my feet and ran, kicking off the stiletto heels I wore. He came after me."

Linn grabbed another napkin and wiped away the tears coursing down her face. "He threw me into the bushes as if I were nothing more than a sack of garbage. After he raped me, he stabbed me—five times. I have the scars across my chest to prove it." *Not counting the ones I carry inside.* "The doctor said it was amazing no vital organs were hit. I don't know how long I lay there before another car came by." She locked eyes with him again. "I swore I would never run out of gas again."

"Do you remember what the man looked like? Can you recall any characteristics about him?" Drew's face softened with sympathy.

Linn sniffed. "He wore a mask and gloves. His clothes were black. He didn't speak. Not a sound. It was too dark to see even his eye color." She blew her nose into the napkin. "Do you think The Photographer could be the same guy?"

Drew scratched his head. "It's occurred to me. It's easy to see why you're so skittish around men."

"Skittish? I'm not a horse, Drew." Her look darkened. "I've been wondering. Where's the picture of Shelly?"

"You're an Arabian. Spirited and beautiful." The phone clipped to his belt rang. Drew yanked it free and flipped it open. "Yeah." His eyes clouded. "Okay. Be there in ten." He closed the phone cover. "We've got a report of another missing woman."

12

*H*er white dress caught the moonlight and served as a beacon in the dark. The Photographer glanced back at the woman lying tied and gagged on the floor of the van. Why shouldn't he take another? She was there, offering herself to him. He smiled and eased the van to a stop on the shoulder of the highway as he experienced a sense of *de ja vu*. His beautiful Linn had done the same once upon a time. It had been the best night of his life.

"Thank you." She leaned away from the car, toward the van's window. "I've got a flat, and I don't have the foggiest idea how to change it." She straightened, flirting, batting her long dark eyelashes. Full lips pouted beneath a straight patrician nose.

The Photographer slid across the seat, exiting through the passenger door in an attempt to keep the woman from looking inside. It wouldn't do for her to see his lady in the back. "Let's take a look in your trunk."

She tottered on high heels that kept sinking into the soft dirt on the shoulder, chattering with a nasal tone back to her car. The Photographer rubbed his temple, fighting away the threatening headache. Sometimes, even a beautiful woman wasn't worth the annoyance.

"My name is Eva. I just can't thank you enough. Really." She played coy, lowering her lashes and giving him just the tiniest bit of a smile. It wasn't until she bent to unlock the trunk that he saw her roots. Black as the night! The long platinum hair was fake. He cursed under his breath.

"Excuse me?" Eva lifted the trunk and turned to him.

He smiled and shook his head. What was he supposed to do now? He couldn't take a pretender.

"I was on my way home. I'd just picked up my son and…"

"You have a child with you?" Anticipation leapt in his chest. A son. Could it mean one of his heart's desires was soon to come true? He would be a father!

Eva nodded and transferred her attention to the trunk, bending to retrieve the crowbar. "Yes." Her voice trembled as she handed the bar to him and took a step back. Her blue eyes narrowed in suspicion. She licked her lips and shot a quick glance in the rear window.

His eagerness made her uneasy. He smiled. "Let's get this tire changed, shall we? Then, we'll send you on your way." She nodded, and he lifted the small spare tire from the trunk. He grimaced as his hands came into contact with the dirty rubber. He'd have to buy new lambskin gloves. This pair was ruined.

The child in the back seat began to wail. The noise vibrated against The Photographer's ear drums, and he dropped the tire. It bounced twice, then fell on its side. He clapped his hands over his ears.

Eva frowned and rushed to her child. "I'll just quiet him. He's probably hungry."

A squeal came from the van to the side of them. The vehicle rocked.

Eva turned, her mouth open in question.

He smirked and raised the crowbar, bringing it down with a satisfying crunch to her head. Blood welled from the hole. She crumbled to the ground.

The infant inside the car wailed louder.

Banging came from inside the van.

"Stop it. Stop that noise." He flung his arm. The crowbar screeched down the metal panel, leaving a gash in the side of the van. He yelled and banged the bar again. "Shut up!" The squealing subsided, and he hurled the crowbar into the field beside the highway.

The baby's wails turned to shrieks and, with eyes narrowed to slits, The Photographer turned his focus on the car. He wrenched open the driver's door to the two-door sedan. The baby lay buckled and red-faced in an infant car seat. The Photographer slammed the front seat forward, grabbed the car seat, and yanked it toward him. It jerked, slinging the baby against its harness. Its shrieks increased in volume, then subsided to shuddering sobs. The Photographer fought harder to free the seat from its bindings. He cursed louder and shot his body forward, stretching to find the seatbelt release.

He glanced through the rearview window. Headlights split the darkness. They were maybe a mile away. Acid rose in his stomach. Eva!

He withdrew, scraping the side of his thigh on the door latch. He dashed to where the woman lay crumpled and swept her into his arms. With no time to spare, he tossed her into the trunk and slammed it closed.

The truck slowed, and The Photographer waved, smiling. His face ached from the effort. The man inside tipped his baseball cap, and accelerated.

The baby's cries subsided to shuddering hiccups. The Photographer stood by the open door and stared inside. The urge to grab the infant plagued him. What a gift the baby would make. If it didn't behave, he would kill it. What power its spirit would release.

Another set of lights pierced the night, and he decided against the baby. Too risky. He dashed back to the van and hurtled down the freeway. He was miles away when he realized what he'd left behind. As if the reminder increased the pain, his hand shot to the side of his leg. The scrape stung. More a scratch than anything, he hoped.

"That'll liven things up, won't it, Amber?" He tossed a quick glance to the bound woman on the floor behind him. "The real game begins. Earlier than originally planned, but what the hell." An iron fist seized his heart, squeezing the breath from him, as visions of the cowboy tenderly tucking Linn's hair behind her ear ran through his mind.

"I hope you're a natural blonde. Eva wasn't. That's why I left her. No cheap imitations for me." Maybe he needed to check his collection. Lift their skirts and take a peek at the carpeting.

His gloved hands tightened on the wheel. "I would have enjoyed the baby, though. I've always wanted a child of my own. That's a pity. It might die out there, all alone. What a waste." He leaned and punched the play button on his compact disc player. Strands of opera music serenaded the early evening, and he lifted his voice in song.

~

Linn couldn't believe how much personal information she spilled to Drew. Her stomach churned. He must despise her now. After all, what self-respecting man wanted anything to do with a former stripper. It didn't matter that she didn't have sex with every guy who tried slipping her money. She actually had rather strict morals, regardless of her past profession. But, she was still damaged goods.

Although Drew said a lot of women worked their way through school by dancing, it didn't change how Linn felt. His kind words and compassionate gaze didn't take away the pain of an unloving grandmother or the horror of an abusive rape. Only Linn could erase the effects. That and a bullet into the man who hurt her.

But first, they needed to save the women he'd captured. They needed a way to draw him out of hiding.

"Thank you for telling me of your past." Drew reached over and patted her hand. He took his eyes off the road for a second, warming her with a look. His gaze darkened. "I would love to see you dance."

"Stop it." She clamped her lips together to keep from smiling. "That will never happen."

"We'll see."

Yeah, maybe they would.

13

*T*he front door of Amber Richards's rented red brick duplex hung open while officers roamed in and out barking orders into radios and jotting notes on yellow pads of paper. The atmosphere hung heavy, tense. Deep lines furrowed the faces of each officer.

Linn sighed. Would the killing ever stop? Although the first victim disappeared approximately three months ago, it seemed a lifetime. She unclipped her seatbelt and turned to Drew. "We need to draw The Photographer to me quicker. Spur his anger. Force his hand. Whatever."

"What are you suggesting?" Drew wrinkled his brow, keeping his hands on the steering wheel and his gaze out the front car window. "Because if it's what I think you're suggesting…absolutely not."

"People are dying." Anger seared through her. "Let's trap him. You'll protect me. I trust you."

"No way." He pounded the wheel, then turned a steely gaze on her. The tic in his jaw told her she had a fight ahead of her.

"It makes sense. If you don't do it, I'll ask Steve to help me."

His eyes widened and he tightened his grip on the wheel. His knuckles whitened. "Don't threaten me. Chavez would never go for it. He isn't going to do anything that puts you in danger."

"Then pretend we're an item." Her stomach dropped. What if he refused? What if the thought of people thinking they dated offended him? Her face heated. Could she pretend? The man oozed sex appeal that even she couldn't deny. He spelled trouble from the toes of his scuffed cowboy boots to the top of his dark curly head.

"Wouldn't work." Drew leaned toward her, and she pulled back.

"Why not?"

He cupped a hand to her cheek.

She flinched.

"Because you can't bear for me to touch you." Drew unclasped his seatbelt and swung open his door. He gave her a wink. "Come on. We've got a lady to try and save."

It wasn't because he repulsed her. Definitely not that. The opposite, in fact. Men made her uncomfortable, and the feelings of insecurity deepened after her attack. Steve was the only one she relaxed around.

There was no relaxing around Drew. He awakened long buried desires. Wants she thought were extinct. Could she let a man touch her in love? She had never tried. Not after that night. What if she couldn't? What if a man's touch sickened her and sent her screaming? Maybe Special Agent Andrew Wayne was the perfect man to try with.

Drew poked his head in the door. "Are you coming?"

She nodded. Her gaze locked with his, and he smiled. Faint wrinkles radiated from the corners of his midnight blue eyes. She took one long step forward, flung her arms around his neck, and plastered herself against him, taking his lips captive.

The feel of them was everything she imagined. Strong, yet soft. Linn closed her eyes, just for a second, stifling the moan rising in her throat. When she opened them again, his gaze grabbed hold, and she knew she was in danger of drowning.

His eyes widened, and his body stiffened, then his arms wrapped around her and tightened. He returned her furious kisses with a tenderness that brought tears to her eyes and sent heat to places starved for a man's attention.

Breathless, she stepped back, straightening her shoulders. "How's that for not being able to stand someone's touch?" She whirled and stalked toward the house, her fingers on her lips.

"Pretty good."

Catcalls and wolf whistles followed her as the other officers clapped and hooted. Linn flushed. So much for her hands off image.

Madden and Steve exited the house.

"Looks like the Ice Queen is melting." Madden laughed.

Linn's gaze slid over Steve's hurt face, avoiding his eyes. "It's all an act. We're trying to draw out The Photographer."

"Can I get in on it?" The captain clapped a big hand on her shoulder. "I'm sure there'll be a line."

She twisted away from him. "Cut it out. That's harassment, and you know it." Not to mention how much the remarks hurt, especially since men did try lining up after one of her dances. They couldn't grasp the concept that she danced, collected her pay, and went home alone. She shuddered, and forced the mental picture away.

"Sweetheart, wait up." Drew loped toward them, Linn's investigative case clutched in his hand. "You forgot this. Must have been the power of my kiss driving everything else from your mind." He winked at Madden. "I still got the magnetism."

Madden laughed. "Linn's inexperienced. She doesn't know any better."

"I said stop it." She grabbed her case. "Don't we have work to do?" The men's laughter followed her into the house. Humiliation filled her, and she dropped her case to put her hands on her hot cheeks. What was she thinking? Right there in front of practically the entire police force.

She lowered her hands and clenched her fists at her sides. How dare he laugh at her? She knew her kiss had knocked his socks off. And the way he'd retaliated, well…

Fingernails digging into her palms despite the soreness around her stitches, she swept her gaze around the small room. If The Photographer was the man who'd taken Amber, she'd let him into the house. There was no sign of forced entry, although the inside showed signs of a struggle.

A cheap laminated coffee table lay on its side, an overturned glass and plate next to it. A ceramic lamp was knocked to the floor, shattering the bulb and the goldenrod colored base. Black residue from fingerprint powder lay over everything. Steve had beat her to the punch again.

Had she let the perp in or had the missing woman left the door unlocked? Was The Photographer someone these women knew or was he charming enough to earn their trust so easily?

She moved her case just inside the door and turned down the small hallway. Three doors decorated the otherwise barren corridor. She took a step forward, then paused and pulled back.

"Remember the last house you went wandering down a hallway in?" Drew pushed past her.

"The other officers have already searched the house."

"Regardless, I'll go first."

"You can go alone." Linn whirled, grabbed her case, and stalked back to the car. The jangle of Drew's cell phone followed her. Within seconds he sprinted toward her. "Let's go. They've found a body. Out on Highway 50. Some driver discovered her. Madden's already on his way."

Linn yanked open her door and slid behind the wheel, daring Drew to argue over her driving. He shook his head, slid across the hood and sat in the passenger seat.

"Don't do that again." Linn started the car and shot into reverse, whipping the wheel until the car spun facing the direction she needed to go. She slipped her sunglasses over her eyes to ward off the setting sun.

"What?" Drew clicked his seatbelt into place, then reached across the front of Linn to secure hers.

She drew in a sharp breath as his arm brushed against her. "Slide across my car. You'll scratch the paint."

He snorted. "This old thing."

"Stop laughing at me."

"I'm not—oh." His eyes widened. "I'm sorry. You surprised me. Next time give a guy some warning before you throw yourself at him."

"There won't be a next time. I've never been so humiliated in my life." She pressed her foot to the gas pedal. The car roared onto the Highway. "You laughed at me." Her voice quavered, and a fresh wave of embarrassment washed over her. What in the hell was wrong with her?

"I was just playing along. I liked it, really. The kiss, I mean." Drew stretched his arm to the seat behind them and retrieved the revolving magnetic light. He reached out the window and secured it to the roof of the car.

"Gee, thanks."

"When the opportunity presents itself, I'll show you just how much I enjoyed your kiss."

What nest of vipers had she opened?

Less than five minutes later, they pulled up behind a dark blue sedan. Madden bent over something in the backseat, and a woman's hand hung from the open trunk.

Linn grabbed latex gloves from the glove compartment of her car and handed a pair to Drew. "Pray he slipped up somewhere."

"I always do." Drew snapped the gloves over his hands. "We've got to get bigger gloves. These cut off my circulation."

"They fit me just fine. If you need bigger gloves, then get some. We're a low budget police department." She slid from the car and slammed the door closed. "You want the body in the trunk or do you want to search the ground?"

"I'll take the body."

"Linn." Madden waved her over. "Help, please."

Her eyes widened at the sight of the infant in the dead woman's backseat. "There's a baby? What do you want me to do?"

"Take care of it."

She backed up, her hands raised. "I don't do babies."

"But you're a woman."

"What's that got to do with anything?"

"I'll take care of the little guy." Drew pushed Madden aside, unbuckled the baby who'd started crying and lifted him to his shoulder. "Hush, now. Shh." The baby stopped crying with the suddenness of a tropical storm. "Has child protective services been called?" Drew paced the area beside the car, gently bouncing the baby.

"I just called them," Madden answered. "They'll be here shortly. The person who made the original call to the station made it from a pay phone somewhere." He laughed. "Wouldn't leave a name. Said they had too many parking tickets and didn't want to risk getting arrested."

Linn rolled her eyes. Was there anything Drew couldn't do? She spotted tire tracks in the soft dirt of the shoulder and squatted beside them, pulling her camera from her case. The tire marks looked bigger than ones left behind at past crime scenes. She snapped several shots of the tracks and straightened before turning her attention to the trunk.

The woman's blood had pooled and congealed, the smell rank in the gathering darkness. Linn pulled the neckline of her shirt over her nose and bent closer. She took pictures of the woman from every angle, then hung the camera around her neck. She turned to scan the field beside the road.

The dry vegetation rustled and crunched beneath her feet as she tottered forward on the uneven ground. She unclipped a small flashlight from her belt and swung its beam back and forth. Small nocturnal rodents scurried from the light's rays.

As she ventured further, the beam of light glinted off a metal surface. Her step quickened. At her feet lay a blood encrusted crowbar. Leaving it where it lay, she lifted her camera.

"Linn, come here."

After snapping one more photograph, Linn turned and jogged to where Drew waited, the baby's sleeping head lolling on his shoulder.

"I think we may have gotten lucky." He motioned his head toward the car. "Take a look at the door latch."

She turned her flashlight on the door. A small smear of blood covered the latch. Linn retrieved her case and withdrew a small vial and Q-tip. "What makes you think this is our guy? The tire tracks don't match."

Madden peered over her shoulder. "Pretty blond woman in the trunk."

Linn swabbed the area. "She's not a natural blond, and her eyes are dark brown." She dropped the Q-tip into the vial and screwed the lid on.

"I found the murder weapon about thirty yards into the field. It's covered with blood. It's a likely assumption that the blood belongs to the dead woman."

"Do you think it's just some freak stopping to take advantage of a woman in need?" Madden straightened, putting his hands on his hips.

"I don't know." Drew stared down the highway. "My gut tells me it's the same guy. I think he saw an opportunity, realized she wasn't what he wanted, and killed her."

"Why kill her?" Linn stored her camera and the glass vial in her case. "Why not just drive away? Why leave the infant by itself? Maybe he was interrupted. None of this matches his MO."

"He doesn't have an MO anymore. He's slipping. Making mistakes."

A white four door Ford pulled up behind them.

"Thank God." Drew shifted the infant to the other arm. "This guy is about to drool all over me." He held the baby away from his shoulder and placed a kiss on his forehead. "Poor little guy."

Madden consulted a small spiral notebook. "The victim's name is Eva Molero. She's a single mother living alone. No known family."

Drew handed the baby to the waiting Social Services worker. His shoulders slumped. "Linn, you got everything you need?"

"I think so." She glanced around the area once more. "The medical examiner should be here anytime." Picking up her case, she turned. "The Photographer is escalating, Drew. He's taking more women and seeming to kill without reason." She lifted her face to stare into his eyes. "We need to provoke him into coming after me."

He folded his arms across his chest. "I said no. It's not a good idea."

"Look." Linn set the case on the ground at her feet. "Either you work with me, or I'll find a way to provoke him myself."

"I won't do it." Drew leaned forward, putting his face inches from hers. "It would be suicide."

"You two are like two junk yard dogs going for each other's throats." Madden stood beside them, his gaze flicking from one to the other. "What is going on?"

Drew straightened. "Linn wants to provoke The Photographer into making a move for her."

The chief glanced from one to the other. "I don't know. It's a bit risky."

"But it'll work." Linn spun to face him. "Drew can keep me in his sight—from a distance. I'll be fine. Look, Mad Dog, women are going to continue to die until we catch this guy."

"Let's see what DNA brings back first."

~

This one wouldn't cooperate at all. The Photographer grasped Amber beneath her arms and tried hauling her to her feet. The girl went limp, sliding from his hands. He grunted and grasped her more firmly. "You are trying my patience."

She continued to struggle, squealing behind the rag he'd stuffed between her lips. Her booted feet hammered the sides of the van as he fought to drag her into the house. He almost dropped her again as her head slammed back into his chest.

Cursing, he slammed her to the ground. Grabbing a fist full of hair, he pulled her head back, then shoved it forward until her forehead collided with the concrete floor of his garage. It worked so well at relieving his frustration, he did it again. Once she lay limp, he plopped to the concrete and sat beside her, fighting to regain his breath.

Why was it getting so difficult? Things had been easy when he'd first come to Upton Falls. It was her fault. Aislinn's.

The first time he'd seen her, she had twirled around a shiny silver pole, swiveling her scantily clad hips to the beat of the music. She had looked right at him. He had done his best to look debonair, even lifting a martini in her direction, like the hero in a Hollywood classic. He didn't drink, but the bar said you couldn't watch if you didn't pay. Her smile had been worth every dollar spent that night, even the bills he stuffed in her thong.

Oh, the feel of her skin under his hand. The smell of her.

He took a deep breath, remembering their moment of passion less than an hour later. She had fought him, adding to the thrill, playing hard to get. But she had been his first, and she would be his last.

When he saw her again, walking into the police precinct with that long, steady stride of hers, he knew fate had put them back together. The wind blew that day, pulling beautiful tresses of hair free from her ponytail and floating them around her face. She'd lifted one gorgeous, long-fingered hand to brush the strands aside. Then, she'd turned around, and he saw the scar. Minor, certainly, but still an imperfection on an otherwise perfect face. Why hadn't he seen it before?

He'd fallen in love in spite of his resolve not to, and promised himself he'd wait until she attained perfection. What was taking her so long? All she had to do was profess her love for him. Seek him out instead of him doing the chasing. With her training, finding him should be such a simple thing.

The Photographer sighed. He grew tired of waiting. His gaze fell on the unconscious woman beside him. Blood pooled beneath her head. He studied her classic nose and smooth chin. The rose petal loveliness of her skin. Even with all the others' unscarred beauty, Aislinn was more perfect than they.

He rose and used his foot to flip Amber to her back. Grasping her ankles, he dragged her into the house, bouncing her head across the door frame.

As he lifted the trap door and rolled Amber into the hole to join Suzy, the other woman looked up at him, her eyes wide in a thin pale face. When was the last time he'd fed her? The Photographer squatted over the hole and squinted. Empty water bottles lay around Suzy's feet.

"I'm sorry, Suzy. I've been so busy with preparations, I haven't remembered to feed you." He held a hand down to her, pulling her weak body up the ladder.

He pulled out a kitchen chair. "Do I need to tie you, or will you behave?"

"I wouldn't get very far." Her voice sounded weak and defeated.

"I really am sorry about your neglect. It's only been a day or two. We need to build you up. You won't photograph well in this condition." He slapped a glass of milk in front of her. "Drink up. I'll make you a sandwich."

With the makings of a peanut butter and jelly sandwich on the counter in front of him, he continued, "This is really nice. It's good to be needed. I've always wanted a large family. I was an only child you know. That's why I've brought you company. As long as the two of you behave—I'll keep you." He wrapped her sandwich in a paper towel and placed it on the table. "The new girl's name is Amber. She needs discipline." He placed his hands flat on the surface of the table, and leaned close to Suzy's ear." Teach her how to behave, Suzy. I'm counting on you."

Suzy nodded. "I'll let her know what happens when we disobey."

"That's my good girl." The Photographer placed a tender kiss on her forehead. Her skin felt greasy to his lips. How could she have gotten this way. He sniffed and smelled the rank odor of her unwashed body. He jerked upright. His spine stiffened. Disgusting! He grabbed her hand and yanked her to her feet.

Pulling her along behind him, he led Suzy to the bathroom where he lowered the lid to the toilet and had her sit. He looked around his stark, tiled room. "Now, I know there's some bubble bath here somewhere. Would you like that?" He opened the cabinet beneath the sink. "Here it is. Smells like roses." He turned the faucet to the tub and poured in a generous amount of liquid bubbles.

Soon, the tub filled with a fragrant mound of cleansing bubbles, and he lowered Suzy into them, clothes and all. He sat on the closed lid of the toilet and watched as she submerged herself.

He scowled when she didn't immediately resurface. Springing forward he shot his arm beneath the water and grasped a handful of her hair, jerking her head above the bubbles. "Not nice, Suzy. You mustn't try drowning. If there is any killing to be done, I'll do it. I say who lives and who dies." He shook her head, knocking her teeth together. "Understand?"

Tears fell down her cheeks, mixing with the suds. She nodded.

"Wonderful." He patted her cheek, a little harder than necessary and resumed his place on the toilet. "There's a washcloth beside the tub. Wash yourself. You really don't want me to wash you. When I was a small boy, my mother had to wash me. It was brutal. She scrubbed so hard in some spots she made me bleed. My mother is an evil woman." He folded his hands and hung them between his thighs. "Aislinn cured me, though. She's my miracle. She taught me not all beautiful women are ugly inside."

14

*L*inn stared out the car window. Trees, darkened by the approaching dusk, whipped past as Drew sped along the highway. She snuck a peek at his stern profile. A muscle twitched near the corner of his lips. She opened her mouth to speak, then closed it, thinking it better not to break the silence.

He appeared to steer loosely, one hand draped over the steering wheel, yet, at closer study she could see his body sat rigid, tension in every line. His gaze cut to hers, and he shook his head. "Not another word, Linn."

"But…"

"I mean it." Drew readjusted his eyes to the highway. "This subject is closed."

Linn crossed her arms and laid her head back against the headrest. Who did he think he was? Her father? She closed her eyes for a second, then went back to staring out the window. She'd do it anyway. Once it was done, he wouldn't have a choice but to go along. Now, she had to figure out how, exactly, to provoke the elusive Photographer. Mere public kisses wouldn't be enough to draw him out.

Her shoulders burned, and she rolled her head to release the tension as Drew turned the car onto her street. He slowed as they neared her house and cast a glance in her direction. No white paper or photograph waved at them from the front door. Linn released the breath she hadn't realized she had been holding.

"Guess he's been too busy to leave any gifts tonight." She shoved open her door and slid from the seat.

"Uh huh." Drew unsnapped the loop around his gun. "I'll still enter the house first and have a look around."

"Be my guest." She waved her arm. "I'll be two steps back, like a good little woman." Linn withdrew her weapon and followed a couple of steps behind him as he headed up the stairs and into the house.

They'd left in a hurry, while it was still daylight, and Linn hadn't thought to leave a light burning. Shadows washed the front room grey. The corners dark and welcoming, inviting someone to hide there. She reached around Drew and flicked on a lamp.

Pain stabbed her eyes, and Linn squinted around the multi-colored dots dancing before her.

"Leave the lights off," Drew hissed.

"I don't like the dark."

With his free hand, he rubbed the back of his neck. "Linn, please."

"Okay." She flicked the switch off. "No more lights, but I can tell you there's no one here." If someone was, and Drew wished to remain anonymous, she'd already ruined their chances anyway.

He turned. "Let me find out for myself, all right? Humor me."

Linn smirked. "Fine."

"What is wrong with you?" He grabbed her arm above the elbow and dragged her along with him as he searched each room, gun held ready in front of him. Once he satisfied himself there was no one in the house, Drew pulled her back to the living room and shoved her to the sofa. "Why are you acting like a child?"

"I don't like being removed from the action. Y'all are treating me like a child, so, I'll act like one." She lifted her chin and narrowed her eyes. "I'm a cop. A good one. Let me do my job."

She stormed into the kitchen and slammed a pot onto the stove, then yanked it back to fill it with water. Slamming open a cabinet, she located and withdrew a box of tea bags. The routine of making tea served to calm her, and Linn leaned against the counter top while waiting for the water to boil and her blood to cool.

The water boiled, directing her attention back to the task at hand. Drinking caffeine would likely keep her awake, but the monotony of the task usually served to calm her nerves. Not tonight. She sighed and turned off the stove. She refused to soften her feelings. Firming her jaw, she marched into her bedroom and slammed the door.

~

Hot water streamed down his shoulders and loosened tightened muscles. Drew couldn't resist humming the tune to his favorite country song. After a brisk rub down with a towel, he tossed it in the corner of the bathroom.

He frowned as he pulled on a pair of clean jeans and another tee-shirt. Being bodyguard to a woman didn't leave him much freedom in the way he slept at night. He preferred the freedom of sleeping nude.

Anticipating the battle to follow, he smiled and went to the living room to retrieve his pillow and blanket from the sofa. He strolled barefoot to her door and rapped his knuckles three times against the wood.

The door swung open. "What?"

"Let me in." Drew pushed her aside, a grin splitting his face.

Her eyes flicked to the items in his arms. "You are *not* sleeping here." She stepped back, hands on her hips. Her cheeks flushed crimson, and her brows drew together.

"I'm sleeping on the floor beside your bed." Drew tossed his pillow to the mentioned spot and spread out his blanket, laying his holstered gun next to the makeshift bed.

"No, you're not." Linn yanked up the blanket.

"Be reasonable." Drew looked down at her. "After the other night, when The Photographer obviously watched you sleep, I don't think you should sleep alone. I thought about camping outside your door, but that leaves us both vulnerable."

"This is ridiculous." She hurled the blanket at him. "You act like you're my father." She tried to shove him, and he took her fists captive in his.

"I'm only doing my job." He pulled her struggling body close to his. "I'm here to protect you, and, I hope, catch a killer. The best way to do this is to keep you close."

Drew gazed down into her upturned face and fell headfirst into sparkling hazel eyes. His gaze was drawn to her parted lips, and he lowered his head. This kiss wasn't one of anger, but of tenderness. The velvet feel of her lips against his, the caress of her breath, sent his emotions reeling. He wrapped his arms tighter around her until her slight form was plastered against his chest.

A small moan escaped her, and she struggled to pull away, only causing him to tighten his hold.

"Stop. Stop." She whispered against his mouth.

Using what felt like inhuman strength, Drew lifted his head and released her. "I'm sorry. I shouldn't have done that." He turned and shook his blanket, once again spreading it on the carpet next to her bed. He looked back at her. "You should get some sleep." And he'd be calling

Steve, as much as he didn't want to, to stay with them to chaperone. Drew couldn't put himself in a situation to repeat a past mistake.

"Drew." Linn stood frozen, her hands hanging at her sides, wide eyes fixed on him.

"Go to bed, Linn." He folded his arms around himself as protection against the chill, and lay his head on the pillow. A few seconds later, a blanket draped over him. "Thanks."

He pounded out the lumps in his pillow. What was wrong with him? Did he have to be reminded that she found him repugnant? Was he on some kind of self-destructive mission? He flopped over to his back.

Attraction muddled a man's mind, kept him from concentrating on the task at hand. He didn't plan on anything happening to Linn. Not on his watch. Not again.

Rasping came from above him as Linn settled into the bed. Within minutes, a soft snoring drifted to where he lay. How could she sleep? Drew put a hand over his chest where his heart thudded, racing. Did that kiss do nothing for her? He ached to sit up and watch her while she slept. He punched Steve's number into his phone. No answer. He left a message and flipped the phone closed. His tortured thoughts whirled until sleep claimed him.

A creak and a muffled bump woke him with a snap. Drew's hand snatched his weapon from its holster. He held his breath, listening for signs of Linn being awake. Her soft snores reassured him she still slept.

He sat up as slow as possible, using caution to remain silent.

A slight light squeezed beneath the bedroom door. Drew kept his gaze focused on the handle. The soft thud of a falling footstep on the carpet. A darkening of the space beneath her door. The knob turned.

Linn murmured, "Drew?"

The shadow retreated. The doorknob returned to its original position with a click.

"Drew?"

"Shhh." He bolted to his feet, yanked open the door, and peered out. Nothing. No one.

He ran toward the living room, and drew his breath in with a hiss when he reached the end of the hall and fell to his knees. Glass shards sprinkled the tan carpet like fallen raindrops, and now, his scarlet blood left spots of their own.

Linn peered around the doorframe.

He held up his hand. "Stay there. Don't come out barefoot."

She disappeared, then padded out in enormous bunny slippers, gun in hand, and rushed past him toward the front door. Within seconds, she was back. She laid her weapon on the carpet and squatted next to him.

"Whoever it was left in a hurry. They left the front door wide open. Let me see your feet."

"We know who it was." Drew crawled a few feet away and sat cross-legged, one stinging foot in his hand. "I'll be fine." Taking a sharp sliver between two fingers, he slid it from the padding of his foot and placed it to the side. "Mean trick, and I was stupid to fall for it. Did you close and lock the door?"

"Of course I did." She took his other foot in her lap and set to work plucking glass from his skin.

The feel of her warm hand on his skin caused his heart to race like a tornado he saw crossing the prairie once. He slowed his own administrations, focusing instead on the head bent before him. Sleep mussed, strawberry-blond hair over a wrinkled man's dress shirt and pink bunny slippers. She'd never looked more beautiful. His gut clinched as he thought of the possibility he might not be able to keep her safe.

Linn peered up at him from beneath lowered lashes. "Does it hurt much?"

"No. Stings mostly."

"Let me get a towel and wipe off the blood. Then we'll have to get you to the bathroom and washed up. These spots will…"

Drew stilled her nervous hands, causing her to finally meet his gaze. "I'm sorry. I don't want you to be uncomfortable around me. Ever. I shouldn't have taken advantage of you at a vulnerable moment. I had no intention of—"

"I know." She swallowed visibly, a blush creeping up her cheeks. "It's okay, really. I…I liked it, Drew. I liked it when I kissed you earlier, too. You just have a way of making me so angry. You're like sandpaper against a raw wound."

"Gee, thanks." He laughed. "If you liked the kiss, why did you stop me?"

She bit her bottom lip. "I was afraid of things going too far. I don't get involved with men I work with."

His heart leapt in his chest. "So, I don't repulse you?"

"On the contrary, I…"

The shrill ringing of the telephone stopped the conversation, and Drew glanced at his watch. Two a.m. Only bad news called so early.

15

*T*he Photographer fled through the backyard and hurtled over neighboring fences. He clutched his right side. Fiery darts stabbed him as he labored for each shuddering breath. Three blocks over he caught the welcome sight of his car. He huddled behind a juniper hedge and cast his eyes up and down the street. What if someone saw him? He'd had the foresight to wear sweats in case someone did question his motives, but even he knew most people didn't go jogging at this time of the morning. They preferred to stay home in their warm beds and wait for the light of dawn to give them reason to rise.

Finding the coast clear, he darted across the dim street and slid behind the wheel of his unlocked car. His heart raced along with the car's engine as he headed home. His breath came in shaky gulps. He struggled against the continuing pain in his side. Maybe he should take up jogging for real. He was terribly out of shape.

Once home, he rushed up the porch steps and slammed the front door behind him. He leaned against it. The sobs he'd held inside burst forth in a dam that threatened to rip apart his very soul.

She'd betrayed him. She'd shared her bed with the cowboy. The thought of what he knew took place behind her closed door burned through his heart like acid. Spinning, he thrust his fist into the wall. A sneer stretched his lips at the sight of the hole he left there.

The thoughts continued to whirl, bringing with them full-color images of Linn and her new love. He clapped his hands over his head but the pictures still flashed through his mind. He pounded his skull with his fists. How could she do this? She belonged to him. From the first time he saw her, dancing like an angel in red, an angel on fire in scarlet lingerie, he'd known he had to own her. Because of him she'd changed her life. Become a lady. A *pure* angel. He slammed another fist into the wall. He'd left his mark on her, damn it!

He needed comforting. He *needed* his Linns. Although he knew the girls he kept in the hole beneath the house weren't really Linn, they would do as a substitute until he claimed the real one.

The Photographer swiped his arm across his watering eyes. There was no need for him to spend what remained of the dark alone. He cast a quick peek at his watch. He needed to be at work in three hours. He hated his job as janitor at the city's discount department store. But, it did parade past him a delectable fare to choose from. Maybe fate would send him another Linn to add to his collection.

Suzy and Amber blinked up at him when he threw the trapdoor open. "Good morning, ladies. I want company." He held a hand toward them. "One at a time, please."

Amber ascended first, her limbs trembling.

"Don't be frightened." He took her hand and led her to a waiting chair. A coil of nylon rope waited on the counter. "I'm sure Suzy filled you in on my expectations. I don't have many." He tied her to the chair and tugged on her bindings to test their strength.

"Your turn, Suzy." He helped the other girl up the ladder. His gaze raked over her body. "You're still so thin. Let me fix both of you something to eat." His mood lifted as he catered to the needs of his girls.

Suzy, the dear thing, moved to the sink, wet a rag, then knelt beside the bound Amber and washed the dried blood from the other woman's face. So like his Linn.

His mind flittered to thoughts of his love. Fresh pain rose, choking him with an iron fist. He shoved the thoughts aside, focusing instead on the two women in front of him. "I'll release one of your hands so you can eat. I'm trusting you to behave." He set a bowl of hot soup before each of them. "Try not to drip on the table cloth. I just washed it."

He slid a chair for himself away from the table and settled back. His own stomach churned, and he couldn't stand the thought of eating anything.

Amber's hand shook, spilling soup down her chin and onto the tee-shirt she wore. As The Photographer scowled at her sloppiness, he noticed the unusual paleness of her face and the fine sheen of perspiration. "Are you ill?" He leaned forward.

She nodded. "I'm hypoglycemic. I can't go hours without eating."

"And you have no right to make demands of me!" The Photographer stood with enough force to send his chair careening into the cabinets behind him. "If not for me, you wouldn't be eating the soup you're slopping down your front." He whirled and pushed his face close enough to Suzy's to spray her with spittle. "Tell her what happens to those who disobey."

Suzy's spoon halted its progression to her lips. She trembled. "You'll be killed."

The Photographer raised his hands above his head. "Yes! We have a winner." He transferred his attention back to Amber, gripping her face in one hand.

"You'd do well to remember that. I desire perfection above all else. Take control of your thoughts and body…or you'll be of no use to me." He removed his hand, leaving red marks on her skin where his fingers had dug into her face. He patted her cheek, stinging his fingers with the force. "Finish your soup."

He paced the room. Why must they make him angry? Why is it so difficult to find perfection in a woman? His mother drilled into his head to search for that perfect someone. She'd said someone like her. Now, she laid like a slobbering, immobile slug in a hospital bed, barely alive. She couldn't do anything for him.

Surely, by combining the traits of several women he could achieve that which he so vigorously sought? His gaze swung back to the two women at the table. They weren't enough. He knew that. He'd have to find another—and soon.

~

As Drew's face paled, Linn's fist tightened around the shards of glass she'd pulled from his foot. Her eyes remained glued on his face as he rubbed the back of his neck. "Are you sure?"

Drew sank to sit on the arm of the sofa. "Give us ten minutes. We'll meet you there." He moved in slow motion as he replaced the receiver.

"What is it?" Linn loosened her grip as the sharps poked the skin of her palm. "Who was on the phone?"

"Maybe you should sit down."

Her heart faltered. "Tell me now. I don't want to sit down."

"I asked for a rush job on the blood on Molero's car. A friend who works at a private DNA firm owed me a favor." Drew limped toward her and stopped when she took a step back. "The preliminary DNA results from the blood left on Eva Molero's car are in." He lifted a hand in her direction then let it fall. "It's Steve, Linn. The DNA matches his."

Her stomach ached as if he'd punched her in the gut. Her hand opened, releasing the bloody fragments of glass. "My Steve?" She shook her head. "No. It can't be."

"Linn." Drew rushed forward and caught her before she slid to the floor. Scooping her in his arms, he carried her to the sofa. "Madden is going to arrest him now. I said we'd meet him at Steve's place, but I can call him back and tell him to go ahead without us."

"I should be there." She forced her face to remain impassive. What she wanted to do was scream and slam her fists into the wall. She refused to believe that her tender partner could be someone as cold-blooded as The Photographer. "I need to see his face when they arrest him. The clues all pointed to him, but I didn't believe them." She folded her trembling hands in her lap. "But, you did. You tried to tell me."

Drew knelt in front of her, taking her hands in his. "I changed my mind, Linn. Something didn't add up."

"You were right." She shook her head. "I'm sorry." She stood and pulled free of his warm grasp. "I'll get changed. You need to wash your feet and get some shoes on."

The walk to her bedroom seemed long. Her steps heavy as she crunched across the glass in her slippers. She didn't realize she was crying until she raised a hand to wipe her face and felt the wetness. Linn stared for a moment at the shiny tips of her fingers, then brushed her hand roughly across her hip.

A myriad of emotions swept through her. Relief at the end of The Photographer's reign of terror. Pain at the betrayal of a friend. Fear and anger. They all swirled through her until she found herself dizzy.

She grabbed the pair of jeans she'd discarded at bedtime and yanked them on under the over-sized shirt she wore. She stuffed her weapon into her waistband, secured her hair in a plain blue ribbon, then grabbed her purse. Who cared whether she looked professional or not? Her world had just crumbled around her feet.

"I'm driving." She stalked past Drew who struggled and grunted to pull on his boots. "Are you going to be all right?"

"Yep." He hopped to catch up with her, and winced. "A bit tender, but I'll survive." He stopped her with a touch on her arm. "What about you?"

Linn shrugged. "I'll be all right. Just one more item of proof to add to my box of rejections."

"Self pity isn't one of your better traits."

She pulled free. "You don't know me well enough to know what my traits are." She swung the front door open. Great. Pouring rain. Perfect weather for her to arrest her best friend.

Drew sprinted ahead of her, and opened the car door. "Thanks." She ducked into the car, avoiding the look of concern in his eyes.

The *thunk thunk* of the windshield wipers kept time with the beating of her heart as she drove them to Steve's house. The tires swished through puddles, spraying the sidewalks on each side of them. Under different circumstances, Linn enjoyed driving in a light rain. The way everything looked so much clearer and brighter. But tonight, the rain intensified her pain and provided the perfect backdrop to the night.

Madden sat in an unmarked car across the street from Steve's, and Linn stopped just a few feet behind him. She sat still, both hands gripping the steering wheel. Her knuckles ached from the pressure. The front door of Steve's house loomed before her. The windows returned her stare, dark and uninviting. Obviously the traitor still slept. His modest sedan sat parked in the driveway.

Linn's gaze scanned the street and surrounding houses. No lights burned. No traffic cruised past. Not that she expected any at this time of the morning, but how could things be so normal when everything was falling apart?

The driver's side door of the police chief's vehicle swung open.

"Ready, Linn?"

"No." She turned to Drew's dark, compassion-filled eyes. "I could never be ready for this."

Madden tapped the car window and motioned his head for them to get out.

Taking a deep breath, Linn released her death grip on the steering wheel. Madden opened the door for her and offered his hand, pulling her from the vehicle. He handed her a black umbrella.

The glow of street lights reflecting in the rain puddles gave Linn the illusion of cleanliness. She felt anything but. Life had dealt her another cruel blow on top of all the previous ones. The fact of Steve being The Photographer angered her and made her feel betrayed, but the idea of arresting the man who'd been her friend, saddened her. There'd been so few friends in her life.

She sloshed through the drizzle, a man on each side of her, and resolved to do what needed to be done. Her foot slipped on the top step leading to Steve's porch, and Drew grasped her elbow to steady her. Lifting one hand, she pounded on the door and stepped back, letting the umbrella fall to the porch as she placed a hand on the gun at her hip.

She rapped again. The faint sound of padded footsteps came to her through the door and seconds later a sleep mussed Steve frowned at her.

He glanced from one to the other of the three standing there, his brow wrinkled. "What's going on?" He glanced down at his watch. "It's early. Did another woman disappear?"

Madden unclipped the handcuffs from his belt. "We have a warrant for your arrest for the murder of Eva Molero and for evidence that points to you being The Photographer."

"What?" Steve took a step back. "I didn't kill anyone. I couldn't." His eyes narrowed at Drew. "What kind of game are you playing, Wayne?"

"Stop it, Steve!" Tears fell down Linn's face. "We found your DNA at the murder site."

"There's been a mistake." Steve shook his head.

Madden turned a pliable Steve around to cuff him.

"Tell them, I'm not a murderer. I wasn't at the Molero site. Linn, you know I'm not a killer."

She shook her head. Acid churned in her gut. Tears burned her throat. "I don't know anything anymore."

Drew put an arm around her shoulders.

"This is your fault," Steve growled. "You've poisoned everyone against me, putting these ideas in their heads."

Madden clicked the cuffs around his wrists. "Come on, buddy. You'll have your day in court." He took Steve by the elbow and led him down the steps. "You two go on home. I'll see you at the precinct in a few hours."

Once Steve sat in the back of Madden's car and the door slammed shut on his stunned face, Linn lifted her hands to her eyes and let the sobs that had been threatening to rise, spill out of her. Completely unprofessional, but the situation couldn't have been a worse scenario.

Drew wrapped his arms around her, pulling her close. He smelled of rain and man.

"Make it all go away." Linn buried her face in the broad expanse of his chest.

"I wish I could." He placed his chin on the top of her head.

"I guess you'll be leaving now." She sniffed.

"I'll be around for a few more days. Until things are settled."

"Thank you for being there. For keeping me safe." How would she survive without him? If any man could get past the barriers she had erected, it was Special Agent Andrew Wayne.

He lifted her stitched hand, and laughed. "Yeah. Real safe. These should be coming out soon, right?"

Linn stepped back, nodding. "After a week." Her heart grew heavy. For Steve or the fact Drew would be leaving? "I want to talk to Steve. I have a lot of questions."

"Okay. Let's go back to your place, shower and get changed, and we'll head to the precinct. You can probably get to him while he's still being questioned."

16

*T*he mirror reflected a face she'd thought long dead. Pale and full of pain. One that dreaded the future, full of distrust. But The Photographer brought that frightened woman back, and Linn had no idea how to deal with her.

Linn reached up and released her hair from its ribbon. Steam rose from the gushing shower, and she stretched to adjust the temperature before stepping beneath the spray.

She tilted her face, relishing in the warm silkiness of the water running across her face and down her shoulders to mix with the salt of her tears. Steve's betrayal pierced her heart with an agony so intense she found it difficult to stand upright and only did so out of sheer determination. Her stomach churned, and she pressed a hand to her abdomen to fight back the nausea.

He knew her innermost secrets and desires. She'd opened herself to him, and he'd taken that information and used it for a diabolical plot to terrorize her. Why? How could she not have seen it? So much for women's intuition.

Finished with her shower, she donned her familiar, comfortable navy suit and pinned back her hair. Her chin quivered as she fought back tears before turning away from the mirror.

She opened the door and froze.

Drew stood before her decked out in a black suit and tie. He'd slicked back his dark hair, taming the curls, and shaved. Shiny black shoes peeked from beneath the suit trousers.

"Wow. Now you look FBI." *And still way too gorgeous for her vulnerable heart.*

"It's a somber day." He gave a sad smile, dimple winking despite his words. "Thought I should look the part."

"You clean up real nice." Linn moved past him. "Let's do this before I lose my nerve."

Drew's hand shot out. "You don't have to. You can wait and ask him when he's behind bars. Let someone else interrogate him."

"No, I need to face him now." She dug through her purse, found her keys, and tossed the ring to Drew. "You can drive."

"Okay." He looked surprised as he caught the keys in one hand.

Linn's mind raced as they drove to the station. The car's tires whirred against the pavement, keeping time with her thoughts and sending up occasional sprays of rain water. Her thoughts spun so fast she couldn't find a solitary one to grasp hold of and dwell on. Her years as Steve's partner collided, tumbling in memory and feeling, one after the other. The knife in her gut pierced deeper, and twisted.

It wasn't lost on her the number of times Drew cast her a worried glance. No doubt he thought she would fall apart. She wouldn't. No way would she give The Photographer the satisfaction of seeing her crumble.

How long had Steve planned to torment her? When had he come up with his mad scheme? The man deserved an award for his acting skills.

They pulled into the parking lot of the precinct, and Linn gritted her teeth. *I'm not going to cry.*

The rain stopped, and the air hung heavy and humid. Linn loosened the top button of her blouse as Drew tugged on his tie. They splashed through the shallow puddles on the concrete and wiped their feet on a rubber mat. Drew clamped a hand on Linn's shoulder and gave a gentle squeeze before he opened the door.

The atmosphere inside the building resembled a funeral home. Silent and full of whispers and furtive glances. A few officers glanced Linn's way, not meeting her eyes, and scurried off to some errand. The receptionist opened her mouth to speak and snapped her lips shut at one look from Linn.

Linn stood in the hallway, arms folded across her chest, and watched as Madden ushered Steve down the hall. Steve glanced her way, his look imploring her to speak. Each time Linn turned her head. She wanted to wait until she could speak with Steve alone. Without an audience and with no interruptions.

She almost lost her resolve when Steve stood against the wall for his mug shot. She squeezed her eyelids tight against the tears that threatened to spill. Her throat ached from her struggle not to cry.

Steve's handsome face paled beneath his olive complexion, his lips a thin slash across his face. His head drooped, and the officer taking the pictures asked him to raise his head and look into the camera. The officer seemed apologetic, sorry for the position Steve was in. In no way did Steve look like a murderer.

Preliminaries out of the way, the officer led him to an interrogation room that contained nothing but a table and two chairs.

Linn stepped through the door and halted, turning to place a hand on Drew's chest. "Let me do this alone, please."

"You can't interrogate him. Conflict of interest, but I'll allow you to speak with him." He stepped back. "I'll be watching through the glass."

"Could you get us some water?"

"Sure."

She jerked at the click of the door and marched to the chair opposite the one Steve sat in. Her heels snapped against the tile floor, echoing in the almost empty room.

The air conditioner whistled through the ducts, and she shivered beneath the suit jacket she wore. Goose pimples peppered Steve's arms.

Slowly lowering herself to the padded chair reserved for the detectives, Linn folded her hands on the cold metal table between them. With a deep breath, she raised her eyes. "Why?"

"Please," Steve's handcuffs clanked against the table. "I didn't…"

"Don't. DNA doesn't lie." Even with the anger burning through her, Linn held out a small ray of hope that something went wrong, and she looked at an innocent man.

"Then someone planted it." He reached across the table to grab her hands and she pulled back. His countenance fell.

"I just want to know why!" She rose and shoved against the table. "You were my best friend! You helped me through some of the worst days of my life. Days when my past would come back to haunt me. A past you gave me, you bastard!" Her words broke. "How could you do this? How could you murder those women and send me the pictures?" She turned her back and rested her forehead against the cool glass of the one-way mirror. "I trusted you."

"I want to shoot you." Linn whirled. "Kill you as you did those women." Her eyes burned.

"I didn't do it." He rose from his chair. "I love you." He took a step toward her.

"Stay in the seat, Chavez." Drew's voice came through the speaker.

Steve fell into the chair. "Search your heart. You'll know I didn't do it."

"I don't know what to think." The tears she'd been holding escaped, running down her cheeks. Spent, her shoulders slumped, and she turned back to him. "It hurts, Steve. It kills me to think you're capable of something like this. All the hours we've spent together. I've told you my secrets." Her voice lowered. "I've told you everything about me. The ugly, the sordid, and the small amount of good. You betrayed everything I thought we were."

"I'm begging you." Tears welled in his eyes. "You know how I feel about you."

She slapped her hands flat on the table top. "Yeah, well The Photographer loves me too." She lifted her hands and sunk the palms to her eye sockets and pressed. "I don't know what to think."

Her mind spun. She straightened and stared into the one-way mirror. Bloodshot eyes stared back at her. In that moment, as she looked at Steve's reflection, she knew the truth. She had no idea how things came to be, but her heart told her Steve was innocent. How could she prove it?

Whirling, she threw herself into the chair and leaned forward, resting her forearms on the smooth surface. She stared deep into his eyes and whispered. "He's going to leave me, Steve. Drew is. Now that they believe we've caught The Photographer, he'll leave."

Hope bloomed in Steve's eyes. He leaned forward, his face inches from hers and in the same silent voice, answered, "You believe me."

She nodded. "I don't know how or why, but God help me, I do. Everything inside of me says you didn't do it. I'm sorry for all the things I said."

"Don't apologize." He smiled through his tears. "We've been thrust into a situation neither of us can understand or control. I'm just grateful I still have my friend."

"Linn." Drew sauntered through the door. "You're too close to this. Time's up."

Face burning, she ducked her head. What did he think of her conversation with Steve? He most likely thought her an idiot. DNA didn't lie.

He unfolded his arms and banged his fist on the table. "Everything points to you, Chavez. Your DNA is on the woman's car."

Linn jumped.

"What do you expect us to think?" Drew paced the room. "Nobody wants to believe you're The Photographer!" He ran his hands through his hair, releasing the curls from their smooth finish. "Not even me."

Linn watched as he paced, the heels of his polished shoes beating a heavy-metal rhythm on the floor. He actually seemed upset to believe Steve guilty of the crime he'd been charged with. If Drew wasn't convinced, then maybe they could get Steve released on a technicality. They just had to come up with one. "What can we do, Drew?"

"What do you mean?"

"To get Steve released?"

He spun on one heel. "We can't get him released, Linn. He's being tried for murder. The evidence points to him being a serial killer."

"I don't think he did it."

"It's not up to you. A jury will make that decision."

"What about you, Wayne?" Steve raised hopeful eyes to him. "Do you think I'm guilty?"

Drew rubbed the spot between his eyes. "I don't know. All the evidence points to you, but...I don't know." He leaned on the edge of the table. "I'm kind of going with Linn's instincts on this one."

"Thank you." Steve's shoulders shook, and he buried his face in his cuffed hands. "I haven't got the first clue how my DNA got on that car or how to prove my innocence. This is an awful thing to say, but I'm hoping for another abduction." He lifted his head. His red-rimmed gaze locked with Linn's. "Maybe I *am* as evil as the killer."

"No, you're not." Linn started to place her hand over his but stopped. The possibility of Steve being The Photographer still hovered in the air between them.

"But you're right," Drew added. "It would help prove your innocence. Until then, you're staying in jail. Solitary confinement—for your protection."

~

The hope on Linn's face slammed into Drew's gut with the force of a sledgehammer. It was obvious to him The Photographer, if he wasn't Steve, had planned the set-up. The difficult part would be proving Steve's innocence.

Drew resumed his pacing. *Did* he believe Chavez was innocent? Linn seemed adamant. Watching her through the mirror as she cried and questioned the man everyone said betrayed her had wrenched his soul.

When the two leaned across the table, he'd sworn they were going to kiss. The vice around his heart squeezed tighter. Was he believing Chavez innocent so he wouldn't have to leave within the next day or two? Did he grasp at straws in order to remain by Linn's side?

He smoothed his hands over his hair. "I'll do what I can. I think I'll visit the victim's car and the murder site. Linn, do you want to come?"

"Sure." She reached across and laid her hand over Steve's. The gesture brought a new welling of tears to the man's eyes. "Don't worry, Steve. Drew will think of something."

"I wish I had your faith in me," Drew said as they left building. "The chances of us proving someone planted Steve's blood in that car…" He halted and slapped a hand to his forehead. "Blood. Why didn't we check?"

He spun and raced back into the building, halting the officer leading Steve to a cell. "Wait. I need him for a minute." Grabbing Steve by the elbow, Drew left an open-mouthed Linn standing in the hall and dragged the cuffed man to the men's room. "Strip."

"Excuse me?"

"Drop your pants."

"Why am I doing this?" Steve unzipped his pants and let them fall to his ankles.

"Take off your shirt."

"I'm not dropping another article of clothing until you tell me what you're looking for."

"A scrape." Drew walked a circle around Chavez. "Something that would have left blood on the bolt of that car. If you don't have any type of scrape, then…"

"I do." Steve turned and revealed a narrow day-old scrape on the calf of his left leg.

Drew sighed and bent to peer at the wound. "This doesn't bode well. How did you do it?"

"I don't know. I run in the evenings. When it's daylight, I do lawn work. I'm always scraping or bruising myself. Can I pull my pants up now?"

"Yeah." Drew scraped his hand across his chin. "That blew my idea out of the water and made you look even more guilty."

"I'm not guilty." His golden eyes hardened.

"And if, after trying to prove your innocence, I find out you do have plans to harm Linn," Drew locked gazes with the other man. " I'll kill you myself."

"You won't find out any such thing." Steve pulled up and zipped his pants before pushing open the door. "Leave me alone and catch the real killer."

"I'm trying to help you, man. Why the attitude?"

Steve spun to face him, his face red. "Are you helping me or Linn? Her heart is going to be broken when you leave, and I'll be here to pick up the pieces."

"I'm helping Linn. I don't plan on leaving her life, Chavez, but my job will take me away from here."

"She deserves more than a long distance relationship."

Drew's heart plummeted as he realized the truth in Steve's words. Linn did deserve more.

"When you leave, and I'm in prison, she'll be alone again."

"What do you want me to do?" Drew whirled. "I can't guarantee I'll get you released. I can't guarantee Linn will never be alone. I can't guarantee anything, except for the fact that I love her."

"You…love her." Steve sagged against the wall.

"Yes." Drew's eyes searched the face of the man before him. Steve's look of resignation contrasted with Drew's feeling of shock. Love? He couldn't believe he had admitted it. His life left no room for a relationship.

Steve's eyelids lowered, shutting off any expression that might give Drew a clue to the man's thoughts. His lips compressed into a straight line, and he set his features into a mask. Taking a deep breath, he raised his eyes. "So, what's the plan?"

"You go to jail, and I try to prove your innocence."

"I'm talking about Linn."

"We take it one day at a time. As long as I can convince my superiors that we might have the wrong guy, I'll remain here on the case. After that…I'll be gone."

17

*L*inn accosted Drew as soon as the two men stepped out of the restroom. She cocked one hip and crossed her arms. "What was so important you had to run off and hide in the men's room?"

"Lower your voice." Drew ushered Steve ahead of them and took Linn's elbow in a tight grip. "I had an idea I thought would rule Steve out as The Photographer. I was wrong."

Practically running, Linn struggled to keep up with Drew's long-legged stride. "Slow down."

"I need to speak with Madden." He pushed open the glass door to the chief's office and ushered Steve and Linn in before him.

The chief's eyes widened as the trio entered his office. His eyes flicked to Steve's handcuffed wrists then swept across the faces of Drew and Linn. He frowned as the three of them plopped themselves into the chairs across from his desk.

Sighing, he took off the black plastic-rimmed glasses perched on his nose and laid them on his desk blotter. He folded his hands in front of him before speaking. "Why is Chavez with you, and why are the three of you making yourselves comfortable in my office? Wayne, you should be booking your flight out of here."

His words pierced Linn's heart. She lowered her head to stare at her folded hands.

Steve and Drew began speaking in sync until Madden raised one finger to stop them. "You first, Wayne. Chavez, keep your mouth shut unless I ask you a question."

"I need you to convince my supervisor that there is a chance Steve may not be The Photographer. I want to stay here and work on the case."

"Excuse me?" The chief leaned back in his chair. The burgundy vinyl squeaked beneath his weight. He folded his hands across his ample middle. "Chavez's DNA is all over Molero's car. The case is finished."

"Mad Dog." Linn leaned forward, balancing her elbows on her knees. "You know Steve. He's been part of your division for years. Can you honestly tell me you believe him capable of these murders?"

"Cops go bad all the time." Madden's chair banged forward. He rubbed his bald head. "You're right. I don't think Steve is The Photographer. But I don't believe Molero was murdered by The Photographer. Not his MO."

"I didn't kill that woman, chief."

"I wish I could believe that, Chavez. Maybe the two of you had a fight. A lover's spat and it got out of hand."

"And I went to the trunk, grabbed a tire iron, and whacked her with it!"

The chief held up a hand. "Settle down before I have you dragged out of here."

"Why can't you let us dig further?" Linn studied his face, noting the worry mark between his eyes which seemed deeper than it had last week. Stubble dotted the man's cheeks and chin. Weariness etched itself in every line of his face.

"You're too close to this, McFarland. I'm removing you from the case. I've wanted to for a long time. Should've followed procedure and done it days ago."

"Chief." Drew rose from his chair and leaned the palms of his hands on the desktop. "Go with your gut on this one."

The big man shook his head. "My hands are tied. Chavez is going to jail, and you are going back to California. Now take him back to holding."

Drew kicked the desk. A mug used as a pencil holder fell over. Yellow pencils rolled across the desk.

"Come on. "Linn grabbed his arm. "Let's go back and check Molero's car again. We can talk to forensics. Maybe we missed something."

His stormy gaze stared into hers, and he nodded. A curl fell forward.

Linn dug her nails into the palms of her hands. She itched to smooth the curl back into place.

Her heart pounded as their gazes locked, and she swallowed against the lump in her throat. Drew gave a slow wink and the connection was lost.

"Chavez." Drew turned on his heel and marched out of the office.

Tossing Madden a small smile of apology, Linn stepped aside for Steve to follow Drew. She backed out, keeping her eyes on the chief who stared after her, and closed the door.

She turned and flattened her face on the rock solidness of Drew's chest. "Oh." Linn stepped back and put a hand to her throbbing nose. "I thought you took Steve."

"I passed him off to a rookie." He took her hand down from her nose. "You all right? Let me take a look."

"I'm fine." Linn ducked beneath his outstretched arm. "Let's go. We have work to do and not a lot of time. You leave when, tomorrow?"

"Yeah, morning."

The outside heat blasted them when Drew opened the door and allowed Linn to precede him to the car. Heat waves shimmered and danced over the asphalt.

"You guys have crazy weather here. Rain yesterday and hot as the desert today. But sticky."

"Yeah." Linn slid behind the wheel of the car. She kept her gaze focused on the steering wheel. "Will I ever see you again?"

"Linn." His husky drawl washed over her and he reached across the gear shift to wrap his arms around her. "You'll see me. As often as I can get away. Nothing can keep me from you." With a finger he tilted her face to look at him. "Besides, I haven't found anyone who can kiss like you."

"Idiot." She punched his chest and slid back into her seat.

Taking hold of her arm, Drew pulled her close, his lips settling on hers. She sighed and closed her eyes, relishing in his tenderness. Butterflies flitted against the walls of her stomach.

"Oh, yeah. You'll see me again." He cupped her cheeks in his hands and, using his thumbs, wiped away her tears.

Linn giggled and sat upright. "Good. Because I'd miss tripping over your cowboy boots."

"The next time, you'll be tripping over them because they're sitting beside your bed." Drew held her free hand as they drove to Eva Molero's murder site. His large hand engulfed her smaller one. The calluses rubbed against the smooth flesh of her palm. She tightened her grip.

~

The vehicle had been moved, but the yellow warning tape still fluttered in the warm breeze. The tall grass in the nearby field waved around the areas trampled by the police.

"I don't think there's anything left to find." Linn removed her suit jacket and tossed it in the backseat. She grabbed a spiral notebook and opened her door before stepping back into the oven of early afternoon.

"We need a miracle." Drew paced the asphalt. He scanned the ground around his feet then squatted beside the shoulder of the road. "Do you keep copies of the pictures you take of crime scenes?"

"Only on active files."

"Do you have copies of the photos from Sara Vern's murder site with you?"

"Yes, why?"

Placing both hands on his thighs, he shoved to his feet. "I'd like to see them. Something doesn't look right to me."

Linn popped the latch on her car's trunk and removed a manila envelope from a file box she kept there. Peering beneath the flap, she located the Vern photos and slid them free.

The one of herself was on top. She captured her lower lip between her teeth. Steve just wasn't capable of something like this, was he?

"Linn?"

"Sorry." She handed him the photos.

He rubbed his chin, his narrowed eyes perusing the photo.

"What?"

"The pictures of the tire marks from the Vern site and the ones here don't match. They also don't match Steve's car."

"Madden would just say he used another car."

"You're right, but, if we can find another piece of inconclusive evidence, it might be enough to take some interest off of Steve. I need to see Molero's car." Drew stood, feet shoulder width apart, and stared across the field.

Linn glanced in the same direction. Many pairs of feet had trampled the dry grass of the field, eliminating any hope of them finding missed evidence. A green field of corn stood proudly to the west.

"Let's take a look." Drew removed his suit jacket and tossed it on the hood of the car. "I'll head this way, you go there. Stay close enough that we can hear each other if we call out."

She nodded. "About twenty feet past where you're standing is where I found the crow bar."

Rolling up the sleeves of his white shirt, Drew nodded. "Doubt we'll find much, but we need to be positive. We can't leave anything out."

Linn pulled her blouse free from the waistband of her slacks and headed toward the cornfield. Why couldn't they have gone first to the air-conditioned garage and checked out Molero's car? The tall, swaying stalks promised shade from the sun's rays and drew her like a magnet. She tossed a glance over her shoulder. Drew strolled, head bent, seemingly focused on the ground beneath his feet.

The dry grass crunched beneath her shoes, leading into the dusty dirt of the cornfields. The stalks towered a foot above her head. Instead of the coolness she desired, the air sat still, dry, and stagnant. Linn lifted her ponytail from her sweaty neck.

Standing on tiptoe, she peered over the stalks. Drew wasn't in sight. "Drew?" No answer. She shrugged, transferring her attention to the ground beneath her.

"This is a waste of time. Why would The Photographer come this far out?" They were grasping at straws. She turned back to the car.

Smoke!

She sniffed again, whipping her head in each direction. From where?

The smell grew stronger, burning her eyes. To her right, the corn crackled, consumed by a fire Linn couldn't yet see. Her heart beat a rapid rhythm. Her mouth dried up.

"Drew!"

Someone dodged across the path.

"Drew, I'm here!" Where was he going?

The man turned.

"Linn!"

The person disappeared.

Fear threatened to consume her as the fire's crackle increased in intensity. Which way to run? She chose her right and shoved aside corn in her attempt to escape the fire's path. The corn stalks slashed back, leaving stinging razor thin cuts on her arms.

A low trench tripped her, sending her sprawling in the dirt. Agony shot spears of its own fire through her ankle.

Using the stalks, she pulled to her feet and bit her lip against the sharp pain in her ankle. She held onto the thick stalks and dragged herself forward, limping, in what she hoped was the right direction.

The smoke thickened and grew dark. She swiped an arm across her watering eyes, and tried to take shallow breaths despite the fear of suffocation whirling through her. She glanced at the blue sky overhead. Black smoke was quickly blocking the view, and Linn had no idea in which direction was freedom.

~

Drew watched Linn disappear into the stalks of corn then squatted beside the faint imprint of a gym shoe. Bingo! His crazy, desperate attempt to find evidence had paid off. It looked like the same print found at the murder of Linn's neighbors'. He slipped the camera he'd grabbed from Linn's trunk off his shoulder. Only one way to be sure.

The camera clicked. He straightened and studied the area around him. A faint spiral drifted above the cornfield. Drew lifted his hand to shade his face. Fire? "Linn?"

Stepping over the footprint, Drew quickened his pace toward the corn. "Linn!"

The smell of smoke grew stronger and the crackle of fire filled the air. A dusky grey cloud hovered over the cornfield.

Drew draped the camera strap over his head, then used both hands to shove aside the corn stalks. "Linn!"

The fire roared now on three sides of the corn field, cutting off their avenues of escape. Drew glanced back the way he'd come, praying he'd have time to locate Linn and get them both out safely before the fire cut off all hope.

"Linn!" His heart flew into his throat. Heat seared his skin. He veered in another direction. "Answer me!"

"Over here."

"Where? Keep talking." Drew followed the sound of her voice to where she sat. Dirt covered the front of her blouse and pants. She clutched her ankle.

"What happened?" He knelt beside her.

"Twisted my ankle. I tried to make it back to the car, but stopped when I heard you call."

Drew slipped an arm beneath her. "The fire's growing. We don't have much time."

She nodded and allowed him to help her rise. Thick smoke billowed over their heads, and she coughed.

"Try putting your shirt over your nose. Breathe through the fabric." Drew tightened his grip around her waist and pulled her along with him. Each direction they turned put them against a blazing wall. With each breath fire seared his lungs.

"We're trapped." Linn clutched the front of Drew's shirt. She breathed in short rapid bursts, her eyes wide in a face pale beneath the dirt. "He's here. I saw him."

Despite the fear rising in his own chest, he tilted her streaked face to his. "We're not going to die . I'll get us out of here."

Stretching his neck to see above the corn, he squinted through the smoke. There. One area the fire hadn't yet reached. "Come on." He half-carried, half-dragged Linn in the direction of the unburned gap. He couldn't breathe. Spots swam in front of his streaming eyes.

She cried out and sagged beside him. "I can't, Drew. I can't go any further on my ankle."

He swept her up in his arms and whirled to catch his bearings. His chest heaved. His eyes stung and watered. The smoke grew thick, obscuring his vision. He ran west and used his body to push through close-growing stalks.

The leaves slapped at him, cutting his arms. Drew hunched over Linn, taking as much of the damage as possible. One sharp leaf cut the skin next to his eye, adding one more sting to the many areas of pain on his body. He lifted his shoulder and wiped the streaming eyes.

Through the smoke he caught another glimpse of the rapidly disappearing gap of freedom. With coughs that threatened to split his lungs, he lunged forward and dove through the opening.

The force of the fall drove the wind from his lungs, and he released his hold on Linn. She squeaked and rolled across the grass.

Gasping like a stranded fish, Drew struggled to his feet and pulled her with him. Once again sweeping her into his arms, he lumbered toward the paved road.

In the distance, the wail of sirens rose.

At the edge of the pavement, Drew dropped to his knees and lowered Linn beside him. The first fire truck braked to a stop a few feet away.

Paramedics surrounded them and hooked oxygen masks to their faces. Two lifted Linn to a gurney and wheeled her to a waiting ambulance. When they wanted to do the same with Drew, he shook his head and pulled away, removing his oxygen mask.

"I'm fine."

"If you'd left when I told you to, you wouldn't be breathing oxygen from a plastic tube." Madden stood with arms crossed.

Drew pushed to his feet and turned to stare where firemen sprayed the flames. "He's still out there, Madden. I know it. I'd bet my bottom dollar he set this fire."

"Why?"

"I might be taking a long shot here." He glared at the chief. "But I'm thinking he wants us dead."

"No need to be sarcastic. I doubt it's our guy. He's sitting in jail right now on a wish and a prayer. This fire might have started by a tossed cigarette."

"Not with the rain we've had or this early in the growing season." Drew growled and turned away. His eyes scanned the burning cornfield. "Linn said she saw someone out there."

"That growl because you're clearing the smoke from your lungs?"

He whirled to face his friend. "You know Chavez isn't a killer."

Madden sighed. "I know, but without proof, he might as well be."

"Then back me up. Let me stay and catch this guy before he kills someone close to us." His eyes searched out Linn. A medic wrapped her ankle in an ace bandage. "It's only a matter of time until he gets her, Madden. With every minute, he's getting closer."

18

Linn drew in a sharp breath as the paramedic inflated the air splint on her ankle. The stabs of pain subsided to a dull throbbing. Thank goodness nothing was broken. Her throat burned from smoke inhalation. Otherwise she was ready to move.

Arms folded and feet planted shoulder-width apart, Drew glared at Madden. Linn's hungry eyes drank in every smear of soot and dirt. Every tousled curl, the sneer on his full lips. The set of his chiseled chin. Her fingers ached to run through his hair, her lips to kiss his. The first man since her attack that she wanted to give herself to, and he would leave soon. Despite his promises, a man that good-looking, that sexy, couldn't, wouldn't suffer long through a long distance relationship. Her heart threatened to stop beating.

He looked her way, and she ducked her head, afraid he'd see the feelings written on her face. She couldn't let herself dwell on what ifs. Her heart twisted as she burned his image to memory. They both had careers important to them. There could be no future together for them. She'd have to be happy with the time they had left.

"You'll be okay." The paramedic removed her oxygen mask. "Might have a sore throat for a few days. Keep the splint on the ankle at all times until the swelling and bruising go down." He handed her a crutch. "Use this and follow-up with your doctor as soon as possible."

"Okay. Thanks." Her eyes roamed over the blackened cornfields.

Spots of burning grass dotted the landscape, and the firemen paced the area with their hose.

After positioning the crutch under her arm, Linn made her way, limping, to where Drew and Madden stood arguing.

"I'm telling you it was him." Drew's brows lowered.

"And I'm saying we have no proof." Madden glowered back.

"About what?"

The men didn't turn at Linn's question, keeping their eyes locked on each other.

"I think The Photographer started this fire, and Madden doesn't. Just a difference of opinion."

"Ask the fire chief." Linn motioned her head toward the field. "He's heading this way."

The fire chief was a man of small stature, even in his fire-protective suit. He removed his mask and rubbed his hand over his bald head.

"Well?" Madden demanded. "Was the fire started on purpose or accident?"

"Good afternoon, yourself." The fire chief tucked his helmet under his arm. "Definitely started. We found a gasoline can and the remnants of a cloth. The arsonist didn't even try to hide the evidence. He made a circle around the section y'all were in. You're lucky to have made it out alive."

"See?" Drew's brows drew together.

"Wayne, this doesn't mean anything."

"This type of thing happen a lot around here or is it just a coincidence this one started with me and Linn in the middle of it?" Drew threw his arms in the air and turned back to the field. "He's playing games."

Linn looked in the direction he did. "I think so, too. He was out there with us. In the corn."

Drew switched hooded eyes in her direction.

"At first I thought it was you." Linn moved the crutch to a more comfortable spot under her arm. "Then you called out from the opposite direction." She remembered the rustling of corn from the east side of the field and pounding footsteps. The stark terror that had flooded through her. "He was coming for me until he heard you. I know it."

The fire chief nodded. "There were man-sized shoe prints around the gas can."

Madden whirled. "You can go now," he told the chief, then redirected his attention to Drew and Linn. "You two find one more piece of evidence to cast a shadow of a doubt on Steve's involvement in

Molero's murder, and I'll keep Drew here in town a few more days." He shook his head. "I hope I don't regret this."

"You won't. I promise." Linn threw her arm around the police chief's neck. "We'll find something. Today."

"You'd better." The big man drew back, then awkwardly patted her between the shoulders.

Drew clapped his hand on the big man's shoulder. "Thank you."

"Go on before I change my mind."

Drew took Linn's elbow in his hand and helped her across the rough ground to their car. "Ready to head to the garage?"

"Yes." She smiled up at him.

"Not tired?"

"Not much. I'll rest later."

She slid into the open car door and pulled her injured ankle in slowly. "Why would he go to such lengths? Why not just grab me like he does the other women? He could have burned me back there."

Drew shrugged. "I believe he was going to take you and leave me. We were separated. That's why he didn't burn a circle around us." He reached over and squeezed her hand. "I'm sorry. I shouldn't have let you get so far away from me."

"You had no way of predicting this. This is so outside the box of what he usually does."

He lifted her hand and brushed his lips across the top. Wings fluttered through her stomach. "You've been my hardest assignment."

"Why?" Her voice hitched.

His dark eyes drew her in, spiraling out of control as he bent toward her. "'Cause this time it's personal." He tugged her to him, wrapped his hand in her hair, and kissed her. One long, lip-moving kiss, and Linn's world stopped.

"Wow," she whispered, after catching her breath.

"Yeah." His eyes smoldered. "That's why this case is so hard." He straightened and twisted the key in the ignition. "Don't look now but Mad Dog is eyeballing us."

Linn turned in her seat and stared out the window.

The chief watched them, a smile on his dark face. His smile broadened, and he nodded before heading toward his squad car.

"I told you not to look." Drew laughed, deep and throaty and steered the car back onto the road. "He's sure to give you a hard time."

Warm feelings engulfed Linn as Drew drove them in the direction of the garage. When he kissed her, she forgot the terror that was her constant companion. When Drew's lips touched hers, she felt clean, as if her past had never happened.

They passed a dark van idling beside the highway. A slender, dark-haired man sat behind the steering wheel. Linn whipped her head around for a better look, and the driver turned toward the passenger seat.

"What is it?"

She focused harder, and the van did a u-turn, heading in the opposite direction. "Nothing."

Why did the man's figure look familiar? Dressed in dark colors, he blended with the van's upholstery. Had she seen the van somewhere before? She peered over her shoulder at the disappearing vehicle.

"Linn?"

"Nothing. I thought I recognized the person in the van, but I wasn't able to get a good enough look."

Drew whipped the steering wheel and spun the car to face the other direction. Squealing car tires, they raced after the van. "Let's follow."

"On what grounds?" The swerve of the car sent Linn's ankle colliding with the door, and she winced.

"A hunch or woman's intuition. You pick."

They raced down the highway, and Linn leaned forward to try to see around corners for the fleeing van. She'd catch glimpses as it turned. Occasionally she'd spot it between trees…then it disappeared.

Drew slid the car to a halt on the graveled shoulder of the road. To their right, ran a weed-infested path strewn with rocks. It led into the woods. The thick grasses looked recently crushed. Tall trees, thick with heavy hanging branches formed a canopy overhead. "Bingo."

He swerved and followed the tire tracks.

Tree branches scraped the sides of the car. Linn groaned at the thought of the damage to her paint job. They bounced over rocks and through holes, jolting Linn's ankle. The throbbing increased. She bit her lip and stifled a groan.

Five minutes later, every bone in her body screaming, they stopped behind the parked van. Drew opened the door, one hand on the butt of his gun. "Lock the doors."

"Drew…"

"Lock them." He stepped from the car and closed the door with a soft click. He waited until she locked the doors, then turned.

Keeping his hand on his gun, he approached the van, remaining in Linn's line of vision. He made his way first to the open driver's side and peered in. Drew shook his head in Linn's direction and headed toward the rear doors.

Her heart skipped a beat as he swung them open. The dark cavern of the van's rear gaped at her. She leaned forward. Empty. No boxes, no carts, and, thankfully—no bodies.

Drew jogged back to where she waited, and she flipped the locks on the doors.

"Strong smell of gasoline," he said, sliding in." Most likely our arson was the one driving the van."

"But no gas can?"

"He left that at the field, remember? But he did manage to spill some. The smell is really strong. I'll call Madden, and we'll let them handle it. Once they get here, we'll head back to the garage."

She leaned her head against the headrest. "We always get just a nibble, then nothing. When are we going to get a full bite?"

~

Drew punched in Madden's number and lifted the cell phone to his ear. "Madden, it's Wayne."

"Got that evidence you were looking for?"

"Maybe. We found the arsonist's van. The guy escaped, but maybe we'll find something that matches Molero's car. There's a spill of gasoline in the van. It's on a dirt road about five miles south of the cornfield."

Madden grunted. "I'll turn around and be there in five."

Click.

Drew turned to Linn. "He's coming. If you'll be all right, I'm going to go back and scout the area a bit more."

"I'll be fine. I'll lay my head back and rest."

He patted her knee. "Lock the doors."

"Yes, sir."

Drew circled the van once more, his eyes scanning the blue paint for chips or rust. *This is one clean guy.* Besides the dirt and leaves from the trail, even the tires were clean.

After widening his circle, Drew spotted tracks heading off in front of the van. Gym shoe tracks with a squiggly pattern in the tread. Pulling his gun from its holster, he held the weapon in front of him. With one more glance at Linn, he followed the tracks.

The suspect appeared to have fled in a hurry. Broken saplings lay bent beside the trail. The ground had dried in the afternoon heat, leaving no footprints. Drew followed the broken branches away from the trail, his eyes flitting from side-to-side in his quest for clues.

Snap!

He whirled toward the sound. A bullet zinged past him. He dove into the thick underbrush. The suspect used a silencer and sent one bullet after another into the brush where Drew hid.

When the bullets moved the air beside him, he flattened himself on the ground and low-crawled deeper into the shrubbery. Sharp rocks and pine needles dug into his flesh, adding to the cuts and scrapes he had acquired in the cornfield.

The gunfire stopped, and he rose to kneel and peruse the area surrounding him. The woods were eerily quiet. Birds, disturbed by the shooting, had flown away. A breeze stirred the leaves above his head and filled the air with a soft whisper.

A scream rent the afternoon.

Linn!

He bolted to his feet, heart pounding, and leapt across logs in his haste. All thoughts of silence were thrust to the back of his mind as he barged through bushes and around trees.

Stumbling into the clearing around the van and car, he released his breath in relief. Linn still sat in the front seat of her car, her face pale as she frantically waved him toward her.

She'd rolled down her window and spoke before he reached her side. "He was here. Staring at me through the window. He wore a ski mask. I'd rolled it down a little to let some air in, and he reached for me. He ran that way." She pointed to the trees opposite them.

"Roll up your window!" Drew whirled as Madden's squad car pulled up behind Linn's mustang, then he sprinted the way she'd pointed.

Fifty yards into the trees, he realized he'd lost the guy—again. He leaned over, balancing his hands on his knees and recovered his breath.

Then he saw it. A scrap of navy blue snagged on a bush.

Drew picked up a small stick from the ground and retrieved the cloth. A piece of cover-all. He lifted it to his nose. The strong smell of gasoline assaulted him. He smiled.

He ambled back, meeting Madden on the trail. "He got away," he said in answer to Madden's unspoken question.

Linn rolled down the car window as they emerged from the trees.

"Was he wearing something like this?" Drew held the stick out to Linn.

"Yes. And the ski mask." She pulled a plastic baggie from the glove compartment and held it open so he could drop the cloth into it. "I guess you didn't find him."

Drew slid his gun into his holster and leaned against the car. "The man's like a ghost. Disappears in the blink of an eye. What happened, Linn?"

"I had my eyes closed. I heard something…like a rustle, then the jangle of the door handle. When I opened my eyes, he was standing there." She shivered. "Staring at me. Just staring."

"Can you tell us anything else? Body build, hair color, eyes?" Madden pulled a small spiral notebook from an inside pocket of his jacket.

"Not big. About five foot ten, slight build. His face and head was covered by the mask." She gasped. "And green eyes. Light green. They shone through the slits in the mask. They were Steve's eyes."

Madden shook his head. "Impossible. Steve's locked up."

"I know, but they were his eyes." She turned her head to look at Drew. "I'm not mistaken. Steve has very unusual colored eyes, and so did this man."

"They are unusual." Drew nodded. "Almost yellow. Are you sure the color wasn't distorted by the sun, or a shadow? He can't be the only person alive with eyes that color."

"What are the odds, Drew? Here in Upton Falls, Arkansas." Linn folded her arms.

He shrugged. "Madden, call the precinct. Make sure Chavez is still there."

Madden flipped open his phone and pressed buttons. "Rozz, I need an affirmative that Steve Chavez is still in holding. Yeah, I'll hold." He rolled his eyes, then snapped to attention. "What do you mean no one can find him? Get me Ryan on the phone. Now!"

Scowling, he covered the mouthpiece of the phone. "They don't know where he is. They let him go to the bathroom, alone, and now he's gone."

"It doesn't make any sense." Drew ran his hands through his hair. What was going on here?

"I'm surrounded by idiots." The chief slapped the hood of the car. He transferred his attention back to the phone. "You have got to be kidding me!"

19

*I*t couldn't be Steve. Linn bit her trembling bottom lip. All the signs pointed to him, but she refused to believe them. "Drew, let's go to the garage."

He nodded. "Madden, phone me when you discover something."

"It doesn't look good for Chavez, Wayne."

"I know. But it doesn't make sense. None of it."

"Stop running your hands through that mop on your head. Your hair's sticking up like some wild, curly dog." He tapped his hand on the door frame in goodbye.

Drew laughed. "Call me when you find him." He slipped around the car and resumed his position behind the steering wheel. "You okay?"

She nodded. "I can't believe it's Steve. I know what the signs say, what the clues lead us to believe, but…"

"I know." He put a hand over hers, and squeezed. "We'll find our answers. I promise."

"Yeah, sure." How? Unless they find Steve and someone else dies while he's locked up, it was hopeless. Linn sighed. The daunting task loomed ahead. Another woman had to die or disappear while Steve was in custody to prove his innocence.

Madden rapped the window. Linn jerked.

The man stuck his large head in the car. "They found Steve in the lounge with Ryan drinking coffee. Coffee! Chavez said I shouldn't get so worked up because he wasn't going far in handcuffs, and since he wasn't guilty he had no reason to run anyway." He lifted his shoulders. "Ryan confirms the story. The man in the woods can't be Steve. You got the evidence needed to stay behind a few more days."

Tears burned Linn's throat. She tried to swallow against the mountain-sized lump lodged there.

"Doesn't mean he didn't kill Molero," Madden said.

"We'll find something on the car that says otherwise." Linn's words lacked conviction. Why wouldn't the chief leave that crazy notion alone? Steve rarely dated, much less be involved enough with a woman to get angry enough to kill.

He clamped one hand on her shoulder and squeezed. "I hope so, McFarland, I really do." He stepped back so Drew could move the car down the path. Another squad car roared up as they exited onto the highway.

"I'm glad it's not Chavez." Drew looked her way. "I know he's important to you."

"He's been a great partner and friend." Linn stared at her folded hands. "Steve has been the only constant in my life."

"Y'all ever been, you know, an item?"

"No." Linn jerked her head in his direction. "I told you that."

"I know what you said." A muscle twitched in his jaw.

"Would it bother you if we had?" Why were they having this conversation? Linn's heart sank to her stomach like a cold stone.

"I don't know. Things like this have a way of bringing people together. Chavez wouldn't mind if you turned to him."

Heat flooded Linn's face. "I love Steve like a brother. Nothing more. I never will. End of subject." She folded her arms and slammed back into her seat. Trees zipped past her line of vision. The setting sun streamed through the branches, blinding her.

"Fine." Drew's drawl lost its warmth.

"Fine."

He's not going to want to be with her. Telling her that Steve would take her in with open arms was his way of letting her down. Linn continued to stare out the window, her eyes pooling with tears. Drew would leave and never look back. He's too good for a girl as damaged as she was. He deserved better. She sniffed and shrugged his hand away when he laid it on her shoulder. "Leave me alone."

If his leaving was inevitable, then she'd do her best to keep her distance. His cologne, something musky and male, drifted across the car. Why did he have to smell so good? Or look so hot? She'd miss his kisses. Linn sniffed again, then wiped her hand across her eyes.

"Look at me." His voice drifted soft across the front seat.

"No."

"Please. I didn't mean anything by it. I'm sorry I got upset."

She forced her face to remain impassive despite the turmoil inside. "It wouldn't work, Drew. Both of our careers are important. A long distance relationship is not what I want. I don't think you want it either."

"Now you're being ridiculous." His words cut to the very center of her.

"Am I?" Linn pressed her lips together.

"Linn."

"Look." The pain in her heart swelled, choking out all reason. "We're not the same. We're different. You're good, I'm not. You're brave, I'm riddled with fear. If I was even an ounce of being the type of cop I want to be, I wouldn't be so afraid." She narrowed her eyes. "Besides, you aren't my type. I can't stand egotistical cowboys."

He opened his mouth to say something.

For several seconds, the atmosphere inside the car stilled, the air thick.

Drew laughed. Silent at first, his shoulders shaking. Then a loud snort like the pop of a firecracker. How dare he? She frowned as his laughter built and exploded, rolling over her. Her mouth dropped, then a wave of heat rushed to her face. If she'd been born a cat, she'd claw him!

"How dare you!" She glared. All thoughts of missing him were thrown out the window.

Drew stopped the car on the road's shoulder, spinning gravel and slammed the gear into park. He clutched his side, still roaring with laughter.

"What's so funny?" She spat out between clamped teeth.

"You." He snorted. "Trying to be tough. You don't mean a word of it. You're so attracted to me you can't see straight."

She doubled her fist and punched him in the arm. Her knuckles cracked. It was like hitting a brick wall. "I meant every word."

"It won't work. You can't make me angry enough at you to leave you alone."

"Why not?" She hit him again.

"Ow." He took her hands captive and drew her close. "'Cause I like this. A lot."

This time the kiss wasn't a soft, tender one. Drew took ownership of her lips, commanding her to respond and holding her hands tight against his chest. She moaned when he took possession of her bottom lip, then moved to her ear, nibbling. His lips seared a path down her neck and, in spite of herself, she wanted it never to end. Heat spread through her lower body. If they'd been anywhere but in the front seat of a car, she would have let him take her, and the hell with the consequences. She would have dealt with the mortification afterward.

"There." He straightened, a grin across his face, eyes darkened with desire. "Tell me you don't like that." He put the car in gear and drove back onto the highway. "Tell me you don't want more."

"You're an arrogant ass." But a desirable one. Her lips tingled from his kiss, and she resisted the urge to run her finger over them. She struggled to slow her breathing. The man's self-control amazed her. How could he stop in a moment of passion? She wanted more. Surprisingly, she wanted what he offered for the rest of her life. How would she live without him?

"Correction. I'm irresistible." He winked at her.

"Neanderthal." She softened and smiled. Knowing him as she did now, and feeling comfortable in his presence, it was going to be impossible not to react to his charms.

The police garage was housed in a large brick building painted an institutional grey. Massive roll-up doors covered one entire side. A window, painted black to prevent passers-by from seeing inside, spread across the front.

"I hope this works." Linn opened her door and, using her crutch, got to her feet. "I've never been hurt this much before in my entire life." Not even that fateful night that brought her world crashing down around her.

Drew took her free arm. "Yeah, I'm a great bodyguard."

"Actually, you stink." She tilted her face to his, squinting against the sunlight. "But I won't fire you yet. If nothing else, you make good eye candy."

He laughed again. She loved the sound. Soft, deep, and manly. Strong and addicting. She followed him inside.

The interior of the garage was marginally cooler than the warmth of early evening and smelled of car oil, grease and wet, musty cement. Linn took a deep breath. Her first boyfriend in high school had been a mechanic, and she'd spent many Saturdays in his garage blasting the gunk of auto parts. Her eyes roamed the cavernous building.

A single mechanic reclined in a worn vinyl chair, feet propped up on a grey metal desk. He wore a dirty baseball cap pulled low over his forehead. Stained coveralls protected his body. A name tag with Larry scrawled in red ink was pinned to the chest pocket. "Howdy."

Despite the man's slovenly appearance, the garage looked immaculate. The man's desk was free of clutter, containing only a computer and a phone. He handed them a clipboard. "Sign in here."

Drew signed and flashed his badge. "We're here to take another look at the Molero car."

The man didn't get up. "Down there." He motioned with his head. "Only one car stored here right now. You'll find it in the last stall. Forensics finished up this morning. We're waiting for the next of kin to claim it."

"This building used to be home to prize-winning Thoroughbreds." Linn skirted a water puddle. "A rich old man owned this building. Treated his horses better than he did his family. When the horse track closed down, the horses were moved. The department bought this building for our garage and did some major renovations."

"Small town life," Drew muttered, heading toward the mentioned stall.

Linn hobbled after him on her crutch. "You got something against small towns? You use what you have. No sense in a perfectly good building going to waste."

"Everybody knows everything about everybody else." He stopped and stared with narrowed eyes into the stall. He turned, calling back over his shoulder. "Stay here. I'm getting the keys. There's not enough room to work in the stall."

Molero's car sat silent, the finish dull under a thin layer of dust. Through the window, Linn spotted the thrown back padded bar of the ancient toddler car seat. The old fashioned style reinforced the feeling of abandonment.

"Got it." Drew jogged to a stop beside her. "What's wrong?"

"The car looks lonely." She shrugged. "I was thinking about the baby."

"The child is being taken care of."

She glanced up at him, surprised.

"I checked. He's with his grandparents. His father took off before he was born, and they haven't heard from him since." One corner of his mouth curled. "I'm a sensitive guy. I've got feelings."

"In touch with your feminine side?"

"I wouldn't go that far. I'm not metro sexual or anything." He opened the car door and slid into the plastic protected seats. "Watch out." He dragged one booted foot through the open door as he backed the car out of the stall.

Linn hopped out of the way. "What exactly are we looking for? Forensics already went over every inch."

"I don't know. Anything. There's something nagging at the back of my mind." He exited the car, leaving the driver's side door open. His booted heels clipped against the cement floor as he walked a circle around the car. "Steve's maybe an inch or two taller than you, right?

Stand over here and lean in, like you're getting something out of the back seat."

"Okay." She leaned her crutch against the wall and limped to where he wanted her. "Like this." She leaned toward the child's seat, careful to keep her weight on her good leg.

~

"Yeah, stay like that." Drew took time to admire her curves before shaking his head to clear away the thoughts. He didn't have time to admire the way her ass filled out her navy pants, or the way her breasts fell forward, outlined in her white blouse as she bent into the car. Dangerous ground for sure. He turned, his boots thudded as he paced, he stopped, then marched again the whole while keeping his gaze on Linn and the car. "Okay, you can come out."

"Now just stand there." He stood beside her, his eyes roaming from her toes to the top of her head.

"What are you looking for?" She squirmed under his scrutiny and crossed his arms, closing off the enjoyable view of breasts in a cold room.

"I'm pretending you're Chavez."

"Excuse me?" She planted her hands on her hips. "In what world do I look like Steve?"

She sure was pretty when she was mad. Drew smiled. Her eyes sparkled, and her cheeks turned pink. He couldn't allow her to distract him from the job at hand.

"Move around like you're struggling to take someone out of the car."

"You have got to be kidding." She glared at him.

"Chavez has a scrape on his leg, presumably from the bolt on this door."

Awareness dawned on her face. "And you want to see if it fits."

"Exactly."

She moved in and out of the car, struggled with the car seat, stood on her toes, and then flat on her feet. Her face gleamed with perspiration.

"You can stop now." Drew took a step and squatted, his face inches from the door frame. He turned and ran his hand up the calf of Linn's leg. The cotton blend slacks rasped under his hand, molding around her shape, and causing his blood to boil. He swallowed against the sudden dryness in his throat. He sighed and stopped at the position of the scrape on Steve's leg. He ran his fingers lightly over the spot. Bingo! As much as he would like to continue to fondle Linn's leg, he had found what he came for.

"And?"

Drew stood. His face split with a huge grin.

"What?" Linn smoothed a wayward strand of hair out of her face. "We just got that full bite you were asking for."

20

*F*ull bite? Linn rubbed the nape of her neck. "I'm confused."

"You said you were tired of nibbles." Drew gazed down into her face, his hands warm on her shoulders. "You got the whole platter, sweetheart. As far as Chavez is concerned, at least. The scrape on Steve's leg is below the knee. There's no physical way he could have scraped his leg on this bolt, unless he's a contortionist."

"So he'll be released, right?" Her heart skipped.

Drew nodded. "I think this might cause enough doubt for Madden to release him—yes."

She flung her arms around his neck and planted a quick kiss on his lips. "Thank you."

"You're welcome." He tightened his arms around her, and she grunted from the pressure.

The mechanic cleared his throat beside them. "If you're done, I'd appreciate it if you put the car back. I'm heading home. The garage doors will lock automatically when you close them."

After watching him stalk away, Linn giggled. "I didn't hear him come up."

"Neither did I." Drew wiggled his eyebrows. "Wanna fool around in the backseat?"

Boy, did she. "Behave yourself." She limped free of his arms, feeling a sense of loss that was becoming all too familiar when Drew released her from an embrace. "Let's get Steve."

"Now?" Drew's face fell.

"Don't be a baby. He shouldn't have to stay in a cell any longer than necessary." Linn grabbed her crutch from where she'd propped it, and hobbled out of harm's way. "Put the car back where it belongs."

He slid behind the wheel and inched the car forward.

The slam of the garage's huge sliding door reverberated through the building. Linn whirled, losing her balance and almost falling. She half-hopped on her good foot, her free arm pinwheeling. "Larry?"

No voice called back.

She looked to where Drew slammed the car door shut. Two steps, and he stood beside her.

Within seconds, strands of *Music of the Night* from the *Phantom of the Opera* blasted through the garage and echoed from the walls. Dread filled Linn. Adrenaline burned through her veins.

Drew grabbed her, slamming her against his chest, and they slid behind the protection of the concrete stall.

The lights went out.

"Now what?" Linn's chest heaved. Her throat seized. Evil lived in the dark. Consuming horror that ate at your soul. "My weapon's in the car. Please tell me you have yours." Her words shook.

"I have it." He withdrew the gun from its holster with a soft swoosh. Keeping his back to the wall, he sidled to the corner and peered around.

Linn's breathing quickened, and she wished again for her gun to wrap her fingers around. The darkness of the garage was thick as syrup. She could vaguely make out the shape of her hand. She fished around for Drew.

She made contact. He grasped her fingers and squeezed. "You stay here. Be quiet."

"Where are you going?" *Don't leave me.* "To get my gun?"

He chuckled, the sound a small expulsion of air against her ear. "If I can. I'm going to look for a way out. Don't be frightened. I won't go far."

"Be careful."

"You're trembling. Not afraid of the dark are you?"

Yes. "No, just the things *in* the dark."

He put his mouth closer to her ear until his lips touched her lobe. "A big tough detective like you." His gun, warm from his hand, found its way to her palm. "Take mine. I'll get yours." Drew kissed her cheek then disappeared into the inky blackness.

The music continued to resonate against the walls of the garage. Linn wanted to cover her ears, curl into a ball in the corner, and hide. She strained to hear beyond the music—for sounds of Drew or a pursuer. Her fear left Drew vulnerable. He was out there, unarmed, at the mercy of a psychotic killer. Because of her.

Cold from the cement wall seeped through her back. She trembled. Her gun hand shook. If she drew the maniac into the open, Drew would be safe, and they could end this reign of terror.

She retrieved her crutch from the floor beside her and struggled to her feet. Her eyes zipped from one dark shape to another. Her lungs wheezed, and she fought to control her breathing, willing herself to remain as silent as possible.

Sliding across the wall, she slipped, losing her balance and her crutch. She landed on her knees. The crutch clattered against the concrete. From the sound, it seemed it lay mere inches away. The cavernous building was so dark the crutch might as well have been yards from her. Linn held her breath against the pain of her fall and the fear of discovery.

The music stopped with the same suddenness in which it'd begun. Linn's ears rang with the silence. The sound of breathing drifted across the great space of the building.

Getting her feet beneath her, she rose and stepped back, again putting her back against the wall. Raising Drew's weapon, she slid across the wall, halting at the rasping noise she made, then taking one step forward, before taking another sideways.

Despite the dark, she felt exposed. Her knees buckled. Maybe she wasn't cut out to be a street detective. Forensics seemed more her thing. The gathering of evidence. The studying of clues. A job that kept her out of sight of murderers. Linn snorted. She hadn't done much good in that arena either. The Photographer still roamed free.

She straightened, shaking, and limped as quickly as she could to the other side of Molero's car. She scanned the darkness for Drew.

A clatter.

Thud.

Linn tightened her grip on the handgun. Drew? As if her thoughts had conjured him, he appeared like a shadow at her side. She choked back a shriek.

"You all right?"

"Yes. You found my gun?"

He slipped it into her hand, and she handed him his.

"Thank you." Linn breathed easier with her trusted weapon.

"There's someone here. I haven't been able to corner him. He *is* like a phantom." Drew's breath tickled the hairs on her neck, and sent goose pimples down her arms. "We'll have to circle around and trap him between us. Are you up to it?"

"Yes." The dark still threatened, and her heart beat erratically in her chest. "I can do this." *It's what I've been trained for.*

"Great. I'll go right. You go left." And Drew was gone. Vanished like a puff of smoke.

Linn took a deep breath and stepped away from the protection of the car. The breathing continued and she could tell it came from a recording. A woman screamed. Linn's steps faltered. The woman wasn't there. The Photographer played mind games, that was all.

Her heart thudded so loud, she was certain he could hear it. The center of the garage was bare of anything to hide behind, and her heart raced faster. With one hand on her gun, and the other stretched out in front of her, she searched for obstacles in her path.

The lights flipped on and she stumbled, blinded by the sudden brilliance. Then darkness again and colored spots swam before her. Then light again, so bright she slipped and fell, this time rolling to her side.

Laughter rang out.

Her eyes squinted against the painful intrusion. Her hip screamed with pain from its impact with the floor. The oily smell of car fluid, auto parts cleaner, and grease, assaulted her nostrils, stinging her sinuses, and soaked through her pants.

Now the less painful darkness was back, along with the lyrics of the night's music.

Where was Drew? She hadn't seen him when the lights flicked on. She hadn't seen anyone. Who spilled the liquid on the floor? The garage had been immaculate upon their arrival.

Linn grunted and pushed to her feet, a throbbing beginning anew in her ankle. She grimaced as she wiped the thick stickiness from her face. Her gun hand slipped as she tried to tighten her grip. Using a clean section of her blouse, she wiped the gun as clean as possible in the dark with filthy clothes.

"Aislinn." A whisper of her name floated to her, mixed with the lyrics of the music. "Aislinn."

Fingers of fear snaked into her mind. She squatted, whipping her head back and forth, straining to see something. Anything. The dark wrapped her in a blanket of cold terror.

The music stopped again, then started a few seconds later. She waited to see whether she'd be blinded by the sudden flood of light. It remained dark but for a tiny flicker on the far side. She hadn't noticed it before and limped in that direction.

Each touch of her foot on the concrete floor sent shards of pain through her ankle. She bit her bottom lip and focused on that tiny flicker of light. No. Wait.

Her steps halted, and she hunkered in the darkness. Why was that one light burning? Why hadn't Drew responded to it? She turned and bit back the pain in her ankle as she duck-walked her way toward a hulking shadow on her right. Her car.

"Aislinn." The music paused. "Come with me."

She slid to the ground, her back pressed against the car's bumper. *Drew, where are you?* Old fears of abandonment welled up to choke her. Was he injured? Dead? She lifted her head.

"You belong to me."

"Shut up!" She opened her eyes as wide as possible. Sweat poured down her temples. Her shirt stuck to her back.

Metal clanked against metal and she jerked, hugging her gun to her chest. The Photographer was coming for her. Not if she got to him first! She closed her eyes, pressed to her feet, then moved to dive around the car, eyes now wide open.

Strong arms wrapped around her and slammed her to the floor. The breath left her body in a whoosh. Her shoulder exploded in pain. As suddenly as she hit the ground, she found herself lifted to her feet and pulled across the garage, then deposited in a heap against another wall.

"What are you doing?" Drew hissed.

"It's you?"

"You were stepping directly into his path."

"I can't see anything. I'm going strictly on sound." She tried to pull away. "We have to stop this. It needs to end."

Footsteps pounded across the concrete floor. Moonlight streamed in through the open office door. A shadow disappeared into the night.

"Now, he's gone. Again." Drew held out his hand to help her to her feet.

"I was doing what you told me." She turned away from him. "Circling." With hands on her hips, she whirled to face him. "Where were you? I searched everywhere."

"Not everywhere or you would have found me." He stuffed his weapon into the holster hanging over his shoulder. His gaze traveled over her. "What did you get into?"

"I slipped and fell in something." She glanced down. Her pants and shirt clung to her. "Ugh. Every inch of me aches, and I'm covered in this sticky mess."

Drew ran his hand over her face and tucked the greasy hair behind her ears. "Want to go home and wash up before springing Steve?"

"No." She searched the floor for her crutch and limped to retrieve it. "I don't want him under suspicion for any longer than necessary."

"You're loyal, aren't you?"

Linn gazed up at him. "Yes. Loyalty is my one redeeming quality."

"I'm sure you have more than one." His gaze landed on her lips. His mouth quirked. "If you weren't so dirty, I might kiss you." He fished the car keys from his pocket. "Let's go fill Madden in on the latest."

~

Risking a glance at Linn's oil splattered profile, Drew grinned. Even covered in gunk she was gorgeous. Like a drowned cat ready to claw apart anyone who got too close. He laughed.

"What?" The object of his scrutiny glared at him.

"Nothing."

"Don't lie. I'm horribly uncomfortable, I'm getting oil all over my car seat, and my ankle hurts. Not to mention running into that psycho every time I venture outside my house." She crossed her arms across her chest. "I am not in a good mood."

"You run into him at home, too."

"Thank for the reminder."

He continued to smile as they pulled in front of the precinct. He thought to ask Linn whether he should hunt down a wheelchair so she wouldn't have to hobble on the crutch, then thought better of it. Her attitude didn't appear to have improved during the drive.

Limping ahead of him, Linn kept her eyes straight and stopped before the door for him to open it. Once he did, she squared her shoulders and stepped inside to startled looks.

Drew grasped her elbow and steered her away from the staring officers. "You really should have let me take you home first."

"I can handle the looks."

"You're gonna freak Chavez out. I think there may be blood beneath all that grime. Did you bang your head?"

"No, I'm fine."

Okay, but he was pretty sure she hit her head. Drew pushed open Madden's office door and ushered Linn in before him.

The big man looked up from the papers on his desk, and frowned. He folded his hands and stared, his dark eyes flicking from Linn to Drew. "What in the world happened to you two?"

Drew opened his mouth to speak and Madden put up his index finger to stop him. His gaze remained on Linn.

"Can I sit down?" Linn motioned toward one of the chairs in the room.

"Not like that you can't." Madden leaned back in his chair. "But you can tell me why you came into my office looking like you crawled out of a barrel of crude oil."

"Madden..." Drew stepped forward.

"I'm not asking you, Wayne."

Drew scowled and transferred his attention to Linn.

She appeared to be leaning heavily on the crutch, using both hands. Her oil-smeared strawberry-blond locks hung heavy in her face. Her shoulders bowed. He ached to take her in his arms and ease her discomfort.

"We went to find evidence of Steve's innocence, and we did. Plus, someone locked us in the garage with Molero's car and played opera music."

"Opera music."

"Like the murdered girl's video. Except this time, he played *Music of the Night*."

Madden lifted a pen from his desk and chewed the end. "And Chavez?"

"Has a scrape on his leg." Drew stepped forward. "I compared the location of the scrape with the door bolt on Molero's car and there is no way that bolt scratched Chavez's leg. It doesn't fit." He placed both palms flat on the desk. "Chavez didn't kill Molero. Someone was in that garage with us today. He's getting braver and closer to grabbing Linn." He leaned forward, his eyes boring into Madden's.

"Sit down, McFarland, before you fall. But make sure you perch on the edge of the seat." Madden shook his head. "I thought small-town crime would be an easy job."

She breathed a heavy sigh and plopped into the chair.

Madden shook his head. "I don't care to know how you found out about Steve's scrape, but I do want to know how his DNA got on that car."

"I don't know." Drew pulled up the other chair and lowered himself into it, the vinyl creaking beneath him. "But it's pretty obvious he's being framed. Someone wants our attention on Steve."

"I don't think so," Linn said. "The Photographer is pretty adamant I see him. I'm not sure exactly what he means by that, but I don't think he wants the attention switched from himself to Steve."

"Then who?" Madden peered over the top of his glasses.

"That's the million dollar question, isn't it?"

The chief released his breath in a huff. "I'll release your partner, then you go home and get cleaned up. Your shift is over, and I don't want to see either one of you until tomorrow. Got it?"

Linn's smile lit up the room. "Got it." She winced getting to her feet, then turned to Drew. "Ready?" As if she'd gotten a fresh burst of energy, Linn limped quickly toward the cell where Steve was held.

Drew stayed a few paces behind. He could kick himself. Would she have been as happy to see him released as she was Steve? He clenched his fists. Of course she would. She'd said as much, didn't she? She cared for him. Chavez was a friend, like a brother. Nothing more.

His heart sank deeper as Linn launched herself into Steve's arms. Neither of them seemed to mind the grime covering her.

"I knew you didn't do it." Her voice was muffled in the other man's chest.

Steve hugged her and turned to Drew, his right hand extended. "Thank you."

"No problem." The tenderness in the other man's eyes as he turned to cup Linn's face was almost Drew's undoing.

"Are you all right? What happened to you?"

Linn's teary eyes lifted to Steve's face. "I'm fine. What about you? I was so worried about…"

"I'll just wait outside." Drew shut the door and leaned against it, closing his eyes.

21

"*A*t least I'm not a fugitive." Steve took a voracious bite out of his cheeseburger.

Linn smiled at her friend's apparent enjoyment. His eyes sparkled as he grinned around his burger.

"I know my manners are atrocious, but you really can't appreciate real food until you've eaten prison food."

"You weren't in prison," Drew scoffed. "You never left the precinct, and I thought you didn't like burgers." He tossed a wadded napkin into his empty red plastic dinner basket.

"I don't like barbecue sauce. There's a big difference between a sugar coated meal and a juicy burger. You ever spend time behind bars?"

"No."

"Then you can't speak for me, can you?" Steve's eyes narrowed as he lifted the burger for another bite. "Especially when the big guy in the cell next to you is someone you arrested. The things he said he wanted to do to me make my ears burn."

Linn's gaze swept from one man to the other. Rays of tension emanated from Drew, deepening the lines around his mouth as he scowled at Steve. She'd never understand men. Drew acted jealous. The thought pushed away the day's earlier terror and sent it to the recesses of her mind. Warmth flooded through her.

Her smile faded. What was she thinking? Once The Photographer is brought to justice, Drew would leave. There wasn't room in her heart for romance, much less a long distance one. Sure, Drew liked to fool around, steal a kiss or two, but a commitment? With her? No, that was impossible to figure.

Shoving aside her half-eaten food, Linn slouched in the booth. She had let her guard down and set herself up for heartache. She had no one to blame but herself.

"What's wrong?" Drew turned sideways in the booth.

"Nothing."

"She's mad." Steve plucked a French fry from his basket. "I recognize the look."

"What look?"

"That look." Steve pointed his fry at her. "The scowl and pursed lips. The deep wrinkle between your eyes, and your neck is red and blotchy." He stuffed the fry in his mouth.

Linn rolled her eyes. "I don't know what you're talking about. I'm not mad." Hurt, sick, devastated, but not mad.

"Yes, you are."

"Whatever." Linn lifted her cup of soda to her mouth and sipped through the straw. The carbonation bubbled past the lump in her throat.

The waitress sauntered to their table, her gaze focusing on Drew. "Can I get you anything else?"

A slow smile eased across Drew's face, smoothing out the lines of tension. A dimple winked from his right cheek. "No, thanks. We're fine."

She laid the receipt on the table. "Well, you just let me know." The woman flashed him another smile, and left.

"Good grief." Linn straightened in her seat and took a huge swallow of her drink. She choked, spewing soda across the table. "Sorry." She grabbed a napkin and held it to her mouth. Her face heated as Drew snorted next to her.

He pounded her on the back. "You okay?"

"Fine." She shrugged his hand off. Glaring at the two men, she grabbed her purse. "Ready?"

"Sure." Drew tossed two twenty dollar bills on the table and slid from the booth. "You sure are prickly tonight."

"Me?" Linn stood and locked stares with him. "You're the one sitting there, not speaking, with a mean scowl on your face. I'm just reacting to the vibes you're putting out."

"I'm confused." Drew ran his fingers through his hair.

"As usual." She shoved past him and limped out the front door of the diner.

"What's that supposed to mean?" Drew caught up with her.

With a sigh, Linn stopped and faced him again. "Look. You're a great detective, but with people's emotions…well, you're lacking in that department. Completely clueless. I don't kiss just any man the way I have you. Think on that." She left him standing with his mouth open.

A light drizzle fell from the sky, misting her hair. She lifted her face, eyes closed, to its refreshing coolness. With the rain, her heated emotions dripped off her.

A horn blared, startling her. Her eyes snapped open as Drew snatched her from the path of a speeding van. The window cracked open just enough for a small, flat, white box the size of a man's wallet, to be dropped on the pavement at her feet.

Linn's heart sank as the lid fell off, revealing the box's contents.

"Don't let him get away!" Drew sprinted down the street, Steve in close pursuit.

Pulling her pistol, Linn aimed at the rear tires of the speeding van. Pop! Pop! She squeezed off two quick rounds.

Her second shot found the target, exploding the rubber. Sparks flew from the tire rim's contact with the asphalt. The van continued to careen around the corner and out of sight.

Drew grabbed the box and its contents, then clutched her hand. "Let's go." He pulled her alongside him and a sprinting Steve to the car. The three hopped in, and Drew sped Linn's car after the fleeing van.

"Which way?" Linn's eyes peered through the gathering dusk. A line of headlights welcomed them around one corner.

"There's been an accident." Drew pounded one fist against the steering wheel, and slammed on the brakes.

"There are no emergency vehicles. Must have just happened." Steve spoke from the backseat. "Let's go see if anyone needs help. We've lost him anyway."

As if one, they opened their doors and exited the vehicle. Shoulder to shoulder they jogged to the front of the line of cars.

"It's the van!" Linn quickened to a limping sprint.

The navy-colored van sat with its front end smashed against a light pole. The driver's door hung open. Linn slid her gun from its holster and inched closer to the driver's seat. Empty.

Her gaze scanned the throng of milling spectators. "Anyone see the driver of this van?"

Most of the on-lookers shook their heads, but one elderly man stepped forward. "A man ran into that alley." He pointed. "I yelled for him to stop, but he kept going."

Drew raced in the direction the man pointed, his gun held in front of him.

"Why can't we get a break?" Linn stared at Steve, who shrugged.

He unlatched the van's back door and swung it open. "Linn."

She stepped to his side.

A young woman lay bound and gagged on the floor. Blue, red-rimmed eyes stared up at them from beneath a tangle of blond hair. The woman cried behind the gag.

Crawling inside, Linn holstered her weapon and knelt beside the woman. Her eyes raked the victim's body, searching for injury. "Are you all right?" She removed the gag.

"Yes. Yes. I'm fine. Please untie me."

"Can you tell me your name?" Linn held out her hand to Steve. "Give me your knife."

Steve placed a silver pocket knife in the palm of her hand, and she cut through the ropes binding the woman's wrists and ankles.

"I...I'm Mary Ann Owens." She wrapped her arms around her trembling body. "He took me...from the grocery store parking lot." She spoke in a horrified whisper. "It was crowded. I thought I would be safe." Mary Ann covered her face and sobbed.

Linn pulled the shivering woman into her arms and met Steve's eyes. "I'll call an ambulance." He pulled his cell phone from his pocket.

"Shh. You're all right now. You're all right." Linn's heart clenched.

Drew appeared panting beside Steve. "I couldn't find him."

"This is his latest victim." Linn smiled wryly. "One he wasn't able to keep." She tightened her arms around Mary Ann. "I'll stay with you until the ambulance gets here."

One arm propped against the van, Drew turned to Steve. "I never even got a glimpse of him. I heard some rattling of trash cans, but I don't know if I was even chasing the right guy." He wiped his perspiring forehead on his sleeve.

"Did you see the man who took you?"

Linn turned to Mary Ann and looked into her eyes.

Mary Ann shook her head, and sniffed. "I came out of the store and walked to my car. My...arms were full of grocery bags. I sat the bags down to get the key out of my purse and...and...woke tied up in this van." She wiped her face across her forearm. "I got a glimpse of the back of his head, but that's all."

"What color is his hair?"

"Dark. Almost black, and it was military short." The woman lunged at Drew and gripped his forearms. "It was him, wasn't it? The Photographer?" She slumped back to the floor. "I almost died today." Her face paled beneath the streaks of tears.

An ambulance screamed to a stop beside the van.

Madden followed in a squad car.

The paramedics took over the care of Mary Ann.

Drew hopped from the van. He approached the chief, spoke for a few minutes, then the two of them joined Linn.

"Let's take a closer look at what's in this box." Drew withdrew the box from inside his shirt. Steve and Linn crowded close.

"We shouldn't be opening this." Steve shook his head. "This isn't protocol. This should be opened in the safety of the office."

"It's pictures," Linn informed him. "Just more pictures. Besides, the chief is right here. Lighten up."

Butterflies took flight in her stomach as Drew lifted the lid. Inside lay a photo of Suzy Green and Amber Richards, peering into the camera from a dark hole.

"They're still alive." Tears welled in Linn's eyes.

"Well at least they were when this picture was taken." Madden took the box from Drew. "Wayne, what do you think he's trying to tell us?"

"I don't think he's trying to tell us anything. He's still playing."

Linn's mind whirled around the idea of The Photographer's game. "I have an idea. The three of you come over to my house. I'll shower, whip up dessert, and let you in on my brainstorm."

"I don't like the sound of this." Steve turned to the other men. "Linn bakes when she's nervous, or trying to butter somebody up."

"You never like my ideas, Steve."

"With good reason. They're crazy and usually dangerous."

She stopped at the car and turned. "Mad Dog, are you coming?"

The big man hesitated, then nodded. "Sure. Chocolate cake?"

"What else?" Linn opened her door and slid into the car. Inside, she laid her head back against the seat and closed her eyes. "It's been a long day."

Drew started the ignition. "Yes, it has."

"Where's Steve?"

"Don't worry. He's riding with Madden."

The tone of his voice cooled the interior of the car. Linn opened her eyes, turning her head to look at him. His profile could have been chiseled in stone, it was so rigid. A muscle twitched in his solidly set jaw. Linn sighed and closed her eyes again. Men.

~

The Photographer watched from an upstairs window as the tow truck hauled away his van. Anger surged inside him at the loss of his newest girl.

The three of them had stood around gloating. *She'd* babied the new girl, wrapping her arms around her. Oh, yes. He'd seen them. Chavez standing around being useless as usual. Aislinn watching the cowboy with love-struck eyes. They'd made him sick.

His hands clenched into fists so tight his nails dug into his palms, inciting small stabs of pain. He took a deep breath and forced himself to relax. He could find another girl. Another beautiful addition to his collection. The city was full of them.

Turning, he caught his reflection in the brass framed mirror, and grimaced. The right side of his face was covered with the bluish-red of a cavernous hemangioma. The mark of the devil his mother said. Ugly imperfection! The mark began at his hairline and extended to his chin as if someone had dipped one half of his face in paint. Dark hair, cut in the common short style of the military, covered his head. Flames reflected in the depths of his pupils and he blinked, extinguishing them.

An old man's body lay sprawled across the twin bed. He'd been surprisingly strong for one so old. The Photographer rubbed at the emerging bruise on his chin. Yet, in the end, he'd been no match for the younger man's strength and now lay dead, strangled by his own belt. Less messy than the knife he had used on the last old couple.

Lifting a vase from the nearby dresser, The Photographer hurled it into the mirror, shattering it. A banging came from the other side of the door along with loud, angry curses demanding silence. He whirled and fled, slamming the door behind him.

He kept his head lowered and turned away, keeping his good side to the few people still milling in the apartment stairwell. Sirens wailed in the distance. His heartbeat quickened.

For years he'd remained invisible. What had he done wrong? The only person he wanted to stand out for was her. Linn, the beautiful woman with the scar on her lip. She'd see past his disfigurement and maybe, his heart beat even faster, she'd come to love him. They had their deformities in common. He was becoming visible to the world around him, and he feared he'd never be able to hide again.

He flew down the nearest alley and leaned, panting against a brick building. His head whipped from side to side as he scanned hopefully for a car. There. One idled in front of a liquor store. A short run, and he hopped behind the wheel of the small Kia sedan.

The fool inside the store didn't notice. The Photographer laughed, softly at first, then louder and louder until his body shook with the force. Tears streamed down his face, and he blinked to clear his eyes.

A surprise waited for Linn and her friends at her house. One they'd get a real big bang out of. And he wanted to be close enough to watch.

22

*T*he measuring and mixing of ingredients for the cake soothed Linn's frazzled nerves. She listened to the quiet, intermittent murmurs of the three men in the living room. The crack of an egg over the bowl's rim sounded loud in the stillness of the kitchen.

Was he watching? She stared out the kitchen window in the night. Right now? Was he watching as she stirred the batter? She hoped so. She wanted the man to see life went on despite his threats. Chills ran down her spine, and she shivered as she remembered Drew's concerns about a bullet. Linn reached up and closed the flowered curtains, shutting off any sinister prying eyes. Then, in a moment of defiance, she shoved them open. He wanted to kill her in person. Not from long distance.

"Need any help?" Steve joined her and leaned against the counter.

"Not really. I'm putting the cake in the oven right now." Linn opened the oven door and slid the glass baking dish onto the shelf. "What's going on out there?"

"Not a whole lot." Steve pulled up a battered dining chair. "I'm a little put out at Mad Dog, throwing me in jail, and for some reason, Drew is really out of sorts."

"You haven't been much better." Linn sat across from him. "And don't be mad at the chief. He was only doing his job."

Steve drummed his fingers against his lip. "What I don't understand is why Drew worked so hard to get me released. I thought the guy hated me."

"He doesn't hate you...and I asked him to help." Linn glanced through the arch leading to the living room where Drew laughed at something Madden said. "You're like a brother to me, Steve."

A wry smile twisted his lips as he leaned across the table. "Admit it. For a minute, you thought I was guilty."

Remorse flooded through Linn and she averted her gaze. "All the evidence pointed to you. It still does. It's a good thing that scrape on your leg didn't match up."

"What changed your mind about my guilt? Why did you continue searching for proof to free me?"

She shrugged. "Drew did. He said something didn't feel right. I trust his instincts. He's good at what he does."

By the time the aroma of baking cake drifted from the kitchen, Drew and Madden made their way to the table. The two large men filled the small kitchen to capacity, bringing in chairs from the dining room.

Madden's huge bulk filled his chair and he leaned backward, folding his hands across his middle. The chair squeaked in protest.

Drew glanced at the window, scowled while closing the curtains, then swung a chair around, straddling it. He crossed his arms across the headrest. "What are you two talking about?"

Steve gazed at him with a sardonic twist to his mouth. "You. Seems I owe you a debt of gratitude."

"Nah." Drew waved his comment aside. "Just didn't want to see an innocent man condemned."

"Well...thank you."

"I did it for Linn." Drew didn't blink as his gaze focused on Steve. "Maybe a little for you."

"Too much testosterone in here for me." Linn rolled her eyes. "Let's talk about the case."

The men transferred their attention to her. Three different colored pairs of eyes stared at her. She squirmed under their scrutiny.

"We have this man, this killer, right under our nose, and we can't find him. He knows everything about me, and we don't know anything about him. Except he has Steve's eyes." Her voice hardened, and she lifted her chin. "But I have an idea. A way to catch him."

"I know I'm not going to like this." Drew rested his chin on his folded arms. "But, go ahead."

She took a deep breath. "We'll set a trap." She raised a hand to stop him as Drew straightened and opened his mouth. "Hear me out. I know you don't care for the idea. We've gone over it before, but this is ultimately my choice." Her stomach fluttered in remembrance of the kiss she'd given him. "I really think it might work.

"The Photographer has a certain image of me in his head. I'll be the total opposite. I'll sleaze myself up and hang out at the nightclubs." Go back to her past. She inwardly cringed. "Drew, you and Steve can go with me. I'll hang all over the two of you. Make it look really good. This ought to provoke him into making a move. It won't be hard. I've lived that life before."

"It'll provoke him into killing you." Drew stood abruptly, slamming his chair into the table.

"Or one of us." Steve folded his arms on the tabletop. "I don't like this idea."

"Mad Dog." Linn shifted her gaze to the chief. "Tell me you're with me on this."

He shook his head. "I don't know, McFarland. It's risky. Possible, but this plan carries a huge risk. If The Photographer does get his hands on you, you're finished. We'd never find you in time."

"I'm willing to take that chance. We have to stop him before any more women are killed." Linn rose from her chair. "This is my decision. You'll have to lock me up to keep me from following through."

Madden pushed to his feet. "You work for me."

"I'll quit." Linn jutted her chin forward. "Then you can't stop me."

"I'll put you in jail faster than you can burn that cake."

"Oh!" She spun and yanked open the oven. Grabbing the nearest dishtowel she pulled the cake from the oven and set it with a clatter on top of the stove. "It looks fine. Let it cool for a few minutes, then I'll frost it."

"Please, guys." Linn placed her palms flat on the counter top and bowed her head. "Please see the importance of what I'm suggesting."

"We can't." Drew grasped her shoulders and pulled her into his arms. "You have three men here who love you. Not one of us wants to stand back and willingly put you in harm's way." He tilted her chin to stare into her eyes. "I won't have it."

"Do you?" Linn whispered. "Love me?"

He brushed his lips across hers. "You know I do."

Warmth infused her body, and she leaned her forehead against the solidness of his chest.

"Ahem." Madden straightened in his chair. "We haven't resolved anything."

"Steve." Linn stepped back, distancing herself from Drew. "Side with me on this."

"I can't." He averted her gaze.

Her mood veered to anger, and she forced the words from her throat. "You're my partner."

"But not your partner to stupidity." He set his lips firmly, his words cool and controlled. "I side with Drew and Madden on this. I will not put you in harm's way or have any part in someone else doing so."

"Darn it!" Linn whirled and yanked a spatula from a drawer. Grabbing the plastic container of chocolate frosting, she slapped gobs of it onto the still warm cake. The force of the spatula against the cake left craters, and pieces crumbled from the cake to the counter.

"Let me." Drew took the spatula from her hand. "You're mutilating it."

"I can't stand it." She turned and leaned her back against the counter. Her gaze roamed over the two men seated at the table. "Women are dying because this psycho has an infatuation with me. Unless he gets me, more women are going to die. We have no idea who, or where, he is."

"He's making mistakes." Steve met her gaze. "Eventually, he'll make a mistake big enough for us to catch him."

"Not soon enough. I feel it. In my bones. Something catastrophic is going to happen." She threw her hands in the air. "But, whatever. I'm outnumbered." She took an offered slice of cake from Drew and handed it to Madden. "Y'all win."

Steve smiled as she offered him a slice. "But you're not going to bow down gracefully."

"No, I'm not." She took her own piece of cake and rejoined the men at the table.

"I'm enforcing a curfew. I got the approval from the mayor this morning." Madden waved his fork in the air. "Dark. No one allowed on the streets after dark except law enforcement. It'll make it more difficult for the perpetrator to find his victims."

"Don't be ridiculous. Besides, he'll manage." Linn shoved her uneaten cake away from her. "He managed to get in my house with Drew here. He likes the darkness. And don't forget the woman today. He took her from a busy grocery store parking lot."

"But he'll be the only civilian out there. We'll see him."

Linn shrugged. "Sure we will."

"Cake was good." Madden patted his stomach. "But, I've got to go. There's work to be done. No rest for the weary they say."

"I'll walk you out." Linn rose and followed him, stepping outside to stand on the front porch. Her eyes scanned the sidewalk and street. Things looked as if a curfew was already in place. No one moved or called to each other in greeting. Pale lights squeezed past tightly closed curtains.

Madden waved as he slid into the front seat of his squad car.

The force of the explosion drove her back, slamming her into the siding of the house. She blinked away stars and struggled to her feet as Drew and Steve rushed to her side. Her ears rang from the concussion.

Engulfed in flames, the squad car no longer resembled its origin. Charred doors lay twisted several feet away. Shattered glass peppered the ground, reflecting the moon's glow like diamonds on the grass.

"Oh, God." A freezing knife pierced Linn's stomach as she stared in horror at the inferno before her. "Mad Dog."

Drew held her back as she tried to move toward the blaze.

She whirled in fury, her doubled fist catching him on the jaw. "We could have avoided this!" She dashed away and folded to the ground. "If you would've listened the first time, we could have trapped him and prevented this."

"Linn." Drew put a hand on her shoulder. "The Photographer had his chance in the garage today. He didn't take it."

"He will. We have to try." She rubbed her knuckles. She couldn't look away from the horrible vision in front of her. Heat from the flames blasted her face.

"I've called the fire department." Steve leaned against the porch railing. "They'll be here in less than five minutes."

Through eyes welling with tears, Linn sat frozen and stared toward the flames licking at the sky. "He's going to go after the people I care about. Starting with Madden." She switched her gaze to Steve. "It'll be you next. He'll save Drew for last. He'll want me there when he kills him."

Her eyes scanned the horizon. "He's watching. Close enough to see, but far enough to get away." Tears burned tracks down her cheeks. She needed to get up. Move. Anything but stay in a crumpled lump on the ground. She'd have to dig deep to find the strength to go on.

~

The blast blinded him through the binoculars. He laughed and blinked against the brief flash of pain. His laugh rolled, thundering over the houses below him. He swung his view to the left, capturing Linn in his sight as she crumpled to the porch. Her two bodyguards flanked each side of her.

"Not for long, my love." He zoomed the lens closer. "Soon, I'll be the only one you'll need."

Linn glanced to where he hid in the thick trees behind her neighbors' houses. She dashed to the center of the yard and scanned the street.

"You see me, don't you?" Tears stung his eyes. "You know I'm here. Finally—you see me." He lowered the binoculars. His heart swelled with love. "Soon, Aislinn. Soon."

His shoes crunched across the rocks as he stalked to his waiting car. He thanked his good fortune in having his mother's vehicle stashed away. The Photographer thought of the lovely woman he'd left in the back of the van, and shrugged. Sometimes bad things happened. It was inevitable.

The wail of sirens in the distance sent shivers of delight down his spine. He glanced at his watch. Late, but the nursing home would probably make an exception and let him visit.

He left the glorious destruction behind him and drove the fifteen minutes to the nursing home.

Highly polished vinyl floors greeted him. His shoes squeaked as he made his way past the reception desk with only a nod of greeting. As he approached his mother's room, a nurse stepped out, her hands full with a tray of medication.

"Mr. Lyman, you're late this evening." A smile split the nurse's face. "You're mother is doing quite well. Had a good day. She's beginning to make sounds and even moved her fingers today. Won't be long until she's able to communicate with you on your visits."

The Photographer forced his lips into a smile. "That's wonderful. Truly it is." His words sounded false, even to him. His mother regaining her speech was anything but good news. "May I visit her?"

"Certainly. She's still awake." The nurse padded away and Peter Lyman erased the smile from his face.

Pushing open the door, he entered the room. His mother lay propped on pillows. The television played softly.

His eyes flicked to the screen to see the next five days forecast. "Any news about me, Mother? I've been busy." He brushed his lips across her forehead. "A girl got away today." Peter perched on the side of the bed.

His mother twitched the corner of her mouth, and a small groan escaped her.

"I thought at first I'd had a bit of bad luck, but other than destroying my van, things are okay." He stroked the top of her heavily blue-veined hand. "There are plenty of girls out there." His gaze moved to the window and he stared into the sky. "The best part is, Aislinn is beginning to notice me." Peter forced his mouth into what he hoped was a smile. "It won't be long now."

Another groan escaped his mother, and his eyes focused with intensity on her face.

"The nurse said you were improving." Peter grasped her frail hand in his and squeezed. "We can't have that, can we?" He leaned close to her ear while continuing to squeeze. "Do you understand?"

Peter straightened and lifted her hand, separating the fingers one by one. "How easy these skinny appendages could be broken. What pain you would endure. Blink once if you understand me."

Her eyes closed slowly.

Replacing her hand on the stark white of the sheet, he patted it. "That's my good girl. You really shouldn't be so appalled. You, after all, taught me all about perfection and the pain that resulted in obtaining it."

Rage flooded through him as he spotted a hand mirror on the nearby table. "A mirror, Mother? Who gave you this? You know they aren't allowed." Peter cupped the side of his face. The scars rose in smooth ridges beneath his palm. He hurled the mirror to the floor, shattering the face that stared in horrific disfigurement up at him.

A nurse rushed into the room, her eyes resting on the broken mirror. "What's going on in here?"

Peter stooped and picked up the pieces. "I knocked it from the side table." He held them out to her. "I am sorry. I went to move it, and my hand slipped. It's a shame really. Such a lovely mirror, but mirrors distress my mother. It's a phobia she has."

The nurse's gaze flicked to the woman on the bed. "I'm sorry. I didn't know."

His hand rested on the woman's shoulders, feeling the small bones beneath the skin. "Don't worry your pretty head about it." He admired the honey colored tresses peeking from beneath her cap. "You're young. Much too young to be a nurse."

A groan rose from the bed, and his mother's fingers twitched.

"Isn't she lovely, Mother?" His eyes caressed the smoothness of her face. "Too lovely to be around death and decay every day."

Peter gave a sudden shake of his head, clearing his thoughts. His eyes focused on the woman's name tag. Clara.

23

"*C*ome on, sweetheart." Drew placed his hands under Linn's arms and lifted her to her feet.

She had run to the middle of the yard, yelled, then collapsed in a heap on top of the grass. She wanted The Photographer to take her. What was he waiting for? No, she wouldn't be a victim anymore. She wanted to draw the creep out and shoot him.

Her eyes stung from unshed tears, and a steely determination came over her. She stood rigid as firemen sprayed arcs of water over the burning car. Steam rose with a hiss from the scorched wreckage. Nothing remained to resemble the great bear of a man who'd been her boss. She shrugged off Drew's hands and turned to face him.

"I want this man brought down."

"We all do." Drew's red-rimmed eyes stared down at her. "Madden was my college buddy. No one wants this more than me." He grasped her shoulders. "We will catch him, Linn. I promise."

She spied her crutch just inside the door. Her ankle twinged when she took a step. An icy resolve had her taking another step, then another, until she'd passed the aluminum tool and reached the kitchen. Her gun lay on the counter next to the stove. Linn lifted it and checked the chamber. "I promise, too."

"Do you want me to stay?" Steve stood in the doorway.

"No." She clicked the chamber back in place. "Go on home. Drew's here. I'll see you tomorrow."

"Linn…"

"Tomorrow, Steve."

She flinched at the hurt reflected in his eyes.

"I just want to protect you." His eyes bore into hers. "Why can't you look at me the way you look at Drew?"

She swallowed hard and tried to manage a feeble answer. Her voice barely rose above a whisper. "I don't know." She'd tried, she really had. But until Drew came along in his scuffed boots and cowboy hat, no man had enticed her. Not since the night of the rape, anyway.

"Yeah. Well." Steve sighed. "I'll see you tomorrow." His shoulders sagged as he turned and walked away.

"Tomorrow." Linn closed her eyes against the forlorn sight. She opened them to see Drew standing where Steve had stood only seconds before.

"You okay?"

"I'll be fine. Tomorrow night I do this. I entice The Photographer to make a move. With or without you, I'll be dancing on a table somewhere."

"It'll be with me." The dimple in his cheek flashed. "Besides, I can't turn down kisses from you. If we're going to play it hot and heavy, then…" His smile faded.

"I'm sorry about Mad Dog." Linn's heart sat heavy in her chest. "He was a wonderful friend and boss."

He nodded. "Madden didn't feel a thing. He said he didn't want to live to be an old man and die after a long illness anyway. Wanted to die a hero." He glanced at his watch. "It's late. Ready for bed? You should probably pack a bag."

"Why?"

"A motel will be safer."

"Oh, no." Linn shook her head. "I'm not going anywhere. The Photographer wants me, and this is where I'll stay." The worries of the day weighed upon her. Linn sagged beneath the weariness. She nodded, and still clutching her weapon, brushed past him and limped to the bedroom.

Drew moved to retrieve the crutch. "I could insist, but I'm too tired to do battle."

"No." She put out a hand to stop him. "I don't need it. He's been trying to beat me down…and I've been letting him. No more. I'll walk and fight under my own power."

The cold metal of her gun rested solid and heavy in her hand. She was tempted to sleep with it under her pillow, but laid it on the nightstand beside her bed instead. The darkness of the weapon contrasted with the white of the crocheted doily protecting the wood.

Linn allowed her gaze to sweep across the lonely room. The corners lay in shadows where the light from her bedside lamp couldn't reach. The window was closed and locked. The curtains drawn against the evil waiting outside.

Grabbing the faded tee shirt she slept in, Linn limped to the bathroom.

When she returned, Drew sat propped against pillows. He had changed into flannel lounge pants. His biceps bulged from beneath his folded arms. Her eyes flicked across his chest. His masculinity sent her heart tumbling somersaults.

"Why are you in my bed?" She took a deep breath and licked her lips. Could she hope she knew the reason?

Cocking his head, Drew remained silent, his dark gaze roaming over her at leisure.

"Goodnight." Pulling back the sheet, she slid between the cool cotton layers.

"Goodnight."

She swore her heart was going to stop beating. Linn pulled the sheet up to her chin and squirmed, avoiding his gaze. She rolled to her side to face the opposite direction.

Drew's nearness assaulted her senses. The fresh scent of his aftershave drifted to her. Every nerve in her body tingled, and she rolled back over to face him.

He returned her stare. "Don't look at me like that. We're not having sex. It's hard enough being in the same room with you as it is without me getting a taste and then walking around with a permanent boner."

"Why?"

His brow drew together. "Why what?"

"Why won't you have sex with me?" Maybe he didn't desire her. Maybe she repulsed him. "It would take both of our minds off the evil stalking me."

"That's exactly why. That, and I got intimate with someone else that I was assigned to protect. She died on my watch." He rolled to his side, propped his head in his hand, and used the other one to smooth her hair behind her ear. "I won't let that happen to you."

"It won't. I'm a cop and capable of taking care of myself, or at least helping." The man had a will of steel. Only a blind man wouldn't miss the tent of his lounge pants or the stormy look in Drew's eyes. "It won't hurt anything."

He sighed. "It would hurt everything. I'd like nothing more than to take you in my arms and make passionate love to you, but I won't. You're too precious to me. I won't cheapen what we have with sex. You know I have to leave after we solve this case."

"That doesn't make any sense." Her heart ached in her chest. "Why are you in my bed?"

"The floor hurts my back." His hand moved to her shoulder. "I'll be leaving soon. I won't do this to either of us, and in case you want to try something while I'm sleeping, I told Steve to return with his things. He'll sleep on the couch."

Her blood pounded. Her body grew hot with humiliation, and she moved to her back. She stared at the ceiling and closed her eyes against the mortifying pain of rejection before she felt Drew's light kiss against her lips.

~

The shrill ringing of the telephone jolted Linn awake. She sprang to a sitting position, her hand reaching for her weapon.

"I'll get it." Drew reached across her to the nightstand. "Drew Wayne…uh huh…" He opened the nightstand drawer, fumbled around inside it, and withdrew a pad of paper and a pen. "Agnes Parsons. Upton Falls Meadows. Got it." Scooting to a sitting position, he replaced the receiver into its cradle.

"What?" Linn swung her legs over the side of the bed and tugged down the hem of her tee-shirt.

"The van is registered to an Agnes Parsons." He tossed aside his blanket. "She's a resident of Upton Falls Meadows. I think we finally got a break that might help us nail this guy."

Rising to his feet, he stretched all six foot something toward the ceiling. "Get dressed. I'll meet you in the kitchen." He grabbed his clothes from the back of a rocking chair and disappeared through the open bedroom door.

By the time Linn joined him in the kitchen, Drew had coffee perking, and the aromatic scent of fresh brewed filled the room.

"Steve already left. He'll meet us there." He poured a steaming cup and handed it to her.

"Thanks." Linn sniffed the aroma rising from her cup. "I can't believe we might actually get a name for The Photographer. That's if the van wasn't stolen."

"I'm hoping Ms. Parsons can give us a clue as to who our elusive killer is."

Avoiding his eyes, Linn leaned against the counter and sipped from her mug. Her emotions ran rampant from embarrassment to mortification, then to sadness. His goodnight kiss had been tender, almost as if he felt sorry for her. She lifted her head to say something, then dropped it back to hover over her mug. She refused to humiliate herself further. Taking a final gulp, she poured the rest down the drain. "Ready?"

The weight of his stare as she left the room threatened to crush her. Her emotions were strung so tight she jumped, reaching for her gun when a shadow passed by the front window.

The doorbell chimed, and Drew moved past her, peering out the window. "It's Steve." He swung the door open.

"Forgot my badge. You two ready?" Steve glanced over his shoulder. "I feel vulnerable standing here. Like someone's looking at me through the scope of a gun."

"We're ready." Linn joined him on the porch, badge in hand. "You left it next to the coffee pot. You drive, and I'll ride shotgun."

"Okay." Steve glanced from Linn to the silent Drew. His eyes narrowed.

"Let's go." Drew stalked past him and yanked the rear seat door open.

Linn struggled to ward off her awareness of Drew in the backseat. She knew she behaved like a scorned teenager, but her emotions still reeled from the previous night's rejection. How pathetic. She'd practically begged the man to have sex. Where did he get his iron self-control? She girded herself with resolve and pushed aside her bruised ego. It was most likely wise not to get involved while in a life or death situation.

Upton Falls Meadows sat back from the interstate on several acres of lush green land surrounded by hundred-year-old oaks. The trees arched overhead, forming a canopy against the morning sun.

A former plantation, the assisted living facility sat upon a small hill like an elaborately decorated wedding cake. A small pond to their right provided ducks and geese with a spectacular home of their own.

"Ritzy place," Drew said. "Must be expensive."

"It is." Steve turned off the ignition. "But if you've got to live like some of these residents, what better place to finish your life's journey, right?"

Their footsteps muted on the thick grass, then switched to dull thuds on the brick walkway leading to the front door. Several orderlies pushed wheelchair-bound patients across the sweeping porch that wrapped around the side of the mansion.

Drew opened the massive double doors and ushered Linn ahead of him.

She flashed her badge to the volunteer behind the reception desk. "We'd like to see Agnes Parsons."

The woman's eyes locked and widened on Steve. "Sure. She's in room 106. Right down the hall. The nurse is with…"

The three of them headed down the hall before the woman finished her sentence.

Room 106 lay around the corner of the L-shaped hallway. An occasional whimper issued from one of the rooms as the three strolled the silent corridor, Linn occasionally slowing to baby her ankle.

Smells of old age and decay, almost masked by the stronger odor of disinfectant, assaulted Linn, and she shuddered.

"You okay?" Drew glanced down at her. His brow wrinkled with concern.

"I don't like hospitals and. . ." She glanced at Steve. "If you tell me this isn't technically a hospital, I'll slug you."

His eyes crinkled at the corners. "I wouldn't dream of it."

Drew placed his hand on Linn's elbow. His touch seared her skin, and he steered her inside the room belonging to Agnes Parsons.

A nurse bent over an elderly woman, tucking and smoothing blankets. "There you go, Agnes. I know you're used to Clara taking care of you in the mornings, but I hope it wasn't too much of a chore putting up with me. I don't know where that young woman can be. It isn't like her to—"

A small gasp escaped as her eyes lit on Steve. "Well, I had no idea. I must not have been around on your other visits. I'm Nurse Dora. Agnes, it looks like you have visitors." The nurse walked closer to them. "Not many people come to visit Agnes."

"We're actually here on business." Linn showed her badge.

The nurse cast a glance toward Agnes. "Well, she can't speak. Had a stroke a while back. Her communication skills are making improvement, but I really don't know what she'll be able to do for you."

Agnes grew visibly agitated, her wide eyes glued on Steve. The right side of her mouth drooped. Her right hand twitched, the finger moving with increased motion.

"I think she's trying to tell us something." Steve pulled a small spiral notebook from the inside pocket of his suit jacket, and placed a pen in the woman's hand.

Tears welled and spilled over when Steve touched her. For several long moments, her gaze remained glued to his face. Finally, she moved her attention to the notebook.

Several agonizing minutes later, Agnes managed to scribble two letters on the paper. P and a rather shaky e.

The nurse peered around Steve. "I think she's trying to write her son's name. His name is Peter. He's her only visitor. Comes quite regular, too. He could be your twin, you know. Are you related?" She looked up into Steve's face.

Linn's gaze met Drew's. "You wouldn't happen to know what kind of vehicle he drove, would you?"

"Sorry, I don't." She shook her head.

Drew snatched the notepad from Steve. "Do you have a full name and address? A place of employment?"

"I don't know about any employment, but his name is Peter Lyman. You'll have to check the front desk about an address."

"I'll do that." Steve squeezed past the nurse, casting another glance at the woman on the bed.

Linn moved to Agnes's bedside. She took the woman's hand in hers, stilling the restless fingers. "Thank you, Ms. Parsons. You've been a big help to us today."

The woman groaned, her eyes moving to the muted television.

The morning news broadcasted the disappearance of Clara Larson, employed nurse of Upton Falls Meadows.

Linn released the woman's hand and placed it carefully back on the bed. "Drew, look."

Agnes curled her fingers, keeping one straight, and pointed at the screen.

"I think she's trying to tell us she knows who has Clara. Give her back the notepad." Linn snatched it from Drew's hands.

Soon, the letters P and e were again scribbled across the paper. Agnes groaned again, her eyes wide, and pointed at the returning Steve.

"There's only a post office box address." Steve's attention seemed to be focused on Agnes. "Lyman pays the bill on time, so no one has bothered getting a street address." His head turned to the nurse. "What's her fixation with me?"

Dora paled. "You look exactly like her son."

~

A hypodermic needle inserted in the neck and the guard outside Agnes's room toppled over. Grasping the man's ankles, Peter dragged him into his mother's room and stashed the guard's body under the bed, before closing the door with a quiet click.

He stared down at the sleeping woman. Rage flooded his body, and he clenched his hands together to still them. She had company today. He'd heard every word. For months the hidden microphone recorded nothing but trivial nursing information, but today...today she'd betrayed him. After all he had tried to do to gain her respect.

"Wake up, Mother." Peter slapped her cheek. "I want you to see my face before you die."

Hatred burned from the old woman's eyes. He flinched beneath her gaze.

"Why? I'm your son. Your flesh and blood. How could you betray me?" He pulled the pillow from beneath her head. "I should have done this when they first told me you were making improvement, but the thought…well, I'm not very excited about killing my own mother. Unlike you, I value the relationship between a mother and her son." Tears stung his eyes.

"I foolishly thought we would be a normal family someday. I'd marry Aislinn and give you grandchildren. Steve would be told about his family and become the doting uncle. We'd be best friends as well as brothers." Peter sniffed. "You've shattered my dreams as you destroyed my childhood. A stroke was too good for you, and my brother would never love me now. I'll have to do away with him, too." He lowered the pillow over her still face and pushed. "Goodbye, Mother."

She bucked and thrashed, whimpering beneath the plump square of cotton and down. Peter stared out the window while her struggles faded. The moon cast beams of silver through the branches of a Magnolia tree. The light formed a rectangle on the ground below. Peter chuckled. The shape was oddly like a coffin.

Minutes later, he unlatched the bedroom window and crawled out. The moon cast shadows in corners and among the trees, providing him with ample hiding places. He scurried from dark corner to shadow until he was far enough away to feel safe sprinting to his waiting car.

Peter stood in the shadow of the overhanging trees as the lights of a car pierced the darkness of the driveway.

He thought of sweet Clara waiting for him at home, and sped away.

24

"*H*ey! Peter Lyman."

Peter peered over the rim of the pit into the upturned face of Clara. His heart warmed at the sight of her standing with hands on hips, eyes flashing. How like his Linn she was.

"These girls are dying. They need food, a bath, and sunshine. We aren't animals to be kept in a hole."

"I've been busy." He turned away. Great. Another whiner. His shoulders slumped. "I need comforting, not nagging."

The door slammed shut behind him as he stalked to the shed behind his house. The sound ricocheted, startling bats from the trees. He watched their flight as their small bodies were silhouetted against the moon and felt the overwhelming urge to cry out his frustrations. Loud enough for his yell to follow them to wherever it is they flew to.

Instead, he laughed. Loud, raucous, and totally unlike him. His mother would be shocked. Shocked? A snort escaped him. She was dead. He killed her, and now he was an orphan. Like Aislinn. They had so much in common.

A rusty metal bucket lay tossed against the wall, and Peter righted it, filling it with water from a nearby hose. He scanned the shelves, grabbed a handful of dusty rags, and tossed them into the bucket.

Water splashed down the leg of his slacks as he carried the bucket back toward the house. All he wanted was to hurl the bucket into the pit and bounce it off one of the women's heads. Instead, he lowered the ladder and motioned Clara to climb to the point where he could lower the bucket to her.

"This water is filthy. Let us up so I can care for these women."

Peter shook his head. "Three against one, my dear. I'm not stupid."

She glared at him. Her gaze stayed glued to his as she backed down, hampered by the bucket.

"I've had a bad day, Clara." He squatted beside the hole. "I know you didn't work at the Meadows for long, but you know what a dutiful son I was. I took time out of my busy schedule to visit several times a week. I was a wonderful son. She was a terrible mother. Abusive, neglectful. She should've been grateful I put her in such a nice home."

Clara's head whipped toward him. "Was? Peter, what did you do?"

"It was a difficult decision, I admit." He lowered himself cross-legged to the floor. "She betrayed me to the police." Peter shook his head. "Where's the loyalty, Clara? How could my mother do that to me?"

"You're a murderer, Peter. You've killed several women, and now your defenseless mother. You're the animal. It should be you locked in this hole."

Rage blinded him, and he shot to his feet, his hands clenched into fists. "Tell her, Suzy. Tell her what I can do to her."

The other girl muttered, too weak to move.

"She needs to eat, Peter."

"Okay!" He grabbed a loaf of bread from the counter and banged open the pantry door. Pulling a jar of peanut butter from the shelf, he tossed both items into the hole. "I suppose you want something to drink, too." Three water bottles joined the food items, and he kicked the trap door closed.

~

Linn sipped her cosmopolitan. The glass stem marker, a ruby revolver, clinked against the glass. She didn't need the markers since she mostly drank alone, spent her life alone actually, but she couldn't resist the trinket she had spotted in a souvenir store.

The visit with Agnes Parsons nagged at her. Fingers kept pointing to a perpetrator who looked like Steve. She was positive she had never seen anyone in Upton Falls who looked remotely similar to her partner. She swirled the drink in her hand.

"What's on your mind?" Drew distracted her, sitting on the sofa and laying his arm along the back.

His close proximity clouded her mind and sent a circus of butterflies tumbling through her stomach. The armrest prevented her from sliding over. She slouched. Anything to keep from touching him.

She raised her glass quick enough to peer over the rim, leaving spots of wet on her blouse.

Drew chuckled, his breath stirring her hair.

Steve watched them, his brows drawn together, a glass of burgundy wine held to his lips.

Linn squirmed under his scrutiny.

"Throughout this investigation, witnesses have mentioned how the suspect looks like Steve. Now, the nurses say the same thing. They're shocked. Like they've seen a ghost. The man I saw outside the van had Steve's eyes." She leaned forward and set her glass on the coffee table.

Steve slid a coaster beneath it. "So, now I'm a suspect again, am I?"

"I don't know what to think." Her head bumped Drew's arm, and he dropped it around her shoulders, sending her thoughts whirling. Why did the man insist on torturing her? He knew she wanted more than his kisses, fiery though they were.

"What about the corn field or the van?" Steve's tone grew belligerent, and he folded his arms across his chest. "I was in jail, remember?"

"Maybe you aren't working alone."

Drew's words were like a sledgehammer to Linn's heart. She'd never considered the possibility of a second person. "I want to go back to the home. We need to question the nurses some more."

"Let's go." Drew jumped to his feet. "We wait much longer, and they won't let us in."

Steve also rose, bringing the two men within a foot of each other. Chartreuse eyes bored into dark blue. Both men's faces were set, chiseled from different blocks of stone. Drew's rugged countenance and unshaven chin thrust toward the smooth, olive complexion of Steve's. Drew towered over the other man by several inches, his shoulders broader.

"You're an arrogant son-of-a-bitch. I thought you were now defending me." Steve rammed a finger into Drew's chest.

"Do you want that finger broken? Why do you think I don't allow Linn to be alone with you?" Drew leaned closer. "Something isn't right. I don't think you're The Photographer, but you're involved somehow. I'd stake my life on it. We *are* staking Linn's."

"You need to get out of my face." Steve two-hand shoved Drew.

"Or what?" Drew's face reddened.

"Guys." Linn pushed between them, placing her palms flat on Drew's chest, moving him back. "Stop. This doesn't solve anything." She glanced over her shoulder. "Let's go. Steve?"

"I'm driving."

Upon arriving at the assisted living home, Nurse Dora informed them Agnes was bedded down for the night and not receiving visitors. Dora apologized profusely, explaining the need for her patient's rest.

Linn pulled a pad of paper from her ever-present bag. "Maybe you can answer some questions. When we arrived earlier, you commented on how much Officer Chavez resembled Peter Lyman. Can you elaborate, please?"

The nurse looked confused, her eyes widened as she gnawed the inside of her lip. "Well…Mr. Lyman's hair is dark, like Officer Chavez's, only he wears it short. Like a military cut. His body build is the same. Slight, but toned." She pursed her lips. "But the face…Mr. Lyman has a birth mark." She cupped the side of her face. "On the entire right side. Poor man. The mark is dark and puffy, kind of scarred. He once said the scars were from a childhood accident. A person can't help but notice."

"His eyes?" Linn's pen moved speedily across the pad.

"Green, I think. I'm not really sure."

"As many times as the man has visited and you've never noticed his eyes?"

"He usually wears sunglasses."

"Inside?"

The woman nodded. "And keeps his face averted. It's hard to say for certain, but I believe if Mr. Lyman wasn't marked, he'd look pretty much like Officer Chavez. I think the man would be handsome, under different circumstances, of course."

"Of course." *Good grief.* "Could he be wearing a mask? His face painted?"

"A mask?" Dora's hand went to her chest. "Why would he do that?"

"I have to insist we see Ms. Parsons." Linn lifted her eyes from the paper in front of her.

"Okay." Dora led them down the hall. Her soft-soled shoes rasped on the tile floor. Flustered, the woman muttered beneath her breath, her short legs moving with small, rapid steps. An empty chair sat beside the door.

"Where's the guard? When was the last time anyone checked on Ms. Parsons?" Drew put his hand on the butt of his gun and stepped in front of the others. "Stay back."

Dora clutched at her neckline. "Well, I'm guessing right before lights out. Thirty minutes, max."

Steve withdrew his weapon and held it in front of him as he plastered his back to one side of the door. Linn took the other.

Her heart pounded as adrenaline coursed through her. Linn held her gun in an iron grip, its barrel pointed toward the ceiling.

The door squeaked when Drew pushed it open, showing them a room filled with shadow. "Police."

Linn spun, putting herself next to Drew. Together, they entered the room. Linn fumbled on the wall for the light switch.

The lights blinked to life.

Dora screamed.

The guard's feet stuck out from beneath the bed. Agnes lay on top, a pillow over her face. The window hung open, curtains swaying with the breeze.

"How did he get in?" Dora rushed to the window. "This only opens from the inside. We're careful about locking all the windows when our guests turn in for the night."

"Don't touch anything, please." Steve stepped beside the nurse and peered out. "We've got footprints outside. I'll call the station and get a mold made. I'll bet they're a size eleven."

Linn used a tissue to grasp a corner of the pillow and remove it from Agnes. She looked down into the pale, still face. "We'll get Peter, Agnes. I promise. Thanks to you, we're a little closer to catching him."

~

Drew watched the straight line of Linn's back as she stood beside the hospital bed. He admired the curves the severe navy suit couldn't hide. How could he leave her when the case was finished? His heart surged, aching, missing her already. Somehow, he would find a way to stay together.

She turned to him with fire in her eyes. "I need my case. It's in Steve's car."

Nodding, he turned and stepped into the hall.

The corridor had come to life. Staff rushed from room to room checking on patients. Muted calls floated through the air as messages were tossed from one nurse to the next. Wailing burst from an open room.

He turned left and marched past the reception desk. Outside, Steve knelt over a set of footprints beneath Agnes's window.

"One set here, where he jumped from the window." Steve pointed. "There's a partial over there." He straightened and glanced down the drive. "My guess is, he had a car waiting. I'll do a perimeter check when I finish here."

"Did you call the station?" Would the deaths and the need to call the precinct ever end?

"Yes." Steve shook his head. "They're sending out David Wazinski."

"Great." Drew rubbed the back of his neck. "This day couldn't be any better."

"Know him?"

"Yeah." Drew sighed as memories of a rooster of a prick assailed. "A greater pain in the ass doesn't exist anywhere on earth." He and Wazinski had a past. One Drew didn't want to dwell on.

"Linn doesn't care much for him either." Steve crossed his arms "He's had his eye on taking the chief's place for quite a while."

Headlights pierced the night. Drew grinned. "Speaking of the devil, here he is now. If you can take Linn her case, I'll take care of Wazinski."

"Sure. My pleasure." Steve glanced toward the approaching car. "Try not to get me arrested, okay? The man's like a piranha, and right now, he's hungry for a suspect."

"I'll try." Drew squared his shoulders.

The man who slid from the passenger seat of the Buick Sedan stood maybe five foot nine inches and pin thin. The hospice lights reflected off his bald head. He marched toward Drew, chin held high.

"Special Agent Andrew Wayne."

"Wazinski." Drew gave a slight nod. His blood boiled just looking at the man. When Drew's fiancé left him because the job took him away too often, the little weasel Wazinski had jumped right in to take Drew's place.

"Too bad about Chief Madden, but I'm the chief now, and I expect to be addressed as such. Do I make myself clear?" Beady brown eyes lifted.

"Perfectly…sir, but I don't work for you." Drew grinned. "The FBI has taken over this case. How's Michelle, by the way?"

Wazinski opened his mouth to retort, then snapped it shut. He spun and continued his march until he'd reached where Linn stood with her long, willowy frame, outlined in the light spilling from the open door.

Shadows of fire licked her hair. Wazinski's steps faltered as he neared her.

"Aislinn."

"David." She stood ramrod straight, her nose in the air.

The new chief joined her on the porch. "We work together again."

"It appears so. How's your wife?" A smile spread across her face.

Their voices lowered. Drew's heart froze. Linn tilted her head closer to Wazinski. It took all the willpower Drew possessed for him to not stomp up the stairs and position himself between the two. He stuffed his trembling hands into his pockets.

Steve handed Linn her case. He stepped between her and the new chief. Drew smiled at the man's ploy to separate them. Jealousy or protectiveness? He leaned more toward jealousy. It fit with Steve's reactions to Drew's own involvement with Linn. But, Linn seemed capable of putting the shorter man in his place.

Withdrawing his hands, Drew pulled out a penlight and moved away from the building's lights. He played the arc of light from side-to-side. His steps crunched across the gravel drive.

Linn's proposition from the night before took top priority in his mind, despite his resolve to focus on his job. Turning down what she had offered took every ounce of strength he had. Especially after seeing the pained look on her face and hearing the soft sounds she made as she slept.

But, the lovely lady wanted to draw The Photographer out in the open. To do that, their romantic entanglement needed to be believable. Drew needed lots of cold showers in order to sleep in Linn's bed and be happy with a teenage make-out session.

A patch of flattened grass grabbed his attention. Two distinct tire tracks. This was where Peter parked. Drew straightened and gazed down the drive to the highway. The man appeared to have walked into the hospice, taken down the guard, and murdered his mother. Then, as if he had no cares, casually climbed out the window and took off. *Peter Lyman, you have guts of steel.*

25

Linn hunched over a cup of coffee and blew into it, watching the swirls radiate from the center while steam rose in her face. She twirled her spoon to create waves in the mocha colored drink.

"Still tired?" Drew lounged in the doorway of her kitchen, feet crossed at the ankles.

"Hmmm." She sipped her drink. "We need to go shopping today. I don't own any sleaze clothes." Not anymore. "We've put off triggering Peter into doing something long enough. It's time to act."

"You're not wearing sleaze clothes." Drew unfolded himself and went to the counter. He grabbed the waiting cup of coffee. "Besides, I'm pretty sure Peter Lyman is aware that we're sleeping together."

"Excuse me? I wasn't aware you had the right to direct my life, and we *aren't* sleeping together!" A flame ignited in the pit of Linn's stomach.

"Actually, we are. We're just not having sex. He doesn't need to know that one important fact." He turned to face her, his eyes clouded. "And, you're right. I don't have the right to dictate anything to you." He left his full mug on the counter and stalked through the open door. "Let me know when you're ready to go."

She flinched at the tone of his voice. "Another great way to start the day." Linn shoved her mug away from her, sloshing coffee onto the table. Drops splashed her hand. She shook them away, hissing against the pain. Dunking her hand into a pot of boiling water wouldn't hurt as much as her heart did at that moment.

Why couldn't she appreciate the time they had left together? What was wrong with her? She sighed. She loved him. Her stomach twisted. When they caught The Photographer, Drew would leave. The thought tore at her soul. She didn't want to go back to her lonely, cold life without him.

Her cell phone vibrated and danced across the tabletop. Spying Steve's number on the screen, Linn lifted the phone to her mouth. "Hey."

"Are you coming into work?"

"Not today. I'm not ready to face Wazinski again. Last night was enough to last the rest of my life. His chauvinistic attitude turns my stomach." Linn grabbed a napkin and sopped up the spilled coffee. "I can't believe they gave Mad Dog's job to that little twerp. He makes me need a shower just by being in the same room with him."

"He's a good cop, and it's not a definite that the job will be his for the long term."

"He's arrogant, chauvinistic, and overzealous. If that makes him a good cop, then…okay, he's a good cop." Linn stood and paced the kitchen.

"If you're not going into work today, what are you doing?"

"Buying slutty clothes."

"Oh."

"It's for, you know, my plan."

"That's tonight?"

"Yes. Be here at eight." Linn closed the cover and met Drew's gaze.

He leaned against the wall, arms crossed. "I'm ready to go shopping."

"Relax, it's not going to kill you." Stepping aside, the solid wall of his chest brushed her arm and threatened to steal her breath as she squeezed past and out of the house. Catching a whiff of his musky aftershave, her senses whirled.

She punched in the code for the garage door and stood back while it rolled open.

"What's up between you and Wazinski?" Drew held the car door open.

"Nothing."

"There's something." He closed her door and jogged around to the driver's side. "You two seemed pretty familiar with each other last night, and today you're avoiding him."

"You eavesdropped?" Heat rose up her neck as Linn turned in her seat to face him.

"No." Drew turned the key in the ignition. "I was standing right there. I couldn't help but overhear."

"We dated once. For a short time. When I was in the academy."

"Was it serious?" His eyebrows raised.

Linn closed her eyes. "He wanted me to drop out. David doesn't believe in women working. I wanted to be a cop. End of love story."

"So it was serious." His gaze brushed across her face as he turned to back the car down the drive.

"Yeah, I guess. He wanted to marry me, and I stalled on giving him an answer. I'm glad I did. I would have wanted to shoot myself within the first year."

Drew faced forward. Linn allowed herself the luxury of studying his profile. The solid chin and straight nose, chiseled lips and swimming pool dimples. Her fingers ached to run through the glossy black curls that brushed the top of his collar. *He's too gorgeous.*

He caught her looking. A slow smile spread across his lips as if he could read her mind.

She sighed, and turned away. *He's too good for me.*

A fresh wave of humiliation washed over her. He didn't want her the night before. She would have given him everything. She envied him his willpower. Knowing how he sometimes looked at her, she knew he was physically attracted to her. She could tell he wanted her, too. Where did his fortitude come from?

"What's going on inside that pretty head?"

"You find me attractive, right?" Linn locked stares with him.

"Oh, yeah." He winked.

"Then…how…?"

Drew redirected his attention to the road. "How was I able to restrain myself last night?"

She nodded, pressing her folded hands between her thighs. Maybe she didn't want to hear his answer.

"It was unquestionably one of the hardest things I've ever done. You're beautiful and intelligent. Vulnerable, yet made of steel. If I would've climbed in bed with you the other night, there'd be no going back. I desire you more than anything else in my life." He tossed her a glance. "You know that, don't you?"

"I think so."

"Neither one of us is ready to give up our careers, Linn."

Could she? For the right man?

"I've made a lot of mistakes in my life." He laughed. The sound low, without humor. "I don't want to make the same ones again. Wazinski's wife is my former fiancé. She left me because I was absent too much. If you and I want a relationship, there are particulars that need worked out first. Until then, I'll restrain myself. It's less painful that way."

"I'll try not to be one of your mistakes." She stared out the window. "Turn right at the stop sign. Do you think you'll be able to endure tonight? I mean, you will have to kiss me." And he had no idea what she could do on top of a table.

"Oh, I promise you, I'll enjoy every minute."

Linn frowned. The fire in her stomach burned fierce. "Bring some ice water, 'cause things are going to get hot."

~

Drew stared across the living room.

"Wow." Steve's mouth fell open when Linn strolled out of the bedroom and struck a sexy pose.

Long legs that never seemed to end emerged from a too-short black leather skirt. The plunging neckline of the sheer black blouse left little to the imagination and covered barely more than the lacy bra under it. High heels added several inches to her height. A curled and teased riotous tumble of strawberry-blond tresses cascaded down her back. Sultry, dusky eyes, outlined in a bright purple, flirted above a siren red mouth.

Drew's heart skipped a beat. His gaze shot to meet the startled one of Steve. The other man's mouth snapped shut.

"Wow is right!" Drew swallowed, hard. This was going to be more difficult than he thought. "You look, uh, well…"

"Like a tramp?" Linn retrieved her purse, tossing her gun to Drew. "I've nowhere to stash this." Holding her arms out, she twirled. "So, how do you like the old Linn?"

"You made a lot of money, didn't you?" Drew stuffed her gun into the waistband of his pants and grabbed his holster. "Once upon a time, I'd have paid a lot of money to see you dance. Privately, of course."

Linn laughed. "I didn't wear *this* much when I danced. These were my street clothes. The type of things I wore after work."

His heart thudded as she pranced past him. The husky perfume she wore tantalized his senses. If he didn't leave, he'd throw her over his shoulder, carry her to the bedroom, toss her on the bed, and screw her senseless.

Steve was still frozen on the sofa. No wonder he never got the girl.

Laughing, Linn crooked both elbows. "Gentlemen, let the games begin."

They made it to Ray's nightclub in record time. A cloud of Linn's perfumed scent hung in the air. Drew did his best not to look at her. Her silky hair brushed his arm. His chest clenched.

Ordinarily, he never would've taken a second look at a woman dressed like Linn is tonight. He preferred his women natural, clean, and wholesome. But this was Linn. A beautiful woman inside and out. A woman who had stolen his heart and refused to let it go. How could he stand by while other men looked at her the way he was? On her back, naked?

He chuckled. Steve still looked shell-shocked. What a change from the police officer in creased navy slacks and blazer he was used to.

The car tires crunched on the gravel of the nightclub drive as Drew pulled into a vacant spot close to the building. He leapt from the car and rushed to the passenger side, opening the door with a flourish for Linn to exit.

Steve slid from the backseat. Each man took one of Linn's arms and escorted her into the building.

Men stopped speaking, several halting drinks on the way to their lips. Woman glared, their gazes raking over her from head to toe.

Linn smiled a tiny, Mona Lisa smile and tilted her chin.

"You okay?" Drew tightened his grip on her elbow.

"Just dandy. Do you think he's watching?"

"I hope so," Steve added. "I'd hate to play this charade for nothing."

"Now, Steve." She flashed him a hundred watt grin. "Don't I look hot?" Hips swaying like a flower in the breeze, she steered them to an empty table next to the dance floor. "Here. We want to be where everyone can see us. And guys, keep the drinks coming."

"Linn, you shouldn't drink. Technically, we're on duty."

"Don't lecture, Steve. I'm not going to drink it, much. I'll be dumping the drinks out, but I want it to look like I'm plastered." Linn accepted the chair Drew pulled out for her. "Get me some cigarettes."

"No. This is ridiculous. If Peter Lyman did his homework on you, which I'm pretty sure he did, he'll know you don't smoke." Steve glowered.

"Fine. Forget the cigarettes." She leaned close and kissed him between the eyes, lingering, keeping her breasts pressed close to his face. "Loosen up. You're here to have a good time."

"Focus on Drew, okay. You're making me uncomfortable." Steve shifted in his seat, then scooted his chair closer to the table.

"I'll play." Drew grinned, knowing what the other man tried to hide. His jeans were getting a mite tight, too. He motioned to the bartender while his eyes scanned the dimly lit room.

Out of the way corners, shrouded in shadows, made Drew uneasy. Occasionally, light glinted off the smooth surface of a glass, but the patrons seated there were unidentifiable. Country music blasted from the jukebox, mixing with the raucous laughter of drunken cowboys and businessmen enjoying the end of the work week.

"Come here." Drew grasped Linn's chair and pulled it closer to his. She smiled up at him, then stood.

She hiked her skirt and straddled his lap. Her eyes darkened.

His heart skipped a beat. Taking a firm grip of her chin, he pulled her close for a kiss.

Linn's arms snaked around his neck, keeping his lips close to hers. "Do you think he's watching?"

Her breath smelled sweet from the frou-frou drink. Why was she talking? He wanted to kiss.

"Who cares? Besides, he's always known where you were before."

She nodded, then nuzzled his neck. "Steve doesn't seem to be having a good time."

Drew planted a kiss in the middle of her delightful cleavage, then lifted his head. Of course he wouldn't. No man with the hots for Linn would relish watching another man kiss and fondle her. Had he been the one watching, he would have pulled his weapon and shot the bastard between the eyes.

The other man ran his finger along the lip of his glass. His odd-colored eyes, hooded and seemed to be focused on Drew and Linn. Every few seconds, he'd flick his gaze to someone strolling past their table, or a couple heading to the dance floor. The sour look on his face seemed to confirm Linn's observation that the man was *not* having a good time.

"This isn't his thing." Linn straightened. "Hey, Steve, scoot closer, and we'll share a fake drink."

"You two play, and I'll work." He shook his head. "Someone has to. Work, I mean."

"I am working." She stood and climbed onto the table, kicking the glasses out of her way. They crashed to the floor. "Now, I'm really going to stir things up."

As a female country singer belted out the lyrics about girls having fun, Linn danced, leaving no doubt in Drew's mind as to her skills as an exotic dancer. She grinded an imaginary partner, gravitated around an invisible pole, and sent every man in the place into over drive. Several minutes into the dance, he stood, offering Linn his hand. "Let's go."

"I'm not finished." She tossed her head back, her hair flying in an arc around her head. She ran her hands down her body and over the curves he longed to touch.

"Yes, you are." He grabbed her hand, pulled her to him, then tossed her over his shoulder. "You are definitely finished."

Linn shrieked and pounded her fists on his back. "How dare you! Put me down. You're ruining my plan."

"Stupid plan anyway. Now, Peter Lyman will think you've had too much to drink and that I had to take you home." He stalked through the swinging doors, waited for Steve to open the back door, and tossed her inside. "Watch her."

Steve nodded. Linn pouted beside him.

Once back at Linn's house, Drew exited the car and entered the house, leaving the other two in the car.

He had one goal on his mind and headed straight to the bathroom. Turning the faucet on full blast, he splashed cold water on his heated face. He raised his dripping head to stare into the mirror, then adjusted the front of his jeans. What was he thinking? It was hard enough to look at Linn under normal circumstances. He would never get any sleep that night.

"Just what did you think you were doing?" Linn stormed into the tiny room and slammed the door.

With slow, methodical movements, Drew patted his face on a nearby towel, then folded it and laid it on the edge of the sink. Turning, he summoned what remnant of control he still possessed, and answered. "Me? What were you doing?"

"Provoking Peter Lyman."

Drew placed both hands on the sink and stared into the bowl. "I'm not made of steel, Linn. You were driving me crazy. Do you realize that?" He turned to face her. "I thought I could handle the charade, but I'm not strong enough." Her closeness was so female, so alluring, he had to take a step back.

"I'm sorry." Linn took her lower lip between her teeth.

"God, help me." He closed his eyes. Every nerve in his body tingled, then he reached for her. He pulled her almost violently into his arms. Tremors coursed through her, and she lifted her lips to his.

She moaned as he ground his lips against hers, plastered her body against his hardness. He groaned and thrust her at arm's length away. "You're killing me." He reached around her and pushed open the door. "Goodnight."

"Drew." She held her hand out toward him.

Squeezing past her, he stepped into the hall.

~

With the fury and power of a volcanic eruption, Peter burst from the cloakroom, knocking aside a female bartender. He rushed from the nightclub in time to see Linn's car speed away.

Trying to make him jealous. That's what she was doing. He knew it. Well, it wouldn't work. The dancing on the tabletop had sent him whirling into the past. His blood boiled. He had taken her years ago, and ached to do so again. She belonged to him.

Peter sprinted to his waiting car and headed in the direction of Linn's house. He parked a block away and jogged to her home where Steve leaned against the porch railing, his fingertips drumming against his lip, pretending to be a better version of Peter. His lip curled.

Where were Linn and the cowboy?

His hand crept inside his jacket, feeling the coolness of his gun's handle. He had a clear shot. Changing his mind, he withdrew his hand. Another time. When Aislinn was there to see it. He wanted her to witness the imposter's death.

Steve closed the front door, then headed to his car, shoulders slumped. The streetlight illuminated as clear as day.

Was he jealous? Did he know he'd lost the woman he loved to another? Peter chuckled and clamped his hand over his mouth.

The other man turned in Peter's direction, a hand over the gun in his shoulder holster. His brows lowered as he peered through the evening light. Steve shrugged then continued on his way. Peter released the breath he'd been holding.

A shadow passed in front of the living room window and from the size, Peter knew it was the cowboy. His hand moved again to the gun in his jacket, then the agent disappeared.

He took two steps and stopped, searching the area for anyone who might spot him. Not seeing another person, he snuck closer to the house.

"Hold it right there."

Peter turned and looked into the barrel of Steve's gun. In one fluid motion, he dropped to one knee, pulled his own gun—and fired.

Steve rushed him. He hit the ground. The shot went wild. The bullet grazed the detective's forehead instead of slamming into his chest. He crumpled to the ground.

26

Linn flew through the air as Drew launched himself at her in a football tackle as soon as her feet touched the front porch. The force of the fall pushed the air from her lungs.

"Stay down." Drew planted his hand on her chest to hold her flat.

"I…will…not." She struggled against him. "Steve's out there. He's in trouble."

"And so is Peter Lyman, who, by the way, wants to kill you." Drew's eyes hardened as he set his jaw. He held her hands above her head, grinding the fine bones together. "And I'm not going to let him have you unless I'm dead."

"Give me my weapon."

"No."

"Give…me…my…weapon." She pulled her legs up, wrapping them around his waist and squeezing until he grunted. "I am powerful enough to break your ribs. Now let me go."

"You win." He pulled the weapon from the waistband of his jeans and shoved it into her hands. "Then stay behind me. Please." He dragged her inside with him while he grabbed a radio from the end table and clipped it onto his belt.

Linn shook free of his hold and checked the cartridge in her gun.

"Where'd you learn to do that?" He rubbed his ribcage.

"Years of dance. It's good for the muscles." She smacked his stomach, hard enough to cause another grunt to escape him. "You should try it." Not that he really needed to. Drew was in the finest shape she'd seen on a man.

"I'll keep it in mind. Ready?"

In unison, they sprang to their feet.

Linn burst through the front door, weapon at the ready. She stepped aside to let Drew in front of her. The night air settled upon her. Goose pimples pricked her flesh.

Keeping back to back, she and Drew moved in a circle. The slow motion ripped at her, ate at her anxiety. But rushing head long into a dangerous situation wouldn't help Steve.

Lights flicked on in houses up and down the street. Residents in robes and nightclothes stepped onto their porches. No bodies lay immobile on the ground. Steve's car remained parked in front of Linn's house.

"Where is he?" She whipped her head back and forth.

"I don't know. Stay close." Drew stepped forward and pulled a small Maglight flashlight from the pocket of his jeans.

Back and forth, the beam moved, illuminating fallen leaves and scattered pebbles. Linn's breath came fast, keeping time with her heartbeat. A neighbor's dog set up a frenzied round of barking. A man yelled out for the animal to be quiet.

A breeze rustled branches in the tree of Linn's front yard. She glanced up. Stars blinked down at her. The far off roar of a jet rumbled across the sky. Ordinary sounds for an unordinary night. Where was Steve? Was he dead? The sky should be covered with menacing clouds. Something to fit the nightmare happening around her.

Together, Linn and Drew matched their steps and raced across the street.

A dark pool of liquid glistened on the sidewalk. She paused with a heart-stopping, gut-wrenching fear. She tugged on Drew's arm. "Look."

He squatted, dabbing his finger in the sticky wetness. "Someone bled a lot." He stood, wiped the blood on his jeans, and studied the area around them.

"Steve!" A sense of foreboding weighed heavy. Her legs threatened to buckle. Linn cupped her hand around her mouth. "Steve."

"He's not here. Look." Drew pointed to a trail of blood leading away from the area where they stood. "Someone was dragged away from here." He grasped her arm and pulled her with him. "We need to call Wazinski."

"We need to find Steve." She yanked her arm free and headed toward the bushes where the tracks disappeared. "Peter Lyman will kill him."

Branches scratched her arms as she fought to push through the thick hedge lining the street. She shoved aside broken limbs, determined to follow the path Steve had been taken on.

"Wait for me." Drew shot out his hand to stop her. "You can't go barging through the bushes looking for a madman."

"Then let's go together, because one way or the other, I'm going through."

Grabbing her hand, Drew pulled her along behind him and shoved aside the branches of the hedge. Ten feet into the alley, the trail disappeared. Red taillights blinked from the far end of the alley…and vanished

Drew unclasped the radio from his belt. "Officer down and presumed abducted. Send backup. Pronto." He rattled off their location as he ran to where the vehicle had disappeared.

Linn pulled a small flashlight from her pocket then paced the alley, eyes peeled for clues. Nothing. The drag marks stopped at the pavement. With the light, she illuminated the surrounding area, hoping to see an unconscious Steve stuffed beneath a bush, or behind a dumpster. Reason told her he was in the vehicle speeding away. Her search was fruitless. She turned back to Drew. "He's gone. Just like the others."

"Keep looking. Just don't go too far from me." Drew's flashlight swept the ground at the other end of the alley.

"Hey! Who's out there?" An angry voice came from the other side of the fence.

"Police. Go back in the house, sir."

"I heard a gunshot."

Drew fished his badge from his pocket and held it over the fence. "Please, sir. Go back into the house."

"Wait!" Linn shoved open the gate and rushed into the man's yard. "Did you see anything? Hear anything besides the gunshot?"

The elderly man shook his head. "It's late. My wife and I were sleeping. The gunshot woke us. It sounded like it was right outside the window."

"Okay." Linn's shoulders slumped. "Thank you."

Sirens wailed in the distance, and she stepped back to join Drew. Within minutes, two squad cars roared to a stop, blocking both ends of the alley.

Linn perched on an overturned garbage can. Her thoughts whirled. She waited for Drew to inform the other officers of the night's events. His comments were surreal. This couldn't be happening. Who was next?

Finished, Drew waved for her to join him and led her back home.

Reentering the house, he closed the door, locked it, and turned to capture her gaze. "First thing in the morning, we'll go to the post office box Lyman owns. We'll see what we can find there. Someone has to know something about the guy. He isn't a ghost. We just have to find the right person."

"I'm going to the papers. I'll do a press release for the local news." Linn dropped to the sofa, heart sinking. "He needs to come after me. Once he does, you'll get him."

Drew knelt before her and tucked a strand of her hair behind one ear. "I'll get him, Linn. Before anything else happens to Steve."

"You'd better." She offered him a smile from beneath her tears. "He's always been there for me. He's the closest thing I've ever had to a family. He's my brother."

He pulled her closer until her forehead rested against his chest. Linn straightened, pulling free of his arms. "Thanks, Drew. I think I'll go to bed. We can't do anything until Peter Lyman contacts us. Give me ten minutes before you come in, okay?"

Eyes filled with compassion, he nodded. "I'll be right outside the door."

She got ready for bed as quickly as possible then called for Drew to come in. Linn lay on her back and listened to the quiet rustlings as Drew situated himself on the bed next to her. The pain in her chest was almost unbearable. The heaviness hindered her breathing, pressing her into the mattress with the weight of a lifetime of hardship. Tears slid down her cheeks, filling her ears and running over to soak into her pillow.

Comfort from Drew was what she needed. His arms around her, his lips on hers.

She squeezed her eyes shut, striving to block out every precious contour of his face. Would he be next? She lifted her hand to trace her lips with her fingertip, remembering the passion of his kiss. When she touched the skin of her scar, Linn yanked her hand away and pounded the mattress.

"You okay, Linn?" Drew's soft voice rose to her.

"Yeah. Sure. I'm fine. Thanks." She lifted the sheet and wiped away the tears. Crying wouldn't find Steve. "Everything's great. Did you speak with Wazinski?" She chose to concentrate on the morning's press release instead of how much she ached for the man beside her.

"Yes. He's put out an APB on Steve and enforced the ten o'clock curfew Mad Dog wanted."

"Is he setting up the press release for the morning?"

Drew's blankets rustled. "Yes, but he's not happy about it. Says you're setting a match to a tinderbox."

"That's the idea." She sniffed.

"Come here." Drew's arms wrapped around her waist and pulled her flush to him, her back to his front. He placed a tender kiss on the nape of her neck that started the tears anew. "I'll hold you all night. Sleep, you're safe."

~

Peter rolled Steve into the pit and watched as he landed in a heap at Clara's feet. "Keep him alive. He may prove useful."

Dragging an adult male and hoisting him into his new van had left Peter winded. He collapsed onto the nearest kitchen chair and tried to regulate his breathing. He slouched and rested his head in the palm of his hand.

What if the cop died too soon? Peter's emotions whirled as he waited for the rush of adrenaline to leave him. His heartbeat slowed, and he wiped perspiration from his brow.

"Even the best laid plans can go awry." Hadn't he read that somewhere? Pushing himself up from the table, he leaned over the pit, balancing his hands on his knees. "Will he live?"

"Yes." Clara dabbed Steve's forehead with a dirty rag. "It's just a graze, but he needs medical care. I need to clean and bandage the wound. He needs stitches. The girls are doing better, too, but they'll need to eat again soon."

"Use his shirt as a bandage." Peter's gaze moved across the faces of his captives. "I'm collecting quite a menagerie, aren't I?" He pulled a length of nylon cord from a nearby drawer and tossed it into the pit. "Tie his hands behind his back. Make sure you tie them tight. I'll hold you responsible if he gets free. You won't like what I'll do to you."

Three girls and now—a man.

Peter shook his head and slammed the door to the pit. He'd better get busy sewing. He suddenly found himself with a desire to see all of his ladies in the red gowns he designed for them. Would they be as lovely in them alive as they would be dead? He grinned and vowed to find out.

Smiling, he took the stairs two at a time and bounded to the small room he used for sewing. He threw open the door and surveyed the mounds of crimson fabric draped over a chair and folded in piles. Identical shades of ruby red silk cascaded from shelves in the closet like waterfalls of blood. How wonderful he had been able to find an internet supplier from China who never questioned why someone would need so many yards of the same fabric.

A work table sat nestled under the window. Peter grabbed the sewing shears. The silk lay smoothed across the table, and he chuckled as the scissors slid through the buttery softness.

Pieces cut, he wrapped them around his neck and reveled in their liquid softness, approaching as close to ecstasy as Peter had ever been outside of sex with Linn. She had felt this soft. He sighed and seated himself before the waiting sewing machine.

The whir of the motor soothed him. Skilled hands guided the fabric through the feed, and he felt the familiar rush of joy as the garment took shape beneath his hands. Soon, one completed gown hung ready in the closet, and he began work on another.

Simple, elegant gowns hung in the room's closet, and Peter stood back to survey his work. He'd design Aislinn's gown differently. More elegant than the others. He wanted it to drape the lines of her slender body, flowing over her soft curves, emphasizing the porcelain quality of her skin. She'd be his queen. The other's would be her ladies-in-waiting. As long as they had a purpose and were obedient, they would live.

He could see her wearing the gown and desire for her grew. His eyes hardened as he focused again on the other gowns. These girls would never compare to his Aislinn, no matter how he dressed them up.

He whirled, stomping back to the piles of uncut fabric. Why did he waste his time on them? Would Aislinn come to him of her own accord if he held the girls over her head? Would they serve as bait, or should he dispose of them and dangle Steve before her as the proverbial carrot?

Peter shook his head. He didn't need to decide now. He would begin on the special gown he had planned for his love. Her time was coming soon.

27

Nausea rose, burning Linn's stomach and into her esophagus as the spokeswoman for the police department, Nancy Rhoades stepped to the microphone. Taller than Linn, she had to lean forward to speak.

Nancy held up her hands. "Settle down. Okay, y'all, come on, now. Detective McFarland will make a brief statement. Please do not interrupt her with questions. Her words are not directed to you." Nancy nodded to Linn and stepped back.

With a mouth full of cotton, Linn stepped to the microphone and cleared her throat. Perspiration broke out on her upper lip as her gaze swept across the faces staring at her. Now was not the time for stage fright.

"Detective, can you tell us—?"

"Officer McFarland, do you think--?"

"Please." Linn's voice was hoarse, barely rising above the din of questions hammered at her. Had no one paid attention to Ms. Rhoades's instructions? Clearing her throat again, she spoke louder, aiming to get through her prepared speech. "Please. Let me speak."

The handful of reporters and newscasters settled down, cameras and microphones waiting. Paper rustled. Flashes went off in Linn's face, and she stepped back. She stiffened and gripped the podium in front of her. There was no other path to take. She had to entice Peter Lyman to come after her.

Linn took a deep breath then stared unblinking into the camera. "My statement is directed toward The Photographer, the man who is ruthlessly murdering the women of Upton Falls." Her gaze locked with Drew's, and he smiled, giving her the strength to continue.

"With absolutely no regard for human life, this man of low character and morals, a man incapable of a healthy relationship with a woman, hunts down our women and, in a sick game, brutally murders them on film, then sends me the photos. We believe The Photographer has also shot and abducted one of this town's finest police officers." She swallowed against the lump in her throat.

"It's obvious to the police department of Upton Falls that I am the target. For reasons only he can understand, The Photographer takes everyone but me. I challenge you, Photographer, to face me. Let the rest of our citizens be, and lets you and I dance alone. Thank you."

The clamor of questions grew in volume. Linn stepped from the podium and marched, without glancing back, down the hall and to her office.

Drew matched her pace, staying close to her side. "You were great."

"I'm trembling." She lifted a shaky hand, wonderfully free of stitches removed before the press conference. "I was absolutely terrified."

Pulling her into his arms, Drew rested his chin on her head. "I just hope we're doing the right thing. If something happens to you…"

A warm feeling of coming home washed over Linn, and she closed her eyes. With a deep breath, she inhaled the scent of him. If she didn't have a show down with Peter Lyman, then Drew would be next. Having something happen to him would be the same as ripping out her heart.

"Hate to break up the little love fest, but that was the most idiotic statement I've ever heard." Wazinski leaned against the door frame. "Do you have a death wish?"

Linn sighed and stepped out of Drew's arms. Pulling her chair closer, she plopped into it, the cheap vinyl creaking beneath her. "We're trying to draw him out and spare any more loss of life."

"Bull shit. By using yourself as bait?" Wazinski lowered himself into Steve's chair. "This is why I don't think women belong in the police force."

"That's exactly what I'm doing." Linn narrowed her eyes at him. "I'm a damn good cop and you know it."

The man shook his head and dug into his pocket, pulling out a small pocketknife. "Foolish, if you ask me." Inserting the blade beneath his fingernail, he scraped across the finger. "We'll just hunt the guy down and take him out."

"Just like that, huh?" Drew perched on the corner of Linn's desk. "Good thing nobody asked you."

Wazinski moved to the next finger, and raised his eyes. "You'd better start asking me. I'm in charge here. I can have you shipped out faster than it'll take to slam the door behind you."

"Not really. The FBI has jurisdiction here. We're the heroes." A slow smirk spread across Drew's face. "You're just the sidekick."

The other man halted cleaning his nails, and paled. "You owe me the professional courtesy of my position."

"I apologize, but you've stepped into the middle of events already set into motion." Drew folded his arms across his chest. "Concentrate on enforcing curfew, and let us proceed as planned. I have your number. We'll call when we know something."

Silent sparks flew as the two men stared each other down. Linn ran her tongue nervously over her lips, fully prepared to intervene and break up a fight between two roosters. Feeling the scar, she stopped and bit her lip.

Wazinski lowered his gaze, resuming his ministrations on his nails. "Be sure you do. It's not only up to the two of you to catch this guy. It's a team effort. One of you will end up dead if you go at this alone."

"We'll keep that in mind." Drew stood and held out a hand to Linn. "Come on. Let's go check Lyman's PO box."

After a quick glance at Wazinski's reddened face, Linn rushed past Steve's desk and out the door. "Boy, you two really don't like each other, do you? He was only trying to help."

Taking her by the arm, Drew pushed open the glass door of the precinct. "We *really* don't like each other, and he was only *trying* to take over."

"What happened between you two?"

"We both applied for the same job, and I got it." He held open the car door. "He hasn't let it go. And he doesn't care for you because you rejected him." He made the comment a statement, but Linn heard the question hidden there. "Plus, I punched him when I found out he was screwing my fiancé."

"Well, he rejected me. He wanted to make me into something I wasn't."

"And that was?"

Linn snorted. "A woman content to stay home and wait on her man."

Drew closed her door and jogged around to the driver's side. "Wazinski's a good officer, just a bit full of himself."

"I don't have much luck with relationships." Linn turned to look at him. "Most men can't get over my past."

"We have a good relationship." Drew winked.

"Don't patronize me!" She yanked her hand free. "You're here because I'm your job."

"That's not true." He twisted the key in the ignition. "It may have started out that way, but that's not the reason I stayed. I thought you knew that. Didn't saying I love you mean anything?" Avoiding her gaze, he backed the car down the drive. The tires squealed as they sped down the street.

Linn continued to stare at his impassive profile. A muscle in his clenched jaw twitched near the corner of his mouth. "It can't be enough."

"I don't care about your past." He swerved the car into the closest clearing on the shoulder of the road and turned to lock gazes with her. "That's behind you. You can do one of two things with your past. You can control it, or it can control you. I suggest you put it behind you." Drew ran both hands through his hair, causing the curls to spring around his head. He sighed. "I care for you very much. My only concern is how we're going to handle this."

"What's to handle?" Her voice shook and butterflies set up a rock concert in her stomach.

"This." Drew waved his hands. "Once Peter Lyman is brought to justice, I have to leave." He speared her with a look. "Are you willing to leave Upton Falls and come with me?"

"No." She shook her head. Tears stung the back of her eyelids. "This is my home. My career is here. I've worked too hard to get where I am. Do you know how tough it is for a woman police officer in a small town where everyone knows everything about you? Are you willing to give up your job and move to the small town for me?"

"This is what we have to handle." He laid his head back against the seat. "One of us has to give. Guess it will be me."

"I bet you came from a privileged childhood with parents and extended family who loved you." She glared. "Am I right? A family you don't want to leave?"

"Yeah, so?"

"Your family probably has money, too, right?"

"Again, so?" He scowled at her. "What's your point, Linn?"

"My point is…my parents weren't around when I was small. I don't know whether they loved me or not. They said they did, but, let's just say physical affection wasn't a big part of my growing up." Pain stabbed her chest. "When they died, I was raised by a religious fanatic who said my scar was dealt to me as punishment for my sins. My sins!" She slapped the dashboard. "I was a child.

"Then, as soon as I turned eighteen, I was kicked out to fend for myself. No problem. I'm a survivor. I moonlighted my way through the academy. Then, when I foolishly believed my life was finally on track, some maniac attacks me on my way home from work." She crossed her arms and stared out the window.

"I'm sorry. I wish I would have been there to save you." He pressed the accelerator and merged back into traffic.

"Nobody was." A well of rebellion rose in her. She gritted her teeth. Linn breathed in deep and slow, willing the dancers in her stomach to settle. Drew mentioned a past of his own. She'd be sure and ask about it when they were on speaking terms.

~

Peter stared in disbelief at the television. The nerve! Aislinn challenged him. All but saying he was impotent and a social reject. He grabbed a crystal vase and hurled it at the television. His traitorous love's face exploded into a million pieces. He was the one in power! He would take her on his time, his way.

The glass shone like black diamonds beneath his feet as he crunched his way into the kitchen. Yanking open the trap door, he peered down into the blinking eyes staring up at him. He needed to spend time with those who understood him.

"Ah, Mr. Chavez." Peter pulled up a chair and leaned over, balancing his elbows on his knees. "I trust you enjoyed a pleasant evening."

Steve lay at the bottom of the pit and pushed himself to one elbow. "It's not the Hyatt."

Peter chuckled. "Now don't go spitting on my hospitality. How many men can enjoy the company of beautiful women, one of whom is a beautiful nurse with nothing to do but care for him?" He leaned closer. "Notice any resemblance between you and I?"

"Who are you?" Steve struggled to push himself up until he sat upright, his back against the wall. "Let me see your face."

"I'd prefer not to at this time. I like the shadows, Mr. Chavez, and the shadows like me. The light stays off."

"What do you plan to do with me?"

"That is undecided at this point. The girls have a destiny with me, you…well, I just haven't decided." Peter kicked the nearby cabinet. "Would you like to hear what your partner is up to? Yes?" He smirked. "She mocked me on television. She defiled my name, calling me weak and of low character. How can she do that? She doesn't know me."

"She knows enough."

Peter lunged to his feet. "She knows nothing!" He paced the floor in front of the pit, then grabbed his camera. Once again bending over the pit, he snapped several shots of Steve's pale face.

"Girls, line up beneath the door. The stench rising from this hole is enough to knock a man over."

"Let us out, Peter." Clara stood beneath him as the others struggled to their feet. "Let us bathe and eat something."

He waggled his finger at her. "I don't think so, my dear. I'm outnumbered, you see."

"Please. Steve is weakened from his injury, and the girls from lack of nutrition. I won't do anything. You know me, Peter. You trusted me with your mother."

"I don't know." He plopped back into the nearby chair and clutched his head. "I can't think right now. I don't think well when I'm angry."

"Let me calm you. I can massage the tension from your shoulders."

"Shut up!" He kicked the door closed. "Stop talking to me."

Peter banged open the back screen door and jogged to his tool shed. Unwinding a hose, he lugged it back to the house, connecting it to the kitchen faucet with a kit he retrieved from a drawer. Once again, he raised the trapdoor.

"I told you to stay beneath the door."

The girls quickly scampered to do his bidding, and he twisted the faucet on. Holding his finger over the end of the hose, he angled the spray into the pit sending the water cascading over the girls. "Don't move!"

"It's freezing." Clara drew Suzy and Amber close to her, keeping her arms around their shoulders.

"Stand there and be quiet. The ground around you is packed solid. I could let this hose run until you drown. Is that what you want?"

"No, please."

He smirked. "Or, I could dangle the toaster down there with you. How about that?"

"You're insane." Steve pushed himself upright, his feet sliding in the mud beneath him. "Let these women out of here."

Peter paused in his dousing of the others. "Why do you think I'm crazy? Crazy people don't have a plan. They aren't able to reason. I, on the other hand, do have a plan." He reached over and shut off the water. "Now, try to stay clean, will you? We'll be having a photo shoot soon."

The slam of the trapdoor reverberated through the kitchen.

Leaving the hose hooked to the faucet, Peter slumped in a chair and cradled his head in his hands. "I may have a plan," he muttered. "But things aren't going according to it." He clenched his hands. "It's all her fault. She's going to have to pay."

28

Drew showed his FBI identification and flashed a dimple at the dark-haired lady at the post office window.

"Oh, yes. Yes. Let me find that for you. Oh." Her cheeks darkened as her fingers flew over the keyboard to the computer in front of her. "My fingers were on the wrong keys. To think we've rented a box to a vicious murderer." She folded her hands under her chin and blinked at Drew. "I sure hope you can catch this guy. I'm afraid to go out by myself."

"You aren't his type." Linn rolled her eyes. Did he have to flirt with everyone who had boobs and a vagina? She studied the way he leaned against the counter, his gaze never leaving the plump woman's face. He most likely made her feel as if she were the most important person in the room. Maybe Linn could learn a few people skills from him.

"We'll catch him. Don't worry." Drew winked.

"What a relief. Here you go." The woman behind the counter handed him a slip of paper. "I saw the newscast this morning." Her gaze flicked to Linn. "You were wonderful."

"Yes, she was." Drew took the paper, scanning the address she'd scrawled there. "Recognize this address, Linn?"

She snatched the paper from his hand. "It's an apartment building about three blocks from here. It's not a very good neighborhood."

"Thank you for your help." He smiled and nodded at the watching postmistress then held open the door for Linn.

"Do you have to flirt with every woman you come into contact with?" Linn glared at him.

"I wasn't flirting."

"You were, too."

"I was only being nice." He held the car door, waiting for her to slide in. "My grandmother always told me you attract more bees with honey than vinegar."

"I'll drive." Linn grabbed the keys from his hand. "You oozed honey. It's called overkill. The poor lady could hardly breathe."

"Jealous?" He slid into the seat she'd declined.

"Hardly."

He chuckled. "I think you are. Don't worry. You'll always be the woman who holds my heart."

"Good grief." She turned the ignition, trying without success to stifle a grin. "We need gas."

Drew stretched to glimpse the fuel gauge. "We have a quarter of a tank."

"I've told you I don't like to slip below that."

"Then stop for gas." Drew clicked his seatbelt across his chest.

~

When they pulled into a convenience store, Linn stopped Drew when he made a move to exit the car. "I'll fill it up. Call Wazinski and let him know where we're going. Professional courtesy, after all." She exited the car and moved around to the pump.

Drew fished his cell phone from his pocket and punched in the set of numbers. "Wazsinki, Wayne here. Linn wanted me to let you know we're heading to the apartments at 1912 Hillside Drive. It's the address listed to Peter Lyman's Post Office box. I'll text it to you, so you have it for reference."

"Didn't figure you'd call on your own."

"Sure, if I'd seen the need."

"Want backup?" The eagerness in Wazinski's voice cut through the phone waves.

"Probably not, but feel free to show."

"I will. Be there in five. Wait for me, Wayne. I mean it."

"No promises." Drew flipped the cell phone closed and returned it to his pocket. He wasn't exactly thrilled to have Wazinski's company but accepted the inevitable. They'd be working the rest of this case together. That thought left a sour feeling in the pit of his stomach.

"Did you call?" Linn joined him in the car.

"Sure did. He's meeting us there."

"Backup is never a bad thing, Drew. Especially since we know Lyman has a weapon and a tendency for booby traps."

"I'm not complaining."

"Yes, you are."

Drew laughed. "You can make the gloomiest day bright."

"What does that mean?"

He laughed again, reaching over to give her hand a squeeze, then leaned in for a kiss.

The Evergreen Apartments sat on the outskirts of town. Drew studied the two-story exterior in silence. Wood siding, painted a garish salmon color and in bad need of a new paint job, flanked the outside of the structure. Mismatched terra cotta tiles covered the roof, some chipped and cracked. Overgrown juniper bushes lined the property.

Drew chewed the inside of his mouth before speaking. "I don't think Lyman lives here."

"Why not?" Linn's head swiveled to meet his gaze.

"It doesn't fit his profile. A male, presumably intelligent and in his mid-to-late thirties, most likely wouldn't live in a place like this. What we do know of Lyman points to his being meticulous. Clean. Hence his choice of murder weapon. Poison is clean. It's also mostly used by women."

"Don't forget the bloody mess he left of my neighbors."

"Still doesn't fit." Drew shook his head.

"Down on his luck, maybe?" She turned her eyes back to the ramshackle apartment complex. "We know he's mental. He could be deteriorating. He did shoot Steve. There was blood. That's not exactly clean."

"Maybe. But I think Steve surprised him." Drew swung open the car door and slid out as Wazinski pulled in behind them.

"What about the bomb that killed Mad Dog?"

"That was to get our attention."

"Thanks for waiting." The chief jogged to their side. "Wasn't sure you would."

"No problem." Drew stuck his hands in his pockets and continued to stare at the building. His gut told him the apartment building was a decoy.

He turned and surveyed the neighboring area. The single-family homes all showed the same signs of disrepair. Drew shook his head. He couldn't picture Lyman living in an under-privileged neighborhood such as this. "Well, let's check this out."

Stepping aside, he allowed Wazinski to lead the way. The manager's office was set off in a corner, hidden by the shadow of a large, untrimmed bush. The sign hung loose, swinging by one nail. A bell tinkled as they pushed open the scuffed wooden door.

"Hello?" Wazinski's voice echoed in the room.

Drew marched inside. No one was behind the simple wooden desk on which sat a desk blotter, telephone, an out-of-date computer, and a straight back wooden chair. A curtained doorway was positioned behind the desk.

"Hello?" he said again, louder.

"Hold your horses," a voice roared at them from behind the curtain.

Drew raised his eyebrows at the other two and placed his hand lightly on the butt of his weapon.

Several minutes later, a large man in a stained green tee-shirt and faded jeans parted the curtains and glared at them from behind the desk. "Yeah?"

Wazinski stepped forward and assumed a position of authority. He flashed his badge. "We understand you have a Peter Lyman residing here. We'd like to see his apartment."

"You got a warrant?" The man crossed his massive arms across his chest.

"We can get one." Wazinski matched the man's stance.

Drew laughed to himself at the picture of David and Goliath being played out in front of him. "Just let us in, man. Make it easy on all of us."

The manager's eyes flicked to the weapon at Drew's side. "Guy hasn't been here in awhile. I hardly ever see him."

"What about paying his rent?" Linn stepped closer.

"Sticks it in the night slot." The man unhooked a ring of keys from his belt loop. "Lyman rented a bottom floor, corner apartment. Follow me."

He squeezed his bulk past them, and Drew got an unpleasant whiff of his unwashed body.

The man led the way down a dark breezeway to the farthest corner of the complex, halting before the door to apartment number 11. "Y'all wanna knock first or just barge in?"

"Unlock the door." Wazinski stepped aside, pulling his weapon. "Then move away."

The manager slid the key into the lock, disengaged it, and stepped back out of the way. "I'll be in my office if you need me."

The other three placed their backs against the wall on either side of the door, Drew and Linn on one side, Wazinski on the other.

Wazinski knocked. "Police, Mr. Lyman. Open the door."

As expected, no answer. Drew stretched his arm to turn the knob then swung the door wide.

It opened to an empty apartment. Not a stick of furniture. No air hissed from the air conditioner, leaving the room stuffy and smelling of mildew.

"A decoy." Drew shouldered his weapon.

"I'll call the crime scene investigators." Wazinski frowned. "You two go see whether you can get anything else out of Mr. Congeniality."

"Yes, sir." Drew gave him a mock salute and turned on his heel. He strode back down the breezeway.

Linn trotted to keep up with him. "You really need to learn to take orders more gracefully."

"Yeah, I know."

The apartment manager leaned back in his chair, feet propped on his desk, when Drew and Linn reentered his office. He folded his hands behind his head. "Figured y'all would be back. What else do you wanna know?"

Drew sighed. "Guess you won't just tell us what you know?"

Linn snorted.

"Nope." The man's lip curled. "You're gonna have to ask. I don't read the minds of pigs."

"Look, mister." Linn stepped forward. "Cooperate, or we'll take you down to the station."

Drew held up his hand to stop her. "Remember. Honey, not vinegar." He turned his attention back to the obstinate manager. "What's your name, sir?"

"Chuck Norby."

Linn scribbled his name on a small pad of paper she had pulled from her jacket pocket.

"Mr. Norby." Drew was careful to make eye contact with the man. "What can you tell us about Peter Lyman?"

"A city fella. Real uppity and proper."

"How long has he maintained a lease at this address?"

Mr. Norby let his feet fall to the ground with a thud and typed something on his computer. "A year ago this past August."

"The apartment is empty. Did he ever reside here?"

Norby shrugged. "Ain't none of my business, long as the rent is paid."

Linn's pen scratched furiously.

"Did he ever mention employment?"

The man shook his head. "I don't ask many questions, Agent. Like I said…"

"You don't care as long as the rent is paid." Linn's pen paused. "Maybe we need to investigate this complex. More than likely, we'd uncover some unsavory tenants. Some illegal practices."

"Look, *officers*." Norby folded his arms on his desk. "I'm cooperating. I'm answering the questions you're asking. You got no reason to drag me down to the hole."

Drew chewed the inside of his mouth. Releasing another deep sigh, he pressed on. "We're not going to take you to the station. Do you, or do you not know where Mr. Lyman is employed?"

"He said he lives off an inheritance."

"An inheritance. Did you verify that with the bank?"

"Of course I did. I ain't stupid. The word around here is that his mother's loaded."

Linn crossed her arms. "It didn't seem fishy that someone with money would rent a place in this dump?"

The man shrugged. "We don't ask a lot of questions as long as the rent is paid."

Drew turned to stare out the window. No one entered or exited any of the apartments. No cars pulled into the parking lot. "What does Peter Lyman look like?"

"A sissy boy." Norby made a noise deep in his throat. "Dresses in city clothes and wears his hair slicked back and cut short. One whole side of his face is purple and kinda swollen. The guy wouldn't ever look straight at me, so don't bother asking what color his eyes are. I never noticed. He always tried to keep his face turned away, but I saw. I don't miss much around here."

"Thank you, Mr. Norby." Drew turned back to the man and extended his hand. "You've been a big help."

Linn handed the manager her business card. "If you think of anything else."

Once outside, she turned to Drew, planting her hands on her hips. "And exactly what did that man help us with?"

Grasping her by the arm, Drew pulled her away from the manager's office and headed to the car. "Absolutely nothing. At least nothing new."

"Then what do we do now?"

"We wait. I've requested Wazinski pull every record the department can find on Peter Lyman. School records, birth certificate, you name it. Anything that will tell us who this guy is."

"We need a big dose of good luck." Linn stalked to the car, yanking open the door.

Drew slid into the passenger seat of the car. Something beneath him crackled. He lifted his rear from the seat and reached to retrieve an envelope from where it had slid between the back and bottom of the seat. "This yours?"

"I've never seen it before." Linn's eyes rounded. I don't leave papers in my car." She snatched it from his hands and ripped it open. She dropped it to her lap. Her hands flew to her mouth. Tears welled in her eyes. "It's a picture of Steve."

Drew lifted the photo by its corner. Steve sat, bound in what was obviously a pit. Dirty and pale, he stared with defiance into the camera. Drew peered closer, spotting the calf of someone's leg in the picture. "Look, Linn. At least one of the women is still alive. She's in this hole with Steve."

29

A sharp knock on the car window startled a gasp from Linn.

Drew rolled the window down. "Wazinski, sneaking up on someone could get you shot."

"Police officers should be aware of their surroundings every second." He nodded at the picture. "What's that? Are you withholding evidence?"

"That doesn't warrant a response." Linn tightened her grip on the steering wheel to keep herself from wrapping her fingers around the chief's throat.

"It's a picture of Chavez." Drew handed the chief the photo.

"You two shouldn't have opened it. Now, it's got your prints all over it." Wazinski scowled as he perused it. "At least we know Chavez is alive."

"I'm not worried about prints, Dave," Linn spit out. The man really was an idiot. She had almost hoped his attitude was a temporary thing. "I'm only concerned with getting Steve and those women all out alive. Lyman never leaves prints. He's too smart for that."

"He'll slip up one of these days."

"He just did." Drew held out the envelope for Wazinski to drop the photo in. "There're no houses in the town limits with basements or cellars. Nothing that looks like a pit. We search the outskirts. My guess is we're looking for an older home."

Wazinski slipped the envelope into his jacket pocket. "Do you know how big the surrounding area is? Miles. Most of Upton Falls' residents live on the outskirts. Some in the mountains. It won't be a small task."

"Then I guess you'd better get all your farm boys out there knocking on doors."

"Look." Linn turned the car key in the ignition. "When you two roosters get finished squaring off with each other, we can get this search started."

Drew nodded. "You're right. I'm sorry." He extended his hand to Wazinski. "Truce?"

The acting chief stared for a moment at the offered hand before extending his own. "Truce."

"Wonderful." Linn threw the car into reverse. "We'll meet you at the station."

As she drove, she shot glances from the corner of her eye at Drew. He scowled as he stared out the window. Linn shook her head. It amazed her how the man's professionalism disappeared when Wazinski was around. They were like two kids on the playground, both wanting to be top dog.

She glanced in her rearview window. Wazinski followed close behind. She smirked. He probably feared they'd head somewhere without him.

"What?" Drew swiveled his head to look behind them. "The guy's like a leech."

Linn laughed. "Stop it. He suffers from low self-esteem."

"No, he doesn't. He's the most puffed up person I've ever met."

"It's an act to hide the truth. You're better at the job than he is, and it bothers him."

"Really?" Drew grinned, watching the car behind them. He waved.

"Stop it." Linn giggled.

Drew turned back around, the grin still on his face. "It's good to see you laugh. Must be a relief to know Steve is alive."

"Very much so." She steered the car into the police parking lot and cut the engine. "Losing Steve would be like…like losing a brother." She turned, resting her back against the door so she could face Drew. "I know it hurts him to know I don't feel more for him, and although he's helped me through so much, I just can't feel for him the way he'd like me to."

"I understand." Drew reached for the door handle. "And I'm glad." He flashed that sexy dimple of his.

Linn inhaled a deep breath and let it out slowly, her stomach turning somersaults. She opened the door, exited, and followed Drew and Wazinski into the building.

"Let's go to the conference room." Wazinski waved them inside the glass enclosed room. "We can use the area map in here."

The conference room contained a large oval table with burgundy vinyl chairs situated around it. An area map took up one wall and an almond phone sat on the table. They really needed to modernize the station.

Linn gazed around the faces seated at the table. Three uniformed officers waited, one clicking a ball point pen. The other two sat with hands folded on the table, trying not to look bored as they waited.

Wazinski took position at the head of the table and with exaggerated slowness lowered himself into a chair. He glanced around the table, halting on each face before stopping and staring at Linn and Drew. Once they'd taken their seats, he pulled the envelope from his jacket pocket and held it in both hands. With a great sigh, he withdrew the photo and slid it across the table.

"Very dramatic," Drew whispered in Linn's ear.

"Shhh. Don't be rude."

Wazinski narrowed his eyes. "We've received another photo. This time, one of our own. Officer Steve Chavez who is, thankfully, still alive. At least, at the time this snapshot was taken." He paused for his words to take effect. "We've determined from the little we can see that we're looking for a home with an unfinished basement, or root cellar. It's clear here in the picture that the walls are dirt."

He swung his chair around to face the map, then stood. "I'd like to divide the outer areas of this map, going door to door. We'll search every house surrounding the nursing home and apartment complex then branch out until we find where Peter Lyman is holding Officer Chavez."

"Chief." One of the officers, the rookie, straightened in his chair. "Do you realize how long this will take?"

A red hue rose in Wazinski's face, giving him a sun burnt look. "I'm well aware of how long it will take, Officer. But at this point, it's all we've got." He pointed to the largest, most remote section of the map. "You and your partner can take this area. Linn and Wayne, this area, myself and Officer Brown, this one. Do not leave a single house, barn, or outlying structure unchecked." He speared them all with a look. "Do I make myself clear?"

The officer who'd spoken up grimaced. "Perfectly."

"Good." Wazinski resumed his seat. "With the ten p.m. curfew in effect, there won't be pedestrians to hinder our progress."

"You want us to search at night too?" The rookie's mouth dropped.

"Afraid of the dark, Officer?"

"No, sir."

"Great. There's plenty of daylight left." Wazinski smiled, his lips spreading into a thin line. "Let's move."

Linn shoved back her chair, the legs screeching against the tile floor. She glanced at her watch. One p.m. and right on cue her stomach rumbled.

"Hungry?" Drew smiled down at her.

"Think we can grab something on the run?"

"I think so." He pushed the door open for her. "A big greasy burger and fries."

"Yum!"

"If the two of you can get your thoughts off your stomachs, there's a killer to be found." Wazinski pushed past them. His shoulder collided with Drew's.

"Settle down, big boy." Linn placed a restraining hand on Drew's chest. The muscles bunched under her hand. "The little ones aren't worth the trouble. I know the perfect place to get that hamburger. Let's eat and then catch us a killer."

~

Dusk dropped across the country like a soft fleece blanket. Peter looked into the reeking pit. Four pairs of eyes stared back. He kicked cursed and kicked over his chair in his haste to bolt to his feet. He snatched his revolver from the counter top. "I'll let you up, but you'll have to all shower together. The man stays below."

He kicked the ladder down and held the gun pointed in their direction as the women climbed weakly up the steep steps. His eyes widened at the gaunt frames of Suzy and Amber. Maybe he did need to feed them more. Take better care of his girls. But, he was so busy. Didn't they understand that? Clara didn't look bad, once he got past the grime.

"Sit." He waved the gun toward the chairs around the table then turned to close the hatch on Steve's upturned face.

The force of a blow to his back drove him to the floor. He roared. Rolling over, he lunged to his feet. The splintered kitchen chair lay on its side. Clara disappeared through the kitchen doorway. "Clara!"

Peter bolted after her, tripping over the upturned chair. He waved his gun toward the women at the table. "Move, and I'll kill you." He pulled himself around the door frame. "Clara, don't make me hurt you."

Her sobs drifted to him as she struggled with the front door bolt.

He grinned, and advanced.

A cleverly aimed kick caught him in the groin.

Intense pain riffled through his insides. His knees buckled. His breath squeaked. Nausea burned his throat.

Peter grappled for her ankle, willing the agony in his testicles to fade. His fingers brushed her skin.

She tripped, falling beside him.

Clara cried out, her hands flailing at him as he positioned his body over hers, pinning her to the floor.

"Settle down." With his free hand, Peter grasped her hands and positioned them over her head. "You're so like her. So full of fire. I think you're my favorite so far. I can't give you what you want. I'm saving that for Aislinn, but I can let you have a kiss." He lowered his face to kiss her.

With an inhuman shriek, Clara raised her head and contacted with his chin with enough force to smash his lip against his teeth. She clawed his face and yanked free.

"Please, God." She crawled to the door and pulled herself to her feet.

Peter cursed and stumbled after her. "You bitch! All I want is to love you."

The lamp from the foyer table hurtled past his head. He ducked then smashed into a coat rack.

Clara threw open the front door and disappeared into the dark night.

Doubled over, Peter pulled a flashlight from the foyer table drawer. "Clara!"

Moving the flashlight's beam across the grass, he limped with slow, even steps, straining to hear any sound she might make. A crashing in the brush to his right had him lurching in that direction. "You can't escape me, Clara. Where will you go? Come back. I forgive you. I understand I should have taken better care of you. What will the other women do without you?"

He stopped to listen. Was that her breathing or the wind?

His breath returned, Peter sprinted around the corner of the house. His flashlight's beam moved across the porch, then the shed. A glimpse of white to his right and he whirled. "I see you, Clara."

Whimpers floated to him on the night wind, and he laughed. "How far can you run?"

30

"*H*mmm." Drew closed his eyes and sunk his teeth into the half pound burger in his hands.

"Disgusting." Linn handed him a napkin. "Don't let that grease drip on my seats."

"It's better than that chicken thing you're eating."

"Whatever." Linn had told him that a burger had sounded like just the thing, until she caught a glimpse of the scarlet ketchup. It reminded her too much of blood and Lyman's crimson gowns.

She spread a thick layer of paper napkins across Drew's lap, setting his insides, and a certain part of his anatomy, quivering when her hand brushed against his stomach. He glanced down at the top of her head. Her actions didn't appear to have any effect on her, and to his surprise, that bothered him. Was she more immune to him than he was to her?

"So, what's the game plan? Where do we start looking in this big, wide, rural area Wazinski gave us?"

"My gut feeling?" He willed his body to settle down and took a deep, steadying breath.

"Yeah." She straightened.

"We start knocking on doors."

"Very funny. I'm serious." She took another bite of her sandwich.

"So am I." A blob of ketchup fell from Drew's burger and plopped to the pile of napkins. Linn raised her eyebrows in an 'I told you so' gesture. "In a town this size," Drew crumbled the messed napkin, "It isn't likely we're going to miss someone answering his door who dresses like a city fella with either very short or slicked back hair and a face that's half purple."

"Don't forget…he also resembles Steve. And I saw those unique colored eyes."

"So we've also been told by an anonymous person in a dark alley. Oh, and the nurse at the nursing home." Drew wiped his mouth on a napkin. "This guy, against all odds, has managed to hide. His luck can't last. We *will* find him." He tossed the messy napkins in the bag Linn held out to him.

She wadded her wrapper around half of her chicken sandwich and stuffed it back into the carry-out bag. "Then let's get this show on the road. You don't need the map, Drew. I know my way around."

He closed the glove compartment and clicked on his seatbelt. "Lead the way, boss."

After a ten minute drive out of town, Linn pulled in front of a small farm house. Three outlying buildings were scattered behind the house. Cutting the engine, she turned to Drew. "This is the first one. I've been here before. Mr. and Mrs. Perry, an older farming couple, live here. Kids all grown and gone."

"Do you know the kids?"

Before she could answer, the front door opened and a plump lady in a flowered house dress let the screen door slam behind her preventing two yapping little dogs from following. She bounced down the stairs. "Linn!" The woman waved and picked up the pace, her heavy legs carrying her in rapid but tiny steps toward the car. "Get on out here. Come in! It's been so long."

"Don't think we'll find our guy here," Linn said around a smile. "But we've been spotted. We'll have to have a glass of lemonade. It's the way things are done around these parts."

"I like lemonade."

She opened her door and stepped out. "Mrs. Perry, how are you?"

The woman wrapped Linn in a great hug, swaying back and forth. "Just wonderful. Can I get you and your friend a tall glass of ice cold lemonade? Sure, I can. Y'all come on in."

Drew smiled at Linn over the woman's head.

"Mrs. Perry." Linn pulled free of her embrace. "This is Agent Andrew Wayne. He's helping on The Photographer case."

The woman grasped his hand in both of hers. "And this town is much obliged, Mr. Wayne. Much obliged." She shook her head. "Nasty man."

"We're just here to ask some questions, Mrs. Perry. We don't want to take up much of your time. We're on a bit of a schedule."

"Okay, Linn. I'll give you a rain check on the lemonade." The woman crossed her arms over an ample bosom. "Ask away."

"We're looking for a man about five foot ten or eleven, dark hair in a military cut, purple patch on the side of his face."

"Hmmm. I don't think I've seen anyone fitting that description. That poor fella would stand out, wouldn't you think?"

"You would think so." Linn sighed. "But it doesn't appear that way." She shook her head. "Then, he can't be from around here."

"Anyone just moved in that maybe you haven't met?" Drew leaned against the car. He really would have liked that lemonade.

"Well," the woman's brow puckered as she thought. "there might be, but we just don't get out much. Running this farm takes up a lot of our time, now that the kids are gone. Let me think for a minute." She folded her hands behind her back and paced.

Drew struggled not to smile at the comical picture she made and earned a fierce warning glare from Linn.

"There just might be, now that I've thought on it. There're a couple of houses been vacant for quite a while higher up on the mountain. One of them is pretty run down so don't really think anyone could live there. The other belonged to the Swansons. You remember them, Linn. Nice couple tried to make a go of farming, failed, and went back to the city. Their place ain't sold yet. Guess someone could be squatting there."

"Anywhere else? Think hard, please, Mrs. Perry." Linn pulled out her notebook and scratched some notes. "Does the name Lyman mean anything to you? Or Parsons?"

"There're a lot of old houses on that mountain I ain't been to. Lyman? No, can't say as I know of any Lymans in these parts, but that don't mean anything. Parsons does sound vaguely familiar."

Linn glanced over at Drew, frustration evident on her face. She closed the notebook. "Thank you, Mrs. Perry. We'll head up the mountain and start checking things out."

Drew held out his hand again for the old woman to take. "We'll definitely take a rain check on that lemonade."

Once back in the car, and Mrs. Perry had returned to her home, Linn pounded the steering wheel. "Nothing. She gave us absolutely nothing."

"Not necessarily. I don't think we need to waste our time on the homes close to here. She'd know whether anyone fitting Lyman's description resided close by. We'll start our search higher up."

"Drew, there must be twenty homes nestled up in that mountain."

"Guess we'd better get going then." He pulled her close, planting a soft kiss on her forehead, and leaving his lips there until he felt the worry wrinkle smooth away. "We'll find him, and we'll find him on that mountain."

The radio on Drew's belt crackled. "Yeah?"

"Wayne, this is Wazinski. Had a call come into the station about fifteen minutes ago. Seems someone at the local Piggly Wiggly recalls a man fitting Peter Lyman's description coming in right before closing time a couple of days ago. Stocked up on bread, milk, peanut butter and jelly. He was in and out real fast."

"We sure it's him?"

"Hard to miss the birthmark, but we're watching the store security tapes to make sure."

"Okay. At least we know he's still here, and hasn't skipped out. Thanks."

Linn's face split in a grin. "That's great news. This is the most optimistic I've felt since this case opened."

"We haven't caught him yet."

"Don't rain on my parade, Drew." She started the ignition and turned the car around in the Perry's driveway.

The mountain road curved sharply, cutting its way up and around the valley, sheltering the town of Upton Falls. No guardrail protected cars from the sheer drops, and Drew's gut clenched.

In a kaleidoscope of green and gold, like the hand-stitched quilts his grandmother used to make, valley spread out beneath them. Drew found himself enjoying the view, discovered he'd acquired a liking for small-town life. The simplicity and quiet of it. Well, quiet once they closed this case on Lyman, anyway.

A family occupied the next home they stopped at, and the husband was more than willing to allow Drew and Linn to search his barn and storage shed. When they moved to the house, the wife ushered her children up the stairs away from them. Finding nothing of interest, Drew and Linn continued up the steeply climbing road, searching the thick forest for the next barely discernible driveway.

Night fell, making the search more difficult. Drew unclipped the radio from his belt and placed a call to Wazinski. "It's getting too dark up here. Can we resume this search in the morning?"

"Not until you're sure you've searched every house to be found on that mountain."

"Hard to search them if we can't find them."

"Linn knows where they are. Plus, she should have a searchlight in her car."

"I don't know where all of them are!" she yelled in the direction of the radio. "And a searchlight would really be subtle."

"Keep searching." Wazinski signed off.

"Great. We've got to be nocturnal to see anything up here."

"Wait. Through there." Drew pointed to an overgrown drive on their right.

Linn swerved the wheel and took them, bumping and teeth clacking, down what could barely be called a driveway. Weeds grew between the ruts, and young saplings fought for life among the rocks.

The drive ended before a ramshackle, one-story building fitting the epitome of a shack. Before Linn had cut the engine, a man wearing faded overalls stepped out of the house and onto the porch, armed with a .22 rifle.

Drew's hand flew to the butt of his weapon as he and Linn emerged slowly from the car.

"Police." Linn flashed her badge. "We'd just like to ask you some questions."

"No need. I ain't done nothing. Me and mine mind our own."

"Sir." Linn took two small steps closer to the house. "Did you see the paper or the news on television regarding the man who's been killing the women of Upton Falls? We're searching for him on this mountain."

"Ain't got no TV or newspaper up here."

Drew shot a hand to stop Linn as she took another step closer to the man. "It's important for us to know whether you've seen or heard of a man around here that dresses in city clothes with a birthmark covering one side of his face."

"I told you. We mind our own. Unless he was dumb enough to come knocking on my door, I ain't seen him. Now, y'all need to git. Don't want to shoot no police officers."

"Well, we don't want that either." Drew pulled Linn back with him. "Give us a call if you hear anything."

"Ain't got no phone."

"Wow." Drew said once they got back in the car. "I didn't think people still lived like that."

"There's quite a few in the South who haven't changed. A lot of poverty around here. Especially on this mountain. Of course, there're some expensive estates up here too." She steered the car tightly around the weedy clearing, her eyes never leaving the armed man on the porch. "A lot of these backwoods people are downright unfriendly. But they don't break the law so, we leave them alone."

Three unoccupied homes, and two more with unfriendly occupants, and they were no closer to finding Lyman than they'd been three hours earlier.

Linn pulled the car over to a clearing on the side of the road and got out. She stepped to the edge of the mountain. "Come here, Drew."

His heart leapt to see how close to the edge she stood. Her toes stopped at the edge. Taking a step nearer, he spotted what seemed to have her enthralled.

Stars so close and bright, like diamonds on a black velvet sky looked near enough he had to resist the urge to reach up and see whether he could pluck one from the heavens. Beneath their feet, winking at them from the surrounding darkness, were the scattered lights of Upton Falls.

"I used to come up here to see the stars when I first moved to Upton Falls." Linn's voice held a hint of awe. "This far away from the town lights, everything seems so much starker. More brilliant."

Drew put his arm around her shoulders and pulled her close. "It's beautiful." He glanced around them. Trees stood black and straight against the night like sentinels against the push of civilization. "I can see why some people would make the drive every day to live up here."

"Teens come up here to party and make-out." Linn leaned into him. "Several times the department has had to break them up. A couple of times, someone has jumped."

"You want to make-out?" He gave her a squeeze.

"Behave. We're on duty."

"Just checking. It doesn't hurt to ask." He took a step back and moved her in front of him, keeping his arms wrapped around her. She felt good, and he rested his chin on her head, inhaling the strawberry scent of her shampoo.

A cry for help pierced the night. As one, Linn and Drew turned to the sound.

A woman stumbled toward them from the darkness of the trees. Her sobs turned into gulps.

Drew released Linn and sprinted to the woman, catching her as she crumpled to the ground.

31

*T*he woman clung to Drew, her gulps subsiding into hiccups that shook her body. She babbled unintelligible words. Syllables ran into each other, tumbling over themselves.

Fear filled his eyes as he implored Linn to take his place. She wrapped her arms around the shuddering woman and pulled her close.

"It's Clara Larson." Drew stepped back.

"Clara." Linn smoothed the woman's tangled hair back from her tear-streaked face. "I'm Detective Aislinn McFarland. This is Agent Andrew Wayne. Let's get you off the road and into the car. Can we do that?"

The woman nodded, sniffing, and allowed Linn to lead her to the car.

"There's a faded quilt in my trunk. Drew, would you get it, please?" Linn opened the passenger door of her Mustang and gently guided the woman inside.

He returned and shoved the blanket in Linn's hands. "I'll call for backup."

Wrapping the blanket around the shivering woman, she knelt beside the car. "Clara. Look at me. This is important. Can you understand me?"

"Yes." The woman took a shuddering breath and clutched the covering tighter around her.

"Were you abducted by Peter Lyman?"

"Yes. Oh, God. I left them. I left the others." She let the blanket fall and grabbed fistfuls of her hair. Moaning, she rocked back and forth with enough intensity to shake the car. "They needed me, and I ran."

"Others?" Hope lept in Linn's chest. "Can you tell me who they are?"

"Uh…uh…two girls. One…is Suzy. The other is Amber. And there's a man. Steve, something." Clara raised wide eyes to Linn.

"It's okay, Clara. You're okay, now. Are the others all right?"

She nodded. "Steve had been shot. A bullet graze along the side of his head. I took care of him, but he needs medical attention. I'm a nurse, but there wasn't much I could do. The girls are starving. Peter hardly lets them out of the pit and barely feeds them. It's like he forgets. Like they're his pets." She choked on her words.

"I talked him into letting us out to get clean and eat. Then…then, I just ran. I kicked him and ran." Clara buried her face in her hands. "I could only think of getting away. He'll make them pay for what I did."

Linn rewrapped the blanket around Clara's shoulders, then turned to Drew, her own tears flowing. "They're still alive."

"He talks about you. About his Aislinn." The woman's words rose softly, whispered on the night breeze. "Talks about you obtaining perfection. He wasn't ready to take you. Now, I think he will be because of me. I'm so sorry."

Fear threatened to choke Linn, and she stepped back into the solidness that was Drew. She touched the scar on her lip. Would fear ever leave her? Would it ever stop it's burning in her gut?

Becoming a cop hadn't relieved the ever present terror that haunted her. She'd thought maybe, hoped, that by helping others she could have let go of the nightmare that followed her. She shivered.

"It's all right, Linn." Drew squeezed her before letting go and reaching for the radio hanging on his belt. "I've got to call an ambulance."

After another glance at Clara, who hugged her knees to her chest, Linn nodded and stepped away, walking again to the edge of the cliff. Her eyes stared across the dark valley. Who was Peter Lyman? Why was he fixated on her? Where had she met him before? Had she wronged him somehow?

The feeling of frustration welled so fast and strong, she swayed, and stepped away from the edge before she took a plunge. Turning, she glanced to where Drew leaned against the car. The woman's sobs reached Linn's ears, and she wrapped her arms around her middle.

Was it possible Peter could be the man from that awful night years ago? The thought shot threads of terror through her. Was it possible someone could hold onto an obsession for six years?

A slideshow of visions from her dancing days passed through her mind. One empty face after another. She could hear the boom of the music. The jeers of the men. With the speed and power of a bullet, she was thrust back to that night six years ago. The night she'd found herself alone on a dark country road.

~

Linn had cursed when the car sputtered to a stop with the gas tank empty. She'd chastised herself for forgetting to fill the tank. She'd worked a double shift that night, and her body ached. Her bones were weary. The thought of walking over a mile to her apartment left her feeling more fatigued, and she'd rested her head on the steering wheel.

She didn't remember how long she'd sat there before she saw the headlights. Fifteen minutes. A half hour, maybe.

She'd gotten out of the car, tottering on her four inch heels, and stepped into the oncoming car's path. The driver halted a mere two feet before her and sat in the dark while Linn blinked and raised her hand against the glare of the lights.

"I've run out of gas," she'd yelled. "Can you help me?" She'd shivered in the cool night air.

The car lights went out, casting her back into darkness. A feeling of evil had washed over her. She'd swallowed against the dryness in her mouth and headed back to her car. When she had heard the other car's door slam, she'd run, kicking off her shoes.

He'd caught her before she could close the door and yanked her from the car. She'd fallen to the ground. The asphalt scraped through the fishnet stockings she'd worn, and she'd felt the blood run. He'd yanked her up, pulling her against his chest. She could smell his Polo cologne. To this day, that scent made her stomach churn.

She'd screamed and fought him. He'd held a knife to her throat, pricking the tender skin beneath her chin. Terror overcame her when she'd reached for his face and discovered the ski mask he wore.

The stranger's voice rasped as he breathed during their struggle. The force of his slap had sent Linn reeling into the door of her car, and she'd slid to the ground, dazed. He'd pulled her to her feet and tossed her into the backseat of her car.

The rape had been violent and swift. He'd chanted over and over with each thrust of his knife, "Now, you're mine. You're mine."

When he'd finished, the man had simply left. Left her sobbing, bleeding, and wounded in the backseat of her car.

She'd stayed there until morning before making her way home. She'd sworn never to run out of gas again and told no one what had happened. Kept her mouth shut, continued dancing until she finished school, and became the only female police officer at Upton Hills.

~

She'd told no one until Steve.

Could that man have been Peter Lyman?

It was a long shot, but the thought drove her to her knees. She ignored the rocks biting into her flesh through the pants she wore and continued to stare over the side of the mountain until Drew joined her.

"You all right?"

"I think I know who Peter Lyman is."

"What?" He knelt beside her.

"I think Peter is the man who raped me. He said I was his now. He said it over and over." She shuddered.

"Why wait so long?"

"I don't know. Guess that's the question I'll have to ask him when we find him. Or he finds me."

~

Peter cursed when he found Suzy and Amber stumbling around his front yard as blind as bats in the daytime. He'd herded them back inside, then grabbed a loaf of bread from the counter. He sent the bread and the girls back into the pit.

He rubbed the barrel of the gun along his birthmark. Rage so intense he feared he'd explode burned through him. He'd messed up this time. Oh, yes. Big time. It'd been bad enough when he'd scraped his leg on that car, then ditched his mother's van. But this…This would lead them right to him. Why'd he listen to that lying devil woman, Clara?

Grabbing his car keys from the table, Peter sprinted out the door and to his van. The woman would stumble to the road eventually, and he knew of a little-used road that would provide him with a shortcut.

"I'll get you, Clara. I'll get you for this." He tossed his revolver onto the passenger seat before turning the key in the ignition and roaring from the driveway, spraying gravel.

The van jounced over the rutted road with enough force to bottom out. His teeth clanked together. At one time, his teeth clicked with enough force he bit his tongue. He issued a new string of obscenities into the night.

As his headlights sliced through the thick undergrowth and trees, his anger grew. His chest tightened. Breathing became difficult. He wiped his forearm across his forehead, wiping away the perspiration.

As he neared the main road, he cut his lights and switched off the van's engine. The headlight beams of another car illuminated the piece of road where he could see through the trees.

Opening his door, he snatched the revolver then made his way as silent as a phantom toward the light. The stupid bitch had made it to safety.

He could see Aislinn and the agent wrapping Clara in a blanket and tucking her out of sight into the car.

Aislinn walked toward the edge of the mountain, and Peter used every ounce of restraint in himself not to burst from his hiding place and take her. He gritted his teeth as the agent joined her. His finger itched to pull the trigger. One shot would take out the cowboy, then he'd dash out to grab…

The wailing of a siren pierced the night, and he whirled to focus his attention on the ambulance and squad car which roared to a stop mere feet from him. Two paramedics slung open the back door and rushed with the passenger board to the waiting car.

Peter's gaze swiveled to the new police chief who stepped away from the squad car and made his way to Aislinn's side. He ached to hear what they said. His finger twitched, and he placed his left hand over the gun in his right.

Once Clara was removed from the Mustang, he swung the gun in her direction, then lowered it again as one of the paramedics stepped into his line of fire. "Patience, Peter. He's not the target." He willed the strawberry-blond haired woman to glance his way.

When Aislinn turned with the arm of the agent around her shoulders, Peter whispered an obscenity and swung his gun arm up. He could take them both down. He could do it now. No, that wasn't his plan.

He took deep breaths. Instead, he focused on the chief-of-police. Time to step things up a bit. His shot shattered the night, then Peter melted back into the trees.

32

*T*he bullet blew the back of Wazinski's head apart.

Covered with blood and flecks of grey matter, Linn dove to the ground. She skinned the knuckles of her hand against the dirt and pebbles as she clutched for her weapon. She winced when she pulled it from its holster and gripped it tight. She scanned the dark line of trees.

Drew fell to his knees beside her, weapon ready, and riddled the bushes across the road with gunfire. Almost immediately, the arrived backup did the same.

The mountain road became a war zone with artillery flying in one direction.

Leaves and branches flew as the gunfire ripped into the forest.

"Hold your fire!" Drew held up a hand. No returning bullets zipped in their direction.

Linn duck-walked to the cover of the nearest squad car and turned her head to watch as the paramedics shuffled, bent at the waist, to Wazinski's body. Blood pooled on the pavement beneath the acting chief-of-police's head.

Knowing the answer, Linn asked anyway. The head paramedic shook his head, his eyes sad, as they transferred the body onto the board.

"Cover me." Drew sprinted into the trees, followed by another police officer. The remaining rookie moved to Linn's side.

Linn's heart leapt to her throat and lodged there as she waited for Drew's return. The minutes crawled by. The ticking of her wristwatch sounded loud in the aftermath of the weapons' fire.

Shouts drifted to her from the cover of the trees. Shadows darted from trunk to bush to trunk. The moon hid behind a layer of clouds, plunging them all into inky blackness. Linn held her breath, willing the clouds to scoot by as she listened to Clara's screams.

The clouds drifted. She released her breath.

Drew and the officer emerged from the woods, and sprinted back to where the others had taken cover behind the parked cars. "Nothing. Not a sign. He's vanished." He spun to bark orders. "Tape off this section. Get a crew here now and stay here through the night. I want these woods combed at first light."

"Yes, sir." The officer scuttled to his partner, relaying Drew's orders into his radio.

"You okay?" Drew squatted beside Linn.

"Yes." She let herself slide until she sat on the cool pavement. "How can he disappear so quickly?" Her gaze flicked to where Clara peered from the back of the ambulance. "He can't be far."

"Do you have a map of every road in these parts? Even the unpaved ones?"

Linn nodded. "Yes, but there may be a couple that aren't listed. Ones that don't qualify as roads. Logging roads cut all through these woods. Some are overgrown and unused."

"We need to follow every one of them." Remaining stooped, Drew grasped Linn's arm just above the elbow and steered her into the car. "We can't do anything more tonight. Let the other officers handle it."

"Why Dave?" Linn slid into the passenger's seat, for once willing to let Drew drive.

"Why Mad Dog?" He turned the key in the ignition and pulled behind the ambulance. "Why not me, or you? Why not Clara? He could've picked any one of us off."

Linn shrugged. "It doesn't make sense. I don't think he wants to shoot me. He's waiting for the opportunity to grab me. But you…" She shook her head. "Peter Lyman has to know it's only a matter of time before you catch him. Clara's escape may be just the break we need."

"We'll follow the ambulance to the hospital and see what else she can tell us." Drew turned to her, a slow, sad smile starting at one corner of his mouth and spreading to the other. "We're getting close, Linn. Real close. And we're keeping him so busy, he hasn't abducted anyone else. Let's be thankful for that, at least. He's getting sloppy. Desperate."

"As big of a pain in the ass as Wazinski was, he still would have preferred taking the bullet over another woman dying."

A light drizzle began to fall, distorting the tail lights of the ambulance. Linn closed her eyes. She couldn't remember ever being this tired. Things like this just didn't happen in Upton Falls. That's why she'd moved here. A sleepy little town with a job that enabled her to help people without much chance of reliving the type of horror she'd experienced in the past. Maybe she fooled herself. Maybe she wasn't cut out for this type of work. Her breath shuddered.

"You okay?" Drew folded his hand over hers.

"Fine." She kept her eyes closed, relishing the feel of his warmth over her cold fingers. "I'm just tired. This case has me whipped."

"Take a cat nap. It'll be at least twenty minutes before we get to the hospital."

Linn must have dozed. She opened her eyes to Drew opening her door.

"Sleep well?" The dimple in the corner of his mouth winked.

"Yeah." She unhooked her seatbelt and slid from the car, her limbs heavy with fatigue. "Can't believe I did."

"Come on, Sleeping Beauty. Work still waits for us."

Drew's hand on the small of her back guided and reassured her as they entered the cold, sterile environment of the small local hospital. Drew flashed his badge, and a nurse directed them to Clara's assigned room.

Linn glanced down. Blood stains covered her jacket. "I've got to wash this off before we speak to Clara."

Drew nodded. "There's the restroom. I'll wait out here."

She palmed the knob and stepped into a salmon-tiled deep freeze. Linn shivered in the air-conditioned room and stepped to the sink. She twisted the faucet to full blast and grabbed a handful of paper towels. Shoving them under the gush of water, she lifted her head. The face staring back from the mirror was spotted with reddish brown, crusty flakes. The strawberry-blond hair hung loose from the ponytail. Haunted eyes stared back.

Linn scrubbed her face until her skin hurt. Transferring her attention to her suit jacket, she grimaced. The suit had gotten the brunt of Wazinski's blood. After removing the notepad from the pocket, she peeled off the jacket and tossed it in the trash.

She shivered in her thin blouse. Reaching up, she released her hair from its band and shook it free, before gathering it back together. Another splash of cold water on her face, and she was ready. Linn opened the door and rejoined Drew.

"Where's your jacket?" His gaze ran over her.

"In the garbage. It wasn't going to come clean."

Drew turned her to face him. "I'm sorry about Wazinski. I know you two were close once." She trembled beneath his hands, and he released her to shrug free of the lightweight windbreaker he wore. "Take this. You're chilled." He draped the vinyl jacket around her shoulders.

"That seems like a long time ago, Drew. I'm fine, but thank you."

The officer assigned to guard duty on Clara stepped outside the room when Drew and Linn entered.

Clara sat clothed in a pale blue hospital gown on one of the two beds in the room. The other bed was unoccupied, and Linn perched on it while Drew lowered himself into the chair closest to Clara's bed.

"We'd like to ask you a few more questions. Are you up to it?" Drew leaned forward, his folded hands dangling between his legs. "Officer McFarland will take notes as you answer."

"I'll help in any way I can."

"We appreciate it. We know you've been through quite an ordeal. This can't be easy for you." Drew ran his tongue over his bottom lip before speaking. "Can you tell us where Peter Lyman kept you? The type of house, shed, anything?"

"It was a house." Clara's brow furrowed. "He kept us in a hole beneath a trap door in the kitchen. I think it was a root cellar. It was cold and dark in there."

"What did the house look like? How far did you run?"

"I'm not…sure. I was unconscious when he took me there, and when I ran, I wasn't looking back. I think I ran maybe a mile. I'm not sure."

"One story or two?"

"Two, I think." She tossed her head on the pillow. "I just don't know. My head hurts."

"Please, Clara. We need to know as much as possible in order to save Officer Chavez and the others."

"It's too late," she moaned.

"No, it's not. Concentrate."

Linn raised her head at the sharp tone in Drew's voice. "Did you see any of the rooms?"

"Just the kitchen. Why?"

Drew ran his hands through his hair. "On a video he sent us, there was a room. A white room. Did he take you there?"

She shook her head. "No. I begged him to let me out of the cellar. I promised him anything."

"What does he do with the girls?"

"Nothing. He just tossed us in the cellar and left us. Once in a while, he'd lift the door and talk, or snap a picture. He complained mostly about Officer McFarland."

"Complain about what?" Linn widened her eyes.

"That you didn't see him. He wants you to see him, whatever that means." Clara closed her eyes. "I'm really tired. Can we stop?"

"Just a few more." Drew reached over and placed his hand on hers. "You had to have noticed something about the house. Anything?"

"The driveway was gravel. I remember that. It crunched under my feet as I ran."

"Good. Anything else?"

"A porch. I jumped off the porch. The house is surrounded by trees. I ran through them. That's it. That's all I know."

Linn paused in her writing. "You know Peter Lyman, Clara. You nursed his mother. What does he look like?"

"Like Steve. He looks exactly like Steve."

33

"*T*his case gets weirder and weirder." Linn followed Drew to the car.

"Yeah, I've been thinking about that." He jogged to the driver's side and folded himself into the seat. "The DNA on Morales's car pointed to Steve. Eyewitnesses, such as they are, all say the suspect looks like Steve. Steve's file shows he grew up in foster homes. Was never adopted. Listed birth mother as unknown. Has anyone checked his original birth certificate? Those files would be closed to a layman, but…" Drew turned the key in the ignition. "We need to speak with forensics. Someone who knows their DNA info inside and out."

"There's a woman with the Burlington police department." Linn leaned to sneak a peek at the gas gauge. Half a tank. "She's really good, unless you want to call someone else. Burlington is only twenty miles away."

"It's nine o'clock. Think it's too late?"

"Let me call her." Linn fished her cell phone from her purse and punched in the numbers. "Helen? It's Linn. Do you have time to answer some DNA questions tonight? We can be there in half an hour."

"Sure. The movie I'm watching is a repeat anyway. Is this about The Photographer?"

"Yes."

"Come on. I've been itching to get my hands dirty on this one."

"Thanks." Linn disconnected the call. "She's ready."

Drew backed the Mustang from the hospital parking lot as a light rain began to fall. "Tell me about the woman we're going to see."

"Helen James is fifty-five and semi-retired. Worked with the local crime investigative team for over twenty-five years. Works mainly as a consultant now. She definitely knows her stuff, and the stranger the case, the more she likes it." A convenience store loomed ahead. "Pull over. I want the largest coffee I can get. Either that, or I'm falling asleep on you."

Drew swerved into an empty space in front of the store and cut the ignition. "A thirty-two-ounce size of carbonated caffeine sounds good to me."

Linn stepped from the car. Drew did the same. Leaving him leaning against the fender, she headed to the front glass door of the store.

A man rushed out.

Linn side-stepped to avoid bumping into him. He wore a sweatshirt jacket with the hood pulled low over his face. She turned and watched the stranger jog to his parked car. Something about the man's build nagged at the back of her mind.

He stopped and turned, a pistol clutched in his right hand.

"Drew!" Linn's heart stopped.

Drew turned.

Pop!

Linn's gut clenched as she watched the first of the bullets strike Drew, spinning him. He dropped to the ground, hidden behind the Mustang. The second shot shattered the Mustang's side window.

Dropping to one knee, Linn whipped her weapon from its holster. Pebbles dug into her knee. She squeezed the trigger. *Snap! Snap!*

The man ducked and sprinted to the opposite side of a four-door sedan where he flung the door open and dove inside. Linn strained to see the numbers on the mud splattered license plate. Within seconds, the shooter sped from the parking lot.

"Drew?" Linn rose and rushed to where Drew sat propped against her car. He clutched his right shoulder. Blood ran between his fingers. "Let me see."

"I'll be fine. Nothing a doctor can't patch up." Blue eyes raked her face. "Are you okay? Did you get him?"

Linn shook her head and placed her right hand against his forehead. His skin was cold and clammy. She grabbed a hand full of tissues from the glove compartment and pressed them against his wound. "He got away. We surprised him. There's no way he could have known we would stop here."

"Let me get you in the car. The rain is really starting to come down." She positioned herself beneath his left arm and helped him to his feet. She glanced toward the convenience store clerk who held a phone to his ear. "Looks like the guy inside is calling the department for us. Will you be all right in the car while I go ask some questions?"

"I told you, I'm okay."

"You don't look it." She shouldn't leave him, but the lure of being this close to Lyman and not doing everything possible, was inconceivable. "Are you sure you won't bleed to death in the next few minutes?"

"I've been shot before. This one is a piece of cake." He reached his hand toward her face and stopped, placing it back over his wound. "Wouldn't do to get blood on that pretty face."

"I don't care about that, Drew." Linn leaned forward and placed a kiss on his forehead. She pushed his wet hair away from his eyes.

"Call your friend and reschedule for tomorrow and go talk to the clerk."

"Will do." She lowered her lips and planted a quick kiss on his clamped ones. "Be right back."

Once free from Drew's scrutiny, her legs trembled, and Linn blinked back tears. Way too close. Her throat tightened at Drew's apparent agony. A few inches and he would be dead.

A bell tinkled as she pushed open the door to the store.

The clerk hung up the phone, face pale beneath his olive skin. "I called the cops."

"Thank you." Linn flashed the man her badge. "I'd like to ask you a few questions."

The man nodded and leaned against the counter, visibly shaken.

"Everyone all right in here?" Linn's gaze scanned the remaining patrons of the store. An older man had his arm around a woman about his age. A teenage boy squatted next to the soft drink dispenser, eyes wide in a pale face.

"Yeah." The clerk nodded. "The shooter seemed focused on the man with you."

"Did you get a good look at the gunman?"

"He wore a hood and kept his face turned away."

"Anything taken?"

"Robbery? No. The man was going to purchase a pack of gum and a soda." The clerk pointed to the counter. His hand shook. "Left them sitting right there. You two pulled up, and he ran out. Just like that."

"Can you get everyone out of the store?" She needed to get back to Drew. "We'll need to ask them questions, so make sure no one leaves the area."

The red and blue lights reached her before the wail of a siren. An ambulance followed close behind, a local media's van on its tail. Linn squared her shoulders, pushed open the door, and stepped outside. Flashbulbs exploded in her face. Reporters emerged from the van and swarmed around her.

"Step back, guys. Police business here. You're in the way." She shoved a microphone away from her face and approached the paramedics. "Officer down in the red Mustang. He's the only injury. Gunshot wound to the shoulder."

"Officer McFarland?" A zealous female reporter shoved another microphone in her face. "Was this the work of The Photographer or a random robbery?"

"No comment." Linn stepped past the woman who followed, tottering on three inch heels. "Look." Linn glanced down in scorn at the woman's shoes, then back to her face. Smooth black hair was swept into a bun. "Step away from me, or I'll arrest you for obstruction of justice."

The reporter clamped her ruby red lips closed and stepped back.

Linn made her way to the waiting officers. "Suspect intended to purchase a pack of gum and a soda until Agent Wayne and I arrived. They're sitting on the counter. Dust for prints. I'll be following the ambulance to the hospital. You guys can handle casing the store, and good luck with the reporters."

The ambulance roared from the parking lot, sirens wailing, and Linn sprinted for the car. She slapped her flashing light to the top and followed close, zipping through red lights in the wake of the ambulance. A smile spread across her face. She'd handled the crisis on her own. Like a true detective. Someone not overcome by fear.

Although her main desire had been to stay by Drew's side, she had done what her job required. She'd returned the shooter's gunfire on instinct. Tonight had renewed a love for her job and reestablished her flagging self-esteem.

She pulled into the closest available parking slot at the hospital just as the paramedics wheeled Drew into the emergency room. Shoving open her door, Linn exited, then slammed the car door closed and jogged by his side as they rushed into the building.

Smells of antiseptic and cleansers assaulted her nostrils, and she wrinkled her nose. An infant wailed behind a closed curtain.

Linn placed a hand on Drew's arm. "How do you feel?"

"Better now that you're here." Drew's pale face turned toward her. "The bullet passed through. They'll patch me up, give me pain killers, and we'll be out of here."

"Shouldn't you stay for the night?"

"Only if I'm dead." He reached over, grabbing her hand. "And it'll take more than a bullet in the shoulder to kill me."

"Still want that caffeine? I could run down to the cafeteria."

Drew glanced at the waiting doctor who shook his head. "Nope. You go ahead. I'll wait here."

~

Peter cursed and slammed his fist into the steering wheel, ignoring the stabbing pain that spread through his knuckles. They'd caught him by surprise. He shrugged. They knew who he was. He slapped the wheel again. His aim was off. He should've killed the cowboy then grabbed Linn. When would he have another opportunity?

His gaze focused on the parked ambulance. She was inside the hospital right now. Just mere feet away from him, yet as inaccessible as if the distance were a mile. He cursed again and contemplated storming into the emergency room and taking her at gunpoint. With all the pigs inside, that would be a suicide mission.

Clara was there, too. He could feel her. He could take care of both of them. So intense was this certainty that he placed a hand on the door latch. He shook his head. Too risky. There'd be another time. A time when it would be just the two of them. Linn and the cowboy. The next time he wouldn't miss.

Peter slid his hood from his head and caught a glimpse of himself in the mirror. He ran a hand down the marked side of his face. How could Linn love someone as ugly as he? Or would it be easier for her having dealt with a disfigurement of her own, minor though it was?

Tears pooled in his eyes, and he slammed his forehead against the steering wheel hard enough to cause spots to swim behind his eyelids. She'd have to love him. He'd make her! She belonged to him. There had been no woman before or after her.

He started the sedan and turned toward home. It had been an eventful night.

The vehicle's headlights pierced the road, illuminating the squad cars still parked on the mountain. Fools. Peter cut the sedan's lights and turned the vehicle to the right and down the overgrown logging road. Once he felt he'd put enough distance between him and the police, he turned the car's lights back on and drove home.

The house drowned in light. Peter grimaced. He'd been in such a hurry to catch Clara, he'd not thought about the lights. He flicked them off as he moved through the foyer and into the kitchen.

Pulling a small flashlight from his pocket, he kicked open the trapdoor and shone the beam into Steve Chavez's eyes.

"Evening, Officer." Peter stuck his hand behind him and pulled up a chair. "Almost killed the FBI agent tonight. I got off two rounds. One hit him then that little firecracker Aislinn opened fire on me."

Steve put up his arm to shield his eyes from the light. "Too bad she missed. Where's Clara?"

"Got away." Peter shrugged. "No matter. It's Aislinn I want anyway. The others are just a diversion."

"Then let the others go."

"No, I don't think so."

"What am I?"

"Bait." Peter laughed. "We know our loyal little lady isn't going to rest while I have her best friend."

"What's your obsession with her?"

Peter pulled back. "I love her. She's mine. I thought I told you." Was it so difficult for people to imagine?

"You're psychotic." Steve shifted his weight, groaning.

"What's wrong? Your wound bothering you? I'm sorry, but your nurse isn't here anymore." Peter bolted to his feet and leaned over the cellar. "You two shouldn't have cooked up such a scheme. It leaves you in a pretty bad fix."

"Let me out of here, and I'll show you what kind of fix I'm in."

"Now, you sound like the cowboy. All tough, when we both know you hide behind Aislinn. She's the real strength in your partnership." Peter reached into the pocket of his sweatshirt and pulled out his weapon. He pointed the barrel toward Steve's head. "I could shoot you where you stand. How tough would you be then?"

Time was running out. He needed a new plan. They'd find him soon. He needed to grab Aislinn now and fulfill their destiny. Peter sighed. "I think I'll visit our detectives at the hospital."

34

*T*he quietness of the hospital cafeteria in the late evening hours slammed against Linn's eardrums as she nursed her cup of bitter coffee. The low murmurings of a handful of hospital staff on break drifted across the room. Out of habit, Linn's gaze roamed the room, noting the points of exit.

Two doors led into the dining area from the hall, and one door led to an outside patio, dark behind the glass. A chill ran down her spine, and she shivered, wrapping her hands tighter around the Styrofoam mug.

Drew had been sleeping the last time she checked on him, and, unable to doze in the uncomfortable chair beside his bed, she had ducked out of the room for another blast of caffeine. She tilted her head to grab a glimpse at the clock on the wall. They'd been here for three hours.

Linn sighed. She loved the man lying wounded in a sterile room, painted mauve and a sickly shade of green. Her heart thumped against her ribcage at the thought. Her—in love. She smiled. She loved everything about him, the dimple, the square chin, the tenderness, and the patience. She loved his bravery in the face of danger.

Love. Was it the feeling of wanting to grab hold of the man and never let go? The feeling of safeness when she was around him? Wanting to wake beside him every morning for the rest of her life?

She stared into the Styrofoam mug, swirling the dark liquid. She never thought love would be possible. As tears welled, she rested her head on her arms.

"Detective? You all right?"

Linn peeked beneath the crook of her elbow and spotted legs encased in the navy blue of the Upton Falls police. "I've never been better."

"Oh, good. I've got the records on Peter Lyman Agent Wayne requested."

Linn straightened to take the offered folder. "Thanks." She pushed her lukewarm coffee out of the way and opened the file. She sped read the printed words. The sound of the flipping pages echoed loud in the stillness of the cafeteria.

Her eyes widened. Peter had quite a past. Originally born Peter Chavez, the man would be 36 years old. Born a twin to one Steven Chavez. *A twin! That explains a lot.* Linn's heart rate accelerated, and she turned pages quicker. Social Services removed the child from his home at the age of ten on grounds of severe abuse and neglect. Linn chewed her lip. Steve had been placed in foster care younger than that. Why had he been taken from the home and not Peter? What took the state so long to take the other twin? Had he been hidden? Was his mother ashamed of the birthmark?

Linn leaned back in her chair. Her mind raced. And when did Peter Chavez become Peter Lyman? She fingered through the folder. No record of adoption. Birth certificate listed Agnes Chavez as birth mother. No father mentioned. Had Agnes remarried a man with the name of Parsons? Had Peter found her later in life? Linn's head ached with the questions whipping through her mind.

Taking a gulp from the tepid cup of coffee, she almost gagged and set the cup back on the table.

She raised her head at the sound of footsteps approaching. A slender dark haired man, dressed in a doctor's white coat, stood a few feet away. His profile was Steve's. "Peter?"

The man dashed to her side.

Linn reached for the weapon hanging in its holster over her shoulder as a needle plunged into her arm. Darkness swept over her, and she toppled from the chair.

~

"Where's Officer McFarland?" Drew slid his legs over the side of his bed as the doctor scrawled a signature across his release papers.

"The nurse said she went down to the cafeteria." The doctor smiled and handed him the release forms and a prescription. "There're enough pain killers here for three days. Keep the arm in a sling and don't use it. I still say you need to stay. There is a risk of infection. I could insist, you know."

"I know the drill, Doctor. Thanks."

Drew slid his stocking feet into the boots beside the bed and stomped, forcing his feet into them. Each jar of his shoulder sent spasms of pain through him. If he'd known he was going to be shot, he'd have worn gym shoes.

The two nurses behind the station smiled as he passed by. He gave a little wave before turning down the hall that would lead him to the cafeteria.

The room was virtually empty. Hushed whispers from a group in the corner. The clatter of plastic trays as a worker gathered them together. But no Linn. Drew approached the young man loaded down with the trays. "Excuse me? Did you see a woman, alone, probably carrying a handgun?"

"Yes, sir. She sat at that table." The man tilted his head to a table where a solitary cup and scattered papers rested. "She was crying for a while, then she collapsed, and a doctor carried her out of here. Took her to the patio. Is she all right? I thought it strange that the doctor took her that way, but sometimes…" He shrugged.

"What doctor?" Dread filled Drew, rushing through his veins as the room threatened to spin around him. "How long ago did they leave?"

"Never saw him before. Thought maybe he was on-call. They left maybe an hour ago."

"What did he look like?"

"About my height. Thin. Dark hair. Purple birth mark."

Drew ripped the radio from its holder on his belt. "This is Agent Wayne. Get me a team at the hospital ASAP. Detective McFarland is missing." He bolted through the exit door with enough force to slam it against the rubber stopper attached to the concrete.

The patio was void of people. Drew stared into the hospital parking lot. No cars moved. No lights shone. His heart plummeted to the pit of his stomach. He spun in a circle, peering into every corner.

Pulling his weapon from its holster, he bolted from the patio and around the corner of the hospital. He darted through the Emergency Room entrance and flashed his badge. "No one leaves the hospital," he barked orders at the administration desk. "Where's security?"

The woman pointed to the right. Drew sprinted in that direction.

A middle-aged man sat behind a desk reading the newspaper. His feet were propped on his desk.

Drew flashed his badge again. "There's been an abduction. Seal all exits. No one leaves."

"But emergencies..."

"I said, no one leaves, I didn't say they couldn't get in." Drew glowered at the man. "Do your job, or I'll find someone who will."

"Yes, sir." The guard jumped to his feet and reached for his walkie-talkie, relaying information to the other guards as Drew rattled off a description of Linn.

"About five-seven, strawberry-blond hair. Scar on upper lip. She's wearing navy pants and a white blouse. Name Aislinn McFarland." Lyman didn't waste any time. Despite his wanting to collapse from the pain of his gunshot wound and his fear for Linn, Drew pushed on, securing all entrances to the hospital.

The police arrived within five minutes of his call. He positioned a man around each door and, although he knew she wasn't there, he ordered the rest to comb the hospital inch-by-inch.

Drew approached the officer by the main entrance. "Do you know a woman by the name of Helen James?"

"Sure I do. She helps out the department quite a bit."

"Got an address?"

The officer pulled a notebook from his pocket and scratched the woman's address on it before handing it over to Drew. "Helen's not going to be up at this time of the night."

"She'll be awake in a few minutes. I need the keys to your car. Have someone gather the papers from the cafeteria table McFarland sat at. Take them to the officers on the mountain. I'll get them later. Is the acting chief here yet?"

The officer nodded and motioned his head toward a man wearing a suit. Then he tossed the keys to Drew who snatched them with his good hand. He fumbled with the keys before tightening his grip, and sprinted out the door to the squad car.

Perspiration beaded on his brow and upper lip. He forced his body past the pain in his shoulder. He thought about the painkillers in his pocket then disregarded them. He needed his senses alert.

~

Fifteen minutes later, Drew pounded on the door of Helen James's home.

"Wait just a minute!" A sleepy voice called from the other side. The rattle of a chain, then the door swung open.

"Ms. James? I'm Agent Andrew Wayne. Detective McFarland called you?"

"Yes, but she rescheduled for later."

"Please. I need to speak with you. It's urgent." He fumbled in his pocket for his badge. "Something's happened to Linn."

Helen swung the door wide, allowing Drew entrance into her home.

~

Peter glanced to where Aislinn sat hunched in the front seat, her perfect profile outlined by the moonlight. His heart swelled, and he reached over to brush aside a strand of hair that had escaped from its clasp. So soft. Like the silk fabric of the dress he'd sewn for her.

He pushed open the door to his car and walked around to the passenger's side, pausing a moment to steal another glimpse of her through the window. So beautiful. He opened the door and clutched her face in his hand. He turned her head toward him and kissed her, the feeling of her lips so sweet he felt an overwhelming urge to cry. He pulled her into his arms and breathed in the scent of her hair. Something flowery. He fought the desire to claim her again.

Right then, right there, but no, this time had to be beautiful. Aislinn needed to come to him willingly.

After carrying her into the kitchen, he propped her into a chair and removed her holster and weapon, placing them on the kitchen table. He grabbed the gun then leaned over and raised the root cellar door. "Company," he sang. "A true prize this time."

"You have Linn?" Steve pushed to his feet.

"Try anything, and I'll snap her neck." Peter stood over the hole and kicked down the ladder. "Come up and get her. I don't want to toss her in."

Steve climbed the ladder. Peter handed Aislinn into his arms. "I know you're injured, but you'd better not drop her."

"How'd you get to her?" Sparks flew from Steve's eyes.

"Took her from the hospital. It was easy. Stole some scrubs and waltzed right in. At first, I bet she thought I was you. Funny, isn't it? But then she saw this." His hand flew to his face.

"Where's Wayne?"

"I can't say." Peter fidgeted as Steve awkwardly advanced down the ladder holding Linn. "I hope he's rotting in hell." Her feet banged against the ladder steps. "You'd better not leave bruises on her."

Steve glared at him then turned to lay Aislinn on the dirt of the cellar floor.

Peter raised the ladder and remained standing above them, staring into the darkness. "Where's Suzy and Amber?"

"Sleeping in the corner. They're too weak to do anything else."

"Wake them up." Peter aimed the weapon toward his captives.

The two girls crawled out of the corner, blinking against the light.

"I'm putting the ladder down again. You two climb up here. If you can't make it, I'll shoot you."

The women cried as they climbed, their eyes never leaving the weapon in Peter's hand.

"Hurry up!" He pointed the barrel in their direction. Once they'd reached the top, he herded them into the foyer and out the door. "Go."

"You're…not…going…to…kill…us?" Suzy leaned against the wall.

Peter shook his head. "Not yet. I have somewhere else for you to stay. I don't want you with my Aislinn. You're filthy." He waved the gun. "Go around to the back of the house."

They stood and stared at him, disbelief on their wane faces.

"Go." Peter ushered them to the shed in the back and deposited them inside his darkroom. "I'll deal with the two of you later."

He closed the door on their screams and pleads, ignoring the banging on the wooden door. With a smile, he headed back to the kitchen to peer again at his prize.

"What did you do to her?" Steve knelt beside the unconscious Linn.

"I just gave her a shot. She'll be all right in an hour or two. You'd better make sure of it."

Earlier that day, Peter had draped the gown he'd sewn for her over one of the kitchen chairs. Now, he ran his hand lovingly over the fabric. "Dress her in this and let her hair down. I want her beautiful when she wakes."

Anticipation was almost too much for him to bear. Her alabaster skin would glow from the sheen of the dress. Her strawberry-blond curls would look richer. Peter tossed the dress then clasped his hands together.

The crimson silk fluttered into the hole like a butterfly.

35

"*P*lease, Agent Wayne, have a seat. Can I get you something to drink?" Helen James's hair was dyed a chestnut brown and sprang around her head like coils. She'd answered the door in a flannel nightgown and blue terry robe. Eyes the same shade as the robe blinked at Drew behind gold-rimmed glasses.

"No, thanks." He perched on the edge of a floral sofa and cradled his injured arm.

Helen took a seat in an armchair opposite him. "Linn said you had some DNA questions. Where is she?"

"Taken from the hospital over an hour ago." Drew leaned back, the pain in his heart unbearable.

"He's got her. The Photographer, I suppose." Helen jumped to her feet and bustled into the kitchen.

Drew threw an arm across his eyes and peered beneath it as she bustled around gathering the makings for coffee. "Ms. James?"

"Go ahead, Agent Wayne. My nerves won't allow me to sit still."

"One of the victims wasn't abducted. She was murdered beside her car and left on the side of the road in her trunk. We believe Lyman had been interrupted by an approaching vehicle. We found blood not belonging to the victim on the door jamb. DNA pointed to Steve Chavez."

"Linn's partner." She filled a kettle with water.

"Yes. For a short while we suspected Chavez, but other events indicated that was impossible. We've never been able to lift prints. Peter Lyman is very meticulous about not leaving any signs behind. We identified him as The Photographer when we found his mother murdered in the hospice, and her nurse abducted."

Helen faced Drew and leaned against the counter. "Does Steve have a twin?"

"We don't know anything about Steve's family. He grew up in foster homes."

"Uh-huh." Helen set the kettle on the stove and turned the knob on the burner before rejoining Drew in the living room.

"Identical twins have the exact same DNA. Did you know that? Although their fingerprints are different. Fascinating, really."

Drew released his arm from the sling, letting it fall to his side. "I was beginning to suspect as much. Just wanted clarification. Peter Lyman has a birthmark that covers one side of his face."

"Won't affect the DNA. A person's DNA is formed upon conception, Agent Wayne, as is the birthmark."

Drew nodded. "Well, you cleared up a few things, but I'm no closer to finding Linn than I was before I got here."

"You'd better be." Helen rose from her chair. "Linn may not have much time. I've been following this case the best I can, and I'm sure you will agree that Mr. Lyman is accelerating in behavior. You love Linn, don't you?"

"With all that is in me." Drew stood and held out a hand to Helen. "Thank you for your time."

Helen ushered him out the front door.

He made his way back to the car and sat behind the wheel, deep in thought. Chavez has a twin. Hence the eyewitnesses saying Lyman looks like Chavez. Easy enough to disappear in a town when you look like someone else. Lyman learned to exist by hiding his mark. So, now, where was he? Drew's eyes were drawn to the mountain towering above the valley.

The radio at Drew's waist squawked. "Wayne here."

"Detective Morrison. We've searched the hospital. No sign of McFarland or Lyman. Forensics did get back with the slug that killed Wazinski. Came from a .45 caliber, shot from approximately 50 yards. Wazinski didn't stand a chance. The slug we found at the crime scene from your shoulder doesn't match. Your's was a .22 caliber revolver."

"So, Lyman owns more than one weapon. A lot of people out here do."

"Just passing on the facts. The car sitting on the mountain hasn't found anything, yet. Still too dark. Dawn won't be here for a few more hours. Where do you want us now?"

"I'm heading back to the mountain. Come dawn, I'm combing those woods and traveling every road. Send your men back there."

"10-4."

Drew looked up to meet the eyes of Helen James peering back at him through her parted front room curtains. She waved and let the curtains fall closed. Teeth gritted against the pain in his shoulder, Drew turned the car back onto the road and headed toward the mountain.

He parked behind the idling squad car and cut the ignition of the one he drove. The driver's door of the car in front of him opened and an officer approached, flashlight in hand.

"Oh, it's you, Agent. Sorry to tell you we don't have any news."

"Already heard. I'm just waiting for dawn."

The officer nodded toward Drew's sling. "How's the shoulder?"

"Hurts."

"We've got…" the officer glanced at his watch, "about three hours 'til dusk. Why not catch some sleep? Give that shoulder a rest. We'll watch things until then."

"Maybe I will. Otherwise, I won't be much use come daylight." Drew fished in his pocket for the painkillers. Pulling out the little orange bottle, he twisted off the cap and shook a tablet into his hand.

The officer handed him a thermos. "The coffee's cold, but it'll wash the pill down."

"Thanks." Drew popped the capsule into his mouth and downed it with the contents of the thermos. He laid his head back, willing a drug induced sleep to take him away.

He startled awake at a tap on the car window.

~

"Steve?" Linn peered into inky blackness.

"I'm here. How'd you know?"

"I was hoping. Oh, Steve." She felt around until she found his arms, then hugged him close. "Are you all right?"

"I should be asking you that question."

"I'm fine." She shivered and pulled back, running her hands over her body. "Oh, wow. Please don't tell me I'm wearing a red dress." Fear prickled her skin. "Who changed my clothes?"

"I did, and yes, it's red."

"And we're in the infamous hole in the ground." Linn moved to sit with her back against a dirt wall. She would not fall apart. She would not let the dark unravel her.

"It's a root cellar. Where's Wayne?"

"Lyman shot him." Linn took a deep breath. "A shoulder wound. I was in the hospital cafeteria drinking coffee while I waited for him to be released. I looked up and saw someone who looked like you dressed in a lab coat. He turned around, and I saw the birthmark."

"Seems I have a twin." She felt Steve scoot beside her, his shoulder touching hers. "Funny the things you learn. I'm sorry, Linn. All my life I've wanted a family. Now I find out I have a psychopathic killer for a brother."

"Sorry for what?"

"He's obviously targeted you because you're my partner." The sadness in his voice ripped at Linn.

"Don't think that way." She fumbled in the dark until she found his hand. "I believe he's the man who raped me. The build's the same. Maybe I'm grasping at straws here, but if I'm right, it's coincidence that you're my partner. I think he laid claim on me a long time ago. Upton Falls is a small town. He followed me here. It's a bonus to him that we became partners." She squeezed his hand. "I'm so glad you're still alive."

"That makes two of us."

"Where are the other girls?"

Steve shrugged. "He took them out when he put you in here. They're in pretty bad shape. He forgets to feed us, and we're lucky if we get water."

Releasing his hand, Linn got to her feet and walked the circumference of the cellar. She ran her hands over the cool dirt that made up the walls.

"There's no way out except the ladder," Steve told her. "I've checked. I've been trying to dig steps into the wall, but I'm not making much progress."

"Clara got away." Linn scooted back down the wall and re-grasped Steve's hand. "She'll be all right."

"That's good. I had hoped so."

A wash of light flooded over them sending pricks of pain into Linn's eyes. She blinked against the intrusion.

"My love. You're awake." Peter stood silhouetted above the cellar. "How touching to see you holding hands with my brother." He pulled over a chair and sat, leaning over the hole in the floor. "Would you like to know how I found you, brother?"

Steve stared without answering their captor.

"Okay, I will tell you. One evening while searching for our birth mother, I stepped into a bar and saw a vision from above. An angel with red hair who's dancing had the power to hypnotize. I followed her home one night. Luck was with me when her car broke down."

Linn shivered at the singsong tone of Peter's voice.

"I stopped and claimed her as my own. She felt so good, warm and moist.

"I was heading for Upton Falls. That's where our mother lived. Agnes Parsons, she used to be Layman, I'm sure you know the name. Unfortunately, she's dead now. How wonderful it was to discover Aislinn moving here. How ironic when fate placed her as your partner. It did bother me when the two of you became so close, and she didn't even know I existed. I made a vow the day you became partners that Aislinn would come to love me." Peter rose from the chair. "But she didn't, and I saw her imperfection."

Linn's hand flew to her mouth.

"No, not the scar, my love. That can be fixed. It was your inability to see me. That's the imperfection I am talking about."

"Then why the other women?" Linn's heart chilled as Peter tapped his fingers against his lip, so like Steve's habit.

Peter frowned. "I needed someone to love me. Don't you understand that? They only filled in until I had you."

"If Agnes Parsons is our mother, why were you with her and not me?" Steve folded his arms across his chest.

"She never kept us together. She kept me locked away in a root cellar until I was ten!" Peter paced across the top of the cellar. "She was ashamed of me! Hid me from the world until one day, I escaped. Do you know what it's like to be sexually abused by a drunken fat ass? I do.

"The cops found me half-starved and wandering around on this mountain and put me in foster care. Seems we've got a lot of money too, brother of mine."

"Peter." Linn struggled to keep her voice calm. He spun and locked gazes with her. "Let me help you. Let us both help you. You don't have to do this anymore. Don't do to others the horrible things your mother did to you. The three of us can be a family."

"Don't tell me what to do." He reached for something and returned with Linn's weapon clutched in his fist. He kicked down the ladder and leveled the barrel of the weapon at her. "Climb up here, and don't try anything funny, or I'll kill Steve."

36

Linn climbed the ladder, clutching a fistful of red silk in one hand to avoid tripping. The ladder rungs bit into her bare feet. The muscles spasmed. When she reached the top, Peter held out a hand to help her and led her to one of the kitchen chairs. He turned and raised the ladder.

"Aren't you afraid I'll run?" Linn watched as he slammed the cellar door closed.

"No. I'll kill Steve if you do. Then I'll hunt down the cowboy and finish him off."

"You mean Agent Wayne?"

"Don't be coy with me. I know he's your lover." Peter sat across the table from her. "I have to admit that hurts. That you would choose a stranger over me. I envisioned us reliving our first time."

"Seriously? You raped me!"

"It was love!"

Linn stared at him in disbelief. How could she get through to a man living in such a disillusioned world? A world of his own making? She needed to humor him.

"What are you thinking?"

Linn snapped back to the moment and stared into the face so like Steve's, yet marred with the ugliness of evil. "That I wish we'd met under different circumstances."

"You wouldn't have noticed me." Peter's shoulders slumped. "You stared right at me and smiled that night as you twirled around the pole. But when I approached you later, you walked right past."

"That's not true. How could I not know you were there? The dancers weren't allowed to fraternize with the customers." Linn folded her hands on the table and leaned forward. "You say you love me. If that's true, then don't you know I'm not one to judge people on looks alone? Come on, Peter. I grew up being made fun of because of my scar. We have something in common."

"Don't be playing mind games with me, Aislinn." Peter's eyes narrowed. "Your scar is barely noticeable. A thin white line. Not like me! Don't play games!"

"I wouldn't think of it, Peter."

"I just want us to be together. Always." He caressed the barrel of the handgun then stuffed it in his pocket. "Come with me. I've prepared a way." He held out his hand for her to take. His skin was cold to her touch.

Her gaze lit on a weapon on the counter.

Peter jerked her, then led her out of the kitchen and down the hall before opening the door on the white room she'd seen in the video. Everything was exactly as Linn had seen, down to the small table with the box of syringes. Her blood chilled.

"No, Peter. Please, not this." His grip tightened as she pulled back.

"This time, I'll film us entering eternity together."

"No. I won't do this." Linn struggled against his tight grip, striking out with a bare foot. She winced as her toe cracked against his shin.

"You can't win against me. I'm too strong for you."

"Please, Peter. Let me love you. Give me a chance to love you."

"Love me?" He faltered. "Could you?"

"Yes, Peter." She stroked his face with her free hand. "Let us be together—alive. Not in death."

"It won't work. I've killed people. They'll send me away."

"I'll vouch for you, Peter. I'll tell them you didn't mean it."

"Stop it. You'll betray me." His eyes hardened. A muscle twitched in his jaw as he clenched it. The force of the slap drove Linn's head back. "They always betray me." He pulled her toward the chair and reached for the box of syringes.

~

Drew headed into the woods where he believed the shot that killed Wazinski had originated. Approximately half a mile in the trees, he found the overgrown logging road. Clutching his arm close to his chest, he jogged down it, his heart pounding. His wound bled, soaking his tee-shirt. He couldn't give up, couldn't quit. Not until Linn was safe in his arms.

Several times he stopped to catch his breath and leaned against a tree trunk for support. He used the radio at his belt to call for backup, letting the searching officers know the approximate location he was headed.

Weeds tugged at his feet as he stumbled over deep ruts in the road. It took every ounce of strength he possessed to keep himself upright and moving forward. He stumbled as he burst into the clearing.

The house loomed large before him. A ramshackle, two-story, white farmhouse with a sweeping front porch and gravel drive. Shingles were missing from the roof, and one edge of the upper story sagged. Clara hadn't been far off in the description of her prison.

Drew stopped at the boundary of trees and pulled his weapon from its holster. Eyes peeled for sign of movement. He bent at the waist and loped his way to the rear of the house. His gaze lit on a grey weathered shack. He paused to catch his breath. His shoulder throbbed.

Forcing himself onward, he bashed the lock on the door with the butt of his handgun. Screams echoed from inside the shack and spurred him on. He flung the door open on the white faces of Suzy Green and Amber Richards. Perspiration dotted Amber's skin.

"You're all right now. I'm FBI. Where are the others? Where's the cellar?"

"In…the…house. The kitchen." Suzy grabbed at his legs. "Please, help us."

"I'm calling to let the police know where you are." Drew grabbed his radio. "Stay here and wait for them. You'll be safe." He closed the door, his heart wrenching at their cries. He gave backup their location.

He tried peering through the house's boarded windows. Nothing. He tried the back door only to find it locked. Could he bust through without alerting those inside? He sprinted to the front door and turned the handle. Unlocked. He grinned.

He stepped into a house as unkempt as the outside. A tiled foyer led to stairs with a sagging railing. Thick carpet covered the floor of the living room to Drew's right. Antique furniture graced the area around a massive stone fireplace.

Keeping his gun in front of him, Drew stumbled into the kitchen and spotted the trapdoor. A rolled up area rug lay to one side. The door squeaked slightly as he raised it. "Linn?"

"Wayne?"

"Where's Linn?"

"Lyman took her. Let down the ladder."

"Took…her where?" Drew lowered the ladder, gasping against the pain.

"I don't know." Steve's head appeared above the hole. "He took her maybe a half-hour ago."

"You okay?"

Steve pulled himself over the edge. "As well as can be expected, considering."

"Backup is coming. The other girls are in a shed out back. See to them, please." Drew whirled to dash down the hall. "Linn!"

~

Peter spun toward the shout.

Linn ducked, throwing herself at his legs. They crashed in a tangled heap on the floor. Her hands scratched and ripped at the pocket of the sweatshirt he wore. Her fingers grasped the weapon.

Peter slapped her hands away.

The gun slid into a corner of the room.

The door shook with Drew's pounding. "Linn!"

She scrambled across the tiled floor, slipping on the long gown. Her chin smacked the hard tile. She bit her lip and tasted blood.

Peter crawled over her. His knees dug into her back as he fought his way toward the whirling weapon.

Bucking, Linn tossed him from her, her fingers colliding with the gun and shoving it farther away. Tears poured down her face as she breathed in great gulps.

"Linn! Answer me!" The door banged against its hinges.

"In here!"

"I'll kill him while you watch." Peter spat, spraying Linn's face with spittle.

Nausea rose in her throat.

He launched himself at her. His hands wrapped around her neck.

She flailed and struck him in the face with her fists. Her nails raked down his cheek.

He howled.

Pulling her knees up, she shoved against him. Sent him sliding across the smooth floor. Sobs wracked her body. She scrambled again for the gun. Her fingers closed around it, and she pushed to her feet.

The first shot struck him high in the shoulder, spinning him in a macabre dance. Whimpers rose in Linn's throat as she squeezed the trigger again. The second shot took him in the chest. He dropped to the floor with a thud.

Linn scooted back against the wall as Peter struggled to regain his footing. His eyes blazed with fury as he spouted curses at her.

The third shot hit him between the eyes.

He fell forward. His body twitched. Blood spread beneath him.

Linn's hands shook. The weapon dropped in her lap, its shiny blackness stark against the crimson of her dress. Her limbs trembled. She wrapped her arms around her knees, hugging them close to her chest.

"Linn!" The door crashed open. Drew paused and stared down at Peter Lyman. He skirted around the body and dropped to Linn's side. "Please tell me you're all right."

She nodded. Sobbing, she threw her arms around his neck.

Drew wrapped his uninjured arm around her. He sat with his back against the wall, and pulled her into his lap. She buried her face in his neck. Breathed in the scent of him. Loving the safety of his arms.

37

*T*wo days later, Linn snuggled beneath the crook of Drew's arm and listened to his heartbeat. She thanked God for every thump against her eardrum. This man had brought her back to life in more ways than one, and, for that, she'd be eternally grateful.

Steve sat in a chair across from them, thinner than Linn thought looked good on him. A white bandage wrapped around his head. Linn giggled.

"What?" Steve's green eyes peered at her over the rim of the cup he had lifted to his lips.

"I'm sitting here with two men and neither one could lift a kitten if they needed to."

"Oh, yeah? You weren't much better off not too long ago." Drew lowered his good arm and tickled her until she squealed for mercy. "That's what I thought." The dimple in his right cheek winked.

"It's good to see you so happy, Linn." Steve lowered his cup to the coffee table, his face drawn in sadness.

"I'm sorry, Steve."

"For what?" Again, his gaze met hers.

"You gained and lost a mother and brother in such a short time."

"Such as they were." He shrugged. "I never knew Agnes Parsons, and she didn't appear to be someone I would care to know. Peter, well, he was a product of his upbringing. I'd say I was the lucky one."

"You don't remember anything before you were sent into the system?" Drew shifted his body so Linn could once again snuggle beneath his arm.

"I've always felt…I don't know…something. Maybe that bond they say twins have. I just put it off as a strong desire to have a family." Steve's fingers drummed against his lip.

"Peter did that, too." Linn announced. "Drummed his fingers on his lip."

"Funny." Steve laughed. A short, derisive snort that lacked humor. "The way family shares characteristics, even without knowing each other. Guess I'll have to break this particular habit."

Linn's heart went out to her friend as her mind replayed the horror of the last few days. She vowed to never wear red again. "So, we've got a few days off. What do the two of you want to do?"

"I'm going to bury Peter. I can at least do that for the poor guy." Steve rose from his seat. "Then maybe I'll head to the coast for a few days. Soak up some sun. What about you two?"

Linn glanced at Drew. "Stay here and get to know this man better."

"I think I'll propose to the pretty lady, then paint the town, such as Upton Falls has to offer." Drew moved his arm and dug in his pocket. He pulled out a black velvet jeweler's box. "Linn, I know I have to leave in a few days, but do you think you can handle a long distance engagement until things get settled?"

The fire in his eyes burned to the center of her, and her breath caught.

"Oh, Drew." She opened the box to reveal a ring with a one-carat ruby stone in the center of a white-gold band encircled with diamonds. "Red?" She looked up at him in shock then switched her gaze to Steve as he laughed. "A red stone? After all we've gone…"

"Easy, sweetheart." Drew chuckled. "It's best to face your fears head on, don't you think?"

"I agree." Steve headed to the front door. "I'll leave you two alone. Congratulations." He glanced over his shoulder and smiled. "Enjoy the ring, Linn. Drew's a lucky man."

She closed her gaping mouth as Steve strode out her front door, then she slipped the ring onto her finger. It fit perfectly, a small heart of fire burning in the center of the stone. "I love it, Drew. I really do." Tears welled. "But red?"

"I don't want you afraid of a color. Having that ring, well, I hope that every time you look at it, you'll have good feelings."

"I will." And she would. She smiled and met his gaze. "So, big boy, when do you think you can finally take me up on that offer I've been trying to give you?"

He rubbed his chin. "Well, I'm not sure—"

Linn tossed a sofa pillow at him and dashed for the bedroom.

The End

247

ABOUT THE AUTHOR

Website at www.cynthiahickey.com

Multi-published and Amazon and ECPA Best-Selling author Cynthia Hickey has sold over a million copies of her works since 2013. She has taught a Continuing Education class at the 2015 American Christian Fiction Writers conference, several small ACFW chapters and RWA chapters. She and her husband run the small press, Winged Publications, which includes some of the CBA's best well-known authors. She lives in Arizona with her husband, one of their seven children, two dogs, one cat, and three box turtles. She has eight grandchildren who keep her busy and tell everyone they know that "Nana is a writer".

Connect with me on FaceBook
Twitter
Amazon
Sign up for my newsletter and receive a free short story
www.cynthiahickey.com

Follow me on Amazon

Enjoy other books by Cynthia Hickey

Time Travel
The Portal

A Hollywood Murder
Killer Pose, book 1

Shady Acres Mysteries
Beware the Orchids, book 1
Path to Nowhere
Poison Foliage
Poinsettia Madness
Deadly Greenhouse Gases

Vine Entrapment

CLEAN BUT GRITTY

Highland Springs

Murder Live
Say Bye to Mommy
To Breathe Again

Colors of Evil Series

Shades of Crimson
Coral Shadows

The Pretty Must Die Series

Ripped in Red, book 1
Pierced in Pink, book 2
Wounded in White, book 3
Worthy, The Complete Story

Lisa Paxton Mystery Series

Eenie Meenie Miny Mo
Jack Be Nimble
Hickory Dickory Dock

One Hour **(A short story thriller)**

INSPIRATIONAL
(scroll down to see clean books without inspirational message)

Whisper Sweet Nothings (a short romance)

Nosy Neighbor Series
Anything For A Mystery, Book 1
A Killer Plot, Book 2
Skin Care Can Be Murder, Book 3

Death By Baking, Book 4
Jogging Is Bad For Your Health, Book 5
Poison Bubbles, Book 6
A Good Party Can Kill You, Book 7 (Final)
Nosy Neighbor collection

Christmas with Stormi Nelson

The Summer Meadows Series
Fudge-Laced Felonies, Book 1
Candy-Coated Secrets, Book 2
Chocolate-Covered Crime, Book 3
Maui Macadamia Madness, Book 4
All four novels in one collection

The River Valley Mystery Series
Deadly Neighbors, Book 1
Advance Notice, Book 2
The Librarian's Last Chapter, Book 3
All three novels in one collection

Historical cozy
Hazel's Quest

Historical Romances
Runaway Sue
Taming the Sheriff
Sweet Apple Blossom

Finding Love the Harvey Girl Way
Cooking With Love
Guiding With Love
Serving With Love
Warring With Love
All 4 in 1

A Wild Horse Pass Novel
They Call Her Mrs. Sheriff, book 1 (A Western Romance)

Finding Love in Disaster
The Rancher's Dilemma
The Teacher's Rescue
The Soldier's Redemption

Woman of courage Series

A Love For Delicious
Ruth's Redemption
Charity's Gold Rush
Mountain Redemption
Woman of Courage series (all four books)

Short Story Westerns
Desert Rose
Desert Lilly
Desert Belle
Desert Daisy
Flowers of the Desert 4 in 1

Romantic Suspense

Overcoming Evil series
Mistaken Assassin
Captured Innocence
Mountain of Fear
Exposure at Sea
A Secret to Die for
Collision Course
Romantic Suspense of 5 books in 1

The Game
Suspicious Minds

Contemporary

Romance in Paradise
Maui Magic
Sunset Kisses

Deep Sea Love
3 in 1

Finding a Way Home

Service of Love

Christmas

Handcarved Christmas
The Payback Bride
Curtain Calls and Christmas Wishes
Christmas Gold
A Christmas Stamp

The Red Hat's Club (Contemporary novellas)

Finally
Suddenly
Surprisingly
The Red Hat's Club 3 – in 1

Short Story

One Hour **(A short story thriller)**
Whisper Sweet Nothings **(a Valentine short romance)**